PRAISE FOR

Tales from the Town of Widows

"Cañón's strong and simple writing, which is touched by humor and magic realism, never falters."
—*The New Yorker*

"Enchanting . . . a rollicking and often shocking tale that Cañón tells with charm and bite."
—*Washington Post Book World*

"Slyly pushing the envelope Aristophanes opened with *Lysistrata*, debut novelist Cañón exultantly sets up the saga of Colombian women on top. . . . Prime magic realism a la [García] Márquez, Cortázar, and Vargas Llosa, updated with a pop-culture twist."
—*Kirkus Reviews*

"Like his villagers, Cañón has built a new world on an old—a realigned literary landscape, with new sex roles, new stubbornness, new glory, and new wreckage. A much-loved tradition of Colombian fiction has been gorgeously reimagined in a novel for a new era of readers."
—Joan Silber

"James Cañón is a gifted storyteller, as full of his radical purpose as Swift, as enchanting as [García] Márquez, as brainy as Pamuk, yet his anger and compassion, as well as his humor, are distinctly his own. His first novel, *Tales from the Town of Widows*, is a book of wonders with great political purpose."
—Maureen Howard

"Start with a broth of magic realism a la Gabriel García Márquez, toss in a soupçon of William Golding's *Lord of the Flies*, add a twist of the musical play *Brigadoon* and even some ingredients from the Book of Genesis, and then top off with some borrowings from post-Revolutionary France, and you have a first novel that is not a derivative pot of unintegrated elements but an inventively rich stew. . . . The characterizations are drawn as compellingly as the storyline itself, which simply gets increasingly delicious as the pages turn."
—*Booklist*

"From its bravura opening, in which the men of a fictional Colombian mountain town have been marched off to fight in a decades-long guerrilla war, leaving the womenfolk to form a new social order, James Cañón's brilliant *Tales from the Town of Widows* has an imaginative reach that encompasses political, philosophical, sexual, religious, and magical realms while it also explores the deeper conflicts between tradition and freedom that underlie this mesmerizing debut novel."
—*Elle*

"Get ready for a refreshing dip into the waters of a rich imagination with this debut novel, which centers on the lives of one hundred contemporary women living in a remote Colombian village called Mariquita. After the village's men are killed or forced to join a guerrilla group, the women eke out a squalid existence, enduring drought, food shortages, and a flu epidemic. Faced with a hopeless future, they reject the traditional male concept of governance and rebuild an independent, caring community closely connected with nature. Contrasting with the humorous if sometimes disturbing events in the lives of these uncommon women is the hostile world of the village men, who are involved in gruesome warfare and torture. The story of these women touches our deepest emotions and reveals fundamental needs and concerns, such as the vulnerability felt by Rosalba, the town's new magistrate, after she accepts the love of another woman. This exciting book confirms the idea that our world would be far better off in the caring hands of women—especially the women from Mariquita. Highly recommended." —*Library Journal*

"The author spent five years crafting his highly imaginative debut about the determination and courage of the women in a small Colombian village, and the result is this stunning, unique novel." —*Pages* magazine

"The book, which tells of a fictional Colombian mountain village whose men have left to join communist guerillas . . . has been compared to the magic realism of Gabriel García Márquez." —*New York Sun*

"Cañón, with his ability to encapsulate epic political history into poignant, poetic prose, promises to evolve into an enduring literary presence." —*Chronogram*

"[*Tales from the Town of Widows*] mixes supernatural and allegorical elements into an account of a dying town." —*Bookslut*

About the Author

JAMES CAÑÓN was born and raised in Colombia. He moved to New York to study English and later earned his MFA in creative writing from Columbia University. Cañón was awarded the 2001 Henfield Prize for Excellence in Fiction. He lives in New York.

TALES
FROM THE
TOWN
OF
WIDOWS

& Chronicles from the Land of Men

James Cañón

HARPER  PERENNIAL

NEW YORK • LONDON • TORONTO • SYDNEY

This book is for
my mother, my grandmother
and every woman in the world.

HARPER ● PERENNIAL

"The Day the Men Disappeared" was first published in the *Chautauqua Literary Journal* in the summer of 2005.

A hardcover edition of this book was published in 2007 by HarperCollins Publishers.

TALES FROM THE TOWN OF WIDOWS. Copyright © 2007 by James Cañón. All rights reserved. Printed in the United States of America. No part of this book may be used or reproduced in any manner whatsoever without written permission except in the case of brief quotations embodied in critical articles and reviews. For information address HarperCollins Publishers, 10 East 53rd Street, New York, NY 10022.

HarperCollins books may be purchased for educational, business, or sales promotional use. For information, please write: Special Markets Department, HarperCollins Publishers, 10 East 53rd Street, New York, NY 10022.

FIRST HARPER PERENNIAL EDITION PUBLISHED 2008.

Art by José Manuel Villanueva López

Designed by C. Linda Dingler

The Library of Congress has catalogued the hardcover edition as follows:
Cañón, James.
Tales from the town of widows / James Cañón—1st ed.
p. cm
ISBN-10: 0-06-114038-4
ISBN: 978-0-06-114038-9
1. Women—Fiction. 2. Kidnapping—Fiction. 3. Guerrilla warfare—Fiction.
4. Colombia —Fiction. I. Title
PS3603.A558T35 2007
813'.6 —dc22   2006043528

ISBN: 978-0-06-114039-6 (pbk.)

08 09 10 11 12   ID/RRD   10 9 8 7 6 5 4 3 2 1

The day will come when men will recognize woman as his peer, not only at the fireside, but in councils of the nation. Then, and not until then, will there be the perfect comradeship, the ideal union between the sexes that shall result in the highest development of the race.

—SUSAN B. ANTHONY

1. Plaza
2. Church
3. Municipal Building
4. Marketplace
5. School
6. Infirmary / Nurse Ramírez's House
7. Police Station
8. Barbería Gómez
9. Cafetería d'Villegas
10. Eloísa's House
11. La Casa de Emilia
12. Magistrate Rosalba's House
13. Señorita Cleotilde's House
14. Virgelina Saavedra's House
15. Ubaldina's House
16. The Moraleses' House
17. Francisca's House
18. The Other Widow's House

CHAPTER 1

The Day the Men Disappeared

Mariquita, November 15, 1992

THE DAY THE MEN disappeared started as a typical Sunday morning in Mariquita: the roosters forgot to announce dawn, the sexton overslept, the church bell didn't summon the faithful to attend the early service, and (as on every Sunday for the past ten years) only one person showed up for six o'clock mass: Doña Victoria viuda de Morales, the Morales widow. The widow was accustomed to this routine, and so was el padre Rafael. The first few times it had been uncomfortable for both of them: the small priest almost invisible behind the pulpit, delivering his homily, the widow sitting alone in the first row, tall and buxom, quite still, her head covered with a black veil that dropped over her shoulders. Eventually they decided to ignore the ceremony and often sat together in a corner drinking coffee and gossiping. On the day the men disappeared, el padre Rafael complained to the widow about the severe decrease in the church's revenue, and they discussed ways to revive the tithe among the faithful. After their chat, they agreed to skip confession, but the widow received communion nonetheless. Then she said a few prayers before returning to her house.

Through the open window of her living room, the Morales widow heard the street vendors trying to interest early risers in their delicacies: "Morcillas!" "Empanadas!" "Chicharrones!" She closed the window, more bothered by the unpleasant smell of blood sausages and fried food than by the strident voices announcing them. She woke up her three daughters and her only son, then went back to the kitchen, where she whistled a hymn while she made breakfast for her family.

By eight in the morning most doors and windows in Mariquita were open. Men played tangos and boleros on old phonographs, or listened to the news on the radio. On the main street, the town's magistrate, Jacinto Jiménez, and the police sergeant, Napoleón Patiño, dragged a big round table and six folding chairs outside under a tall mango tree to play Parcheesi with a few selected neighbors. Ten minutes later, in the southwest corner of the plaza, Don Marco Tulio Cifuentes, the tallest man in Mariquita and owner of El Rincón de Gardel, the town's bar, carried out his last two drunk customers, one on each shoulder. He laid them on the ground, side by side, then closed his business and went home. At eight thirty, inside the Barbería Gómez, a small building across from Mariquita's municipal building, Don Vicente Gómez began to sharpen razors and sterilize combs and brushes with alcohol, while his wife, Francisca, cleaned the mirrors and windows with damp newspaper. In the meantime, two streets down at the marketplace, the police sergeant's wife, Rosalba Patiño, bargained with a red-faced farmer for half a dozen ears of corn, while older women under green awnings sold everything from calf's foot jelly to bootleg cassettes of Michael Jackson's *Thriller*. At eight thirty-five, in the open field in front of the Morales widow's house, the Restrepo brothers (all seven of them) began to warm up before their weekly soccer game while waiting for David Pérez, the butcher's grandson, who owned the only ball. Five minutes later, two old maids with long hair and slightly square bodies walked arm in arm around the plaza, cursing their spinsterhood and kicking aside the stray dogs that crossed their way. At eight fifty, three blocks down from the plaza, in the house with the green facade located in the middle of the block, Ángel Alberto Tamacá, the schoolteacher, tossed in bed sweating and dreaming of Amorosa, the woman he loved.

At three minutes before nine, on the outskirts of Mariquita, inside La Casa de Emilia (the town's brothel), Doña Emilia (herself) passed from room to room. She woke up her last customers, warned them that they were going to be in serious trouble with their wives if they didn't leave that minute, and yelled at one of the girls for not keeping her room tidy.

IMMEDIATELY AFTER THE ninth stroke of the church bell, while its echo was still resounding in the sexton's ears, three dozen men in worn-out greenish uniforms appeared from every corner of Mariquita shooting their rifles and shouting, "Viva la Revolución!" They walked slowly along the narrow streets, their sunburned faces painted black and their shirts sticking to their slender bodies with sweat. "We're the people's army," one of them declared through a megaphone. "We're fighting so that all Colombians can work and be paid according to their needs, but we can't do it without your support!" The streets had emptied; even the stray animals had fled when they heard the first shots. "Please," the man continued, "help us with anything you can spare."

INSIDE THEIR HOUSE, the Morales widow, her three daughters and her son, were clearing the dining table. "Just what we needed," the widow grumbled. "Another damn guerrilla group. I'm so tired of these bands of godless beggars coming through here every year."

Her two younger daughters, Gardenia and Magnolia, rushed to the window hoping to catch a glimpse of the rebels, while the widow's only son, Julio César, clutched his mother fearfully. Orquidea, the oldest, looked at her two sisters and shook her head in disapproval.

Orquidea Morales had lost interest in men some five years before. She knew they didn't find her attractive, and at her age—thirty-one—she wasn't about to expose herself to rejection. She had pointy ears, a hook nose and a mouth too small for her big, crooked teeth. She also had three warts on her chin that looked like golden raisins. When Orquidea was born, these unpleasant protuberances had been on her cheeks, but as she grew up, they'd migrated down to her chin. She hoped the warts would keep moving and eventually settle in a less visible part of her body. Orquidea claimed to be a virgin, a statement that had been confirmed repeatedly by the unkind men of Mariquita with remarks like, "If all virgins had bodies like hers, they'd remain untouched forever." She had inherited her late father's breasts: two dark little nipples side by side on her flat chest. But despite her sisters' recommendation to stuff oversized brassieres with corn husks, she decided to wear nothing underneath her immaculate white blouses. Orquidea didn't have a waistline or any curves. She was a walking rectangle with a very charming personality. She was capable of engaging in long conversations about Napoleon Bonaparte or Simón Bolívar, Shakespeare or Cervantes, Iceland or Patagonia, but also humorous topics like Colombian politics. She had educated herself by devouring most of the books available in the small library of Mariquita's school. But despite her erudition and broad views, she was a devout Catholic. She believed with all her heart that the pope was the emissary of the Lord, and her fondest dream was to have him sign her Bible, "To Orquidea Morales, my most devoted follower. Yours, John Paul II."

When she was younger, Orquidea had had a suitor: a farm worker named Rodolfo who thought he could improve his living conditions if he married her. But in 1986, when the first Marxist guerrilla group had come to Mariquita looking for recruits, Rodolfo surprised Orquidea by joining the rebels. It upset her so much she had diarrhea for two months. Finally, one day after using the toilet, she came out of the outhouse and said loudly and confidently, "I just finished shitting out my love for Rodolfo!"

Since then Orquidea had had neither boyfriend nor diarrhea.

"PLEASE COME OUT and join us at the plaza for a short talk," the guerrilla went on shouting through the megaphone. "We're not going to hurt anyone. We're fighting for your rights, and for the rights of every Colombian citizen." He repeated the same lines over and over, louder each time, but aside from the schoolteacher, two drunkards, an insomniac prostitute and three stray dogs, no one accepted the rebel's invitation.

"Can I go, Mamá?" Gardenia Morales said to her mother, who was washing the dishes with the help of Julio César.

"You have no business attending Communist meetings."

"But I have nothing else to do."

"Go find your sewing case and finish the quilt for the magistrate's wife. We're going to need the money soon."

"It's Sunday, Mamá. I want to go out."

"You heard me, Gardenia," the widow said, raising her voice as well as her eyes.

Gardenia strode away angrily, leaving behind a nasty smell. Julio César covered his nose and mouth with both hands and mumbled through his fingers, "Please, Mamá, don't get her upset."

Like her two sisters, Gardenia had been named after a fragrant blossom. When she was irritated, sad, or disturbed, however, her body gave off a smell quite different from the one emitted by that delicate flower. No matter how many times she bathed in warm water scented with roses, honeysuckle and jasmine, or how many times she sprayed her body with sweet-smelling perfumes, when she was agitated, her pores gave off a carrion-like stench. Dr. Ramírez—the only doctor in town—had been unable to cure the odor, and the witch doctors her mother had taken her to said Gardenia was possessed by an evil spirit. Nothing could be done, so the Morales family had learned to live with the recurrent stink. Even so, Gardenia was a handsome woman. She was twenty-seven, and she constantly challenged her sisters to find a single spot or wrinkle on her face. She had big black eyes and full lips that concealed two perfect rows of white teeth. Her eyebrows were thick, and she never plucked them, though she did curl her eyelashes on special occasions. Her long, delicate neck was permanently adorned with an aromatic necklace of dry cloves, cardamom seeds and cinnamon sticks on an invisible nylon thread. Behind her left ear she tucked fresh-cut flowers, angel's trumpets or lilies of the valley, whichever smelled best that day. She stuck out her tongue, almost involuntarily, every few seconds to wet her lips, a habit that the pious women of Mariquita took for a hint of lust. But like her older sister, Gardenia was a virgin. She'd had three suitors from nearby towns, all of whom ran away as soon as they figured out the source of the stench. Even when the second guerrilla group had come to Mariquita looking for recruits in 1988, Gardenia was one of the few women that the lascivious, girl-chasing revolutionaries didn't bother to court.

SINCE THE VILLAGERS chose not to come out of their houses to attend the guerrillas' meeting, the insurgents opted to go from door to door asking for voluntary contributions, hoping to interest any young, healthy man in joining their movement. But only a small number of families answered their doors. The people of Mariquita had grown weary of being harassed by the many groups of rebels who went up and down the mountains asking for money, chickens, pigs and beer; enchanting the most ingenuous women with their macho attitude and their olive-drab uniforms, winning their hearts and their maidenheads and finally, after a week or two, leaving them behind with bad reputations, swelling bellies and few possibilities of marriage.

When Magnolia Morales, who hadn't moved away from the window since the rebels arrived, informed her mother that the guerrillas were knocking on all doors, the widow quickly wrapped the leftovers of their breakfast in plantain leaves and left the small bundle outside on their doorstep.

"We should at least hand them the food, Mamá," Magnolia said. "They're Communists, not dogs."

"Oh, no," said the widow emphatically. "If I open that door, they'll start lecturing us about communism and flirting with you girls. Absolutely not."

"I just want to talk to them, Mamá. I'm not going to run away with some guerrilla."

"Talk to them through the window," her mother said. She pushed a heavy wooden chair against the door.

Magnolia Morales, the youngest of the three sisters, was twenty-two but looked much older. Her breasts were flaccid through the almost transparent blouses she liked to wear, and her hips were wide and nearly flat. She had the legs of a man, hairy and muscular, which she disguised with dark-colored stockings. Her face wasn't missing anything: she had two dark eyes with their respective eyelashes and brows, a mouth, a nose and plenty of undesired hair. In the past she had plucked out bristles and the excessive mustache, but the obstinate hair—like the guerrillas—always came back. Finally, she decided to let it grow as fast and long as it pleased, and so it did. The hair on her head fell freely to her waist, black and shiny.

Magnolia definitely wasn't a virgin. "If she charged every man for her favors, she'd be a millionaire," the old maids used to say. The girl had such a bad reputation in town that she might as well have sold herself. In truth, she had not slept with many men, just the wrong ones: the ones who told. When she first heard the rumors, she locked herself in her bedroom for over six months, thinking people would forget about her damaged reputation. In 1990, however, when the third guerrilla group arrived in town, Magnolia came out of her seclusion, hoping to meet someone new. That's when she realized that her reputation was the least of her problems; the rebels had persuaded most of Mariquita's single men to join the revolution. Suddenly, Magnolia's dearest dream of getting married to a handsome, wealthy man was unrealizable. Even her second dearest dream, getting married to any man, seemed remote. Devastated, she'd lingered awhile by the window of her bedroom, watching the large group of bachelors march out of town with the guerrillas, slowly waving her hand in the air, weeping as the last man disappeared from sight.

THE GUERRILLAS, FORTY of them, gathered once again at the plaza at noon. They sat down on the ground in the shade of a mango tree and made an inventory of the items they'd collected: two live, bony chickens, four pounds of rice, three liters of Diet Coca-Cola, six panelas, three small bundles of leftovers and a handful of rusty coins. They also had a new recruit, Ángel Alberto Tamacá, Mariquita's twenty-three-year-old schoolteacher. He was the only son of a legendary rebel killed when Ángel was only a few months old. Ángel had been raised by his mother, Cecilia Guaraya, and her second husband, Don Misael Vidales, a wise man who had moved to Mariquita many years before with nothing but his goiter and three large boxes full of books, and who three months later had become Mariquita's first teacher ever. From his mother Ángel had learned good manners, discipline and perseverance. From his stepfather he learned mathematics, geography, science and communism.

Unlike most young men in town, Ángel Alberto had never served in the military. Don Misael had called someone who owed him a favor, who in turn called someone else, and after an endless number of someones reminding others of their unpaid favors, Ángel's name finally reached an influential person who freed him from his obligations to the country. Don Misael then began training Ángel as his successor in Mariquita's elementary school. Having taught two entire generations to read and write, add and subtract, multiply and divide, the old man had grown tired. His eyes were becoming weak, and so were his arms and legs. He could easily count the strands of hair left on his shiny head, and his goiter was now so big he had given it a name, Pepe, and had considered claiming it as a dependent on his income tax form.

Before turning eighteen, Ángel Alberto Tamacá became Mariquita's youngest teacher as well as the town's agitator. He publicly despised the two traditional political parties and shouted slogans against the government of the moment: "Capitalist pigs, exploiters!" To his students he became "El Profe," to the magistrate and the sergeant "El Loco." The priest called him "El Diablo," and most men called him "El Comunista." The women, on the other hand, called him by different coquettish diminutives: "Papacito," "Bomboncito," "Bizcochito," and so on.

Ángel's new job gave him confidence and sharpened his leadership skills. In his spare time, he started going from house to house teaching from the *Communist Manifesto*. Soon afterward he created what he called "The Moment of Truth," a Sunday afternoon meeting at the plaza—inside the school if it was raining—where he talked about the doctrines of Marx and Lenin, read the most famous speeches of Fidel Castro and Che Guevara, recited Neruda's poetry and sang the most controversial songs of Mercedes Sosa, Silvio Rodríguez and Violeta Parra.

The Moment of Truth only attracted a handful of people at the beginning, but after Don Misael started serving beer, it became the most popular event of the week. Within a few months, people began to repeat socialist poems and Communist speeches. They memorized "La Maza," "Si Se Calla El Cantor," and other revolutionary songs, for which they invented lively steps and poses, creating a unique dance that was a mix of tango, salsa and sanjuanero. Five newborns were christened after legendary Communist philosophers, rebels and places: Hochiminh Ospina, Che López, Vietnam Calderón and Trotsky and Cuba Sánchez. *Communism*, once a foreign term for most villagers, became synonymous with Sunday-afternoon entertainment.

Ángel was aware that the villagers didn't take his doctrines seriously, but he was proud of having raised their political consciousness. Nothing pleased him more than hearing a couple of older men talk about Karl Marx as if the philosopher were their next-door neighbor and they fully understood and agreed with his ideas, and weren't just two old drunk men. Ángel, however, couldn't help being disappointed when on election day, after a couple of years of indoctrination, the majority of the villagers temporarily forgot about Marx and Lenin, Castro and Che Guevara, and voted for the candidates of the two traditional parties.

Despite his Communist leanings, the news about Ángel joining the rebels came as a surprise to everyone in town, because he'd had several opportunities to join in the past and never done so. No one in Mariquita thought that El Profe, El Loco, El Diablo, El Comunista and

El Bomboncito would be courageous enough to take such a bold step. What they didn't know was that this time, Ángel had a reason to leave town. He'd fallen in love with Amorosa, a prostitute from La Casa de Emilia who'd recently left Mariquita without so much as an adios. Ángel was suffering the pangs of her departure. He couldn't eat, sleep or think about anything else but her. He needed to go away with the guerrillas, or with the traveling circus, or with the Capuchin friars, or simply vanish with the torrential rains of November before he went mad.

THE GUERRILLAS BEGAN to eat the food and drink the sodas they had collected. When they were finished, Commander Pedro, a tall, brown-faced man with a scar that ran down the side of his neck, parallel to his jugular, walked slowly among his troops, staring at each rebel without saying a word. "Matamoros," he finally called out. "Let me have a word with you. In private." The two men left the group and walked across the plaza, stopping in the center by a half-mutilated statue of an anonymous hero. They spoke in whispers. It was clear that the matter they were discussing was serious, even dangerous, because both men looked tense. They shook hands solemnly and went back to the troops. Commander Pedro handpicked six rebels, including Ángel Tamacá, and ordered them to prepare to leave. "The rest of you follow orders from Matamoros," he said. Five minutes later, Commander Pedro, Ángel and five other men made their military farewells and headed toward the mountains.

Matamoros was a tall man in his twenties, handsome except for his missing right eye, which he had lost three years before after being shot in the face in a military confrontation with the Colombian army. His four upper front teeth were lined with gold, as if to compensate for the lack of expression on his face. With so much gold in his mouth, each order he gave seemed to carry additional weight. Matamoros waited ten or fifteen minutes before instructing his anxious men, then grabbed the megaphone and began shouting:

"We're very disappointed with the people of this town—"

The guerrillas got to their feet.

"We asked for food, and you gave us your leftovers—"

They adjusted their rucksacks on their backs.

"We asked for money to continue fighting for you, and all we got were your worthless coins—"

They checked their old rifles for bullets.

"We asked for young men to join us, to help us free our country from imperialism, and except for your teacher everyone scurried like roaches into their houses—"

They broke into squads of five.

"You're selfish cowards who don't deserve our willingness to die for you—"

They lined up and pointed their guns at the sunless sky.

"Listen carefully, people, because I'm only going to say this once: if you're older than twelve and have a pair of balls between your legs, you *must* join the revolution today. Come to the plaza right now, or you'll be found and executed!"

And, finally, they waited for Matamoros's last command:

"Comrades: in the name of the Colombian revolution, take what's yours!"

The rebels fired several shots into the air, then went around the village kicking doors open, stuffing their rucksacks with food and money, dragging young and older men out of their dwellings, pulling them from under their beds, from inside their wardrobes or trunks, and shooting those who resisted. The first man struck by a bullet was Don Marco Tulio Cifuentes, the owner of the town's bar, who got shot in the leg when he tried to escape by way of the roof of his house. In her distress, Eloísa, the wounded man's wife, pounced on the aggressor and hit him repeatedly with her bare hands. This so infuriated the rebel that as soon as he managed to free himself from the madwoman, he shot Don Marco Tulio twice through the head. Two streets down, Police Sergeant Patiño and his two officers rushed out of the magistrate's house (where they were hiding) with their guns. When they saw the many guerrillas, the two officers dropped their guns on the ground and threw up their hands. The sergeant, however, managed to kill a rebel with a single discharge of his revolver. His heroic action was reciprocated by nineteen shots that pierced his body from all different directions. Before collapsing, the sergeant's body froze like a statue in a fountain with jets of blood showering the ground. Soon after, the remaining men—including el padre Rafael—timidly came out of hiding and began marching, heads down, hands in the air, toward the plaza.

THE MORALES WIDOW circled her living room. With her eyes half closed and her hands locked behind her back, she thought about how to prevent the rebels from taking her thirteen-year-old son Julio César. Orquidea, Gardenia and Magnolia stood in a corner holding hands, waiting for their mother to calm down. Suddenly, the widow had an idea. She gave specific instructions to her three daughters and started searching for the old first-communion dress that her girls had worn on three separate occasions. She found it wrinkled in a trunk under her bed. It will serve the purpose, she said to herself. At that moment, the widow remembered that there was a God and a group of saints to whom she could turn in difficult situations, and though time was pressing, she lit candles in front of the numerous images scattered around the house. Then she began saying her prayers while looking for her frightened son. "Padre nuestro que estás en el cielo . . . Julio César! Santificado sea tu nombre . . . Julio César! Venga a nosotros tu reino, hágase tu voluntad . . . Julio César! Where the hell are you?" She found the slender little boy hidden under his bed, his body shaking in terror. "Hurry, put this on," she ordered, throwing the fluffy white dress on his bed. "Dádnos hoy nuestro pan de cada día . . ." The widow repeated the words mechanically, interrupting herself every few moments to hurry Julio César. She helped him zip up the back of the dress, wrapped his little head in a white silk kerchief and secured it with a plastic tiara. The speechless boy pointed at his bare feet. "Don't worry about the shoes," she said, then pushed him out into the living room.

When Matamoros and four of his men strode into the Morales's house, they found Orquidea, Gardenia and Magnolia knitting peacefully in the living room, their mother making guava preserves in the kitchen, and Julio César sitting in the wooden rocking chair like a small Virgin Mary, a Bible in his hands and his heart in his mouth. Matamoros stood by the door, a long rifle in his hands. The other four guerrillas went around the house, disturbing the quietness of the rooms with the tread of their soiled boots, searching every corner for men old enough to fire a gun.

"The only man in this house was Jacobo, my husband," the widow said to Matamoros, pointing at a large, framed picture of a man who could pass for Winston Churchill, which hung on the wall. "He died of cancer ten years ago." She covered her face with both hands and cried out loud through her fingers.

"Don't you have any sons, señora?" Matamoros asked, looking at Julio César out of the corner of his eye.

"No, sir," she sobbed. "God blessed me with four beautiful girls."

"I see," he said, and started walking back and forth, now staring at the boy. The three girls became increasingly distressed, and, as was to be expected, Gardenia began to sweat out her rank fumes. "What's your name, little girl?" Matamoros finally said, addressing Julio César. The boy grew pale and his mouth hung open. At that moment, the four guerrillas joined their superior in the living room.

"Negativo, Comandante," one of them shouted. "Not a single man in this house."

"Let's go, then," Matamoros said, motioning to all of them to go out.

"Comandante," said one of the rebels, a leer on his small face, "may we fuck the girls?"

"Afirmativo, Comrade," the commandant replied. "That is, if you don't mind the smell of shit in this house." He spat on the floor. Suddenly the rebels noticed the stench and quickly went outside; all except the youngest one, who untied the red bandanna from around his biceps, covered his nose and mouth with it and walked toward the three girls. He looked no older than fifteen, a dark-skinned Indian boy missing one of his upper front teeth. He stood next to Orquidea, squeezing her nipples with one hand while holding his ancient rifle with the other.

"Please don't," begged Orquidea, pulling away from the boy. "I'm a virgin."

"So much the better," sneered the boy, bringing his hand down to her crotch. Gardenia shut her eyes and lowered her head. Magnolia smiled at the boy and placed her sewing instruments to the side, hoping she would be next. But the guerrilla had already turned his lustful eyes on Julio César, who was rocking the chair much faster. "She must be a virgin too," said the young rebel, and approached the boy. The three sisters jumped up, screaming, and their mother, who had been silently praying, cried out, "Don't touch my little girl!" She ran to her son's side. "Do whatever you want with the other three. Take me, if you wish, but please not Julia."

"And why not?" the boy asked cynically.

"She's just a little girl. She hasn't even received her first Holy Communion."

The boy laughed loudly through the cloth that covered his mouth. "Well, she will now," he said, grabbing his own crotch.

The widow had a sudden impulse to smack the insolent boy across his face. Feeling empowered by this urge, she stood between him and her son. "I won't let you have your evil way," she said purposefully.

"Señora, I'm warning you: get out of the way."

"You're supposed to be fighting for our rights, not violating them," she said accusingly, her hands on her hips. "We women have rights, too, and my daughters and I will do whatever it takes to protect ourselves from wretches like you."

"You women don't have nothing," the guerrilla boy said disdainfully. "This is and will always be a land of men." He struck her down with a single punch to the face, shouting, "Come near me again and I'll shoot you!" He let his belt out, unbuttoned his dirty pants and began to pull them down slowly. Julio César rocked his chair rapidly, weeping, while Orquidea and Magnolia bit their nails in a corner. Gardenia, visibly agitated, sat down and fanned herself with the bottom of her long skirt, fouling the air in the room with her perspiration. The stench was now insufferable. The guerrilla fell on his knees and threw up. While he was still retching, Doña Victoria got up off the floor, opened the door and pushed and kicked the half-naked boy out with her bare foot. She watched him and his rifle roll down the step and hit the ground, then shut the door with a slam.

As Gardenia's fears diminished, the smell went away. The widow went around with a bottle of rubbing alcohol, making her daughters and son sniff it until they recovered from the shock and the disgust. All five sat together around the dining table, holding hands, the old matron saying a few prayers between tears and nervous giggles.

Outside, the firing in the streets went on, punctuated from time to time by the heartbreaking cry of a new widow, and the weeping of another fatherless child.

WHEN THE SHOOTING stopped an hour later, the Morales widow went outside. The left side of her face was already swollen. The women of Mariquita had gathered on both sides of the main street, leaving just enough room for the line of men and boys being taken away by the guerrillas. These men were the Morales widow's neighbors and friends: the ones who'd welcomed her, her husband and their two older daughters when they first arrived in Mariquita in 1970; the ones who'd brought her handpicked flowers after she gave birth to each of her two youngest children; and years later, the ones who'd consoled her when her husband passed away. These were the only men she had known in twenty-two years. And those young boys marching next to them, their younger sons, were the ones who stopped by her house every afternoon to do homework with Julio César, the ones who helped her carry her basket of groceries from the market, and the ones who played soccer every Sunday morning in the open field in front of her house.

The widow saw the women weep as their men filed past them with their heads down. She saw Cecilia Guaraya give her old husband a pair of spectacles, and Justina Pérez give hers a set of dentures. She saw Ubaldina Restrepo give her youngest stepson, Campo Elías Jr., her own rosary. She saw others hand their men family photos, food wrapped in banana leaves, toothbrushes, alarm clocks, love letters, cash. She saw the women cry as they held their men tight against their bodies, sobbing as they kissed them for the last time. They knew they would never see them again; that those husbands, sons, cousins, nephews and friends were dying right there, at that very instant, before their eyes.

In sad moments, the widow always felt nostalgic for her late husband. This time, however, she didn't cry. She thanked God in her head for giving Jacobo the cancer that had allowed him to die at home, in her arms. She felt very sorry for the rest of the women in town, and couldn't help letting out a long sigh when she saw the last two men vanish amid the clouds of dust raised by their marching feet.

The Morales widow turned around slowly. Just as slowly, she walked toward her house, followed by a long echo of wails. She stepped inside, held the doorknob with both hands and pushed the door closed with her forehead. She stayed like that, weeping, for a long time.

Her dearest Mariquita had turned into a town of widows in a land of men.

Gordon Smith, 28
American reporter

"John R.," 13
Guerrilla soldier

It was Sunday afternoon. I was sitting in a clearing next to the guer-rilla camp waiting for John. He had agreed to meet me there for an interview.

The guerrilla camp was a small settlement located in the high-lands of the country, about three days away on foot from the closest town.

Suddenly John emerged from the woods, a little boy wrapped in an oversize olive-drab uniform with a rifle slung over his shoulder. His face was small and shiny with sweat, splashed with freckles. A shadow of soft hair above his upper lip suggested a future mus-tache. His hair, what I could see underneath his hat, was black. He looked no more than twelve, maybe thirteen. We shook hands and exchanged smiles.

"Sit down, kid," I said, making room for him on the tree trunk where I was sitting.

"No, gracias," he replied, shaking his head. "I'm good here. And by the way, I'm no kid. I'm fifteen."

His voice hadn't broken yet, and he spoke loudly, as if to com-pensate for it.

I'd first seen John during a soccer game that had taken place only two hours earlier in the same clearing. John seemed to be the youngest of both teams—a child playing jokes on his comrades. "The Boy Soldier," I thought, would make a good title for the story.

But the boy I had in front of me now wasn't the same John I'd seen earlier. This one pretended to be older and taller than he actually was. He lifted one of his legs and pulled out a pack of Marlboros from his sock. He smacked it three times on the palm of his free hand before offering me one. I'd given up smoking about a year ago, but I figured a cigarette might help break the ice between us, so I took one. Next, he produced a lighter shaped like a small replica of a cellular telephone.

"This is a good lighter," he said, handing it to me. "It was made in Estados Unidos."

"How do you know that?" I asked. On the lighter I read "Made in China."

"A gringo gave it to me. He came here to interview our coman-dante."

I wasn't the first foreign reporter to brave the dangers of Colombia in search of a good story. In the two years I lived there, I met a lot of guys from different parts of the world who were inter-viewing guerrillas, paramilitaries, army soldiers, coca growers, or, like me, all of them.

"And how do you know he was from Estados Unidos?"

"He looked like you, pale and blond, with blue eyes. And he talked funny like you."

John and I each took drags on our cigarettes, but I choked on the smoke and began to cough.

He burst into laughter, "Haha-haha-haha-haha . . ."

This was the John I'd seen earlier, the mischievous laughing boy; his "hahas" made him unique. I put out the cigarette and watched him laugh until I got my breath back.

Then, abruptly, he said, "I'm only thirteen." He looked down, as though ashamed of being a child. "I don't tell nobody, though. There's this guy who said he was fourteen and they don't respect him no more. Like you need to be full-grown to kill people."

When I'd chosen John as the subject for my interview, the commandant had given me the boy's file. According to it, John hadn't yet been in battle. I doubted that. I knew commandants doctored their recruits' files, especially if they were underage.

"How many people have you killed?" I asked him.

"Haha-haha. Like you keep count," he said. "I just close my eyes and fire until I don't hear no fire back." His effortless answers made me think he was telling me the truth. "What about you?" he asked. "Have you killed someone?"

I shook my head.

"Really?" John seemed genuinely surprised. He laid the rifle on the grass and sat next to it, his knees pressed together against his chest and his arms wrapped around them. The message was clear: he no longer needed to feel any older or taller. He'd killed people. I hadn't.

"What do you think about when you're in combat?" I went on.

"Most of the time I don't think nothing, but sometimes I think I'm saving my own life, you know? It's either my life or theirs, and God doesn't want *me* yet."

"Oh, so you believe in God."

"I sure do. I say my prayers almost every night, and always before a battle."

"And do you think God approves of you killing others?"

He considered my question for a while before declaring, "I think God doesn't want me killing them anymore than he wants them killing us."

Next, I asked him questions about the daily life of a guerrilla and learned that they get up at four and fall in at five; that daily duties are assigned at five thirty. A party of two cooks all three meals, two parties of three go hunting, two parties of four scout the area for possible invasion forces, and the rest do guard duty. In the afternoon, they exercise and do target practice.

"This camp's nothing compared to training camp," John assured me. "There, you learn to shoot pistols, rifles and machine guns, and how to spot aircraft, and where on the fuselage to aim. It's awesome!" He said all this in his child's voice, and I thought again about the file that the commandant had given me. I pulled it from my backpack and reread the page. It said John's real name was Juan Carlos Ceballos Vargas and that he was sixteen; that his parents had died in a car accident when he was a baby; that the boy had spent his entire childhood in an orphanage, from which he'd been dismissed when he turned fifteen; and that he'd voluntarily joined the guerrillas in November of 2000. I decided to find out how much of the information on his file was true.

"Is John your real name?"

He shook his head.

"What is it then?"

"I don't tell nobody my name."

"That's fair," I said. "I like John. It's a nice name."

"It's not just John," he replied. "It's John R."

"I still think it's a fine name. Did you choose it yourself?"

He nodded. "You seen *Rambo*?" He asked this as though *Rambo* had just been released.

"All three of them," I admitted.

"Me too. He's awesome! Remember his name? Rambo's name?"

I had to think for a moment. It had been years since I watched *Rambo III*. I knew it was a common name. Michael? Robert? John?

"John!" I announced. "Oh, I get it. John R."

He smiled. "My grandmother had a TV. She let me watch sometimes, till she sold it. She started selling everything she had to get us food till there was nothing else to sell in that house."

"Where is your grandmother now?"

He shrugged.

"What about your father? Where is he?"

"In jail. He got twenty years for killing a neighbor who stole a pig from us."

"And your mother?"

"She got shot in the head," he replied, matter-of-factly, as if that were the only way someone's life could end. "That man my father killed, he had a son who was a policeman. He put my father in jail, then he killed my mother."

"Did someone turn the policeman in?"

"Haha-haha," he answered.

"How old were you when this happened?"

He pushed his left hand outward in front of my face, the way little boys tell their age. Five fingers.

"And how old where you when you joined the guerrillas?"

"Eleven."

"Do you know what this is?" I asked him, flashing the file in front of his eyes.

He glanced at it and shook his head. "I can't read. I never went to school."

"Here, I'll read it for you," I offered, and began to read each line slowly. He listened attentively, but the expression on his face didn't change.

"I wish that was true," he said after I was finished. "It sounds a lot better than my life." His eyes, black and sad, fixed on mine. I looked into them and saw a little boy learning how to shoot a pistol, hunting birds in the forest, saying prayers on his knees before going to war, opening fire on someone else's enemy with his eyes tightly closed. I scrunched the file into a ball and threw it away.

"Just one more question," I said, noticing he was now looking at his watch. "Tell me what made you join the guerrillas."

"I was hungry."

John R. grabbed his rifle and stood up. It was almost four in the afternoon, and he was scheduled for guard duty from four to eight.

"Promise you won't twist what I told you to make me look like a bad guy," he said.

"I promise," I assured him. To prove it, I kissed a cross made

with my thumb and index finger, a gesture widely used by Colombians to indicate they'll honor their word.

Then he asked me for a present. "Anything," he said.

I looked inside my backpack. There was a change of underwear,
a toothbrush, a travel-size toothpaste, two sets of batteries, aspirins,
antibiotics, a roll of toilet paper and a beat-up copy of *One Hundred
Years of Solitude*, which I'd just started reading. Nothing John R.
would want. But then, in the side pocket, I found a Christmas floatie
pen I'd gotten the last time I visited New York.

"Feliz Navidad, John R.," I said, handing him the pen.

"Navidad? But it's only April."

"Any time's good for Christmas."

I gave him the pen and told him to tilt it back and forth, and saw
him watch Santa and his reindeer float smoothly over a miniature
snowy village.

"Haha-haha." His face lit up. "Is it made in Estados Unidos?"

"I'm not sure," I confessed.

His lower lip dropped in disappointment.

I took the pen back from him and carefully checked it. At last I
found, on the little silver ring that divided the upper part of the pen
from the lower one, engraved in very small print, the three words
John R. wanted to hear.

"Sí," I said. "Made in USA."

He thanked me four or five times, turned around and headed
for the camp, tilting the pen back and forth as he walked, saying
"Haha-haha," again and again until his little body disappeared into
the woods.

CHAPTER 2

The Magistrate
Who Didn't Know How to Rule

Mariquita, October 29, 1993

F OR MORE THAN A week, Rosalba had been closely watching the
sky. Each time she looked, the clouds and the sun, the moon and
the stars, everything above her village had seemed a little farther away.
Today, as she stepped outside of her house and looked up at the sky
once more, she decided that her green eyes weren't lying. It was true:
Mariquita was sinking. She crossed herself and started down the street,
toward the plaza.

Rosalba viuda de Patiño, as she liked to introduce herself, was the
widow of the police sergeant. She was a comely woman with a pale complexion, thin arms and legs, a small waist, and the largest bottom of all
the women in Mariquita. She wore her long chestnut hair gathered up
in a chignon at the nape of her neck, and she had a mole between her
eyebrows that looked as if a fly had settled on her forehead. When she
laughed—a rare occurrence since her husband's death—she squinted
and her mouth opened in an oval wide enough that the many silver
fillings of her molars flashed. She was forty-six, but the deep creases
around her eyes—which now lingered after she stopped laughing—and
the thin, freckled skin of her hands made her look much older.

Walking down the main street, Rosalba noticed a few new piles of garbage and rubble. They kept rising everywhere. With the village sinking, it was just a matter of time before the widows and their children found themselves immersed in trash. The rickety old man with the rickety old truck that used to come to Mariquita once a week to collect the garbage had stopped coming soon after the day the men disappeared. With the town's treasurer and the magistrate gone, who was going to pay for his services? Not the widows. They had other priorities, like feeding their children and themselves.

"Damned old man!" Rosalba said without stopping. She turned left at the corner and encountered a new deserted house, the Cruzes'. Since the men disappeared, several women had left Mariquita with their remaining children, their elders and whatever they could manage to carry on their mules or their own backs. In less than a year Mariquita's population had been significantly reduced. Abandoned houses had sprung up on every block and were soon dismantled. Roofs, doors, windows, flooring, everything was removed that could be removed until all that was left of them were four adobe walls with two or three openings of various shapes. Rosalba knitted her brow and kept walking.

Lately, she had gotten into the habit of sitting on a bench in the plaza to watch the villagers going about their ordinary occupations. Indifferent old women draped in black lace on their way to church; young women shouting at intervals that they were selling fresh arepas, used clothes, soap, candles, etc.; half-naked children following them, begging for the things they sold, waiting for the women to lower their guard so they could steal something, anything, from them. After a few minutes, the tediousness of the routine would prove unbearable, and Rosalba would find someone to talk to. Today she sat down on a bench half covered in bird droppings. The bench faced the distant sun, which was just breaking through the also distant morning clouds.

Three biblical-looking women wearing long nightgowns and bearing large water jugs appeared from around a corner. Orquidea, Gardenia and Magnolia, the Morales sisters, were on their way to the river, which was nearly an hour away on foot. Long ago, the men of Mariquita had dammed and channeled a nearby stream to provide running water for kitchens and laundry areas in the village. Now it was nothing but weed-infested tubes. A year of unusually dry weather had dried up the stream and the aqueduct and ruined most of the crops, leaving the women and children in the grips of famine as well as drought.

"Good morning," Rosalba shouted to the Morales sisters.

None replied.

Rosalba looked around for someone, anyone, to talk to; to complain to about the poor manners of the three sisters and other things that bothered her. There was no one.

"Everyone must be busy doing nothing," she said bitterly, addressing an old mango tree that stood next to her. "I've never seen women more passive than the widows of this village. We're running out of food and don't even have manure to fertilize the soil. It's true that we're going through a dry spell, but we can't blame nature for our hardship. Not when we haven't done a thing. All this time we've been sitting here, complaining, waiting for the news of our predicament to travel across the mountains and reach Mr. Governor. For Mr. Governor to meet with his council. For them to notify the central government. For Mr. President to meet with his congress. And for the congress to authorize Mr. President to authorize the council to authorize Mr. Governor to authorize someone else to offer some assistance to a bunch of stupid widows in some dry region somewhere . . ."

A small flock of half-starved pigs appeared, followed by their shepherd, Ubaldina viuda de Restrepo, who was yelling abuse at them. She was the widow of Don Campo Elías Restrepo—once the richest man in town—and she had lost him and seven stepsons to the rebels. Ubaldina kept her pigs in a little barbed-wire-fenced shed at the rear of her garden. She herded them around town twice a day so the animals could feed themselves on trash. She had marked their left ears with red paint, and she counted them several times a day to make sure none had been stolen.

The pigs stopped every few seconds to ransack each pile of garbage they came across. "Move, you stupid beast!" she yelled at the skinniest one. It was well behind the rest.

"When am I getting my chops, Ubaldina?" Rosalba shouted. She hadn't eaten meat in over three months, even though she had paid, long ago, for two full pork chops.

"Maybe next week," Ubaldina replied. "I still haven't sold the ears and the feet."

Ubaldina, who had been left with two useless refrigerators at home after Mariquita's electricity had been cut off, would only kill an animal when every part of it had been sold.

"A disaster for the poor is an opportunity for the rich," Rosalba whispered to the tree. "You know how much that greedy woman charges for a pound of meat of those garbage-fed pigs? Three thousand pesos! To be able to afford some, I had to rent the back room of my house to Vaca. You know, the cobbler's widow, the big-eyed Indian who's always chewing her cud. Why, of course Ubaldina knows that! I told her myself. She simply doesn't care. But I'm not the only one. You know Lucrecia Saavedra? The old seamstress? The poor thing had to barter her spare pair of scissors for tripe to make soup!"

As Rosalba was complaining to the tree, a small convoy of green Jeeps spattered with mud pulled into town. The women rushed out of their houses, imagining that it was relief sent by the government. Fifteen strangers in military uniforms got out of the Jeeps in complete silence. In the same silence they went about the filthy streets of Mariquita, followed closely by unclothed children and mothers with their hands outstretched, chanting, "Please, please, please . . ." The soldiers asked a few questions of el padre Rafael, the priest (the only man the guerrillas hadn't taken). They wrote their findings in small notebooks. They also took photographs of the dilapidated plaza, and of the large group of women that had gathered around the Jeeps to beg.

The oldest of the military men climbed onto the hood of his Jeep and tried to appease the widows. He was a short, fair-haired fellow with an ill-favored aspect. His skin was sweaty and shiny, and his face had scars of various shapes and lengths. "My name is Abraham," he began in a gentle voice that didn't match his appearance. "We're not here to give our condolences on your loss, though all of you have our deepest sympathies. We've come to evaluate the material damage done to your village so that you can be compensated accordingly." He reinforced his statements with swift motions of his small hands. "Unfortunately, it's going to take some time before any help can reach you. You see, our nation's undergoing yet another undeclared civil war. Many villages were attacked by guerrillas and paramilitary groups before yours, and so . . ." Despite the disheartening news he was delivering, the little man appeared to have hypnotized the women and children. They stared at him entranced, as though waiting for him to lay eggs or sweat milk. Only one woman remained in full control of her senses: Rosalba viuda de Patiño.

"We appreciate your honesty, señor," she interrupted Abraham's speech. "But tell us, who's going to provide us and our children with food until we get some rain?"

"I'm afraid that I don't have an answer for that, señora, but—"

"And what about clothing? These rags we have on will soon fall apart." She quickly turned toward the women and said, "Are we supposed to walk around naked like Indians for the rest of our lives?"

"Señora, listen to me—"

"No," Rosalba interposed, turning to the man. "You listen to us. Did you by any chance take pictures of our empty cisterns and our trash piled up everywhere? Did you write in your little notebook that our village is sinking?"

"Or that we haven't had electricity for a year?" Ubaldina, the pigs' owner, echoed her.

"Or that the only telephone in town doesn't work?" shouted Magnolia Morales from the back.

More women began to angrily shout their complaints, making Abraham nervous. He knew that if the storm of protests turned into a riot, he and his fourteen men alone would not be able to control it. Not only did the women outnumber them, but they and their children were also hungry. People were more likely to revolt when they had empty stomachs.

Suddenly, Rosalba broke into tears. "What are we going to do?" she wailed. "We're all going to die of hunger, buried in rubbish, and only the vultures will notice."

"Señora," said Abraham, bewildered by Rosalba's shifting attitude. "What this town needs is a strong leader like you. Why don't you take up the office of magistrate until the government decides what to do?"

"I know nothing about civil law or judicial procedures," she confessed to Abraham, wiping the tears from her eyes with the back of her hands, "but my husband was Mariquita's police sergeant. A very brave man who sacrificed his life fighting the rebels."

"That alone," Abraham replied, "makes you the perfect leader for this village."

He didn't intend for Rosalba to take his suggestion seriously; he only wanted to stop her from wailing. But the woman, who was not accustomed to compliments of any sort, surprised him by accepting the job. Abraham got down off the Jeep and hand-wrote a document designating her the acting magistrate. Then he made it official by singing, tunelessly and along with his soldiers, the Colombian national anthem.

*   *   *

ON HER FIRST full day as magistrate, Rosalba left for her office at seven. She wore a white apron on top of her black dress, and carried a broom, a mop and a bucket filled with soapy water. She also had a stub of a pencil tucked behind her ear, and, in the pocket of her apron, a small notebook and her pistol. As she went down the main street, she thought of the grand things she would do for Mariquita. Every time an idea came into her head, she stopped, put down the cleaning supplies, pulled out her notebook and pencil and wrote it down on her list of priorities. *Bring back running water into town. Develop an irrigation system for crops. Send someone into the city for some fertilizer and seeds.*

Mariquita's municipal office was a small house by the plaza. On the front wall was a plaque that still bore the name of the former magistrate, Jacinto Jiménez. The guerrillas had executed him in front of his horrified wife and children, then taken away his eighteen-year-old son. The poor Jiménez widow cried for days. But then, one morning, she packed her clothes and her many pairs of shoes and together with her two daughters left for Ibagué, where she soon married a butcher who made her happy again. Before she left, she gave Rosalba (they'd been very good friends) the key to the municipal office.

The magistrate was surprised at how easily the key turned in the lock after almost a year. She pushed the door open and was greeted by a number of squeaky bats that had made the office their home. She stepped aside, repelled. The hideous creatures fluttered around and crashed into the walls, disturbed by the shaft of light coming in through the door. Rosalba waited for them to quiet. Then, with an air of determination, she went inside, unlocked and opened the only window and watched the flock of bats swoop past her head and fly out of the building. She began dusting the furniture of her office, interrupting her duties now and then to write in her notebook. *Organize cleaning squads to sweep the garbage off the streets.* She brushed the cobwebs from the corners of the ceiling. *Have a team of women sow rice, cotton and drought-tolerant sorghum.* She rearranged the bookcase and the shaky coatrack and moved the desk from one corner to another. *Restore electricity seven days a week.* She swept and mopped the floors twice. *Make the telephone work again.* She brought in a beautiful begonia in a flowerpot and placed it in a corner. *Reopen the school.* Finally, the magistrate burned eucalyptus leaves to free the room from evil spirits.

When she was finished, Rosalba stood behind the old mahogany desk and looked around. Her office was now the cleanest and neatest place in the entire village. She was content. She squeezed her opulent behind into the chair and slid her hands across the smooth surface of the desktop. "I'm going to bring Mariquita back to what it used to be," she said. "No, what am I saying? I'm going to transform it into a much better village than the men could have ever created. I know how to do it. After all, I'm a born leader."

ROSALBA WAS FROM the town of Honda by the Magdalena River. When she was fourteen, her mother choked to death on a fish bone. Rosalba took charge of the house and her four younger brothers, assigning chores to each member of the family, from simple tasks like peeling potatoes to more difficult jobs like grinding corn in the wooden mortar. Even her youngest brother, who was only four, had a duty: to bring water from the river for cooking and cleaning. Rosalba's strict enforcement of the rules earned her the resentment of her brothers. Everyone had to be up at six in the morning and in bed by eight at night. A daily sponge bath in the cold water of the river was mandatory. Prayers had to be recited before every meal and at bedtime. Bowls of steaming soup had to be eaten completely. "Por favor" and "Muchas gracias" were required at all times, while complaints, fights and curse words were considered punishable offenses.

Rosalba gave everyone haircuts the last Sunday of every month and clipped their nails every other Saturday. She cooked three meals a day for the entire family, washed their clothes and took care of her small garden, where she grew lettuce, cilantro, onions and carrots. On Saturdays and Sundays she and her brothers went to the public school, where they learned to read and write. She practiced her cursive handwriting until it was neat and beautiful.

She was extremely careful with the little money her father gave her, but the other members of her family didn't approve of her priorities. While her brothers wore the same old plaid shirts and jeans every day, passing them down as they got too small, Rosalba had windows installed in the front of their mud shack, and the earthen floor covered with tiles. She bought herself a portable transistor radio to listen to the news and soap operas, from which she learned about wealthy land-owners madly in love with beautiful young servants. Rosalba preferred the news. She was courted by several fishermen, from whom she accepted the best catches of the day, but no invitations to dinner or to the Sunday afternoon dancing party. Her expectations for herself went far beyond fishermen.

It was not until her father remarried a few years later that her dictatorship came to an end. Doña Regina, her stepmother, had rules of her own. The woman freed the boys from their duties and assigned all the household chores to Rosalba—all but the gardening. Doña Regina was an enthusiastic gardener. Rosalba thought her stepmother was wicked. How dare that odious woman come into her newly renovated house and tell her what to do? Look how well-mannered her brothers were. They were much better trained than the stepmother herself was. The woman often complained about Rosalba's cooking, she never said "Por favor" or "Gracias," and she cursed in front of Rosalba's brothers. The situation worsened when Doña Regina began talking to her husband behind Rosalba's back.

"She spends most of the money on lottery tickets," Doña Regina lied. "Meanwhile we have to eat rice and chicken gizzards every day. Look how hungry your sons are." She pointed at the youngest one, who was naked on the floor, eating the scraps he found inside his own nose. In the face of such evidence, Doña Regina was immediately authorized to manage the family budget. She went food shopping that same day and came back with bags full of delicacies they hadn't seen in more than three years: steaks, pork chops, cheese and even a cake. The next day she bought shirts for the four boys and her husband, and a dress for herself. She bought nothing for Rosalba. Not even batteries for her portable radio, which Doña Regina considered an extravagance.

The tension between the two women kept growing, and after countless arguments and fights, Rosalba finally left on a sunny Monday morning. She took only her radio and a sharp knife and walked south, ignoring the many truck drivers who offered her a ride in exchange for her favors. Before the end of the day she made out a village in the distance: Mariquita, at that time a settlement of less than one hundred people. Rosalba could never explain to herself how or why, but at that precise moment she knew that there, in that distant village, she would live for the rest of her life; and there, in that village, she would never be just an ordinary woman. Never.

TWENTY-EIGHT YEARS LATER, Rosalba found herself sitting in the most important chair in Mariquita, surrounded by its four most significant walls. The wall on the left displayed the Colombian flag, frayed at the edges, its three colors almost faded into one. The wall on the right was blessed with a large wooden crucifix with a headless Jesus (the woodworms had been nibbling at it for quite a while). The wall in front of her desk was adorned with a framed picture of the current president of the republic. And the one behind her had a replica of the national coat of arms, which read "Libertad y Orden"—Freedom and Order.

Rosalba rose and walked to the window. She felt daunted by what she saw: a dilapidated plaza surrounded by dying mango trees, stone benches covered in bird droppings, a few broken lampposts and a tangle of wires that once had brought electricity into town five days a week, and which now dangled pointlessly between moss-covered poles. She went back to her desk, disappointed. Not so much in the view as in herself. She had seen this same ruin every day for the past year. Had she really expected the plaza to look any different through the window of her magisterial office? What a fool she was! Mariquita would only show improvement when she, Rosalba, put her management skills to work. She was a strong and capable woman. *Have a team prune and water the mango trees.* She'd always been the decision maker. *Get the benches cleaned.*

A voice in the distance interrupted her train of thought. "Compañeras!" she heard a woman yell. "We're all suffering from hunger and from the loss of our male relatives. Let's put ourselves in the hands of the Lord. Only He can save us." Rosalba rushed back to the window.

The voice belonged to the Jaramillo widow. She stood, a little stooped, in a corner, inviting the community to join her in saying a public rosary. She was wearing a red dress and had an oversized chaplet tied around her waist. The magistrate was incensed. First, how dared the Jaramillo widow wear a red dress when the entire town was in mourning? And second, how could she expect so much from God? What had He done for Mariquita? Their village was in wretched poverty, marked for doom as surely as the Jaramillo widow. And what had the Lord done for that pious woman? She had lost her entire family: her husband and two younger sons had been shot dead by guerrillas when they refused to join them, and Pablo, her eldest, had left for New York long ago in search of a better life and never been heard from again. The Jaramillo widow was thinner and poorer than ever. There was even talk about her going mad. And yet there she was, shouting that only the Lord could save Mariquita. . . . Suddenly, the magistrate realized that she had a very strong rival and that it wasn't the Jaramillo widow. The Lord Himself was out to defeat Rosalba.

Her biggest challenge now would be to persuade the women to forget about miracles and put their faith in the only flesh-and-blood leader there was in Mariquita. She knew she'd have to work hard to convince them that it was she, not the Lord, who'd eventually bring back the electricity and running water. She, the magistrate, who'd reopen the school. She who'd procure the seeds and fertilizers that would provide the villagers with food. Rosalba walked back to her desk, straightening her shoulders with each step. She seized her list of priorities, and, feeling the fear rise up in her, she wrote: *Win the villagers over to my side. Forbid the use of bright-colored garments at any time.* Finally, *Change the plaque outside the municipal office to read "Rosalba viuda de Patiño, Magistrate."*

THE PROSPECT OF competing against the Lord was terrifying. Until today, Rosalba's relationship with Him had not been entirely bad. In fact, going to church had been the first thing she did the night she arrived in Mariquita in 1964. She remembered clearly how el padre Bartolomé, a ninety-three-year-old priest, had listened patiently to her sad story and offered her shelter in exchange for work in his kitchen. Rosalba quickly organized the priest's untidy house and created a weekly schedule of hearty meals, which were highly praised by the priest.

At the same time, her green eyes and generous behind caught the attention of the only three single men in town. They saw her every Sunday afternoon sitting alone on a bench by the plaza, reading or listening to the news on her portable radio. She seemed unapproachable in her fluffy white dress and straw hat that the priest had bought for her, and for that reason the three young men contented themselves with watching her from the ice cream parlor. It was Rosalba who took the first step by showing them her perfect teeth. They waved. She closed the book she was reading—the life of Joan of Arc—and looked the other way. The nervous men tossed a coin to decide who would have the opportunity to approach her first.

Vicente Gómez was the lucky one. He smoothed down his bushy eyebrows with his forefingers and walked boldly in her direction. After the formal greeting, Vicente found himself answering a list of questions for which he wasn't prepared: "What do you want to be in five years?" "How many children would you like to have?" "Will you let your wife manage your family budget?" "What do you think of wives ruling their homes?" "How often do you bathe?" "Do you like listening to the radio?" Vicente couldn't understand why she asked so many questions, but he answered all of them: He wanted to be a barber, have six children, manage the budget himself, and let his wife rule the house. He bathed every other day and thought the radio was the greatest invention of all times. Rosalba sent him home with a kiss on his cheek. Do I want to be a barber's wife? she thought.

Rómulo Villegas came next and wasn't even allowed to finish the inquisition. He said he was going to open a cafeteria, have at least a dozen children, manage the budget and rule his house. At that point Rosalba turned on her radio, brought it to her ear and opened her book, pretending Rómulo wasn't there.

At last it was the turn of Napoleón Patiño. He was a slender man with long, greasy hair and bulging eyes. He looked vulnerable with his hands hidden inside his pockets and his head sunken between his shoulders.

"How often do you bathe?" Rosalba asked right away, detecting a peculiar stink.

"Every Monday."

"I'm not surprised." She sniffed once again and wrinkled her brow. "And your fingernails. How often do you clip them?"

"I don't clip them. I eat them." His voice was low-pitched, and he avoided Rosalba's eyes. She proceeded with her questions and found out that Napoleón would like to be a police officer, have one child, allow his wife to manage the budget and rule the house, and he owned a radio. He's not bad looking, she thought, but he cannot be just a police officer. He'll be the police sergeant of Mariquita.

After exchanging glances, love letters and poems for nearly three months, Napoleón and Rosalba got married and rented a house near the plaza. Many years later they would buy it in partial payments from Don Maximiliano Perdomo, a rich landlord who owned half the houses of Mariquita and the surrounding coffee farms. The young couple witnessed the slow growth of Mariquita: they helped build the first elementary school in 1968, and the telephone office in 1969. They encouraged their friends Vicente Gómez and Rómulo Villegas to pursue their dreams. In 1970, Napoleón became the first man to have his hair cut at Barbería Gómez, and early in 1971, the couple ate the first meal ever served at Cafetería d'Villegas. In 1972, together with their neighbors and friends, they planted young mango trees along each side of the unpaved streets. The following year they watched the first lampposts being installed around the plaza. Theirs was also the first home in Mariquita with a black-and-white television set—an enormous apparatus standing on four thick feet, like a cow, with a small screen encased in the middle and three round dials on the right side. Rosalba bought it on her first trip to Ibagué in 1973. In 1974, Rosalba and Napoleón ate lunch at the same table with the governor of the moment, who came into town to inaugurate a paved road that connected Mariquita with larger cities in the south.

The road made the village an attractive stop for people traveling between Fresno and Ibagué. People stopped to drink batidos of fresh fruit, use the public lavatory, stretch their legs, or just appreciate, and even take pictures, of the color-coordinated houses with their facades painted yellow, blue and red, like the nation's flag, and their roofs covered with terra-cotta tiles.

With its warm days and cool nights and the genuine hospitality of its inhabitants, Mariquita was a pleasant place to live. For that reason, some of the visitors who stopped by never left, like Don Jacobo Morales and his pregnant wife Doña Victoria, who arrived in 1970. They were on their way to Ibagué to deliver their third child in a private hospital, but after she drank a guava shake, Doña Victoria's contractions began, and she was immediately admitted to Mariquita's cozy infirmary. Seven hours later, she gave birth to a little girl and named her Magnolia. Doña Victoria spent the customary forty-five days recovering in the Patiños' home, until she managed to convince her husband to sell their country house and move to Mariquita.

Poor Victoria, the magistrate thought, as she dusted the framed picture of the president one more time. After all she went through to keep her son Julio César from being taken by the guerrillas, and now he won't speak or stop dressing like a girl. I should pay her a visit soon. The shrill cry of a cat outside made her go to the window and peep out. The cry could have come from any of the four corners of the plaza. Rawboned dogs and cats rummaged about in the piles of garbage, fighting Ubaldina's pigs and Perestroika, the Solórzano widow's cow, over rotten scraps of food, corn husks, plantain leaves and human waste. Watching them, she became nauseated. The magistrate decided that everything looked much worse through the window of her new office.

She vowed to clean up the plaza. After all, she was Rosalba viuda de Patiño: competent, efficient, resourceful. She had spent her life cleaning up messes. This wouldn't be any different. Besides, it would put her ahead of the Lord in the eyes of the villagers.

She rushed back to her desk, and as her posterior landed on the chair, the zipper of her dress broke. Annoyed, she shook her head and went over her list of priorities. *Organize cleaning squads to sweep the garbage off the streets* was number four. She frowned. With great care and the help of an eraser, she shifted the order, so that cleaning the streets became her number-one priority without hurting, in any way, the aesthetics of the list. Her handwriting really was exquisite. Another cat cried in the distance. She rolled her eyes and kept working on her list: *Visit Victoria viuda de Morales. Have my two black dresses mended.*

Rosalba owned many dresses, but only two of them were entirely black. She'd been wearing them ever since her husband was killed, and now they were frayed at the collar and hem. Before she hadn't cared. She was in mourning—what did it matter if her clothes were tattered? But now she was the magistrate. She had to maintain a neat appearance. She'd have the old dresses patched over until they gave way. Then she'd have a new one tailored. Black, of course. It was the least she could do to pay her respect to the exceptional husband she had once had.

NAPOLEÓN PATIÑO HAD done everything in his power to please Rosalba. He'd have been content to remain a police officer for life, but Rosalba wanted more for him, and so he had worked diligently to earn the respect of his superior. Rosalba vividly remembered the proud look in his eyes when, after ten years, he was finally promoted to sergeant.

Her friends also regarded Rosalba very highly, and her husband's salary allowed her to refurnish her house and buy a record player. The only thing marring her happiness was that after their third year of marriage, Napoleón was unable to get an erection. He tried eating bull's penis soup and fish eggs, and drinking a fermented corn drink with honey and brandy. He also visited doctors in Fresno and Ibagué, but Rosalba's sexual life remained limited to the sporadic caresses of Napoleón's fingers, or her own. She consoled herself by thinking, At least I have his devotion.

Being the police sergeant of Mariquita had been an easy job at the beginning. Except for the sporadic fights among drunkards in El Rincón de Gardel—the town's bar—and the disputes of prostitutes over the wealthy patrons in Doña Emilia's brothel, Mariquita was a peaceful town. There was no record of any person being killed or even seriously wounded. The doors and windows of every house remained wide open, except when it rained, and at night to keep wandering bats from landing on the beds. Nobody argued about politics. Everyone got along because their magistrate was designated by the central government. No matter what party he belonged to, he got equally drunk with supporters of the Partido Liberal and of the Partido Conservador. Naturally, there was some envy and hostility in Mariquita, especially among single women. On warm evenings they gathered in small groups around the plaza and savaged one another with caustic remarks about hair, outfits and reputations. But, as el padre Bartolomé used to say in his tuneless voice, "Overall, the good men and women of Mariquita observe each one of the Ten Commandments."

"WHAT A GOOD soul el padre Bartolomé was," Rosalba said, staring, vigilant, at the crucifix on the wall. She remembered how peacefully the old priest had died after falling asleep in the middle of a mass.

And then el padre Rafael had taken his place. When she'd first met him, Rosalba thought he was a virtuous and educated man endowed with celestial gifts. But throughout the years she'd realized that el padre

Rafael was much more astute than he was virtuous or educated. She didn't like him, but she had respect for him, especially now that he was the only "real" man left in town. One "real" man and God knew how many women. Wasn't it the job of a magistrate to find out how many men had been taken and how many women were left? She would think so. The figures needed to be reported to the central government. Perhaps if they saw the count they would speed up the financial assistance. *Take a census*, she wrote in her list. She'd simply ask el padre Rafael to ring the church bell many times. People would rush to the plaza, and then she'd count them.

At that precise moment el padre Rafael rang the church bell, summoning the devoted to attend the early service. Since the men disappeared, he'd become lazy. He rose late, and he'd cut the daily religious services from three to two. He also was no longer fond of fixed schedules because, he would say, "Any time is good for God." Mass was celebrated whenever it pleased him, and lunchtime was the only time of the day he announced with twelve resounding chimes. Now that Rosalba was at odds with the Lord, she could demand that el padre stop celebrating mass altogether. She could even run the idle priest out of town. But that wouldn't be right, and she wanted to compete fairly. Instead, she wrote, *Demand that el padre celebrate mass at seven in the morning and at six in the evening seven days a week.*

"Rosalba," a woman called through the window.

Who could it be bothering her this early? And why couldn't they come knock on her door? *Make myself available only by appointment*, she wrote.

"Rosalba, you there?" a different voice shouted.

She moved to the window. About a dozen women in black, and a few naked, lice-ridden children with snotty noses, had crowded together outside the municipal office. They held their cupped hands, empty baskets, pots and gourds out to the magistrate. All of them had the same sorrowful look on their faces, as though they were in the most horrendous pain and Rosalba had the cure.

"What's happening here?" said Rosalba, annoyed by the unexpected company. "What do you all want?"

"Help us, Rosalba," the old Pérez widow begged, waving her container in the air.

The others joined her, "Help us. Help us."

"If you want to talk to me, you must form a line," the magistrate demanded.

The sight was quite overwhelming, even for a woman of her strength and bravery. Rosalba thought they should all be taken into custody for begging. But who was going to do it? Ever since her husband got killed, Mariquita hadn't had anybody to maintain the public order and enforce the laws.

"You're the magistrate, Rosalba. You must help us," the Jaramillo widow demanded.

She wanted to yell at them to be quiet, to go away, to leave her alone.

"We're hungry," a different woman shouted.

She wanted to scream that she was no Jesus Christ to feed great crowds with little food.

"Help us. Help us."

Rosalba thought that the baskets, pots and gourds were getting too close to her. And that the women's bony hands were bound to strangle her. She felt short of breath, terrified. She walked a few steps back and slammed the window closed, padlocked it and threw the key in the wastebasket. Those women were awfully impatient. Couldn't they wait until she was settled? Limp with exhaustion, she leaned with her back against the window and let her body slide down the wall until her buttocks landed softly on the immaculate floor of her office. She felt like weeping, but she didn't. If a man could do this job, so could she. There was no such thing as the weaker sex. Women were made of flesh and bone, just like men. A woman with her two feet planted where they should be could work like a man, or even better. She imagined what a man would and wouldn't do in a situation like this. A real man would never be scared of a bunch of starving women. And he'd never hide from them. A man would go out there and confront them, scold them, threaten to imprison them. And if a man were smooth, like a politician, he'd promise them the universe. Rosalba too could do that. Yes, she would go out there and confront the women. She would tell them that they had to be patient until she could figure things out. She might even promise them food and clean water. Maybe electricity. Although she knew that in a poor, broken town like Mariquita, any promise would be hard to keep.

Resolute, she rose and walked up to the door, but the memory of her husband's last words kept her from turning the knob: "Never go anywhere without a gun," he had said to her. Then he'd put on his sombrero, kissed her on the cheek and began taking chairs and tables outside so that he could play Parcheesi with his neighbors. Months later, Rosalba learned from a neighbor that her husband had won the first game before he got shot.

The magistrate opened the first drawer on the right side of her desk and searched for her pistol. She checked it for bullets. There were three, which was all that remained from her late husband's ammunition. She held it firmly with both hands and looked around for a proper target. Her eyes found the picture of the president of the republic hanging on the wall. He was sitting behind a desk, his arms wrapped around his chest and his head leaning slightly to the right. His graceful posture and confident, almost sardonic smile disturbed Rosalba. "What are you smiling about, Mr. President?" she said out loud. "Are you making fun of a poor woman who doesn't know how to manage a town full of widows? And you, where were you that day our men were taken away?" She stopped, as though waiting for the picture to reply. "All this time you've been sitting on your scrawny ass on your comfortable chair, hiding behind your stupid desk with your arms crossed and that phony smile of yours." She turned her eyes slightly to the right. "And you," she said to the crucifix on the wall. "Where were you the first night we went to sleep and realized that our husbands would never again be in bed with us? Where were you when we wandered around the streets with our noses close to the ground, ransacking the entire damn village for food?" Soon she decided that it was no use talking to a headless crucifix, and so she looked back at the picture and fixed her eyes on the small white spot between the president's eyebrows. "You scumbag!" She lifted her gun slowly. "You piece of crap!" She was lost in reverie when she saw, from the corner of her eye, a dazed bat fluttering around. But she wasn't finished with the picture: "Mr. President, you're not even worth one of my bullets." She waited until the bat landed on top of the bookcase. Then she aimed the gun at it and shot it.

The loud discharge caused the women and children gathered outside to flee, and Rosalba to get in a fluster. She grabbed her list and added the following tasks:

Hire a policewoman. Ubaldina viuda de Restrepo? Cecilia Guaraya?
Demand that no woman complain ever again.
Forbid gatherings of more than two people.
Prohibit the use of the word "Help."

The church bell rang in the distance, announcing noon. So far Rosalba had cleaned her office thoroughly, relocated each piece of furniture, written a thoughtful and comprehensive list of priorities, and shut, permanently, that terribly harmful window of her office.

But she wasn't entirely comfortable with her performance.

She closed her eyes and tried to visualize the ideal view of Mariquita through that window: a clear blue sky; the air perfumed with the scent of magnolias and honeysuckle; nightingales and canaries singing melodious tunes on her windowsill; a lively plaza surrounded by tall mango trees full of ripe fruit; little girls jumping rope on the sidewalk; healthy boys playing soccer on the clean main street; young men and women walking about hand in hand, in love; older couples sitting on immaculate benches, feeding each other flavored ice cones.

The magistrate opened her green eyes and sighed with resignation.

She was now ready to acknowledge what in her heart she had known all along. Finally, she had clearly seen and understood what her first priority truly was, and how to achieve it.

She reached for her notebook and her pen, and at the top of the list, above everything else, she purposefully wrote:

Beg the Lord to send us a truck full of men.

Javier Vanegas, 17
Displaced

When I was a little boy, my only dream was to become a professional magician. I even learned a few cool tricks. My two best ones were the Appearing Bouquet of Flowers (which I produced from my ragged sombrero) and the Vanishing Coin (I made a coin disappear out of my open hand). I often performed them for my friends in our village. They were the only kind of entertainment we had. I used to call them "Tricks of Fun."

But when I turned thirteen, I had to give up my dream because I had to start helping my father with the little piece of land he owned. We raised chickens and pigs, and, like everyone else in the region, cultivated coca. My two little sisters and I picked the coca leaves, and my father processed them into coca base. Our village had long been under the rule of guerrillas, so we were only allowed to sell the product to them, although the paramilitaries, who controlled the village across the river, paid much better for it.

One day, fed up with the small amount the guerrillas paid, my father hid some coca base in his boots and some more in my sombrero, and together we canoed over to the forbidden village and sold it. The following evening, five armed guerrillas came to our house and kicked the door down. My sisters started crying, my mother screaming. One of the men hit my mother in the stomach with the butt of his rifle.

They pulled my father and me out and took us to a little mound nearby where it was very dark. I was shaking. "You sold coca to the paras," one of the men said to my father. "You broke one of the rules, and you must be punished." Father, who had been quiet

all this time, began wailing and begging for mercy. Then I heard
a boom, like a big explosion, and Father dropped to the ground.
"You go tell your mama that she has until tomorrow night to leave
town," the man who'd shot my father told me. Then they were gone.
We packed a few clothes and some kitchen stuff and left that same
night for the city.

That was four years ago. Since, we've become slum dwellers
crammed into a one-room shack with only two rough beds made of
planks and no running water or electricity. We can't find any kind
of work, so every day my mother and my sisters sit on a sidewalk in
front of a busy church with their hands outstretched. As for me, I
have become sort of a magician. My best tricks now consist of making food appear out of someone else's rubbish, and making money
disappear from men's pockets and women's purses.

I call these "Tricks of Survival."

CHAPTER 3

The Rise and Fall
of La Casa de Emilia

Mariquita, May 12, 1994

DOÑA EMILIA WOKE UP to a sunbeam on her haggard face. She was momentarily blinded by the radiance of the early light, but once her eyes adjusted, she saw only a red sky. For a moment she thought she might be dead, her soul descending to hell, but soon she felt the slimy tongue of a dog licking her cheek, the dog's fusty breath in her ear. She had spent yet another night on a bench in Mariquita's plaza. Scattered on the ground were the plantain leaves that had held her dinner. The stray dogs and cats had licked them clean.

Five days before, Doña Emilia had decided it was time to die. She was seventy-two, and for the last eighteen months, since the day the men disappeared, she had lived on her savings, down to the last cent. She publicly announced her decision to die, stating that old age, poverty and solitude didn't mix well, then sat on a bench facing the half-mutilated statue, waiting for death to come and claim her. Rosalba, Ubaldina (the pigs' owner and newly appointed police sergeant), and the Solórzano widow (the village's cow's owner) took pity on the old woman. They thought she had lost her mind. They gave her blankets the first night and agreed to take turns bringing her food and Perestroika's fresh milk. The first day Doña Emilia gave half the food to the dogs and cats, but on the second day she decided that death would not visit her soon enough if she continued eating, so she began feeding everything to the growing pack of animals that kept her company. She only took a sip of milk each day. And so she began to slowly die, part by part. First, her hands closed into tight fists she couldn't unclench; soon after, she stopped feeling her feet and ankles; then her eyes sank into her skull, and the wrinkled skin of her small face became translucent. Her sight and hearing, however, were still working fine. So was her mind, still sensible and lucid enough to comprehend that an old woman with a terrible reputation and no family or money didn't have the slightest possibility of surviving in a town of widows and old maids.

Doña Emilia struggled to sit up. She looked around, noticing for the first time the old mango trees that a team of widows had recently revived by order of the magistrate Rosalba. They were thick with foliage and fruit. She fixed her eyes on a ripe mango hanging from the tallest branch. It was no ordinary mango: it was larger than most, and its color was the kind of orange-yellow she had only seen on summer days when the sky was on fire, as the sun went down. She didn't crave the fruit, but she thought it would be wonderful to spend what was left of her life admiring the beauty of that mango. She stared at it for a long time without blinking, until her eyes began to idly close, almost as though she were finally dying.

She recalled, one more time, her life before Mariquita's men had disappeared.

*   *   *

ONLY TWO YEARS before, she had been the successful owner of La Casa de Emilia, Mariquita's brothel. La Casa was a grand old house with thirteen bedrooms, six full bathrooms, two recreation rooms, an interior courtyard, and twenty-four windows and twenty-three doors, all of which Doña Emilia had had modified to open outward. "Always move forward," she used to say. "Every time you open a door toward the outside, you're taking another step forward." To enter the brothel a customer had to go through a door first, then a narrow hallway, then another door followed by a velvet curtain that finally opened into a bright, large room furnished with folding chairs and naked tables lined against the walls. A corner cupboard and a small counter served as La Casa's bar. Doña Emilia herself tended it, offering aguardiente and rum by the bottle only. Occasionally she would sell bottles of smuggled whisky she bought from black marketeers. Music was provided by an antiquated Toshiba phonograph that played, loudly and continuously, whichever records the madam whimsically chose: boleros when she was dispirited, tangos when she felt nostalgic for her youth, salsa when she was cheerful, and so on. Next to the barroom there was the red room, so called because the only light in it came from fat red candles sitting on shelves on the walls. The red room was furnished with wicker armchairs, colorful cushions and a hammock slung from hooks, and it was reserved for those who preferred a mellower ambiance. Access to the rest of the house—the thirteen bedrooms, the communal kitchen and the dining room—was through a locked gate. Each girl had a copy of the key hanging from a cord around her neck.

With its twelve loving girls, its free-flowing liquor, music all night long, tidy bedrooms, clean bathrooms and showers, and incense burning throughout the house, La Casa was the finest and cleanest brothel for miles around.

Doña Emilia had been born in that same house. Her mother, a prostitute, had bled to death soon after giving birth to her. The owner of the brothel, a spinster named Matilde who was too stout for her dresses, said she hated babies. She'd drop the child off at a convent she knew. "This kid will make a good nun," she said. But the eleven girls who worked for her, all of whom dreamed of babies but didn't like the idea of having a big belly for that long, agreed to raise the little one together and take turns mothering her. Matilde accepted on one condition: she didn't want to hear the baby cry. Ever. And so Emilia, who was named after Emilio Bocanegra, the first customer to come into the brothel after she was born, had eleven mothers but no father and family name; she simply was Mariquita's illegitimate daughter Emilia. Her mothers cooed to her, played with her, and loved her, each woman in her own way. And when Emilia cried, she promptly was lulled to sleep with the only cradle song the women knew. Something about chicks saying pio, pio, pio.

Over the years the eleven girls were replaced one by one. Three of them grew too old for the job. Four went back to their native villages to marry their childhood boyfriends, who, unaware of the girls' job, patiently awaited their return. Three more realized that they weren't suited to prostitution and left for the city to get jobs as domestics. The last one claimed to have gotten the divine call to serve God. She offered to take ten-year-old Emilia to the convent, but Matilde, now older, heavier and lonelier, said she would keep the girl.

Matilde didn't want the young girl to follow in her footsteps. Every morning, she sent Emilia out on the street with a basket full of fruit to sell, just to keep her away from the brothel. Up and down the streets of Mariquita walked Emilia in her pink dresses, shouting her fruit, "Guayabas!" her black hair in braids, "Naranjas!" her long arms swinging back and forth, "Mandarinas!" a large basket gracefully balancing on her head.

But the girl was doomed to be a prostitute.

One breezy morning, a gust of wind blew Emilia's basket out of balance, and the fruit scattered everywhere over the ground. A group of boys who were playing soccer on the street saw it happen. They roared with laughter, pointing their little fingers at her, calling her names. Emilia knelt down and began to weep. The boys ran after the fruit and gobbled it up. The girl went back to Matilde and told her she wanted to work doing what all her mothers had done.

The very first time she performed she didn't get paid. She was thirteen and a virgin, and the pain was so severe that she pushed the client off her body and hid beneath the bed. The very last time she performed she returned the man's money. She was sixty-eight, and her upper dentures fell out during an oral session. Her client, an adolescent with a pimply face, had no complaints, but the old lady thought it unprofessional and insisted the young man take his money back. Doña Emilia's long career was filled with hundreds of anecdotes. On slow nights she used to sit in the red room surrounded by all the girls, light a thin cigar, pour herself a glass of apple wine and share her stories with them. She never mentioned the names of the patrons.

After the day the men disappeared, there were too many slow nights at La Casa. In addition to tale-telling, the old madam held nightly meetings with her twelve girls to encourage them to hold fast to their profession, and to keep up their spirits. "We've come a long way together, my dears," she told them. "It's true that we haven't had a customer in days, but I have a feeling that our men will soon be returned by the guerrillas. I just know they will." But as the nights went by without a single patron, the girls started losing their patience. One night, after three weeks, they decided to confront the old woman:

"Doña Emilia," said Viviana, the most articulate of the group. "It's been almost a month since a man walked through that door. Let's face it, the men of this town are gone for good." The other eleven girls nodded in silence. "We can't just sit and wait for a miracle to happen. We all have families to support back home." She paused briefly, as though thinking through what she was about to say, then added, "We've decided to start touring the farms nearby. There's got to be farmers and coffee pickers in need of our services."

Silence.

"Maybe you and we can work a deal," Viviana continued after a while. "Maybe we each just rent a room from you. That way we keep doing what we know, and you become—an innkeeper. You make money, we make money, and everyone's happy. What do you think?"

All twelve sets of eyes turned to Doña Emilia for an answer.

The old madam appeared to be calm, but her hands had begun to shake, causing the wine in her glass to rock gently. She settled the glass on a table and her hands on her lap, one holding the other tightly. "There's a thing no woman can afford to lose," she said condescendingly. "Her dignity. Each of you was hired because you fulfilled the requirements to perform for the rich: business gentlemen and landowners. These farm workers you just mentioned, dear"—she was now addressing Viviana alone—"they're indeed agreeable people. In fact, I'm acquainted with a few of them myself. But they're *common* laborers, a different clientele entirely. They're unclean and smell of soil." Then, addressing the entire group, she said, "I'd hate to see you lower yourselves."

"That's easy for you to say," said La Gringa, named for her dyed yellow hair. "You have savings and no one to support."

"When it comes to what we do, men are men no matter what class they belong to," said Negrita. There was resistance in her voice.

The other girls soon joined the discussion by getting up, nodding and shouting their discontent. Doña Emilia realized she needed to offer a solution quickly, before the situation got out of control. "Please calm down," she said. "I understand why you are upset, but you must believe in me. I guarantee you that as long as La Casa de Emilia is open for business, you'll always have a room to sleep in and plenty of food." She sounded almost maternal.

"We don't want any damn food!" snapped Zulia.

"There's no need to curse, dear," Doña Emilia tenderly said. "La Casa is indeed going through a difficult time, but I'm convinced that together we can overcome every obstacle. Give me until tomorrow night to come up with an alternative solution." The old lady had the ability to inspire affection in her girls. They agreed to wait and went to sleep.

The following night they met in the same room. Wearing a confident smile on her face, Doña Emilia began: "From now on, and until business improves, each of you will receive a basic salary." She had decided to invest her life savings in her girls in return for one thing: "Since you have nothing to do at the moment, I want each of you properly trained. In the pleasure business you're never too old to learn something new."

Doña Emilia herself would conduct individual sessions with the girls. She'd teach them everything she'd learned throughout her more than fifty years of experience: unique sexual positions and techniques, but also personal hygiene and social skills. During the course of their training, she'd have them role-play and take oral tests.

The second part of Doña Emilia's plan included a promotional tour through selected towns the guerrillas had not yet stripped of men. Furthermore, she was going to hire a photographer from the town of Honda to take pictures of each girl for a portfolio. The portfolio would be shown to potential customers in other towns so they could appreciate in detail what La Casa had to offer.

When the madam finished her improvised speech, the twelve girls gave her a standing ovation. While they mostly cared about money, the idea of having their pictures taken, some of them for the first time, had touched their softest spot, their vanity. They were uneducated women whose identification cards read, "The aforementioned is unable to sign her name." Nearly all had been brutally raped at an early age by their own male relatives. Three of them had borne children but left them with their own mothers and fled. All of them had spent their adolescence and adult lives going from town to town, wishing that the next town would be different, but finding out it was just the same.

Doña Emilia had shown them kindness and respect. Deep inside they were fond of her and admired her success. More than one girl saw herself in the small lady.

THE ONE-HOUR INDIVIDUAL training sessions started the following day. Six girls in the morning, six in the afternoon, plus two hours of role-playing at night. "The difference between a prostitute and an Emilia's girl," she lectured her pupils, "is that a prostitute spreads her legs and lets the man do the work, while an Emilia's girl does the work from beginning to end." Each session was focused on a different technique to satisfy a man. One session was on finding the areas of the male body that were especially sensitive to sexual stimulation.

The anus, Doña Emilia said, was number one, even though most men denied themselves that pleasure. Another session was on contracting the muscles inside their vaginas, which most of them didn't even know they had, to squeeze a man's penis during intercourse. Doña Emilia claimed that when she was younger, she'd mastered this technique to the point where she could bring men to orgasm without moving her body at all. The madam also talked to the girls about the importance of self-confidence: "Only a self-satisfied woman can fully satisfy a man," she said. And finally, she taught them ten of the most uncommon sexual positions she knew men liked but were too embarrassed to ask for from the mother of their children. These acrobatic challenges she'd given her own names to, like the Gluttonous Cow, the Colombian Roller Coaster and the Cuckoo Clock. Doña Emilia always ended each session with the same advice: "Remember to be respectful to your clients' wives if you ever see them on the street. After all, it's thanks to them that we're in business."

A photographer came from Honda to work on La Casa's portfolio. Each girl had three portraits made: one in casual clothes, one in underwear, and one in nothing, with her hands covering her private parts. For her own pictures, Doña Emilia took the photographer's suggestion and wore conservative, dark-colored suits.

With the portfolio under her arm, the madam began her promotional tours. She took a different girl with her every time, visiting neighboring towns like Fresno, which was about sixty miles west of Mariquita through neglected curvy roads, but also others that weren't very close, like the town of Dorada, a hundred-and-twenty-mile trip to the north. They went from business to business, requesting private interviews with the owners. Once Doña Emilia had the owner's attention, she was very straightforward: "Do you like women?" After the positive answer, she would whisper, "Then you've got to come see my girls," and promptly unfold La Casa's portfolio before the astonished man's eyes. She urged the men to make appointments at once, recorded them in La Casa's engagement calendar, and handed out her business card with the motto, "When was the last time you were in a house with twelve naked women? Welcome to La Casa de Emilia."

IN THE TOWNS of Lérida and Líbano, the news of the retrained girls of Doña Emilia's house was gladly received and rapidly spread among the men. Traveling out of their villages eliminated the risk of being caught by their wives and neighbors.

In Honda and Dorada the response was also great. So great was it that on weekends the men chartered vans and Jeeps to do round trips to La Casa.

In the weeks following Doña Emilia's tours, La Casa experienced a rapid surge in business. Likewise, Doña Emilia experienced a growing desire for money to pay off her investment. She adopted extreme measures to ensure a good profit. Before taking a man to a room, each girl had to make him buy a bottle of liquor. The period spent with a client was shortened from twenty to fifteen minutes regardless of the man. Business hours were extended during the week, and on weekends the brothel was open twenty-four hours, with only four girls allowed to sleep at a time. Working overtime was strongly recommended, although not required. Smoking breaks were canceled, and breaks between clients shortened to five minutes. Customers could extend a session only if the girl didn't have a waiting list. Finally, repeat customers, older and handicapped men, had priority at all times. These measures caused mixed reactions among the girls, but the madam wouldn't accept any argument.

Customer satisfaction reports improved tremendously. According to Doña Emilia's latest survey, 90 percent of those serviced were satisfied, versus a mediocre 60 percent reported the week before Mariquita's men disappeared. To get this information, the old madam made it a habit to personally say good-bye to her clients, ask them whether or not they had enjoyed their session, and give them a red rose, "For your wife or your girlfriend," she would say.

*   *   *

WHAT AN ENTREPRENEUR I was then! Doña Emilia said to herself as she opened her eyes. She was relieved to see the large mango still hanging from the tallest branch of the tree, and wondered who would be the fortunate one to eat it. A flock of birds, she thought. Yes, a flock of pretty white little birds would appreciate its soft pulpy flesh and sweet flavor. An approving smile appeared on her face. Or perhaps a dog. . . . At the moment she had a number of them sleeping at her feet. No, dogs swallow without tasting what they eat. That wouldn't do for such a special mango.

Her thoughts were interrupted by a group of women talking in loud voices. Four girls were approaching her. Magnolia Morales was among them; Doña Emilia could recognize the girl's shrill voice anywhere. She once had seen in a store a talking doll that had the same screeching voice as Magnolia. The girls stopped before the old woman, murmuring something unintelligibly; soon they were but guffaws of laughter that rang in Doña Emilia's ears long after they were gone. I only hope none of those women gets to eat that mango, she thought. Those despicable old maids don't deserve such a treat. Her eyes narrowed with hatred, and she bit her lower lip with her dentures.

The former madam had good reason to despise the spinsters of Mariquita. After all, it was because of them that La Casa had gone out of business.

*   *   *

ALMOST TWO MONTHS had gone by since Mariquita's men had disappeared, and while the widows were mourning their husbands, the young women were getting restless. They couldn't accept the idea that they lived in a town of widows and spinsters; that they, too, were fated to be single forever.

Magnolia Morales led a small support group for young women, which met in the middle of the plaza every night after the public rosary was said. They talked only about men; not their own male relatives, but their boyfriends, suitors or the ones they had secretly loved. Topics like the worsening drought, its consequences on their crops and the forthcoming shortage of food were positively banned from their meeting. Instead, the young women shared romantic anecdotes and stories of their sexual experiences, and showed one another pictures of their departed men as well as presents they had been given: dried flowers kept pressed between books, pieces of hair, even male underwear. Night after night they fantasized about the glorious day when their beloveds would be returned to them.

One evening, the girls heard the roar of a car approaching the plaza. They jumped up. Not a single car had driven along Mariquita's dusty roads in a while. Four men in a beat-up green Jeep drove past them without so much as a honk or a courteous wave. The girls looked confounded. A few minutes later, another Jeep with five men drove by the plaza. Magnolia ran toward the road with her hands and kerchief flying in the air, shouting for them to stop. But they drove past without noticing her. Magnolia was upset and frustrated, but not defeated. She waited calmly until she heard yet another car approaching the plaza. Then she ordered the girls to line up across the street, their hands linked together in a human chain. The driver, a balding, middle-aged fellow, pulled over and rolled down the window of his red Jeep. Three other men traveled with him.

"Good evening, gentlemen," said Magnolia, addressing the driver.

"How can we assist such lovely women?"

"We were just wondering where you all have come from and where you're headed. Our village is quite far from the main road—"

"We're from the town of Honda, muñeca, and we're going to visit the girls of Doña Emilia," said the driver, producing the business card the madam had given him.

"Doña Emilia said she had twelve pretty girls available," the harsh voice came from the back of the Jeep, "but I only see nine of you."

"I'm sorry to disappoint you," Magnolia replied, her voice sarcastic, "but we're not ladies of the night. We have nothing to do with that woman."

"Well, if that's so, then clear the way, preciosas. We have some urgent business to take care of," said the driver. The other men laughed.

Magnolia signaled the girls to clear the road, and the men were soon gone.

The girls went back to the plaza and sat on the ground. They tried to go on with their nightly meeting, but the strong, virile smell of the men perfumed the air, and their voices and laughter echoed in the women's ears.

"This is unfair," said Sandra Villegas. "I'm sitting here longing for a man, while those whores are getting paid to sleep with several a night. I'm getting tired of living on memories. These pictures will only yellow and the faces on them disappear."

"It's only been a couple of months," replied Marcela López, who had been engaged to Jacinto Jiménez Jr., the former magistrate's son. "We must remain loyal to our men."

"I have no man to be faithful to," said Magnolia, the most experienced of the bunch, "and neither do you," she added, jerking her chin at Pilar Villegas. "You and I could team up and compete with Doña Emilia's girls." The girls laughed hysterically, and their meeting broke up uneventfully.

The following night, Magnolia canceled the girls' meeting and, together with Pilar, went to the outskirts of Mariquita. They wore tight, sleeveless dresses and colorful makeup, and wore their hair down around their shoulders. They smelled the men before they heard the roar of the car or saw the lights. When the driver saw them, he slammed on his brakes and honked. Magnolia stopped, waved at them and continued walking, slower. Pilar kept going without looking back, her legs shaking. The four men craned their necks. They were elegant young men with shaved faces, and they smelled of cologne. "Wait," one of them yelled through the window, his nostrils flaring. They jumped out of the Jeep and ran toward the girls.

"What pretty flowers have fallen from heaven!" one of them said. "May I ask where you're going at this time of night?"

"We just needed a breath of fresh air," said Magnolia, fanning herself with her hands.

"I see," said the same man. "Are you two from La Casa de Emilia?"

"Not exactly," replied Magnolia. "A few of us operate independently." Between sentences, she stroked her tongue flirtatiously around her lips. She said Pilar and herself would be willing to make love to one of them each that night, free of charge, on two conditions.

"Anything you want, muñequita," said the youngest one, stroking his crotch.

"Firstly, you must promise you'll treat us as if we were made of crystal. And secondly, all of you must promise never to go back to La Casa de Emilia."

"I swear to God!" replied the youngest one. He kissed a cross he made with his thumb and index finger. The other three repeated the gesture and sealed the deal by swearing to God in unison.

The men tossed a coin to decide which two would have the honor to be intimate with the girls. The losers, they agreed, would wait in the car, smoking cigarettes and drinking cheap brandy. The youngest one won the right to choose first, and he took Magnolia behind a large rubber tree. They undressed quickly. She kissed him with passion as he slowly immersed himself in her flesh. They lay on top of the thick, waxy leaves fallen from the rubber tree. They moved together, legs and leaves an impenetrable tangle. The other winner, a rather short fellow with a good amount of brilliantine smeared on his hair, took Pilar behind the bushes. She made the man scan the grass for ants and scorpions first, then covered the ground with his and her clothes. They lay on top of the clothes and he began stroking her face, her hair, her breasts. "You're the most beautiful woman I've seen," he said, and gently moved inside her. For a moment she thought they were making love on a cloud, floating in the air. Then they exploded.

The sky was covered with hundreds of stars.

The following week, Luisa and Sandra Villegas joined Magnolia and Pilar in their adventure. They met in the abandoned school to change into their tight dresses and put on makeup.

"We must not get pregnant," Magnolia instructed her pupils. "Some men are quicker than others. You must keep looking at their faces, and when you see their eyes grow smaller and their mouths grow wide, that means they are close. Right then you have to push them off you."

"What if they're too heavy?" asked Sandra.

"Then you shouldn't be on the bottom," Magnolia replied.

She suggested they go down the road in pairs, keeping their distance. She also gave them whistles, which they had to keep around their necks at all times. "Blow them only if you're in danger."

In two weeks, Magnolia and Pilar persuaded eight other girls to join them, and she organized four teams of three each. They helped the new recruits with their outfits and makeup, and shared their experiences with them. They agreed to keep their business a secret from everyone in town, especially the priest, but also their mothers—the poor women didn't need another reason to grieve. The girls also reserved the right to refuse any man for any reason. They demanded no money in exchange for their favors, but rather let the men compensate them however they chose. "That way we can protect our dignity," said Pilar. Each girl picked a spot of her own and kept it free from bugs, weeds and other unwanted plants. A few of them even planted flowers around them and stored bread and sweets nearby in case their customers were hungry. And a month later, when the rainy season came, they helped each other build tents with bamboo sticks and large sheets of plastic.

Meanwhile, at La Casa, Doña Emilia suffered a noticeable decrease in business. She asked her girls to make sure their clients were completely satisfied, to always thank them for coming, and to invite them back.

"Remember, they're traveling from far away," she said. "The time they spend here with us must be worth it."

But the competition was fierce.

Desperate, Doña Emilia made a few more trips to nearby towns. In Honda she was informed about a group of beautiful young girls from Mariquita, who walked up and down the roads, accepting all sorts of goods in return for the men's ephemeral love: perfume, pieces of jewelry, clothing and appliances. Doña Emilia was told that most of them were pleased with just a box of chocolates, a bunch of red roses, or a handwritten love poem. By then, Magnolia and her team had built a makeshift tent village, which they kept moving to avoid being caught by el padre Rafael or the widows.

The men referred to the tent town as "the magical whorehouse," the one that sometimes was and sometimes wasn't. Looking for the mysterious tents along the tortuous roads, behind the woods and between the arid hills only added to a man's excitement. He'd search high and low—for hours, if he had to—but he always found it. And when he did, he soon disappeared between the arms and legs of a passionate woman, the moon shining down on their nude skin. Legs tightened, hips rocked, hearts sped up, sweat flowed, bodies lost control of breath, moans were set free, wails, screams—a man, a woman, a burst of fire under the sky.

TO TRY TO regain their customers, Doña Emilia and her twelve girls agreed to lower their rates and create more incentives. Sunday through Thursday would be two customers for the price of one. On Fridays, early birds would pay only half the price. And on Saturdays they would introduce Emilia's Fiesta: a three-hour party, which included food, drinks and the right to join all twelve girls, naked, in the red room—all for a fixed rate.

Doña Emilia traveled to Fresno, where she printed flyers with La

Casa's weekly specials, and handed them out herself in the surrounding villages. The old lady had turned into a saleswoman, traveling every day from town to town, her portfolio under her arm and a paper bag full of flyers in her hand. She spent long nights sitting alone in the barroom of La Casa, smoking her thin cigarettes and drinking apple wine straight from the bottle, thinking up fresh ideas that could keep her business afloat. But there was nothing she could do. How, she thought, could she compete with a group of invisible lustful women, romantic ghosts willing to have sex in exchange for a little taste of affection? She cursed the Communist guerrillas for taking her customers away, and wept inconsolably for each of the men who had disappeared.

Soon her lungs began to refuse the smoke of her cigarettes. She developed a nasty cough that could no longer be cured with the usual milk and horseradish sweetened with honey. She lost several pounds, and she got drunk with only a few sips of wine. And so the morning she heard the twelve girls packing their bags, she didn't try to stop them. Instead she rose from her bed, splashed fresh water on her face and went to the kitchen to prepare their last meal together.

A few hours later, when the twelve girls came out of their bedrooms with no makeup on, dressed in conservative outfits, and with their suitcases hanging from their shoulders, they found the old madam sitting in the dining room, her hands clasped together on top of the table. She was wearing a fancy gown of red silk that covered her body from the neck down. Her gray hair hung loose down her back, and there was something saintly about the expression of her face, something blissful and dreamy. The large dining table was covered with a white tablecloth and was beautifully set with cloth napkins, silver platters, casseroles and utensils and crystal glasses filled with wine. Spread over the table were baskets with corn bread, plates with fruit and cheese, a large bowl of steamy potato soup and oval dishes with roast turkey, white rice and red beans.

"Well, my dears," Doña Emilia said. "The time has come to say farewell." She looked down at her translucent hands, her eyes filling with tears. Viviana was the first one to hug her, and then one by one the other eleven girls took their turns. They wiped the tears from the madam's creased cheeks, kissed her small, trembling hands and stroked her hair. When the girls finally took their seats, Doña Emilia stood and raised her glass of wine. In a broken voice she proposed a toast.

"Here's to you, my brave girls, my disciples, who for years bore your own crosses by putting up with the men of Mariquita: sometimes abusive, sometimes rude, but always splendid.

"Here's to the men of Mariquita, our men, and to La Casa de Emilia, where they've been missed the most."

All thirteen women sipped their wine, sat down and began eating in silence. When they finished, Viviana proposed they all put on their work clothes. And so they wore their brightest dresses and helped one another to apply their makeup. Doña Emilia invited the girls into the barroom, where she played festive music. They danced and drank throughout the night, sharing their most amusing anecdotes, telling jokes, making new toasts, laughing and crying and laughing some more.

The following day, when Doña Emilia woke up, she found herself alone in the room, surrounded by dirty glasses and empty wine bottles. She imagined the twelve girls walking down the road, the sunlight shining on their greasy faces, dreaming, perhaps, of that day when they too could be contented with a bunch of red roses or a handwritten poem in exchange for their love. Doña Emilia wished for that fate for each one of them and closed her eyes, hoping she would never have to open them again. She'd decided to close down La Casa and to live for as long as her remaining savings allowed.

The magical whorehouse, the one that sometimes was and sometimes wasn't, one day disappeared forever and only love was to blame. The twelve young women found themselves in love, each one with a different man. Magnolia fell for a married barber named Valentín, a middle-aged, dark-skinned fellow who wore a stubborn hairpiece that moved all over his head. When he visited her tent, Magnolia talked incessantly about wedding gowns made of silk and engagement rings shaped as hearts. She also insisted on reading to him, by the light of a candle, a love story. Valentín thought the girl a little insane and stopped coming. Night after night Magnolia waited for him. She refused all others and turned down their gifts. Under her tent she mostly cried. Sometimes she arranged her provisions and weeded and watered her plants. But mostly she read the same old stories to herself and cried.

Eventually, the twelve girls concluded that God had given them two eyes to better look at men, two ears to better hear what men might want to say, two arms to embrace them and two legs to wrap around them, but only one heart to give. Men, on the other hand, loved with their testicles, and God had given them two.

And so one night the men couldn't find the magical whorehouse. They looked for the tents along the tortuous roads, behind the woods and between the arid hills. They searched high and low for weeks but never found them. The women had gone back to Mariquita, back to their spinsterhood and their sad nightly meetings filled with memories, back to fantasizing about that glorious day when the town's bachelors would be returned to them.

*   *   *

THEY RUINED MY business for nothing! Doña Emilia said to herself. Suddenly she heard, in the distance, a street vendor shouting her goods in a rather delicate voice: "Guayabas! Naranjas! Mandarinas!" Then she saw her, a young girl walking gracefully while balancing a large basket on her head. The old woman carefully observed everything about the girl, who looked no more than twelve: her pink dress, her black hair in braids, her long arms and small waist, and had the odd feeling that she'd known her for a long time. The girl also noticed the old woman. She smiled and gently waved. Doña Emilia smiled back. She was just about to ask the girl to join her at the bench when a gust of wind blew the girl's basket out of balance. Guavas, oranges and tangerines scattered over the ground. The girl knelt down and quietly began to gather them and put them in the basket. Doña Emilia wanted to help, but when she tried to rise from the bench she couldn't feel her legs.

And then there came a stronger gust of wind, and the mango, the one the color of sunset, dropped to the ground, right next to the girl. Doña Emilia saw the girl smile, saw her take the mango in her hands and put it in the basket, saw her stride down the road with the basket on her head and slowly vanish into the wind.

Feeling jubilant, Doña Emilia leaned back against the bench and fixed her eyes on the sky, only this time she couldn't see that it was blue.

José L. Mendoza, 32
Lieutenant-colonel, Colombian National Army

One thing I've learned in the army is that the less contact you have with your victim, the easier it is to kill him. I once let a man talk to me for too long before I shot him, and I still regret it. We had received a call from the police station of a small village in the mountains. They were being attacked by guerrillas and needed reinforcements. The roads were terrible, so we couldn't get there until the following morning, and by that time the rebels, we thought, were gone with whatever was worth anything. I was walking around the town counting dead bodies, unaware that at that moment, a guerrilla in a tree was aiming his Galil at the back of my neck with the clear intention of blowing my head off. One of my officers spotted him and shot him in the arm before the guerrilla could do anything. He was a brown-skinned, small-eyed Indian guy. We herded him and three more rebels we captured into a drainage pit.

When we gained control of the village, I asked the Indian to come out of the pit—I didn't want to shoot him in front of the other three. He knew what I was about to do, and so he claimed that he was too weak from all the blood he'd lost. I should just let him die in the pit. I shouted to him to come out, and he begged me not to shoot him. He said that his mother had had a stroke and that his two younger sisters had been seriously burned in some fire and that they were alive but they couldn't move their legs and that their faces were completely disfigured and that they were counting on him to support them and that he was a good man who had been forced into becoming a fighter and that if I could find it within myself to pardon him he'd quit the guerrillas and join the national army. . . . It was like he'd memorized the whole speech. And I don't know why, but I kept listening to his damn story and staring at his eyes, which had grown larger with fear. I let him talk and talk until he got tired and stopped. Then I knelt down in front of him, placed the tip of my revolver on his forehead, and told the other men in the pit that he had tried to kill me from behind and that it wasn't manly. "This is how you kill a man," I said, and shot him. At the sound of the blast, my eyes, involuntarily, closed. When I opened them, the Indian's body was still standing in the pit, but his head was gone from the nose up. His hair, his brains, his small eyes . . . they simply weren't there anymore. His mouth was, though, the muscles around his lips quivering as if they were trying to articulate something else he'd forgotten to tell me.

CHAPTER 4

The Teacher Who Refused
to Teach History

Mariquita, February 11, 1995

C LEOTILDE GUARNIZO WAS A sixty-seven-year-old spinster. She had short gray hair, a smooth mustache and white bristles on her chin. Thick spectacles rested on her round nose, which looked like an upside-down question mark, giving her face an enigmatic air. There was something masculine about her mannerisms: the way she sat with her legs wide apart, her fierce stomping gait and the way her right hand clenched instinctively when she felt threatened, as though ready to knock someone or something to the ground. Her countenance was completed by a frown that seldom relaxed. In short, she was the image of severity gone gray.

Cleotilde had been on an aimless journey when the bus by which she was traveling broke down. Night was beginning to fall, and Cleotilde was afraid. She hired a country boy to take her, by mule, to the closest village. She would spend the night there and resume her journey at dawn.

The boy dropped her and her suitcase at Mariquita's plaza and left. The village was especially quiet that night, and in the absence of light looked like a ghost town. Cleotilde's legs began to shake. Aimlessly and with great effort, she walked a few blocks until she saw a gleam of light in a small window. She hurried up to the house and knocked on the open door. Soon a young girl wrapped in a black shawl came into sight, a candle in her hand. The girl couldn't have been older than ten, maybe eleven.

"Come on in," she said in a sweet voice. She walked ahead, with the candle lighting a long, narrow hall. "My name's Virgelina Saavedra, and this is my grandmother, Lucrecia viuda de Saavedra." The girl pointed at a pale, old woman sitting on a rocking chair.

"I'm Señorita Cleotilde Guarnizo. At your service," she said, and then, addressing Lucrecia, added, "and I'm looking for a warm place to spend the night."

"You can stay here if you like," Lucrecia replied indifferently. "We have a spare hammock and a blanket somewhere."

Cleotilde hated hammocks. She couldn't understand how anybody could sleep while hanging in the air like sloths. Of course she wouldn't say that to them. They seemed like friendly country people. "I really appreciate it," she said.

Lucrecia motioned to her to sit. There was only one chair available, which made it easier and less awkward for Cleotilde. She set down her suitcase and sat and looked around, half smiling at the walls. The room was dark and stuffy, scarcely furnished, with a pile of cooking firewood sitting in one corner and two black scrawny cats lying in another. Cleotilde hated cats even more than she hated hammocks, and couldn't help wondering whether the ones in sight were alive or dead. They might as well be a part of the house's indigent furniture.

"Fidel and Castro," Lucrecia said suddenly. She appeared to be scrutinizing Cleotilde's face and body for some sign of wealth. She might ask Cleotilde for a donation before she left the next day. Lucrecia had already bartered, for food, most of her seamstress's equipment.

"I beg your pardon?" Cleotilde returned. She felt as though Lucrecia were scrutinizing her face and body for some sign of wealth. She truly hoped Lucrecia wasn't expecting her to pay for putting her up for a night. Cleotilde had barely enough cash in her purse to pay for the bus ticket that would take her far away from this decayed village.

"I said Fidel and Castro. Those are the names of the cats."

"Oh," Cleotilde returned. "Interesting names for a couple of cats. Are they alive?"

"Uh-huh," Lucrecia uttered. She paused, as to indicate a change of subject, then added, "As you can see, we're very poor."

"Oh, aren't we all?" Cleotilde interposed. "This war has left us all in financial straits." She wondered if Lucrecia knew the word *straits*. "You can't even tell who's worst, the guerrillas, the paramilitaries, or the government. . . . With the situation the way it is, tell me, who's going to employ an old woman like myself?"

"Nobody," Lucrecia replied, looking a little frustrated that Cleotilde's speech had ruled out any possibility of her making a few pesos that night. "We have nothing to offer you but coffee. You want a cup of coffee?" she said.

Cleotilde thanked her, saying that it was too late for coffee, that she asked for nothing but a place to sleep and a candle. "I like to read before going to sleep, don't you?"

"I don't read or write," the woman stated resolutely, as though she were proud of it.

"Sweet Lord! I can't imagine not being able to read." Then, addressing Virgelina, who was trimming the wick of a fresh candle with her teeth, she asked, "Do you read?"

The girl shook her head.

"Little girl," Cleotilde said, raising her index finger in the air. "You ought to know that education is a tool for success."

"Women around here don't need no education," Lucrecia said bitterly. "Besides, the school's been closed for over two years."

"Two years? How dreadful!"

Virgelina handed Cleotilde the candle and an empty Coca-Cola bottle to serve as a holder. "The magistrate promised us the school will reopen soon," the girl said softly. "As soon as a teacher gets hired."

"A teacher?" Cleotilde said, getting up from her seat. "Isn't that a coincidence? I'm a licensed teacher."

"Well, if you're interested, then you should stop by the magistrate's office tomorrow," Lucrecia suggested. "She's been interviewing candidates all week."

"You don't happen to know what the salary is, do you? Not that it matters much, for I'm a single woman without any financial obligations. Of course I'd have to rent a room and buy food, but how much can one spend on food in a small village like this. Really? That much for a pork chop? Well, I don't like meat, anyway. It's bad for you. It causes arthritis. Do you really? I have the remedy for that: crush a live scorpion and put it in a bottle with rubbing alcohol for a month. Then rub the alcohol on your joints every night before going to bed. It's a real godsend. An Indian told me about it. An Indian woman, of course, because men don't understand a woman's pain. They don't understand a woman's anything. No, I'm not married. Every man I ever met was a pig. Maybe the men of this village are different. . . . What do you mean, no men? Only the priest? Really? Communist guerrillas, eh? Well, that's wonderful! Terrible, but wonderful. I'd heard about towns of widows, but I'd never been to one. Uh-huh, the war, always the war. Men keep waging wars, and we keep suffering the consequences. At least you didn't have to flee and leave everything behind like I've seen people do. . . . So tell me about your magistrate. Is she friendly? Is that right? Well, nobody's perfect. Yes, I might apply for the job. Just for the sake of it, because I'm not sure that I want to stay in this village. All right, since you insist so much, I'll have some coffee. Just half a cup. Thank you."

THE FOLLOWING MORNING Cleotilde was up at five as usual; she rose at the same time every day no matter where she slept or how late she went to sleep. She got dressed in the semidarkness of the living room, where Virgelina had slung a hammock for her the night before. She put on a black pants suit and black running shoes and, carrying an ancient leather case with her credentials, went out into the dawn mist. Cleotilde imagined there would be other candidates, and she wanted to be the first one interviewed that morning. She was confident that she would get the job. In her long career as a teacher, there wasn't one position she'd applied for that she hadn't gotten. But before accepting the job, she needed to convince herself that Mariquita was a peaceful place where she could spend the rest of her days, a place where she'd feel safe and, as she was fond of saying, close to heaven.

For a moment her case felt heavier than usual. Then she thought, Who am I trying to fool? The contents of the case hadn't changed in years; she had. She was old now, old and frail. It didn't matter how straight her back looked when she walked, or how authoritative her voice sounded when she scolded misbehaving children—she was just a frail old lady terrified of many things. Terrified most of all of the night: of its murkiness in which dire things happened; of its prolonged silence that was nothing but the absence of the sounds she wanted to hear; of the crying ghosts she saw and heard in every corner; and of the horrible dream that kept coming back, torturing her night after night: a dream of men and blood and red velvet curtains.

THE SUN BEGAN to shine on everything: the terra-cotta tiles that roofed most of the houses, the puddles of rainwater in the unpaved streets, the long black hair of a small group of young women carrying large baskets of dirty laundry on their heads, singing and laughing as they strode by. They looked curiously at Cleotilde. The only travelers who stopped in Mariquita these days were fortune-tellers, doctors without degrees, fugitives, displaced families and those who had lost their way. On occasion a caravan of merchants arrived, their mules loaded with goods the villagers couldn't afford or no longer had use for—perfume, Coca-Cola, razors—but also others that were indispensable—coal, candles, kerosene, bleach for the magistrate and supplies of hosts and wine for the priest.

"Good morning, señora," one of the women called.

"Señorita," Cleotilde corrected her, but she spoke too softly, and the woman didn't hear her. Nonetheless, Cleotilde decided that the women of Mariquita were diligent and friendly. She turned left at the next corner and in the distance made out a boy and a girl holding a howling dog. She decided to greet them, her prospective students. Being from a small village, they would be shy and insecure; therefore, she decided, she'd be gentle with them. When she was close enough, she lowered her spectacles and noticed that they were barefoot and wore ragged clothes. She also noticed, to her horror, that the girl was holding the dog's mouth shut while the boy forced a stick into its bottom.

"What are you doing?" Cleotilde cried out. She slapped the boy on his back. The boy released the dog and kicked Cleotilde in the leg. "You crazy old woman!" he yelled. Then he ran away with the girl, laughing heartily. The dog ran away also, the stick still hanging from its bottom. Cleotilde was furious. She sat on the sidewalk to check her leg. Just a little red spot. Hopefully it wouldn't turn blue. She didn't bruise easily; not for an old lady anyway.

She picked up her leather case and limped two blocks down, shooing away the many stray cats and dogs that surrounded her, begging for food. At the next corner she turned right and was met by a group of half-naked children gathered beside a mango tree, chatting. Cleotilde thought they looked more civilized than the others. She would talk to them. "Good morning, boys and girls!" she chirped. "How are you all doing today?"

The children began laughing and whispering to each other.

"Isn't this a beautiful morning?" Cleotilde looked up at the sky, smiling with pleasure. The morning was indeed beautiful. "What's your name, son?" she said, pointing at a gangling boy who was scratching his armpit.

The boy quickly looked at his friends, as though for approval, and then, grinning, said, "My name is Vietnam Calderón, but they call me El Diablo." Making a monstrous face at Cleotilde, he said, "Boooooo!" All his friends laughed.

"Now, that's not polite, son," Cleotilde said calmly. In different circumstances she would have grabbed the boy by his ear, smacked him in the face, made him kneel down and apologize to her. Then she would have made him write, one hundred times, "I must respect my elders." But she had just arrived in Mariquita and didn't know the boys or their mothers. She stared at him long enough to remember his freckled face if she ever saw him again.

"I am Señorita Cleotilde Guarnizo," she said sternly, "and I might be your next teacher!"

"We don't want no teacher!" a little girl yelled from the back.

"Go away," a boy echoed. Soon they were all shouting in unison, "Go away! Go away!"

Ah! If only I had a ruler, Cleotilde thought.

"Go away! Go away!"

She threw them a disapproving look, then turned around and began walking in the direction of the plaza. She hadn't gone more than a few steps when a pebble hit the back of her neck. Her right hand clenched, and she turned to the children sharply, a flush of anger brightening her cheeks. The children stood defiantly, each holding a slingshot with the elastic strip drawn all the way back, ready to fling pebbles at the old woman.

"You little wretches!" she yelled, shielding herself with her case. This safety measure was perfectly timed because, without delay, a rain of pebbles flew at her, hitting her mostly on her legs but also on the tips of her fingers that showed on both sides of the case. "You scoundrels!" she screamed. "You rabble!" The children ran away, laughing and congratulating one another on their aim.

Cleotilde trembled with rage. If she stayed in this village—which she seriously doubted she would after this incident—the first thing she'd do as their teacher would be to punish them for such an affront to her dignity. She was imagining this punishment when five middle-aged women dressed in black appeared from around a corner, their heads slightly tilted and their hands joined before their chests. As they walked, the women sang, with great passion, a local version of the Hallelujah song. They must be the mothers of some of those little rascals, Cleotilde thought, giving them a withering look. She kept walking along the un-paved street until the wicked chanting of the children and the singing of their indifferent mothers were but an echo in the distance.

CLEOTILDE WAS THE first and only candidate to show up for an inter-view that day. She sat very still in the waiting room of the magistrate's office, the leather case resting on her lap. Her hands were shaking. She folded them on the case and decided to disregard the episode with the children and concentrate on the interview. But she couldn't concen-trate because Cecilia Guaraya, the magistrate's secretary, was repeat-edly hitting and cursing a rusty typewriter whose ribbon kept slipping out of place. "Damn you, you son of a rat! You load of pig's shit!" Cecilia shouted.

After a long wait, a broad-hipped woman came out of the magis-trate's office, a bucket in one hand and a broom made from branches in the other. Her head was wrapped in a colorful kerchief and she wore an apron on top of her black dress. Cleotilde seemed surprised. If the magistrate can afford a cleaning woman, she must be able to afford an excellent schoolteacher like myself, she thought, nodding her head. The woman, meanwhile, laid the cleaning tools next to Cecilia's desk and wiped her hands on her apron. Cleotilde noticed that the woman's apron was tattered and her shoes worn out, and this made her recon-sider her earlier assumption. Maybe I'm wrong, and this poor thing earns a starvation salary, she said to herself. Then she had a bad idea. She waited for the woman to look her way and gestured to her to come closer.

The woman looked confused. She looked at Cecilia as for guid-ance, but the secretary was completely absorbed in her task. And so she drew near Cleotilde.

"How much does she pay you to clean her office?" Cleotilde whis-pered, pointing toward the magistrate's office.

"I beg your pardon?" the woman said, looking insulted.

"How much does the magistrate pay you?" Cleotilde repeated furtively.

"I am the magistrate," the woman said.

Cleotilde covered her mouth with the tips of her fingers and gave a nervous laugh. "I apologize," she managed to say. Then, rising from the chair, added, "I'm Cleotilde Guarnizo, your humble servant."

"Rosalba viuda de Patiño," the other said harshly. "Magistrate of Mariquita."

Neither of them made an attempt to shake the other's hand.

THE MAGISTRATE WAS furious. Her secretary had warned her about the stranger sitting in the waiting area. "She seems weird," Cecilia had said. But now, standing in front of her, Rosalba decided that the old woman *was* weird. "Please come this way," she said, wondering when the outsider had arrived, where she came from, where she was staying, and, most importantly, why she, the magistrate, hadn't been informed about it. What if the government had sent the old woman? What if someone out there, a commissioner of some sort, had finally received the official report of the census that the magistrate had taken long ago, and which she made Cecilia type and send out with anyone and everyone who passed through Mariquita?

"Thank you," Cleotilde replied, entering Rosalba's office. The teacher had already decided, in her mind, that the confusion had been the magistrate's fault. She had met with magistrates and mayors before, even with governors. But she'd never been received by a dignitary dressed as a servant. She thought it inappropriate. And what was the purpose of all those cleaning rags piled up on the windowsill? And that smell, ugh! How much bleach had the woman put on the floor?

"Please have a seat," Rosalba said, pointing at a sad-looking chair, the stuffing showing through splits and holes. "My secretary told me that you're here to apply for the schoolteacher's position."

"That's correct."

"Good. Let's start then. Do you have related experience, Señora Guarnizo?"

"Señorita, Magistrate," the old woman corrected her. "And yes, I happen to have nearly fifty years of teaching experience, twenty-seven of which can be verified by looking over my portfolio under the section titled Cartas de Recomendación."

"Very good, Señorita Guarnizo. Very good," Rosalba said, a little intimidated by the teacher's husky voice, and by the complexity of the large case that Cleotilde had carefully begun to fan out on top of her mahogany desk. The documents were meticulously organized into several labeled sections, which included the names of the schools in which she had taught, subjects, periods of time, awards and distinctions and letters of recommendation. There was even a whole section with photographs and résumés of distinguished people she had tutored during the past twenty-seven years—now doctors, lawyers, architects and beauty queens.

"I'm impressed, Señora Guarnizo, but—"

"Señorita, Magistrate!" the teacher interrupted. "After spending sixty-seven years in chastity, one likes to be acknowledged with the proper title."

"Please forgive me, Señorita Guarnizo. I can't help feeling a little— intrinsic addressing a woman older than myself as 'señorita.' I feel almost—concupiscent." Overwhelmed by the old lady's self-confidence, Rosalba made a great effort to find words that sounded as pompous as the teacher's. "As I was saying, I am very impressed with your credentials of the past twenty-seven years, but where and what were you teaching before that?"

"I am afraid, Magistrate, that for personal reasons I won't be able to answer that question." Cleotilde's reply provoked a long, uncomfortable silence, which she had to break herself because Rosalba was pretending to read, in detail, every document in the teacher's portfolio. "Do you have any other questions, Magistrate? Questions concerning my more recent experience? I'll be more than happy to answer those for you."

"Let's see," Rosalba said, closing the portfolio. She thought carefully about what to ask. It had to sound smart. "Do you have a—plan of action for the students of Mariquita, Señorita Guarnizo?"

"I'll be very pleased to develop one as soon as I'm offered the job, in which case I'll converse with the prospective students to evaluate their current degree of knowledge."

"Very good, but do you have any idea of what subjects you'd like to teach? It's been so long since I attended school. I don't even know what they teach these days."

"I'm perfectly capable of teaching language arts, science, mathematics, social studies, geography, and ethics."

"What about Colombian history? Can you teach Colombian history? It was my favorite subject in school."

"I can teach that, too, Magistrate," Cleotilde said, "but I won't." She pushed her spectacles up her nose with her index finger. "And before you inquire about the reason why, I shall inform you that it's also due to very personal reasons."

Rosalba wondered if Cleotilde had been in jail for twenty years. *To get twenty years, she must have killed someone.* Or maybe she'd been shut away in a mental hospital. *She surely looks off her head.* Or perhaps the señorita had been really a señor before. *That mustache sort of gives her away.*

"That's all right," the magistrate said, looking around to avoid the teacher's piercing eyes. "Our students already have firsthand knowledge of civil wars and massacres. That's half our country's history right there."

"And how many students are we talking about, Magistrate?"

Rosalba promptly opened a drawer and pulled out a sheet. "According to our latest census we're a total of ninety-nine people, out of which—children grow so fast, there's always one or two I have to move into a different category. Let's see: thirty-seven widows plus forty-five maidens, minus . . ." She lowered her voice but continued adding and subtracting. "Fifteen children!" she announced after a little while. "But

I'm sure a few of the young women will also be interested in learning a thing or two. So I'd say about twenty students total."

"A very good number," Cleotilde observed.

A speck of dust on the floor caught the magistrate's attention. She couldn't understand how it had escaped her relentless broom and mop. She was tempted to pick it up, but in the mighty presence of Cleotilde, the magistrate felt self-conscious, vulnerable.

"Well, you seem to meet all the requirements that I have—conspired for this position," Rosalba said, still looking around. She was now avoiding not only Cleotilde but also the speck of dust, both of which were staring defiantly at her. "I shall come to a final decision in the next couple of days, then I'll make an official announcement."

"I'm looking forward to hearing your decision, Magistrate," Cleotilde replied. "And I trust that you will take into consideration the many benefits of filling the position with an individual who not only possesses extensive knowledge, but who is also qualified to teach discipline and proper conduct. You are aware, I'm sure, that these attributes have somehow vanished from the children of this town and—"

"Oh, believe me, Señorita Guarnizo. The police sergeant and I are perfectly aware of that situation. That is, in fact, the main reason why we want to reopen the school. Be assured that I'll consider that before selecting our new teacher. Now, if you will excuse me, I have a full agenda today."

Both women smiled insincerely.

Then a strange thing happened. As Cleotilde rose from the sad chair, her face lined up with the framed picture of the president of the republic hanging from the wall behind her, and the magistrate was appalled to notice that they had identical devious smiles. Cleotilde also seemed to have grown a few inches during the interview. In fact, the teacher looked taller than any woman or man Rosalba had ever seen. "Have a good day, Señorita Guarnizo," she managed to say, while pretending to take notes in an upside-down notebook.

As soon as Cleotilde stepped out of her office, the magistrate picked up the speck of dust from the floor and disposed of it. "What is the matter with me?" she said. "I ought to be ashamed to let an old spinster intimidate me in my own office." The last time she had felt that way was when she was sixteen and her evil stepmother was making her life miserable.

But Rosalba was no longer a naive young girl. "I'm no longer a naive young girl." She was a wise, sophisticated and experienced woman. "I'm a wise, sophisticated and experienced woman." She refused to feel threatened by a weird old spinster who had come into her office putting on airs, fancying herself as someone more intelligent, more educated and more capable than the magistrate herself. "How dare she come into my office in black when she's nobody's widow, and wearing running shoes when she can hardly walk?"

Rosalba ordered Cecilia to find out everything there was to know about the mysterious foreigner.

After the interview Cleotilde went to the market. She sat at a rustic table under a tent where the Morales widow and her daughter Julia—formerly known as her son Julio César—served meals and snacks. Cleotilde ignored the widow and the girl's inquisitive looks and ordered breakfast. While waiting for her food, she remembered the incidents with the children and wondered whether or not she should take the job—she had no doubt the magistrate would offer it to her—and stay. Living in an isolated village without men was especially appealing to her, but she was greatly troubled by the children's behavior, and also by their mothers, who acted as if it was nothing to worry about.

Julia Morales placed a cup of steamy black coffee in front of Cleotilde, then went to the grill and laid a half-cooked arepa over a weak fire. The old woman followed her with her eyes, thinking that she was a strange-looking young girl. Maybe it was the extravagant makeup she had on that made her look queer. She took a sip of coffee and looked around the marketplace, trying to find something positive to make her change her mind about Mariquita. Half a dozen faded tents were scattered over an expanse of clear ground. Under them the townspeople sold—or bartered—candles, coal, kerosene and prepared foods and beverages. Among the tents, lying on empty sacks spread on the ground, were potatoes, onions, corn ears and oranges. Not much variety, Cleotilde thought, but she had seen much worse. In the middle of the market an open cooking fire burned fitfully; next to it a mad-looking old woman leaned above a metal pot filled with water, stirring and sweating; a little farther down a burro gobbled a bunch of dry plantain leaves, while dogs and cats roamed around looking for something to eat. Suddenly a group of lookalike children appeared from around a corner, running. Cleotilde immediately recognized one of them, Vietnam Calderón, "El Diablo."

"We've got one! We've got one!" the boys announced enthusiastically. They gathered around the mad-looking woman and handed her a birdlike creature they had just killed with their slingshots. Smiling a toothless smile, the woman dipped the bird into the hot water, took it out and started plucking it, while the children shouted out different stories of the way they had killed the bird.

"They're good kids," the Morales widow said, noticing the contemptuous look Cleotilde gave the children. "They go out of their way to bring something for the Jaramillo widow to put in her pot. That poor woman is half crazy and has nobody to look after her." She nodded repeatedly, saying, "Very good kids indeed."

"They're savages, is what they are," Cleotilde declared harshly. She hoped the widow was the mother of one of them. If she was, Cleotilde would give her a piece of her mind.

The Morales widow got closer to Cleotilde and spoke in a whisper, "You see the two boys over there, just to the right of the burro? The taller one's Trotsky, and the other one's Vietnam. The poor things were forced to witness the killing of their fathers at the hands of guerrillas."

The widow's disclosure shocked Cleotilde. She frowned and bit her nails. "I'll take my arepa now," she demanded. Julia turned around and gestured to her mother that the arepa wasn't fully cooked. "It isn't done yet," the widow said.

"That's all right," Cleotilde said. "Give it to me the way it is!" Julia sneered at her and turned the corn griddle over and waited for it to cook longer. But Cleotilde didn't see this because her eyes were again fixed on the children. "Their mothers don't seem to care much about them," she went on.

"That might be true, lady," the Morales widow replied, "but God knows those poor women work day and night just to put a piece of bread on their tables." She heaved a sigh. "Being a widow is not an easy thing. I'm sure you know that."

"No, I don't," Cleotilde snapped. "And before I lose my temper, let me ask you one more time, may I please have my arepa now?"

The widow walked over to the grill and scolded her daughter for not listening, then put the arepa on a plate and placed it in front of the old woman. "I'm Victoria viuda de Morales," she said, holding out her hand to Cleotilde.

"I'll have some more coffee," Cleotilde replied rudely, slamming the empty cup on the widow's outstretched hand.

While eating her breakfast, Cleotilde reflected on the Morales widow's observation. Perhaps the children of Mariquita were not consciously evil. Maybe the war and the violence they'd witnessed had made them oblivious to the pain they caused others. Most killers started that way, hurting their animals and slinging pebbles at defenseless old women, and before you knew it, they were shooting guns and killing people in the most atrocious ways, because the scoundrels didn't even bother learning how to kill. But Cleotilde could save them from such dire future. If she took the job, she could teach them discipline and manners and turn them into honorable citizens. With regard to the mothers, she decided that they were just ignorant country people who took for granted that their only responsibility as parents was to feed their children. If she chose to stay in Mariquita, Cleotilde would have a word or two with them.

The Morales widow was gone by the time Cleotilde finished eating. Julia was sitting alone in a small table in the back, peeling fat red potatoes. "How much do I owe you?" Cleotilde asked. She hoped it wasn't more than five hundred pesos. She was running out of cash.

But cash wasn't on Julia's mind. The girl walked over to Cleotilde's table and relentlessly scrutinized her for valuables. She pointed at a gold ring on the old woman's right hand.

"I beg your pardon?" The teacher was outraged. "You can't put a price on this ring, dear. It was a present from my mother, and I've never removed it from my finger."

Julia lowered her head and began counting on her fingers, then gestured that she would serve Cleotilde three meals a day for fifteen days in exchange for the piece of jewelry.

Cleotilde looked at the ring. If she decided to stay in Mariquita, it was an offer worth considering. But the ring was her only connection to her past. Then again, it was also her only connection to that horrible and recurrent dream of men and blood and red velvet curtains. "Feed me three meals a day for two months, and the ring's yours," she said. "It's twenty-four-karat gold!"

Julia drew near the teacher and bent over to take a closer look at the ring: it was shaped like a python, with two tiny red stones for eyes. Julia had never seen anything like it before. All right, two months it is, she gestured with a long sigh.

After shaking hands on their deal, Cleotilde started pulling the ring off her finger, but it wouldn't come off. Julia, who was very diligent when she wanted to be, fetched a tin can where they kept the old stinky lard that was to be reused. She scooped some, rubbed it around Cleotilde's finger, and tried to remove the ring. At that moment, while Julia twisted and pulled, Cleotilde felt like her memory was being squeezed, forcing out a jumble of indistinct images: angry men, machetes, a gold ring, marigold flowers, blood, screams. Soon, however, the flashbacks started coming together, slowly and clearly, turning into a vivid recollection of the most traumatic episode of her life.

Like a film being played back in her mind, Cleotilde saw a small village of white houses roofed with terra-cotta tiles, and front yards overflowing with bright golden marigold flowers. The village, she remembered, was called San Gil. There, in a little house, lived a young woman named Milagro with her parents and brothers. She was a history teacher; a good teacher who could recount everyone of her nation's many civil wars as though she had fought in each one, and narrate, year by year, the inconclusive strife between the two traditional political parties.

One night she was sitting on her steps when she saw a large group of men armed with machetes rushing up her street, shouting out slogans against Liberals. She ran inside and hid behind a red velvet curtain. Soon the men burst into her house and forced her family into the living room. From her hiding place, Milagro watched the men gouge out her father's eyes and pull out her mother's nails before hacking them to death. After that, the men beheaded her younger brothers and dismembered their bodies. Before leaving, one of the men heard Milagro's sobs. He found her shaking behind the curtains with her hands wrapped over her mouth. He laughed and eased her down on the floor. Milagro didn't resist. She went soft and limp, staring blankly past him, grinding her teeth furiously. He ripped her skirt, and she firmly crossed her legs. He hit her across the face, and she tensed her body. He fastened his mouth on hers, forced himself inside her, and she just lay there, grinding her teeth. When he was finished, he noticed a gold ring on Milagro's finger. He grabbed her hand and tugged on the ring, but it wouldn't come off. He got angry and cursed her and tugged some more, harder each time, without results. He cursed her again, twisting and pulling and twisting . . .

"Stop!" Cleotilde yelled at Julia, who was still trying to remove the ring from the woman's finger. Cleotilde's body was now trembling. She reared up and glanced around, trying to reorient herself to the present. She noticed the people near her, the color of the sky, the shapes of things. She listened to her own heavy breathing, to the chirping of birds and the barking of dogs. She touched her arms and face and hair and rubbed her palms against the sides of her own legs to feel her clothes. Suddenly, she stamped her feet on the ground and, addressing no one in particular, shouted, "This happened long ago, and she survived. Milagro survived!"

Thinking she was facing a lunatic, Julia rose and moved away from Cleotilde, slowly and without taking her eyes off of her.

Cleotilde sank into the chair from which she had risen, closed her eyes and let the rest of her memories take the form of pictures, sounds, smells, body sensations and feelings, and come out of her mind once and for all.

She saw Milagro weep as she buried the bodies of her relatives in the back of her house. She saw her join hundreds of refugees from several towns who were fleeing to safer places. Then she saw Milagro cut her hair short and heard her change her name to Cleotilde Guarnizo. As Cleotilde she went from town to town hating men and teaching children the nation's history, which she recited from memory. She had a prodigious memory. However, when she was asked about her birthplace, her family, or the reason for her aversion to men, Cleotilde's memory didn't serve her well. She couldn't remember a thing about her past.

"She's pale." "She's shaking." "Maybe we should call the nurse." The old woman could hear different small voices in the distance, whispers that seem to come from nowhere. "I think she's just dreaming." "Lady, wake up!" Did they belong to her past or to her present? "Who is she, anyway?" "A traveler. She's staying with the Saavedras." "I think she's on her way to Dorada, or maybe Honda."

Cleotilde now recalled that when she turned thirty-seven (or maybe it was thirty-eight), she decided to settle down in Dorada (or maybe it was Honda). Soon she found a job in a respectable school where she was given an updated textbook of history to teach. As she started preparing her lessons, poor Cleotilde realized that some of the tragic historic events that she was about to teach, she herself had witnessed: the political civil war of 1948 known as La Violencia, where urged on by the ruling classes, thousands of peasants armed with machetes had begun massacring other peasants (Liberals beheaded Conservatives, and Conservatives butchered Liberals), and the military dictatorship that came after it. Chaos, pain, hunger and devastation were recounted in the book, supplemented with terrifying photographs and testimonials of people who, like Cleotilde, had seen their families and friends being mutilated and killed. Cleotilde immediately stopped teaching Colombian history, and before long found herself on the road again going from village to village, running away from her past, eluding new civil wars that in this country never ended, loathing men, dreaming that horrible dream. Then, one night, she arrived in Mariquita.

The memories, though intense, were no longer frightening. Cleotilde's breathing had become regular, and a healthy rose color appeared in her cheeks. She opened her eyes and saw a number of faces clustered around her.

"Are you feeling all right?" the Morales widow said. "You were shaking."

"And gasping for breath," Francisca viuda de Gómez added. The other women nodded.

Cleotilde rose and moved vaguely among the women, glancing from the one to the other with a blank expression. "I feel well," she said. "I feel really well, thank you." After hearing this, the women went back to their tents.

"Where's the girl?" Cleotilde asked the Morales widow. "Your daughter. Where is she?" The widow pointed at the back table, where Julia was slicing potatoes. Cleotilde walked up to her. "I have something that belongs to you, Julia." She slipped the ring off her finger in one smooth motion and put it on the table, next to the girl's hand. "It was the heat," she whispered. "My fingers swell up in the heat."

Julia put the ring on her middle finger and held her hand up for Cleotilde to see, gesturing that she really, really liked the ring. Cleotilde smiled, then started down the mango-shaded street, followed by the many sets of eyes that watched her suspiciously from tents and corners.

MEANWHILE, IN HER office, Rosalba debated whether or not she should offer the job to Cleotilde. She had already met with four other candidates so far that week, none of whom had a portfolio, a résumé or even teaching experience. One of them, Magnolia Morales, had arrived at the interview wearing shorts, slippers and rollers in her hair. When Rosalba asked her, "What makes you think you are qualified for the job?" Magnolia replied, "I read and write and I can recite the alphabet backward faster than anyone I know." Another candidate, Francisca viuda de Gómez, had brought a live, scrawny pig with her. After an intense verbal encounter with Rosalba's secretary, Francisca had dragged the noisy animal inside the magistrate's office and offered it in exchange for the job.

In the magistrate's mind there was no doubt that Señorita Guarnizo was the only applicant capable of doing the job. She was confident and experienced; perhaps *too* confident and *too* experienced. What if she wanted to enforce her own rules in town? What if she secretly aspired to be a magistrate? Besides, Rosalba knew nothing about her whereabouts before 1973, and the reason why she refused to teach Colombian history. Rosalba had been so intimidated that she'd forgotten to ask Cleotilde the most basic questions, like "Where are you from?" "Do you have any living relatives?" "Are you a hermaphrodite?"

THE FOLLOWING MORNING, Rosalba got to her office earlier than usual and immediately began to clean. She had learned, through her gossipy secretary, that Cleotilde Guarnizo had arrived in town two nights before and that she was staying at Lucrecia and Virgelina Saavedra's home. The woman's origins were unknown, but Rosalba was determined to find out from the teacher herself. With that in mind, she had invited Cleotilde for a second interview. This time, however,

Rosalba would be in control. She'd be the one leading the interview, asking questions and demanding answers. She'd rehearsed her introductory speech at home, in front of a large piece of mirror that hung in her bedroom, and then at the office in front of Cecilia.

When Cleotilde showed up, Rosalba's office was spotless, and the framed picture of the president of the republic had been removed from the wall. The magistrate herself looked elegant in her long-sleeved black dress with a lacy collar. Even her hair, gathered in the same old chignon at the nape of her neck, seemed neater and smoother than before. Cleotilde, dressed in a navy blue pants suit and pointed leather boots, walked inside the office with a vigorous stride. She sat rigidly across from the magistrate's desk, her legs slightly apart.

Rosalba began her speech with aplomb: "You are one of two finalists for the job, Señorita Guarnizo. I must admit that I'm very impressed with your portfolio. I can't think of a better candidate to fill the post. I am, however, a little troubled, since I've been informed that you are not formally settled in Mariquita, and we don't really know much about your former life . . ." She paused, giving Cleotilde the opportunity to disclose a few details about her mysterious life.

But Cleotilde didn't. Instead she fixed her eyes on the magistrate's, making Rosalba fix hers on her own restless hands lying on her lap. They sat silent till after a while Rosalba went on, "As you can understand, our children's education is vital to us here in Mariquita." She couldn't remember any of the questions she had prepared for Cleotilde. "I don't doubt for a second that you are—educated and experienced, but I was just wondering, I'd like to know. Well, *we* would like to know, after all I'm nothing but the voice of the villagers . . ."

At that moment, a beam of sunlight came through the window and illuminated Cleotilde's face with a distinctive glow. This time the magistrate saw a sixty-seven-year-old woman of grand stature. Her gray hair, smooth mustache and white bristles, her clenched hand and permanent frown, were all pieces of the woman's unspoken past; a past that commanded nothing but a great deal of respect.

"We were wondering if—if you would like to take the job. Do you want to take the job, Señorita Guarnizo?" Rosalba asked.

It had taken Cleotilde a lifetime to confront her fears, but only two days to accept the fact that even with all its poverty and chaos, with its wild children, their indifferent mothers and its incompetent magistrate, Mariquita was the closest to heaven she would ever be. Today, for the very first time in her life, she felt thoroughly prepared to wed herself inseparably to something, anything.

"I do," she answered resolutely.

Ángel Alberto Tamacá, 35
Guerrilla commandant

We had been marching for days and used up all our food supplies. Right before sunset, we came upon a small thatch-roofed hut. I decided they would feed us. A middle-aged, thickset woman opened the door before we knocked, as if she had been waiting for us, and went back inside without saying a word. We followed her. The house was just a single room, dark and small. It reeked of dead animal. A man lay on the ground against the wall, covered partly with a white sheet and partly with a swarm of green flies. The woman was applying compresses to his face. He'd been badly beaten.

"They killed the pigs and the chickens and ate all the food," she informed us, with not a trace of resentment on her face.

"Who did it?" I asked.

"The paramilitaries. Who else? They accused my husband of helping the guerrillas. Look at what they did to him." She lifted the sheet. The man's arms were crossed over his belly. Both hands had been chopped off, and the stumps were wrapped in bloody rags tied up with string.

"Shhh," she said to the man. "It'll be all right." She gently covered his arms with the sheet.

I got closer to the man and felt for the pulse on his neck. He was dead. He had been dead for hours. "Señora," I said, "this man has passed." And then, "I'm sorry."

The woman soaked the rag in the water, wrung it and patted the man's face with it. "It'll be all right," she repeated with a tender smile, shooing the flies away.

"Señora," I tried again. "Did you hear what I just said?"

"I'm afraid I don't even have coffee to offer you," she said, addressing the men behind me. "You see, they killed the pigs and the chickens and ate all the food."

We crossed ourselves and left in silence.

CHAPTER 5

The Widow Who Found a Fortune Under Her Bed

Mariquita, August 1, 1996

T HE DREAM WAS SO incredibly vivid that when Francisca viuda de Gómez woke from it, she was awfully disappointed. In her dream she'd been in the kitchen, making lard soup for dinner, when she heard the church bell ringing insistently. She ran to the window and in the distance made out an endless line of male figures slowly coming down the mountain, toward the village. Mariquita's men were coming back from the war!

Feeling more obliged by her moral duties than delighted by her husband's imminent return, Francisca went outside to meet him. She stood under the mango tree across the street and waited. As the figures neared her house, Francisca noticed two things: the former guerrillas were all faceless, and except for their olive-drab peaked caps and knee boots, they were naked, with small penises and enormous testicles. Now, how would she recognize Vicente, her husband? She remembered that he had a distinctive scar shaped like a five-pointed star on the right side of his forehead. But each of these marching figures had the same flat, pale surface where his face used to be. The sun was setting, and there she stood, watching the mysterious figures march along the street, giggling nervously.

ANOTHER RAINY SEASON had begun, and a new leak had appeared in Francisca's roof. She pulled a chamber pot from under her bed, put it next to the armoire where the roof was leaking, and watched how the rainfall mixed with her urine, creating tiny bubbles. She remembered that it was the first day of the month, and the thought put a smile on her face. With visible excitement she fetched, out of the drawer of her night table, a cloth bag and an ancient book of divinations called *Veritas*, which contained one thousand oracular messages. *Veritas* could only be consulted once on the first day of every month, by following two simple steps: First, formulate an explicit question while addressing the book. Second, pick, at random, a small numbered ball from a bag that contained one thousand of them. The chosen figure corresponded to the message that would answer one's question. Francisca carried *Veritas* and the bag to her old rocking chair and sat down, and as she lifted the book from her lap with both hands, she said loudly to it, "Veritas, tell me, What's the secret to happiness?" She had been asking the same exact question every month for the past few years. All the answers were vague and unintelligible, written in old-fashioned Spanish that Francisca could hardly read. Still, she found *Veritas* quite amusing and looked forward to the first day of every month.

She introduced her hand into the cloth bag and gave the thousand little balls a vigorous stir before drawing out the one with the number 739 written on it.

739. TRANSFORMATION

ARCANE: . . . And the light it gave off was dazzling and the heat was scorching and the flames overwhelmingly high, and yet fire and heaven never united.

EXEGESIS: All transformations in life must be considered in accord with the effect they bring about.

JUDGEMENT: If it brings you unhappiness, rid yourself of it.

Francisca repeated the prophetic message time after time, like a prayer, somehow sensing that, this time, *Veritas* had answered her question, and that the answer would have a great impact on her life. She put the book and the bag away and looked around the room thoughtfully. The one thing that brought her the most unhappiness was Vicente, her husband. But how to get rid of someone who dwells in one's mind? The thought of it left her exhausted. She went back to the rocking chair.

Almost four years had gone by since the day the men disappeared from Mariquita; four years since Vicente Gómez, Mariquita's barber, was kicked out of his house by guerrillas, brutally beaten and then forced to join them. All this time Francisca had secretly hoped that the insurgents would eventually realize that except for cutting hair, shaving beards and trimming mustaches, Vicente was of no use to a group of revolutionaries, or to the world, and kill him. She closed her eyes and made an effort to remember what Vicente looked like sitting on the toilet. This was a harmless memory exercise that she did almost every morning, the sole purpose of which was to let out some of the frustration she had accumulated over the years. To her surprise, today she only pictured the toilet—its white ceramic bowl, its hinged, plastic seat and lid, even the silvery flushing device. She tried a second time, and again she saw nothing but the deserted toilet. She was delighted to realize that without the help of his picture, she was no longer able to visualize her husband's face. Like those of the men in her dream, Vicente's face was nothing but a flat, pale surface with no facial traits whatsoever. Perhaps getting rid of her largest source of unhappiness was not as difficult as she had imagined.

The message had said something about transformation, and so

Francisca decided she would change her life. She would introduce the changes gradually, so as not to upset the priest or the most puritan women. First, Francisca would wear her long hair down. She had beautiful coal black hair, too beautiful to be kept up in a graceless bun. Second, she'd request permission from the magistrate to wear dresses that were not black. After all, the other day she'd seen Cleotilde Guarnizo, the new schoolmistress, in a dress with yellow buttons on it. Then she'd concentrate on fixing her dilapidated house: mend the leaks and fill the chinks in the walls. She would have liked to paint her entire house bright red, but she couldn't afford to. For the time being, all she could do to transform her house was to rearrange her scant furniture.

She began this task by pushing the shabby cedar armoire from one corner to another, except this time she placed it at an angle. She noticed that the part of the wooden floor on which the armoire had been resting, though covered with dust and cobwebs, was still smooth and glossy. It had taken her two years to convince her stingy husband to floor their house with pine boards. He'd argued that it was an unnecessary expense, and she'd replied that the dust from their earthen floor was killing her slowly. She even pretended to have a persistent cough, allergies, asthma and other respiratory problems. But it wasn't until she claimed that the continuous inhalation of dust was keeping her from becoming pregnant that Vicente hired a carpenter, not only to floor their house with the smoothest pine boards he could find, but to polish them twice, three times, four times or, like he told the worker, "Until I can see my wife's underwear reflected on them."

Their marriage had not always been bad. Francisca remembered how much her husband used to enjoy making her believe he was truly guessing the color of her underwear. Eventually it became a daily game, and the merry couple agreed on a prize for the winner: every time Vicente guessed correctly he'd get a long kiss, but if he failed he'd give Francisca five hundred pesos. She found the game to be erotic, and so she bought revealing lingerie in unusual colors. Every morning he guessed right, and she rewarded him with a long kiss that usually led to passionate sex. As a result, Barbería Gómez often opened late for business. Francisca had figured out from the beginning that it was the shiny floor that gave away the color of her underwear, but she didn't confess to him that she knew until after seven months. And even when she told him, they laughed together and kissed some more, and he gently rubbed her belly, surprised that it was almost unnoticeable. She was six months pregnant.

But now, all that was left of their love and merriment was a small, shiny rectangle on the lower part of her house, covered with dust. She dragged the rocking chair close to the window and emptied the chamber pot, which was on the brink of overflowing. She pulled and pushed the bed in every possible direction, and finally resolved to leave it in the middle of the bedroom so that her broom and mop could easily access all four corners of the room when she cleaned it.

It was then, after moving the bed around, that Francisca noticed a small piece of paper showing through the crack of a loose floorboard. It was a will signed by a Señorita Eulalia Gómez, stating that she had left her entire fortune—two hundred million pesos—to Vicente. Eulalia had been Vicente's great-aunt, his only relative—a wealthy spinster who had died of old age in Líbano, her hometown, fifteen years before. With the help of a hammer Francisca pried up the board and found buried, under the dirt floor, underneath the bed where she had lain for many years, a large bag filled with bank notes. She felt a sudden rush of anger furiously traveling through her body. She moved randomly about the room and didn't stop until she caught a glimpse of her own reflection in a piece of mirror hanging from the wall. She approached the mirror, cautiously, as though afraid it would cast back a monstrosity. But all she saw was a pitiful thing, a foolish woman who had spent more than half her married life living in poverty while her husband had a fortune buried under their bed. She abruptly flew into a rage and went around the house breaking dishes and glassware, knocking pictures off the walls, kicking chairs and tables and ripping down curtains.

Finally, when she was completely exhausted, she fell to her knees with her hands flat, hitting the floor with her forehead, weeping.

She stayed like that for a long while, recalling how her husband had begun to change after he noticed that Javier, their son, wasn't growing up as fast as the rest of the boys of Mariquita. And when Dr. Ramírez finally confirmed that their son was a midget, Vicente stopped talking to her for almost a year. He threw a large party for Javier's fifth birthday, but the morning after, he locked his son in a room and forbade Francisca to let him be seen by anybody in town. He cut her weekly allowance in half, as if the size of their son dictated the amount of money she was permitted to spend. He started drinking every night and stopped eating at home, and when Francisca asked him for money to buy an extra pound of rice or a loaf of bread, he refused. Instead, he accused her of being a greedy, wasteful wife who spent her allowance heedlessly. For years Francisca lived poorly, buying only the bare essentials for the house, wearing torn clothes, looking for sales and discounts, begging for bargains, stretching to the maximum the insignificant amount of money that Vicente gave her weekly, and which he cut down even more every time he looked at his son.

And then Javier died. When the doctor pronounced his death due to malnutrition, Vicente blamed it on his wife. He told everyone in town that Francisca was a cruel, horrible mother and a coldhearted wife. And she believed it. She even wished herself dead because she'd birthed a midget and let him die and was most likely going to lose her husband too: that charming man who used to notice the color of her underwear and who was late for work every morning so that he could stay home making love to her.

Francisca rose from the floor and walked around the house collecting all her husband's belongings—clothes, pictures, hats and shoes, shaving cream and his small collection of long-playing records. Then she gathered her own mourning apparel—dresses, veils, stockings, mantillas, scarves and any other piece of black cloth she came across. All these she crammed into a cardboard box and set in the doorway, then kicked it out violently, shouting: "If it brings you unhappiness, rid yourself of it!" Feeling proud of herself, she went back to her bedroom and dug her fortune out of the hole. The bank notes were all the same denomination—ten thousand—and they'd been arranged with the face of Colombian heroine Policarpa Salavarrieta facing up. Francisca had never seen so much money. She couldn't imagine how she would ever spend two hundred million pesos. Perhaps she should move away from Mariquita; go to a big city where she could start a new life, a real life with a large house, a handsome husband and healthy children. Mariquita had nothing to offer a rich woman like herself. Yes, it was true that these days some women were farming and that food, though sometimes limited, was not lacking. But with food or without it, Mariquita was a miserable village where nothing happened. The only reason she'd stayed was because of her friends. She had very good friends; kind and loyal friends, like Victoria viuda de Morales, Elvia viuda de López and Erlinda viuda de Calderón, to name a few. What would happen to them if she left? Perhaps she should take some of them with her. Six or eight. Six sounded more realistic. But which six? Oh, what a dilemma! To think she had to wait a whole month before being allowed to consult *Veritas* again.

So many things could happen in a month . . .

She looked through the window. The rain had stopped, the sky had cleared and already someone had taken away the box she had thrown out onto the street. A bright new world was awaiting Francisca. She stacked her money on top of shelves and tables and chairs. Then she went to her room to get dressed.

When Francisca left her house, she had on a pair of red slacks and a yellow blouse that revealed a lot of cleavage. She'd brushed her hair long and smooth and put makeup on her face, and she had a bag slung over her right shoulder. She strode purposefully toward the market where she was known as "La Masatera," because it was there, under a faded green tent, that she had sold the best masato in town for some four years. Her recipe for the fermented maize drink had been passed down among her ancestors for generations. When Francisca arrived, her friends and neighbors were meekly setting up their stalls and bringing out their scanty merchandise for selling and bartering. Some stretched their necks, some strained their eyes; all wanted to make certain that the woman violating the magistrate's ban on bright-colored clothing was indeed "La Masatera." Walking among her friends, Francisca, with her handbag full of pesos, felt somewhat different—a little prettier, a little more interesting.

She stood in the middle of the market and waited for the crowd to gather around her. Once she got everyone's attention, she bluntly said, "I found a fortune buried under my bed." She paused and waited for her friends' reaction, which had already occurred in the form of astonishment, a form that Francisca, a rather thoughtless individual, mistook for incredulity. "Don't you believe me?" she asked, her hands on her narrow hips. Before the women had the opportunity to reply, she opened her bag and flashed large rolls of bills. "And this is not even a hundredth of it," she boasted in case there were any doubts. "I'm having a dilemma, though. Shall I stay in town or leave? What do you all think?" Disconcerted, the women looked at one another, Francisca's words jumbled up in their minds. Francisca observed them long and hard. Poor things! she thought. They could never help me find an answer because they're content here. They're convinced that this is all they can manage. They're so doubtful and insecure, so poor. She gave money to all her friends, then excused herself and headed for the magistrate's office.

"The magistrate wishes not to be interrupted this morning," Cecilia said without taking her eyes off of the typewriter. "Come back in the afternoon." But Francisca was determined to see the magistrate. She took a couple of bills from her bag and with feigned discretion placed them on top of Cecilia's typewriter.

"Perhaps if we pretend that you didn't see me . . ." Francisca said. It took Cecilia a few seconds to establish the connection between the pesos in front of her eyes and the widow's unfinished sentence—after all, no one had ever bribed her before—but once she understood the deal she snatched the money and made it disappear between her generous breasts.

The last time Francisca had been inside the magistrate's office, she had brought a live pig and offered it in exchange for the schoolmistress's job. Naturally, she'd been thrown out of the building. But today it was different: Francisca was rich. She straightened her shoulders and pushed out her chest and went inside the office. She found Rosalba sitting at her desk, writing what looked like a letter on a piece of yellowed paper.

"Magistrate, I came to see you because I'm in a quandary," Francisca said at once. "And since you're the most rational person in this town . . ."

Rosalba looked up when she heard this flattery.

"You see, I found a fortune under my bed this morning, and now I can't decide whether or not I should leave Mariquita."

The magistrate's eyes traveled quickly from the widow's groomed hair to her knees—which was all she could see from behind her desk. "It looks like someone needs to be reminded about Mariquita's law," she said, looking aggravated.

"Magistrate, this morning I learned that if something brings you unhappiness, you ought to rid yourself of it," Francisca went on. "Unhappiness is all this town brings me. So on the one hand I think I should leave, but on the other hand I don't want to abandon my dear friends to their terrible fate here."

"Did you hear what I just said, Francisca?"

"Of course I could take a few of them with me, but which ones? And what would happen to the ones left behind? Please tell me, Magistrate, what would you do in my situation?"

"Well, first I'd change back into mourning clothes, and then I'd contribute half of my fortune to Mariquita's ruined treasury."

It was obvious to Francisca that the magistrate, like her friends, wouldn't help her choose from the equally undesirable alternatives with which her new wealth had presented her. She abruptly turned and walked out of the office, thinking that, after all, Rosalba was not as rational as she'd thought.

Outside a large crowd awaited her. The rumor had spread that Francisca had found a fortune and was giving money away. "Please help us!" they all said, their hands outstretched. The youngest one stroked Francisca's hair, another one massaged her hands; one even knelt before her as in worship. Francisca got furious because these women had no self-respect. Why did they have to demean themselves? When she was poor, Francisca had never kowtowed to anyone for money. Not even her husband. "Have some pride!" she yelled at them, swatting at their obsequious hands as if they were stinkbugs.

She hurried back to her house. Three of her friends were sitting on the steps, waiting for her.

"We need to talk to you, Francisca," said the Marín widow, whose head and upper face were wrapped in a black veil, making her broad nostrils look as though they were her eyes. Francisca invited the group into her house.

"You shouldn't leave Mariquita," Police Sergeant Ubaldina said in a solemn voice.

"You must wait for your husband's return," the Calderón widow added.

"Vicente's dead," Francisca declared. "And so are your husbands." She told the women about her dream and what the book had said, and then, to give some credibility to her outrageous statement, she asked each woman to close her eyes and imagine her husband's face. After a short while, she asked them to tell her what they had seen. The three women were horrified to discover that all they remembered was hair coming out of a long nose or a large cataract in a black eye; that they had been weeping over an unkempt mustache, a gold tooth, or a hairy mole on a prominent chin. They couldn't remember their men's individual smells either, or the sound of their voices. Their husbands were but dusty pictures and trunks filled with wrinkled clothes that sooner or later would be eaten by insects. The three widows realized that their men had died in their hearts, and this thought filled them with guilt.

But the guilt didn't last very long. Encouraged by Francisca—who now, being wealthy, was also assumed to be smart—the three widows went home and changed into bright-colored dresses. Before noon they met Francisca on the outskirts of Mariquita. Each widow had brought a bag filled with her husband's belongings and her own mourning clothes. They piled up clothes, pictures, books, baseball caps, unopened packs of cigars and even a billiard cue. At the count of three, Francisca shouted, "If it brings you unhappiness, rid yourself of it!" and set fire to the pile. They sat there, staring into the growing blaze, giggling nervously as the flames gave forth light of various brilliant colors.

Before the end of the day Francisca went to church, confident that el padre Rafael would give her some good advice. The little man was fond of expressing his opinions and making recommendations. She knelt down behind a side panel of the basketwork folding screen that for years had served as the confessional. The screen, which had three panels, was intentionally folded in the shape of a letter U. Every evening before mass, the priest sat inside the U to hear confessions through the long, narrow openings he had cut on each side. Francisca didn't need to tell el padre her story or ask for guidance—the magistrate had already told the priest everything he needed to know, as well as what counsel to give the confused woman.

"You should stay in town, dear," el padre began, his tone more a subtle mandate than a wise word of advice. "Mariquita's biggest problem is not the lack of men but the lack of resources. How much money is it you found?"

"Two hundred million pesos."

"Very good. Now, if you invest a part of your money in a lucrative business here, you'll be reactivating the town's economy. Say, for instance, that you decide to reopen your husband's barbershop. First you'll need to hire people to do the construction work, which means you'll create jobs, which means people will get salaries and spend their money in our own smaller businesses, which means there will be demand for other products and services. You'll be helping Mariquita tremendously, and at the same time you'll profit from your investment." El padre's voice was low-pitched, his sentences calculated. "Trust my words, dear!" he said with fervor.

From where she was kneeling Francisca couldn't see the man who spoke the words she was compelled to trust, and she thought it was for the best. Ever since the first time she met him, Francisca had been somewhat troubled by the priest's strange looks: his bald head never seemed a part of him—it was too large for his small frame—and his face, flaming pink, contrasted sharply and oddly with a black soutane that concealed the rest of him as if something deceitful and mysterious were living underneath it. Francisca had no other choice but to trust the man's words. After all they were the only words of advice she'd been given concerning her quandary. She was silent for a while, contemplating her options. And then, as she glanced at the background of fading images and pews riddled with woodworm, she said, "How much do you want for the church, Padre?"

The question caught the priest by surprise. "I beg your pardon?"

"I'm taking you up on your recommendation, Padre. I want to have my own business, and your church seems to be the most lucrative house in town." Her voice dropped to a whisper. "How much do you want?"

"The house of God is not a commercial establishment!" he burst out.

"Oh, Padre, you know very well it is too. People come here to buy peace of mind. They pay you to intercede for them with your invisible Lord." The words poured easily from her, arousing el padre's ire.

"Be silent!" he shouted, his face redder than usual. "I will not have you speak about the Holy Church in your worldly terms." He rose hurriedly and started to leave. But then stopped suddenly, as if he had forgotten something important in the confessional, and turned back.

Addressing the screen behind which Francisca knelt, he said, "By God, you'll be sorry you said that."

IF SHE COULDN'T have the church, Francisca would have to make do with renovating Vicente's old barbershop and reopening it as a beauty parlor. Of course she wouldn't rely on Mariquita's women to support her business—they were too plain. Instead she would attract refined women from other villages. They would be so pleased that the next time they would bring their friends, who would in turn bring theirs, and before long Francisca's salon would have its own distinguished patronage. Very soon I'll be a business owner, she thought before going to bed, and that thought stayed with her even in her sleep that night.

The next day she hired Orquidea, Gardenia and Magnolia Morales to repair the run-down barbershop for her. Francisca asked them to remove from the walls two yellowed posters—one advertised pocket combs, the other brilliantine—and several hooks where men used to hang their hats and coats. She ordered them to take down the unpolished framed mirrors, the counters and shelves and drawers, and to take out the two old conventional barbershop chairs. She continued having things removed and thrown out until the old Barbería Gómez was nothing but an empty room with a rusty metal door. As Francisca exited the shop, she was suddenly reminded of her husband; not by his personal equipment and furniture, which now lay in a defiant heap in front of the building, nor by the two incomplete words cheaply printed on the glass window: BARBE ÍA G MEZ; but by a crack between the doorway and the sidewalk, which was still filled with burnt matches, cigarette butts, candy wrappers and large amounts of dirty hair. She ordered her three employees to clean the crack and fill it in with putty.

Before going to bed that night, she looked at herself in the mirror. She wasn't pleased with what she saw: a slender forty-six-year-old woman hoping to look thirty but actually looking over fifty. Her hair was smudged with gray, and the deep creases under her eyes looked more like ostrich's feet than crow's. Her hands were scarred by burns and cuts that would forever remind her that, unlike most women in Mariquita, she was unfit for the kitchen. She decided that, like the old Barbería Gómez, she too needed a major renovation.

The following morning Francisca put on her best dress and shoes and packed a large amount of money in a bag. The rest of her clothes and food supplies, she put in boxes and left on her doorstep for someone poor to take. She went to the old barbershop and assigned specific duties to each of the three Morales sisters. She'd be back in two weeks, she told them. She stopped by the school and, after having an argument with the rigid schoolmistress, got permission to take Vietnam Calderón for a few hours. The boy carried her on one of his mother's three mules to the main road, where Francisca took a bus to Ibagué, the closest city.

When she arrived in Ibagué, she hailed a taxicab and asked the driver to take her to the best hotel in town. There she took a room. Later that day she went shopping at fashionable clothing stores. "I'd like to see trousers," she said to the sales clerk. "Trousers and blouses in bright colors."

She spent several hours trying on pants and blouses and coats of different styles, lengths and colors. She paid dearly for dozens of outfits and pairs of shoes with heels so high she couldn't walk in them. Then she bought purses and belts to match them, and costly brooches and jewelry and silk scarves and gloves and hats and stockings to complement them. That night, when Francisca got back to her suite in the hotel and her new wardrobe was delivered, she unpacked all the bags, unwrapped each item and carelessly threw everything on the large bed. She lay naked on top of the jumble of clothes and accessories and luxuriated in the feel of silk blouses and scarves against her skin. She covered herself with a fur coat and closed her eyes. As her fingers traced the soft fur and the scent of animal skin mixed with the sharp smell of her perspiration, she began to fantasize. She pressed the tips of her fingers into her cheeks and fancied that her face was covered with animal fluff. She stroked her long hair and imagined that it, too, had turned into fur; that that magnificent coat, those clothes and shoes and belts surrounding her, had changed her into something else, a wild creature she'd always longed to be. Feeling afraid of her own reveries, Francisca opened her eyes. The coat still wrapped around her body, she rose from the bed and looked at herself in the mirror. She was still the same Francisca: old looking, with wrinkles around her eyes and scarred hands. What the mirror didn't reflect and she couldn't yet recognize, however, was another woman, a completely different Francisca growing fast inside the old one. That night she fell asleep thinking about what she would do next.

The following morning Francisca mistakenly wore a blouse that didn't match her trousers that didn't match her shoes that didn't match her belt that didn't match her purse, and she put on colorful makeup that, somehow and separately, matched everything she had on. She made an appointment with Ibagué's most renowned hairstylist, a tall and strong man with long, black hair, who was nicknamed Sansón. Francisca walked into the salon looking like something which was in the process of transforming into something else, but was still far from achieving it, like an egg being hatched.

"I want to look like that," she told Sansón, pointing at a stunning woman on a shampoo advertisement taped to the wall. The man glanced at the picture and back at her.

"It will cost you a fortune to look like her," he earnestly said.

"Then you'd better start right away," she retorted. Sansón dyed Francisca's hair, cut it, brushed it and blow-dried it; his assistants plucked out her eyebrows, curled her eyelashes, clipped her nails and toenails, painted them, massaged her feet, removed her light mustache, gave her a facial and applied fresh makeup to her face. By the end of the day she not only felt like a completely different woman, she looked like one too. She didn't resemble the woman on the advertisement in the slightest, but her new appearance gave her an unquestionable air of refinement far beyond her expectations.

The following day she registered for an intense one-week etiquette course with Don José María Olivares de Belalcazar, an old man who had fled his native Spain after the kingdom fell into the dictatorship of General Franco. Once in America, Don José María gave himself a noble title, marquess of Santa Coloma, which automatically made him a member of the small privileged upper class of Ibagué. (As the old adage says, "He who goes abroad presents himself as count, duke, or lord.") The marquess made his living teaching etiquette because, according to him, "We discovered South America some five hundred years ago, and still these barbarians don't know how to hold a fork." Francisca was indeed the perfect illustration of his prejudiced statement: uncultured, unrefined, even vulgar. She learned from the marquess the most conventional rules of dining out. "First rule: Unfold your napkin on your lap soon after the host, *not before*. Second rule: The napkin remains on your lap throughout the entire meal and should be used to *gently* blot your mouth." And so on. She also learned to use the correct silverware by starting with the utensil that was farthest from the plate. In her house in Mariquita there was only one fork, and it hadn't been used since her husband had disappeared. Francisca preferred to eat with her fingers and a wooden spoon.

With her fine clothes, new looks and good manners, Francisca finally hatched out. She dined at fancy restaurants and visited exclusive social clubs. She went to bars and cocktail lounges. She got drunk more than once, vomited inside a taxicab and in the lobby of the hotel, and had sex with another woman.

Francisca had secretly wanted to have sex with a woman since she was young. She had once tried to make a sexual advance to a mildly retarded girl who came to her door selling blood sausages, but when Francisca tried to feel her breasts, the girl dropped the sausages and ran away screaming. But here in Ibagué, she was a foreign woman in a foreign city. Most importantly, she had money to buy whatever she wanted, including sexual favors from one of the hotel's chambermaids. What happened was this: After Francisca threw up in the lobby of the hotel, the desk clerk called a young chambermaid and asked her to take Francisca back to her suite. In her room, Francisca couldn't contain herself. She threw herself upon the maid. The maid refused her instantly, but after Francisca put a wad of pesos in the pocket of her apron, not only did she surrender to Francisca but she also seemed to enjoy herself.

Francisca liked having sex with a woman. Perhaps when she got back to Mariquita she could order one of her employees—Magnolia, most likely—to have sex with her, and then have her mend the leaks in her roof, and have sex with her again, and then make her paint the walls of her house blue, and then repaint them red, then yellow, then green, and have sex with her in between each color, and when she ran out of colors she'd go into shades, a little lighter, a little darker, and so on.

Before going back to Mariquita, Francisca ordered new equipment, furniture and supplies for her beauty parlor. She gave the salesman a deposit, and he promised to deliver everything within two weeks to an address in Mariquita—a village he had never heard of and couldn't locate on a recently updated map.

IN THE MEANTIME, in the unheard-of village of Mariquita, the magistrate had met privately with the priest to mastermind a legal way of taxing Francisca's fortune (currently there were no written laws pertaining to fortunes found under someone's bed). They agreed that since the money had been found in Mariquita's territory, Francisca was required to pay a percentage of her fortune for the support of the local government. Rosalba asked el padre Rafael how he felt about making the tax a round 50 percent. The priest said he liked that number very much because he had just turned fifty. He added in a brooding tone that Francisca should also be enforced to pay a percentage of her fortune for the support of the local church and the clergy. He asked the magistrate how she felt about making the tithe 20 instead of the customary 10 percent. The magistrate said that twenty was a lovely number, that

when she was twenty she'd been the most beautiful woman in Mariquita. The priest said that she still was. They enacted the agreed percentages into law before Francisca came back.

Francisca and her shopping bags and new suitcases arrived in
Mariquita in a rickety 1947 red Jeep Willys a little before sunset. The
Jeep went sluggishly up and down the main street, from the church to
the market, from the market to the school and twice round the plaza,
its obnoxious horn beeping incessantly. Everybody stopped what she
or he was doing and took to the streets, the women wishing the driver
was a handsome man, the children hoping they could get a free ride.
They drew near the slow car, giving whoops of joy. The chauffeur was
a hoary man about as rickety as the car he drove, who kept his head so
close to the steering wheel that it looked as though the tip of his chin,
not his hands, was directing the course of the Jeep. Alongside him, her
back and shoulders squared against the passenger seat, was Francisca,
smiling at her friends and neighbors. But no one recognized her. Not
when the Jeep stopped in front of her house and the ancient driver
walked around the car to open the door for her; not when one of her
feet came out of the car, high-heeled, followed by one of her hands,
well manicured, and a forearm full of rattling golden bracelets; not
even when Francisca stood firmly on the ground, smoothing with the
palms of her hands the creases that the long trip had left around the
waist of her silky crimson dress. Only when Francisca opened the door
of her house did a woman ecstatically groan, "Why, if it isn't Francisca,
La Masatera!"

The large crowd stood watching the driver bring into Francisca's
house bag after suitcase after bag. Watching them go past, each woman
began condemning, in her own mind, Francisca's extravagance.

When the driver was gone, Francisca invited a small group of her
friends inside her house. The rest of the people took turns looking
through the window as Francisca tried on clothes and shoes and piled
them up in every corner of her house, reminding them of their hardship. Among the women watching the spectacle from the outside was

Rosalba. She was feeling guilty about having issued the questionable decree that would dramatically tax Francisca's fortune, so she'd come out in search of vindication for her behavior. But after gazing intently through the window Rosalba realized that Francisca had enough clothes to dress, at least once, the entire population of Mariquita, and as many pairs of shoes as a centipede had legs. Meanwhile nearly all the women in town had worn, day after day for almost four years, the same black dresses presently brimming with darns and patches. And those who had been stupid enough to listen to Francisca and burn their mourning outfits soon discovered that their colorful clothes were now too loose or too small, or had been eaten by moths. Most women had already worn the soles of their shoes so thin that they could feel the bumps on the ground. Some had even chosen to walk barefoot. Rosalba had no reason to feel guilt. Francisca's avarice had vindicated the magistrate's maneuver.

The next day was Saturday, market day. Early in the morning some women went fishing, others hunting, a few chicken throats were slit, grain was gleaned and the largest oranges and guavas picked from the trees. Products that were in short supply suddenly became available, and only the freshest, best produce found its way to the marketplace, where shortly after six all kinds of buyers and sellers convened to trade their goods. Francisca got out of bed early. She was hungry, but there was nothing edible in her house—before leaving for Ibagué she had purposely emptied her pantry. Now it was time to stock up her kitchen with the best products she could find. As she was preparing to leave, she heard a couple of knocks at the door. She opened it and found the magistrate, the priest and the police sergeant standing rather solemnly at her threshold. Francisca showed them in.

"I'd gladly pull a chair for you to sit if I could find any," she said, scrutinizing the room—filled with piles of goods—for some sign of a seat.

"That's not necessary," the magistrate interposed. "I'll be brief." She produced a slip of paper from her handbag and handed it to Francisca before beginning her formal statement: "A law has been passed that entitles the administration of Mariquita and the Roman Catholic Church to tax any amount of money found within the village's perimeters."

"Is that so?" said Francisca, showing no surprise.

"The document you're holding contains all you need to know about the law, including the percentages you must pay," el padre Rafael added, ratifying the magistrate's notification.

Francisca flushed but didn't answer at once. She was aware of the seriousness of the notice, which, of course, called for a sensible answer given in a seemly choice of words, a refined lady's reply. "Get out of my house, you rabble!" she shouted at Rosalba, then tore the slip of paper and threw the pieces at her.

Police Sergeant Ubaldina stood between the two women in a conciliatory manner. This wasn't necessary, however, because the magistrate remained surprisingly composed.

"I warn you, Francisca," Rosalba said. "I will no longer allow any woman of Mariquita to go to sleep with an empty stomach while another is belching pork chops."

"To hell with the women of Mariquita! I'm not sharing my money with anyone. Out!" She now pointed at the door, which she had left open.

"Think about it, dear," el padre Rafael intervened. "Your good looks and fine clothes might make you stand out for a while, but you're still a widow in a town of widows. Your soul, on the other hand—"

"To hell with you and your stupid church. Out!"

"You have until sunset to come to my office and pay the applicable taxes on every centavo you found, or I'll have you banished from Mariquita," the magistrate declared. Then the police sergeant, who until then had been quiet, couldn't contain herself any longer. With a sardonic smile, she said to Francisca, "If it brings Mariquita unhappiness, we'll rid ourselves of it." The three turned at once and walked out of the room.

Francisca leaned her back against the door, feeling restless. What was she going to do now? She couldn't report less than what she had unearthed because el padre Rafael knew the exact amount. Should she stay in town and contest the magistrate's resolution? Or should she leave? She was in the same dilemma as two weeks before. No, it was worse now because the magistrate had only given her until dusk to make a decision. It was the magistrate's threat, however, that incidentally helped Francisca decide that she would not go anywhere. Who did Rosalba think she was, to determine who got to stay in the village and who had to leave? If anyone should be asked to leave, it was Rosalba herself. She hadn't even been born in Mariquita. Francisca would stick to her original plan of opening her beauty parlor, and she'd fight the magistrate. There had to be a law that protected a rich widow from being banished from her native village.

With that thought in mind, Francisca went to the old Barbería Gómez. The place looked just the same as when she had left for Ibagué. The Morales sisters hadn't done a thing. Furious, Francisca went to the market looking for new employees, but no one there accepted her offers. Then she went about the village asking every person to work for her, increasing the salary as she moved from door to door, turning friendly, even pleasant, but no woman wanted to work for Francisca. She felt tired and hungry—with all the problems of that morning, she had forgotten to eat. She went to the Morales widow's tent and ordered breakfast from Julia. The girl gave Francisca one of her worst looks, which said, among other things, that her presence was no longer welcome in their eatery. Francisca moved around the market attempting to purchase food from her old friends, but her business wasn't wanted anywhere. She offered to pay twice as much money for a couple of plantains, three times as much for a yucca, and still the merchants refused to sell to her. She thought that her friends from the market, like the magistrate, were testing her pride. But Francisca viuda de Gómez had never gone down on her knees to anyone, and she was not just about to start doing it now that she was rich.

She went home hungry, feeling as though parasites were eating her intestines. All she had left in her kitchen was some water in a vessel and a gallon of kerosene for the stove. She boiled the water, poured it into a cup and added the last scrapings of salt left in a plastic container. She took small sips of the tasteless infusion, hoping that the strong feeling of hunger would go away. But it only became stronger as the clear liquid reached her insides.

Evening was nearing. Francisca sat on the floor and started playing with her nostrils: she covered the one on the right, and with the left one she smelled the stew of giblets that was being cooked next door. Then she covered her left nostril, and with the other one she detected the smell of tripe soup. She closed her eyes and continued this, her senses traveling from kitchen to kitchen until she was able to tell what each family would be having for dinner that night, and even which families were going to bed with nothing in their stomachs, like herself. Maybe she should pay the taxes so that everyone in Mariquita could eat well and wear clean clothes. Or maybe not. Why should anyone be given something if they hadn't worked for it? She had offered them a well-paying job, and they had all refused her offer. Well, then, they deserved to go to bed hungry, she concluded.

She took the last few sips of boiled water, and suddenly started seeing, one by one, her own fears entering the house. Loneliness was the first to arrive—alone, of course. Francisca recognized it immediately because it coyly scoured the entire house for the right place to dwell. It finally settled inside the inner pocket of one of Francisca's new fur coats and didn't move again. Guilt came soon afterward, pointing at her with long reproachful fingers. It slid itself into a red silk blouse and, poking its fingers through the long sleeves, continued nagging at Francisca. Then, hand in hand, came Rejection and Abandonment. They moved freely about the room, disregarding Francisca. Before long they picked a pair of fancy spike-heeled shoes and each disappeared into a different shoe. Francisca realized that her fears had come together with her fortune. They had only been waiting for the right occasion, a moment of complete weakness and despair, to reveal themselves. At present they hid among her dear new garments, from where they watched the swelling unhappiness of her eyes. There was only one thing to do.

She rose from the floor with trembling hands and legs and undressed completely. She piled up, in the middle of her living room, all her new clothes and shoes, her expensive accessories and her stacks of pesos, all of them. Then she drizzled, with the only liquid left in her house, the heap of goods in a ritualistic fashion: her right arm turned into a long feather flying gracefully in the air. She stepped back from the pile and looked around her house, giggling. She went inside the kitchen, grabbed a box of matches, walked toward the door, opened it, turned around, struck a match and threw it onto the drenched pile. She waited for the flames to swallow the pile and sear the roof. Then she stepped out, shut the door and walked slowly across the street to the mango tree, giggling, giggling. The sun was now setting, and there she stood, stark naked, watching the smoke and the flames come out through the holes in the roof and the open window; hearing the church bell peal insistently and the many voices of neighbors and friends calling for water; giggling, giggling, giggling.

Jesús Martínez, 48
Ex-colonel, Colombian National Army

A man had just moved into the room down the hall, but no one in the house had seen him yet. "He's an ex-guerrilla who suffers from amnesia," our landlady confided to one of the lodgers. "Please don't tell the colonel. He's crazy!" I'm not crazy, just pissed off. Ten years ago, a guerrilla land mine blew off my feet in combat, ending my military career. But in this second-rate lodging house, secrets aren't kept much longer than a few minutes. And when I heard about it, I thought, Amnesia? I'll help that motherfucker get back his memory, and then I'll blow his fucking head off.

In my room, I loaded my pistol and hid it under a white poncho neatly folded on my lap. I drank half a glass of rum and lit a cigarette, took two drags on it and stubbed it out in the ashtray. I checked my hand. It was steady enough to shoot him. I wheeled myself to the door and opened it slowly, wincing when it squeaked. After looking in both directions, I wheeled myself down the narrow hallway. I wasn't nervous. My heart didn't beat any faster than it usually does, and I didn't gasp for breath. My hands worked the wheels until they put me barely two inches away from my victim's room. I heard him cough, the bastard. I knocked three times on his door with my left hand. My other hand was under the poncho, clutching the pistol so tightly that it was beginning to hurt. He coughed again. I'd soon put a stop to his coughing, I thought. There was a brief silence. Then I heard a familiar sound, but before it registered in my mind, the door opened abruptly and there he was, right in front of me, the new lodger, the ex-guerrilla, the monster. He had no legs, only stumps, and he, too, was sitting on a wheelchair.

We stared silently at each other for a while. As if looking at ourselves in a mirror.

"Hi," he finally said, a friendly smile on his face. "Vicente Gómez, at your service," he added, holding out his hand to me.

I let go of my pistol, still hidden under my poncho, and involuntarily waited a moment before shaking his hand. "Jesús," I said. "Jesús Martínez. I rent the room at the end of the corridor."

"It's a pleasure meeting you," one of us said.

"The pleasure's all mine," the other replied.

CHAPTER 6

The Other Widow

Mariquita, December 7, 1997

A S HE HAD EVERY night for the past five years, Santiago Marín sat on his steps, shirtless and barefoot, staring into the darkness, waiting for Pablo. Tonight he also lit candles to the Virgin Mary, who according to tradition, traveled on December 7 from house to house and town to town, giving away blessings for every candle burned.

He heard the roar of a car in the distance. At first he remained uninterested, but when the sound became louder, he quickly gathered his long hair into a ponytail, wiped a rag over his oily face and lit one more candle. Then he saw the headlights of a car coming down the rise. The last car to drive on the unpaved streets of Mariquita had been the rattletrap of a Jeep that had brought Francisca viuda de Gómez and her numerous suitcases back from her trip to Ibagué over a year ago. Except for its black color, the car approaching town tonight was no different: an old, beat-up Jeep with a loud engine. The driver went twice around the dilapidated plaza before stopping at a corner to greet the town's magistrate, the priest and the schoolmistress, who, together with numerous women and children holding candles, had come out of their houses to welcome the visitor. After assuring the magistrate twice that the government hadn't sent him, and getting directions, the man drove slowly through the growing crowd, down a narrow side street, and pulled over in the middle of the block, in front of the Jaramillo widow's house, across from Santiago's.

"Let me out," the driver said to the half-naked children surrounding the car, a hint of irritation in his voice. The women pulled their children aside and waited quietly. "Get out of my way," he yelled. He sounded arrogant and contemptuous despite his slanting eyes and dark skin, despite his straw hat, ragged poncho and sheathed machete at his waist that clearly indicated he was a man of Indian descent—nobody important. He stood in front of the Jaramillo widow's doorway, thinking perhaps that the noises made by his car and the crowd were enough to draw the woman out. The widow hadn't lit any candles tonight because she'd lost hope of blessings a long time ago (she had gone mad after her husband and two of her sons were shot dead by guerrillas, and at present she had nobody to look after her). When the Jaramillo widow didn't come out, the arrogant driver knocked on the door and waited. He knocked a second time, then a third and a fourth, louder each time until the widow finally opened the door, barely poking her nose around it. The man whispered something to her, and without replying the insane woman slammed the door in his face.

"Bitch!" the man shouted. He began kicking the door with his pointy leather boots. "Open the door, you bitch. It took me hours to find this damn hole." The crowd stepped back. The enraged man continued kicking the door and shouting abuse. "If you don't pay me right now, I'm going to dump that sickening piece of shit on your steps," he yelled, pointing toward the car with his index finger. "And you know what else I'm going to do? I'm going to take the damn suitcase with me. That's what I'm going to do."

Santiago quietly observed the scene from across the street. He asked his two younger sisters to go inside the house, and his mother to observe from a prudent distance. He didn't move. He remained on the same spot where he'd been every night for the past five years, lighting more candles to the Virgin, hoping for more of her blessings, staring into the darkness, waiting for Pablo to return to him.

*   *   *

PABLO AND SANTIAGO had both been born on the morning of May 1, 1969. Pablo was older by two and a half hours. Dr. Ramirez, the physician who delivered them, liked to say that except for a dark birthmark under Pablo's right eye, the two boys looked identical when they were born: "Like twins, only born to different mothers."

Growing up, Pablo and Santiago were the only children on a lonely street of Mariquita. The street was narrow and unpaved and lined with young mango trees. The houses had mud tile roofs, their adobe facades forever hidden under layers of dust. This street was known as Don Maximiliano's street, because he owned all the houses up and down each side. He also owned three coffee farms near town. During harvest season, most of the men he hired to pick the crops were from around Mariquita. The women stayed home and tended their children, along with their cassavas, potatoes, cilantro and squash.

The two boys spent most of the day playing in the backcountry. They always went to one or the other's house for meals, then went out again. It was not unusual for their mothers to see Pablo and Santiago walking around Mariquita hand in hand. "They're like blood brothers," their mothers agreed.

The two boys' favorite game was playing father and mother by the river.

"I'll be the father," Pablo said.

"You're always the father. I want to be the father, too," Santiago complained. But he gave in every time. Pablo disappeared behind the bushes and pretended he was on Don Maximiliano's coffee plantations. Santiago stayed by the bank impersonating his own mother: carrying water from the river in big clay pots, cooking, watering the garden, cooking again, washing clothes, cooking one last time. After a few minutes Pablo came out of the bushes, acting dirty and tired.

"Buenas tardes, mi amor," he said, kissing the back of Santiago's neck.

"How was your day?"

"Oh, just the same. Too much work."

The two boys sat on the ground and ate a pretend meal of rice and beans. After dinner, Pablo took his shirt off and lay in the grass, facing the sky, his hands beneath his neck. "I'll do the dishes later," Santiago said, and quickly moved on to a part of the game he liked better: the massage. He began with Pablo's feet, gently rubbing each of his twelve toes (the boy had inherited his father's six-toed feet). Santiago worked his way up slowly, massaging Pablo's calves and knees and thighs, spending a good amount of time on his chest. When Santiago pinched Pablo's little brown nipples, Pablo began to howl. And when Pablo began to howl, Santiago knew it was time to start playing with his friend's small penis, pulling on it as if it were a tit on an udder, laughing heartily at the way Pablo's body wriggled with pleasure, like a puppy. When Santiago stopped, Pablo took him in his arms and walked with him into the river. There, with the water up to his waist, Pablo rewarded Santiago with a tender kiss for being a good wife. They spent the rest of the day swimming naked in the river, drowning crickets, peeing on anthills, throwing stones at wasps' nests and running back into the water. The kiss, however, was the part of the day Santiago liked the best, a true expression of love that to him was worth the boredom of impersonating his mother every day.

At night, the two boys sat on logs of wood outside Santiago's house and listened to his grandmother's magical tales, like the one about the old woman who turned into a cat to deceive death, or the one about the rich princess who didn't know how to laugh. Almost every night Pablo and Santiago slept together on the bumpy earthen floor of Santiago's house, wrapped in the same white blanket, dreaming different dreams.

*   *   *

Resolutely, the driver went back to the Jeep. He opened the back door and pulled out a shabby leather suitcase, unzipped it, took out a large white towel and zipped it back up. Before carrying on with whatever he was doing, the angry man looked toward the Jaramillo widow's door, as though giving the woman a last chance to come out and settle up with him. Then he set the bag aside and from inside the Jeep he carefully pulled out a body by the legs. The body didn't move, didn't make any sound. The women stepped a little closer, illuminating the scene with the light of their candles. "Back off!" the driver yelled. He hastily stripped the body naked, revealing a scrawny man covered in sores and bruises, and took a cap off the man's head with a swipe: he was almost completely bald.

"I'm cold," the unclothed man cried softly.

"Ohhh!" the crowd whispered in unison, relieved to find out that the stranger wasn't dead. The driver removed a golden chain from the naked man's neck and a flashy watch from his wrist and put both things in the front pocket of his own dirty pants. Then he tried to pull off two rings from one of the man's bony fingers.

"No," the naked man moaned. "Not the rings, please." He firmly clenched his hand.

"Shut up," the driver ordered. "You swore she was going to pay me for bringing you here, but she's not, so you'd better let go of those damn rings now."

"Please, not the rings."

"Let go, or I'll cut off your hand," the driver shouted, reaching for his machete.

"Ohhh!" the crowd whispered again.

"Stop, please. Don't do it. For the love of God, don't." The despairing voice belonged to el padre Rafael, who had just been notified of the situation and now rushed to the scene together with the magistrate and the police sergeant. "Please let that poor soul die in peace." He halted some distance away from the sordid sight and, producing a chaplet from within the pocket of his soutane, began murmuring a rosary. A few widows promptly joined him.

The frustrated driver ignored the priest's request and kept struggling to open the scrawny man's hand, but he wouldn't let go.

"You leave that ill man alone right now, or I'll blow your brains out." The threat came from the magistrate, Rosalba viuda de Patiño. She stood right behind the driver, pointing a pistol at his head. Next to her, holding a revolver with both hands, was the police sergeant, Ubaldina viuda de Restrepo.

The driver turned his hateful eyes on the women and spat on the ground. He seized the white towel and wrapped it around the scrawny man, then carried the bundle of bones on his shoulder to the Jaramillo widow's door, laid it on the ground near the steps and kicked the door three more times. "He's outside your door," the driver yelled. "Naked, because I'm taking his clothes. You hear me?" He went back to the Jeep, ignoring the two guns that followed his every move, and collected the ill man's clothes and shoes and stuffed them into the shabby leather suitcase. He closed the back door, got inside the Jeep and started the engine. Through the window he screamed the words Santiago, sitting across the street, had been so afraid of hearing: "It's your own son dying outside, you heartless bitch. You're going to hell!"

Santiago remained still, staring in an absent way at the mass of familiar faces crowded before him; unable to see how they abruptly went from distressed to solemn. He didn't see the women put their heads in their hands, or hold their quivering lips with the tips of their fingers. He didn't hear their crying, or the loud engine of the Jeep as it drove away. At the moment, the throbbing of his heart in his chest was the only movement there was about him.

*   *   *

PABLO AND SANTIAGO began working the lands of Don Maximiliano Perdomo on a cloudy day in 1981. It was common for parents to send their male children to work as soon as they turned twelve, and sometimes even before if they were required in the fields. Harvest season had begun and hands were needed at Yarima, Don Maximiliano's largest coffee farm. The two boys arrived at the farmhouse early in the morning and met with Doña Marina, an unfriendly midget who was in charge of the workers' housing. She looked at the boys with disdain, grumbled something they didn't understand, and, with her tiny fat hand, gestured that they follow her. Pablo and Santiago walked behind Doña Marina along a narrow, muddy path, kicking away the geese that chased the little woman as if she were one of them. Doña Marina took the boys to a large shelter where Yarima's coffee pickers stayed during harvest season. She told them where to find the straw baskets they would tie around their waists, and sent them over to the plantation. "Follow this path until you see coffee trees," she squeaked, and then, giving them an obliged look, she added, "Thank you for keeping those beasts away from me."

The beans on most of the coffee trees had turned a dark cherry color. From the highest part of the hill the farm looked like thousands of Christmas trees decorated with little red lights. The steward ordered Pablo to follow, for half a day, an older Indian man with a long ponytail hanging down his back. Santiago followed a man nicknamed Cigarrillo, because he always had a cigarette in his mouth. The two men were to teach the two boys the easiest, fastest way to collect beans. Pablo and Santiago wished they could trail their own fathers, each with more than thirty years of experience in the coffee plantations, but they had been sent to Cabrera, a smaller coffee farm where bad weather was causing the crop to fail.

"Watch my hands, son," Cigarrillo told Santiago. His fingers fluttered like birds among the branches, hardly touching them, as dozens of red beans fell into his basket. "We only want the coffee cherries that are ready, the ones you can pluck with your own hands." His face was sunburned, his mustache unkempt. "If there are any green cherries mixed, the coffee will taste bitter, and if there are any overripe cherries, it'll taste sour." Santiago checked the man's basket for green or over-ripe cherries and found none. "A skilled picker will pluck the entire ripe crop in just one pass," Cigarrillo went on, "and he should collect no less than one hundred pounds of coffee beans per day." When the basket got full, he said, the picker must take it to the coffee mill, next to the storage building, where Doña Marina, the midget, would weigh and mark down the amount of coffee gathered, then he should go back to the plantation and do it all over again. Coffee pickers got paid, partly in cash and partly in produce, every Saturday according to the amount of pounds each man had picked during the week. "The most important thing," Cigarrillo added, "is to have fun while you're working. Sing songs, talk to the trees, tell them jokes. Pretend the trees are hundreds of naked women lined up, waiting for you to pull their tits." The man guffawed. Santiago feigned a smile. He would think of pulling Pablo's penis instead.

The first night in Yarima's shelter Pablo and Santiago pushed their straw mats together to sleep close, like they always had. They held each other's hands to say their prayers, and when finished they kissed good night.

From a corner, sitting on his mat, Pacho, a short, pudgy young man with rosy cheeks, watched the two boys by the light of a Coleman lamp. "Look what we got here, guys," the young man shouted so that everyone in the shelter could hear him. "Two fags kissing each other and praying to God." He stood up, seized the lamp and strode toward the boys. "Kissing and praying—you know how fucking wrong that is?" he asked, in a tone that seemed much more like an answer than a question. He shook his head censoriously before adding, "It's very fucking wrong." Santiago and Pablo didn't comprehend what the man was saying, but whatever it was, he'd made it sound as though they had committed a terrible sin. They leaned into each other, distressed. The man stood over them now, his torso enlarged and distorted by its proximity. "That's so sweet," he said, imitating a woman's voice. "Come on, I want to see the two of you kissing again."

"Shut up, Pacho," Cigarrillo grumbled from his mat, half asleep. "Leave those kids alone and let us sleep."

But the men, who in the past few weeks had done nothing except work, were eager for any kind of entertainment. A few of them sat on their mats and made ready to watch the spectacle from a distance; others got up and gathered around the boys, calling for the show to begin immediately.

"Come on, mariquitas. We don't have all night," said a guy missing nearly all of his front teeth. He stroked Santiago's bottom with his bare foot.

"I'm frightened, Pablo," Santiago whispered in his friend's ear. "Let's kiss one more time so we all can go to sleep." Pablo shook his head.

"Kiss him, kiss him," the aroused spectators sang in unison.

"Please, Pablo, just one more kiss," Santiago whispered again, his soft voice choked with panic, his heart pounding against his small, bony chest.

"Kiss him, kiss him—"

Santiago asked so insistently that Pablo felt he must do it. All right, he said with his head. The two boys held each other tightly. Santiago glanced at the men, from the one to the other, to indicate that he and Pablo were ready to please them, then gently kissed his friend's trembling lips for just a moment, until the first kick separated their faces. The stirred men fell upon the two boys like hungry beasts, thrashing their slight bodies with furious fists, stomping them with enraged, crusty feet. Numbed by fear, the boys didn't feel the heavy blows that came from every side. They hardly screamed, hardly cried, hardly saw or heard anything.

"Stop it now!" The sudden shriek came from the door. "Get out of the way! Move!" The voice was unmistakable. Carrying a lamp that was half her size, Doña Marina was pushing her tiny body through the crowd. The men went back to their mats, laughing and whispering. Pablo and Santiago raised their beaten faces from their mats and began to cry. "Good Lord! What have you done to these poor kids?" Doña Marina laid the lamp on the earthen floor and stroked the boys' heads with her little hands. "These kids just got here today," she said to no one in particular. "They haven't done anything to you. Why would you hurt them?" she shouted. "Why?"

"Because they're faggots," a voice replied from the back. "That's why." She looked toward the corner from which the voice had come, but there was no one to see: the men had blown out the light of their lamp, leaving most of the room in complete darkness. "You're all going to pay for this," she yelled into the darkness. "No breakfast for anyone tomorrow." Doña Marina kindly helped the boys rise from their mats. She took them back to the farmhouse where she lived with the cooks and the maids. She disinfected their cuts gently and without making any comments or asking questions, but when she began dressing their wounds, she suddenly said, "I know you boys aren't *that*, what that rascal said." Her voice had an undernote of warning that the boys, still utterly distressed by the thrashing, couldn't recognize. "I know you're not. I just do." She was quiet again, as if she were finished talking, although in her mind she was choosing her next round of words carefully. Only when she started applying cold compresses to their swollen faces did she continue, "If you were *that*, what the man said you were, I'd advise you first to keep it to yourselves, and second to be very careful around here. The countryside is rough. But since you're not *that*, I won't advise you nothing." She gave them a conspiratorial smile and continued treating their wounds. When she finished she took them to the storage building where, she said, they would sleep from then on.

When she left, Pablo and Santiago hugged each other and wept quietly. One stroked the other's broken nose with the tips of his fingers. The other kissed his friend's swollen eyes time and time again.

They slept together inside a coffee sack.

*   *   *

EL PADRE RAFAEL and his followers had stopped reciting the rosary and joined the rest of the crowd in relentless gossiping. Now and then they glanced over their shoulders at Santiago, wondering when the full impact of the tragedy would hit him and what his reaction would be. Nurse Ramirez warned the entire group not to get near the ill man, then pulled el padre Rafael and the magistrate aside to talk to them.

"Whatever illness Pablo has, it might be contagious," the nurse began in a small voice, shooting the magistrate a warning glance. Mariquita's children, she argued, hadn't been vaccinated against anything in over six years. They would not survive an epidemic. She recommended locking Pablo up in Francisca's burned-out shack until he died—which from the man's looks should be soon—then incinerating his body. The magistrate and the priest seemed appalled by the nurse's advice.

"We can't leave one of our own to die like that—isolated, in a dump, surrounded by . . . rats and creatures," the magistrate said, her agitated voice rising above a whisper.

"I agree," el padre Rafael interposed. "Pablo Jaramillo must die like a Christian and get a Christian burial."

"The future of our village is uncertain as it is," the buxom nurse retorted. "I only know our children is all we have. If we lose them—" She didn't finish her sentence. Instead she put a fatalistic look on her face, a face with a large witch's nose and sad fish eyes. "Just think about it," she added.

They thought about it, together and for less than a minute, and concluded that they had no alternative: Mariquita's future must come first. "But who's going to take Pablo to Francisca's old house?" the magistrate asked. El padre shrugged and the nurse shrugged and the magistrate, shrugging, asked yet another question: "Wouldn't that person have to be quarantined?"

At that precise moment Santiago rose, a candle in his hand, and began walking slowly across the street, toward Pablo. Pablo lay curled up on his side, his face turned to the door of his mother's house as though waiting for it to open. Santiago stood next to him, contemplating by the light of the candle the little there was to contemplate, struggling to recognize his old friend. Perhaps this was an error. Perhaps the Jeep driver had mistakenly driven into the wrong town, the wrong street. It had to be an error. Pablo was such a handsome man: tall, dark, well built, with thick, black hair . . .

"Santiago? Is it you?" Pablo said, somehow sensing his friend's presence.

Santiago nodded mechanically as Pablo turned himself languidly onto his back. With great difficulty Pablo drew his left arm from under the towel in which he was wrapped, uncovering the upper part of his body, and stretched it out to touch Santiago, but Santiago was a little too far away, and Pablo's arm fell limply to the ground with a graceless plop. "The rings," he mumbled.

Santiago looked at Pablo's skeletal hand wiggling like a worm in the dirt. Two solid gold bands clung to his ring finger. "What about them?"

"Take one," Pablo said in a whisper. "I promised you a ring. Remember?"

*   *   *

IT WAS JUNE of 1984. Pablo and Santiago had just turned fifteen. They'd left Yarima to work, on Doña Marina's recommendation, at Don Maximiliano's country house, located about three hours away on foot from Mariquita. The wealthy landowner had had it built on a mesa five years ago, and it was a monument to his poor taste and lack of imagination. Casa Perdomo was a wide, graceless box with interconnecting rooms and few windows, as if purposely designed to prevent light from invading its dwellers' privacy. It had taken Don Maximiliano several months to convince his wife to leave the city and move into it. To compensate for its ugliness, Doña Caridad had stuffed the house with furniture of remarkable quality, turning each room into a jumble of fancy tables and chairs and cabinets and beds, all of which largely contributed to a permanent state of confusion.

Following Doña Marina's indirect advice, Pablo and Santiago had introduced themselves as first cousins. They were soon entrusted with the house's maintenance—painting and repainting the walls, fixing broken doors, replenishing the stoves with firewood, keeping up the plumbing system, stocking the storage room. There was always something to do. The two young men shared a small windowless bedroom in the back of the house, next to the maid's room, furnished with two trunks for their few clothes, two folding beds and a lamp. At the end of the work day, Pablo and Santiago had only to enter that room and close the door to experience a mighty sense of calmness, safeness and intimacy. The room's absolute quiet, its refreshing lack of adornment, the lamplight casting shadows that swayed on the white walls—it all created an isolated world where everything seemed possible for the two young men, even their secret love and growing desire. Inside that bedroom, massaging each other's feet, calves and knees was no longer part of a childish game, but an essential part of their life together; kissing was no longer a reward but a desirable way of reminding one another, without words, of their most intimate feelings. Inside that bedroom there was no husband or wife, only two young men, each in love with the other.

The Perdomos' only daughter, Señorita Lucía, had recently arrived from New York, where she was attending college. She came every June and stayed until the end of August. This time, however, she hadn't traveled alone: a twenty-seven-year-old man named William had come along to ask for her hand in marriage. William was neither ill-featured nor handsome but somewhere in between: tall and pink, with a small nose and green eyes. His face, conspicuously covered with freckles, at first bore a haughty expression, but after noticing the genuine affection and hospitality of his hosts, it revealed an air of innocence and modesty that made a lasting good impression on the Perdomos. William wore nothing but khaki trousers and heavily starched light-colored shirts. He spoke atrocious Spanish in a voice almost imperceptible, as though to prevent listeners from noticing his poor pronunciation. Doña Caridad thought this quite charming and took every opportunity to make conversation with him. He stayed for only five days, long enough for mosquitoes and other insects to scar his foreign skin and scalp. The night before he left, William made his engagement to Señorita Lucía official by putting a golden ring on one of her long fingers during a formal dinner.

Once her fiancé was gone, Señorita Lucía became demanding. "Pablo, bring my breakfast to the porch." "Santiago, brush my hair." "Pablo, get my sunglasses." "Santiago, massage my feet." She was rather unattractive: lanky, with dark shadows under sleepy brown eyes and thin lips that disappeared every time she smiled. And though she was barely twenty-three, her teeth already had lost their original color and now looked as though partially covered with rust; the result, Doña Caridad used to say, "of that nasty smoking habit that you must quit before your fiancé finds out." The girl's eyebrows were the subject of criticism and mockery: she had plucked all the hair from them and replaced it with two fine tattooed lines that she made thicker, darker, or longer—but always uneven—every morning using eyebrow pencils. The Perdomos' only daughter also had a personality unsuited to the countryside: she was gentle and sensitive, with refined manners, perhaps too refined for rural life. The summer heat was "abominable," mosquitoes "insufferable," local running water "filthy," and so on. She wore high heels, makeup, and jewelry every day and sat out on the porch smoking, browsing through bridal magazines and reading love stories.

"Was that story about death, Señorita Lucía?" Santiago asked her one day, after the girl had put her book down.

She smiled. "No, silly. It was about love." She was lying stretched in a hammock, alternating the reading with short puffs of a thin cigarette dangling from her slender hand. Santiago stood beside her, fanning away the mosquitoes and gnats that buzzed around her.

"But you looked like you were in pain."

"Love can make you feel pain sometimes."

Santiago thought about this for a moment. It wasn't love that had caused him and Pablo pain; it was hate, the unjustified hate that the coffee pickers felt toward them, and which—despite Doña Marina's opportune intercessions—had cost them more than one beating and continuous verbal abuse. Perhaps he should tell Señorita Lucía that he and Pablo were not first cousins, but two boys in love. She would certainly understand. She seemed like a woman who understood things. Besides, she was getting married, which made her an expert on matters of love. But Santiago had promised Pablo he wouldn't tell anyone.

"What's the story about?" he asked.

Señorita Lucía let the cigarette smoke dribble out the side of her mouth, making a sound like a gentle breeze. "It's about a man who goes to war." She paused briefly to think. "No, it's rather about the girl the man is in love with . . . forget about it, Santiago. It's too complicated."

"Please, Señorita Lucía. I want to know."

She looked at him curiously. Unlike his cousin Pablo, Santiago looked delicate, almost effeminate. His voice hadn't broken yet, and there was no sign to indicate that an Adam's apple would ever protrude from the front of his neck. He was slender, smooth-faced, and he clearly had a great feeling for love stories and dramas. She stubbed out what remained of the cigarette in an ashtray.

"All right," she said. "The story is about Ernesto and Soledad, a young man and a young woman who are deeply in love. They're engaged and already planning their life together—where they'd like to live, how many children they'd like to have, that sort of thing. But then a war breaks out, and Ernesto's ordered to go far away, across the ocean, to fight the enemy. Soledad swears undying love to him, and he promises he'll return and marry her. But weeks and months go by without any word from Ernesto. Every night poor Soledad stands in front of her window wishing to see Ernesto's green eyes glow in the night, but she doesn't see them. One day, after years of waiting, Soledad learns from a war veteran that Ernesto was badly injured and as a result lost his memory. He now lives in a remote country, happily married. She's brokenhearted, but her love for him is so strong that she decides to keep her promise to him. And so every night Soledad stands by her window lighting candles, waiting for Ernesto to come back to her."

By now Señorita Lucía wore the same mournful expression Santiago had noticed earlier. She lighted another cigarette and took several puffs. "That's it," she said.

"That's it? What about Ernesto? Does he ever come back?" He was clearly disappointed with the ending.

"Nobody knows. That's what I love about this story; one must imagine what happens after."

Santiago didn't know what to say. He continued fanning her, thinking about a satisfying ending for the story, then said, "I think Ernesto ought to get his memory back somehow, then go back and marry her."

Señorita Lucía gave him a sympathetic look. "I think he'll never go back." She paused briefly. "And Soledad will stand by that window, waiting, for the rest of her life."

Santiago thought that was a cruel and absurd ending. "That wouldn't be right, though," he said. "That man promised to go back and marry her. He must keep his word."

"I have an idea," she said with a refreshing gesture. "Take the book with you, read the story, and then we will each write our own endings and compare them."

"I can't read or write," he said.

Santiago's confession was no surprise to her, and although she was far from being socially concerned, it disturbed her conscience. "How old are you?"

"Fifteen."

"Well, at least you seem to know the numbers."

"I know some."

"What about Pablo? Can he read?"

Santiago shook his head, but his face remained calm and content. Señorita Lucía held the cigarette close to her mouth, and without inhaling she, too, shook her head.

SEÑORITA LUCÍA TURNED out to be a great tutor: charismatic, dynamic, articulate and patient. Every night after work, Pablo, Santiago and two maids joined the Perdomos' daughter in the kitchen for a two-hour lesson. First they learned the vowels, then the consonants, and then the construction of simple phrases and sentences. Pablo was a fast, eager learner. He quickly memorized the alphabet and soon began writing long, intelligible sentences. Santiago was the opposite. He scribbled letters and grouped them in no particular order, making no effort to learn. His nonchalant manner disconcerted Pablo—Santiago had always been enthusiastic about learning anything. Perhaps he just learned reading and writing at a different pace, slower than Pablo's, slower than the two maids'. Or perhaps he was jealous of the attention Pablo frequently received from Señorita Lucía, who was unstinting in her praise for his intelligence and willingness to study.

After each class, the maids went to their room and Santiago went to his room and Pablo and Señorita Lucía moved to the porch. She was quite talkative, and Pablo was a good listener. They had long conversations, mostly about her life in the United States, and she showed him pictures and postcards of impressive cities and exotic places. Sometimes Pablo asked questions about New York, and the girl's detailed and embellished answers made him fantasize about a majestic city with high-speed cars flying in the air; massive, indestructible towers touching the sky; lush gardens suspended from the clouds; a land flowing with money, where gold coins grew out of holes in the ground everywhere, like weeds.

Living in such a place was at first merely an idle reverie, but it soon became an obsession with Pablo. He thought about moving to New York day and night. He visualized himself dressed in khaki trousers and starched shirts, like Don William, walking along broad avenues; or sitting behind a desk in his own office; or contemplating the city skyline through the large windows of his own house, his pockets permanently filled with bank notes. He thought about moving to New York so much that it began to seem achievable. He wished for it with such devotion that at length the opportunity to fulfill his dream arose. One night, after a serious conversation with Señorita Lucía and before going to bed, Pablo broke the news to Santiago.

"I'm leaving with Señorita Lucía. She said she'd help me get there. She knows how."

To Santiago the idea was preposterous. "That must be an expensive trip, Pablo. Where are you going to get the money to pay for it in two weeks?"

"She's going to lend it to me."

"But where would you live?"

"She'll let me stay at her house for a month or so, until I get settled."

"And how're you going to find work over there?"

"She's going to help me get a job."

"But you don't speak their language."

"She said I'm smart. I can learn it fast."

"But all you know how to do is fix things."

"She said that's a well-paid job in New York."

"I don't know, Pablo . . . it can't be that easy."

"It's not impossible."

The silence that gathered between Pablo's last answer and Santiago's next question was long, unbearable.

"What about us?"

"Don't worry about us, Santiago. I'll come back to get you. And I'm going to bring enough money to buy my family and yours their own coffee farms." His eyes grew wide with excitement, his nostrils swelled. "Oh, and I'm going to write you a letter every week; that way you'll know I'm thinking about you all the time."

Santiago sank into his bed without speaking.

Señorita Lucía had never looked as hideous and wicked as she did, in the eyes of Santiago, during the two weeks prior to Pablo's departure. It was her fault that Pablo was suddenly going away, her fault that from then on Santiago's days and nights would seem endless. She must have found out that Pablo and Santiago were in love and thought it "abominable," "insufferable," and "filthy." She might look friendly and caring on the surface, but deep inside, she was just as evil and hateful as the coffee pickers who used to beat them up. She couldn't separate them with her fists, so she had opted to use her cleverness.

Santiago avoided coming across Señorita Lucía during the day. In the mornings, as usual, he brushed her long hair, though not as gently as he used to. And in the afternoons he stood by her, fanning away mosquitoes while she read, except now he refrained from asking what made her chuckle, heave long sighs or shed tears. He, however, didn't miss any of the reading and writing classes she taught at night. In fact, he made an effort to learn fast because, he reasoned, he must be able to read the letters that Pablo would send him every week and write him back. During the course of the two weeks Pablo didn't talk about anything except his forthcoming adventure, and that made Santiago furious. Santiago didn't care to know that in New York every house had a television set, or that people in New York could afford to eat chicken every day if they wanted to. A week before leaving, Pablo made a two-day trip to Mariquita to collect his legal documents and say good-bye to his parents and two brothers. It was then that Santiago truly understood what his life would be without him. For a short time he entertained the idea of going to New York with Pablo, but he soon abandoned the thought. He was the oldest of three children and the only son, and he'd promised his father he'd help support the rest of the family in Mariquita. And he, Santiago Marín, was a man of his word.

The Saturday before Pablo left, Santiago stole Señorita Lucía's engagement ring. He only wanted to try it on his own finger to see what it felt like to be engaged. He had learned from the maids that she removed the ring from her delicate finger every morning before taking a bath, and that she placed it on top of her night table, next to a framed picture of her future husband. That morning, Santiago waited to hear the water of her shower running, then tiptoed into her bedroom. The room smelled heavily of cigarettes, and her clothes and shoes were scattered all over the floor. Standing in the middle of the room, he broke out in a cold sweat, and his hands began shaking. What was he doing? He started thinking about the grave consequences his brave act might have for him and for Pablo, but then he saw the ring in the exact place the maids had said. He stared at it for a moment or two, his hands tightly clasped behind his back. Then he snatched it and held it up to the light: a solid gold band crowned with three tiny clear stones. He tried it on each of his ten fingers but didn't think it looked particularly good on any. It'd certainly look good on Pablo's, though. He fancied Pablo's hand writing a letter, *My dearest Santiago*—the three stones sparkling on his ring finger—and decided, in a moment of excitement, that Señorita Lucia's ring would be his and Pablo's engagement ring. He put it in his pocket and hurried out of the bedroom.

Back in their room, Santiago told Pablo to close his eyes. "Don't open them until I tell you so," he said. "Now give me your hand. The right one." He put the ring on Pablo's little finger, the only one that was small enough. "Before you open your eyes, you must promise me that you'll always keep this on your finger; that you will never take it off, not even when you bathe."

"I promise," Pablo impatiently said, and then, opening his eyes, he hollered, "This is Señorita Lucía's engagement ring! Did you steal it?"

"Don Míster William can buy her another one."

Pablo quickly removed the ring from his finger and slapped it in Santiago's hand. "This is wrong. You should be ashamed of yourself."

He walked out of the bedroom, shutting the door with a slam. Santiago lay on his bed and wept softly against the pillow. The world he and Pablo had built together was suddenly shattering around him. He was about to lose the one person he loved.

A few minutes later Pablo came back into the room. "I know why you took that ring, but that doesn't make it right," he said. "You must return it right away before she notices that it's missing." Santiago sat on the bed and nodded. "Look at me," Pablo whispered, turning Santiago's chin toward him with his hand. "I'm going to make lots of money, and I'm going to buy us two rings, you hear me? And they'll be ten times, a hundred times, better than that one, you'll see. And when I come back, I'll put one ring on your finger, and you'll put the other one on mine . . . no, don't cry. Please don't. I promise I'll be back and we'll be together. Yes, forever. Shhh . . . it'll be all right, Santiago, my Santiago. I'll be back soon. I promise. Shhh . . ."

*   *   *

THE CROWD HAD dispersed after the nurse's warning. Only a handful of women had remained near the pitiful scene, watching through their windows and doors. Among these women was the magistrate. Rosalba was keeping an eye on the two men from the window of Cecilia and Francisca's house—after setting her own house on fire, Francisca had been allowed to move into Cecilia's late son Ángel's bedroom in exchange for working in the garden and kitchen.

Pablo lay on the ground with Santiago standing over him. Both wept, their suffering partly illuminated by the pale light of the candle in Santiago's hand.

Santiago knelt down and planted the candle on the ground. He held Pablo's hand, damp and flaccid, in his. Pablo was nothing but bones, bones that might have collapsed if his skin hadn't encased them. His arm, his neck and the exposed part of his body were covered with purple blotches and bright red sores. A thin layer of translucent skin clung to the bones of his face. His eyes were sunken and gloomy, and his thick eyebrows had turned into flimsy lines of sparse hair. Only the birthmark under his right eye remained whole, dark, defined, its intense blackness magnifying the cadaverous paleness of a face that held no trace of the man Santiago loved, the one he had been waiting for.

"Take one," Pablo muttered. "The rings. Take one."

Santiago carefully slid the top ring off Pablo's finger and rubbed it in circles on the ill man's palm. "I want you to put it on my finger," he said. "You promised you would."

Pablo nodded. Yes, he remembered his promise. He, too, wanted to put the ring on Santiago's finger. If only his arm had a bit of strength left . . .

Santiago made him hold the golden band while he slid the ring finger of his right hand all the way through it. Then he took the second ring off Pablo's finger. "Give me your right hand," he said, though by now he knew that Pablo had lost control of most of his muscles. He said it just to hear his own voice; to make sure he was Santiago Marín and the man before him was Pablo Jaramillo and this long-awaited moment was really happening. He reached for Pablo's right hand and gently put the gold band on the man's ring finger. For a little while the two rings were side by side, sparkling in the candlelight. Two solid circles of gold with no stones to detract from their plain beauty. Pablo smiled, his trembling smile a series of muscular contractions.

Santiago held his own hand up, turned it around, made a fist and released it without taking his triumphant eyes off the golden band on his finger. It was official: he was finally engaged to Pablo.

*　　*　　*

NINETEEN EIGHTY-EIGHT. FOUR Augusts had gone by, and Santiago still hadn't heard a word from Pablo. Señorita Lucía and her husband had visited once, but they had no news of him. "I don't know where he is," she said. "William and I moved to a new house, and we haven't heard anything from him since." But Santiago wouldn't give up. Before the couple went back to the States, he gave them the stack of letters he'd written to Pablo. "New York is a big city, Santiago. It'll be impossible to give him your letters without knowing his address."

"Please, Señorita Lucía, take them with you. Just in case you ever see him on the street."

"I'll take them. Only I can't promise you that Pablo will ever read them."

Santiago was now in charge of overseeing the Restrepos' house. He kept an inventory of provisions and cleaning supplies and was given a weekly budget to keep every item up to par. He was responsible for hiring maids and gardeners and for keeping the altar of the house decorated with fresh fruit and flowers. He worked from six in the morning to six at night, making sure he didn't have time to himself. *Himself* was a terrible word he'd been forced to learn after Pablo left; a state of solitude and desolation he confronted every night in his bedroom. What if Pablo had lost his memory, like Ernesto in Señorita Lucía's story? What if he'd met someone else and forgotten about Santiago? From time to time the doubts overpowered his hopefulness, making him weep softly. He rewrote the ending of Señorita Lucía's story over and over, and when he couldn't think of one more possible way to finish it, he rewrote the entire story.

His version of the story went like this:

Once upon a time there were two young men named Pedro and Samuel, who were deeply in love with each other. Like every good loving couple they wanted to get engaged, but were too poor to afford the high cost of the rings. Pedro, then, decided to leave for Nueva York to work and save money to buy their engagement rings. They were very sad when they said good-bye. They cried and swore undying love. Pedro promised to write every week and to return to be with Samuel forever. A year passed, and Samuel didn't receive any letter from Pedro. But Samuel didn't worry. He trusted Pedro and was certain that he had a good reason not to write. Every time he was struck by some doubts, he'd drive those evil thoughts out by saying to himself, "Pedro loves me. He's coming back." Samuel waited a long time but never gave up hope.

One night, he was bathing in the river when he heard someone call his name. He looked around and saw Pedro coming out of the bushes. He wore a perfectly pressed white suit, red tie and white patent leather shoes, and he carried two suitcases. Samuel thought he was just seeing things. But no, it was really Pedro. He rushed out of the water and kissed him. Pedro opened one of the suitcases. The inside was filled with the hundreds of letters he'd written to Samuel, all of which had been sent back to him for one reason or another. Then Pedro opened the other suitcase. Inside there was a neatly folded wedding gown.

"This is for you, Samuel," Pedro said. "I want us to get married. Now."

"Oh, Pedro! I don't know what to say. We're not engaged yet," Samuel said.

"I'm sorry. I almost forgot," Pedro replied, pulling a little box from his pocket. When he opened the box, a light nearly blinded Samuel. It was a gold engagement ring crowned with a big diamond. "Would you marry me?" Pedro asked.

"Yes," Samuel answered with a smile. They kissed. Then Pedro gave Samuel the suitcase with the wedding gown and asked him to get dressed. Samuel was aware that the groom shouldn't see the bride before the ceremony, so he went behind the bushes. The gown was really nice: all white, sleeveless, with a low-cut neckline and a long skirt shaped like a bell. The train was about three yards long. The gown came with a veil and a pair of white shoes. Samuel had no doubt this was the most expensive wedding gown in all New York, but he didn't feel bad because he knew he was worth it. He put on the gown and veil and arranged wild flowers into a colorful bunch, then came out of the bushes. Dozens of people had gathered, waiting for Samuel to come out. These people were relatives and neighbors that Pedro had invited beforehand.

They clapped and cheered as Samuel walked slowly through them with the flowers in his hands. Samuel met Pedro at the end, near the bank. Pedro lifted the veil and was pleasantly surprised to see a full moon reflected in each of Samuel's eyes. "I love you, my darling," he said. They kissed and at that moment a brief shower of rice rained down on both of them. Pedro took Samuel in his arms and walked into the river until the warm water covered his waist.

"We're the happiest couple on earth," Pedro said.

"We are, my love," Samuel echoed.

They promised that they would never again be separated and lived happily ever after.

SANTIAGO READ THE story every night before going to bed, like a prayer. At length he memorized it and was able to recite it to himself throughout the day.

*   *   *

SANTIAGO WRAPPED PABLO back up in the white towel, picked him up in his arms and started down the street with him. The widows lingering on the block glanced furtively at Santiago's pained face as he passed them by. They shook their heads, crossed themselves, whispered prayers and rubbed their prying eyes.

"Bring him in, son," Santiago's mother shouted from her door. "We can spare him something to eat."

Santiago kept walking in silence.

"He must be cold." She sounded overly distressed. "Let me get some clothes for him." Her shouts got louder as her son moved farther away with Pablo. From behind, they looked like a large black cross vanishing amid the dusty lights of the many candles that faintly burned on both sides of the road.

"Where are you going with that man, Santiago Marín?" the magistrate called from Cecilia and Francisca's window. "You'll be put in quarantine, you hear me? Don't go saying I didn't warn you."

Santiago didn't reply, didn't stop or look back. He gazed fondly at the bundle in his arms and brought it even closer to his own body.

The full moon lit the narrow footpath. Only once did Santiago stop to rest. He knelt on the side of the path with his buttocks on the back of his heels and Pablo in his lap.

"Where are we going?" Pablo said in a low voice.

"To the one place you ought to see." Their deep voices did not agree with the sounds of the night, the rustling of the branches, the creaking of the trunks, the noises made by frogs, cicadas, owls and other night creatures.

"I want to see the plaza . . . and the church."

"They're all the same as when you left."

It was hot. Beads of sweat appeared along Santiago's forehead and ran down his face. He closed his eyes and imagined that the man in his arms was a basket filled with purple orchids; just as delicate, just as beautiful. He rose, half smiling, and went on, slower than before because enormous clouds had blocked out the moonlight and he couldn't see well. His feet would take them to where they were going.

"Take me to see my father," Pablo said.

"He's gone, Pablo."

"Then . . . take me to see my brothers."

"They're gone, too."

SANTIAGO DIDN'T TELL Pablo how they died. He didn't tell Pablo that five years before Communist guerrillas had assaulted Mariquita, claiming their men. That the rebels said they were fighting so that no Colombian should go a day without eating a good meal, and then ate their food and drank their water. That they said they were leading the country toward a society in which all property would be publicly owned, and then went from house to house raping their sisters and mothers. That they demanded that every man older than twelve join them, saying they would give each one a rifle, a freedom rifle to fight against the government, to defend their rights. But when Pablo's father asked for his right to choose not to join the movement, they shot him dead with one of the very freedom rifles they handed out. Then they killed his two brothers, too, because "Colombia doesn't need any more cowards."

Santiago didn't tell Pablo that the guerrillas took all the men away; that he, Santiago, had escaped the forced recruitment because he was still employed in Don Maximiliano's country house; that he went back into town as soon as he heard about the assault; and that he promised his mother and sisters not to ever leave them again after what he saw: houses burned down to nothing, mad widows weeping among the rubbish, old women praying on their bare knees with their blood-stained hands pressed together and their eyes tightly shut, young girls furiously rubbing their abused bodies with mud, cursing their lives, naked little boys and girls crying and roaming the streets, shouting for their fathers and brothers.

Santiago didn't tell Pablo any of that. He just went on, following his own feet that knew the trail better than him.

"But, Mamá . . . she's in the house. I heard the driver . . ." Pablo's voice grew weaker every time he spoke.

"Yes, she's there; she hardly ever leaves her house. But when she does, a parrot's on her shoulder and three old dogs follow her closely. She doesn't talk to anyone."

"Is she insane?"

"She's happy. Happier than most of the widows in town. She's not alone. Every relative she lost, she replaced with an animal."

Pablo pressed his face hard against Santiago's chest and wept softly.

THE MOON BROKE through the clouds, larger and brighter, shining down on the two men. When Santiago sighted their destination at last, he slowed down, but his breathing still came fast, the warm air coming in and out of his lungs in convulsive short waves.

"We're here," he whispered. They were by the river, where he and Pablo had played father and mother so many times. Santiago stood on the bank, watching the water flow steadily, listening to its bold splashing sound. "Look how beautiful it is," he said. Pablo looked up, and it was extraordinary and moving to see a full bright moon reflected in each of his sunken eyes, lighting up an otherwise lifeless face. "I love you," Santiago said, tightening his grasp on Pablo and walking purposefully into the river as they used to do when they were children. The cold water gradually covered his naked feet, his ankles and calves, his knees and thighs, his waist. Then he stopped, kissed Pablo lightly on the lips and watched him smile, watched his eyes grow wide and his nostrils swell like they had when he'd wanted to leave for New York.

Pablo was ready to leave again.

Santiago looked up at the moon and stretched out his arms, as if he were offering a sacrifice. He fixed his gaze on Pablo's face, filling himself full of the man he loved, and gently began to release his hold on him, his solid arms slowly separating from the smallness of his lover's back, giving him to the current like a gift. Pablo's flimsy figure drifted away from him, down the river, now disappearing into the water, now rising back to the surface, until all that was left of him was a white towel caught up in an eddy, bobbing up and down.

Or maybe it was the full moon now shining on the water.

Manuel Reyes, 23
Guerrilla soldier

When I came to, I was lying on my stomach in a field of grass. My body hurt, and my nose, mouth and throat burned. I lifted my head. A man was sitting in front of me, his face painted black and green. It took me a few seconds to notice other things about him: a patrol hat, a lit cigarette dangling from his mouth, a camouflage uniform, a Galil rifle held between his hands, aimed at my forehead.

"You have no idea how happy I am you're alive," he said cynically.

I slowly began to trace, in my mind, the events leading up to that moment. Falling overboard, water rushing in my mouth and nose, my arms struggling desperately against the current, trying to stay afloat. I couldn't remember anything else.

The man identified himself as a paramilitary soldier. He told me he'd get two hundred thousand pesos if he brought me back to his camp alive. "You ought to be thankful. You're the lucky one," he said, the cigarette smoke dribbling out the side of his mouth. "See that guy next to you?" I turned my head to the side. A half-naked man lay flat on his stomach, hardly a yard away from me. "The poor bastard drowned. He's still worth a few thousand pesos, though."

He got up and ordered me to pick up the corpse and carry it. His camp was about two hours away on foot. When I turned the body over to put it on my shoulder, I realized it was Campo Elías Restrepo Jr., my best friend in the guerrillas. Right then I remembered the rest: Campo Elías and I had developed a perfect plan to escape from the guerrillas, from the war. The night before, while on guard duty, I'd handed my gun to a comrade (deserting with his gun is the worst offense a fighter can do against his former group) and told him, "Look, comrade, I'm gonna be taking a crap behind the shrubs over there." I couldn't tell him I was fleeing. The guerrilla rule is to kill anyone who proposes to sneak off, even if he's your commander. I rushed down to the abandoned shack, where Campo Elías was waiting for me with the makeshift raft he'd built. We'd been crossing the river when our raft got caught up in a whirlpool and overturned.

He's just pretending to be dead, I thought—that was part of our plan—but when I picked him up, his head went limp. His face was pale, his lips purplish. His eyes were wide open, but only the whites were visible, like he'd decided there was nothing else worth seeing and turned them backward.

I began to walk quietly with Campo Elías on my shoulder, wondering what would happen to me, thinking that he—not me—was the lucky one: he'd escaped from it all.

CHAPTER 7

The Virgin Sacrifice

Mariquita, April 22, 1998

I T WAS THE PRIEST'S own idea to break the Sixth Commandment of God's law. One day he decided to pay a visit to the magistrate to discuss what he called "a pressing need for procreation." He went to her office early in the afternoon, wearing his black polyester soutane despite the relentless heat that followed a fierce three-day storm. He brought his altar boy, fourteen-year-old Hochiminh Ospina, who was on probation for eating an entire week's supply of hosts. The boy, who was fat and soft and flabby, hated the job, especially when, as on this day, he had to carry around el padre's gigantic Bible. "Can't we take a smaller Bible?" he asked every time, and every time he heard the same answer: "No." El padre was convinced that a big Bible made him more important and added weight to his moralizing discourse.

Inside Rosalba's office, the priest stood next to the window reading aloud an extensive selection of excerpts and psalms about procreation. The magistrate thought they were rather tedious and wondered why the priest didn't just get to the point.

"Praise be to God!" he exclaimed after he finished. He slammed the Bible closed, peered over the tops of his reading spectacles and declared, "It's our obligation to ensure the survival of our species."

"I agree with you, Padre," the magistrate replied. "Bringing men back to Mariquita has been one of my priorities since I was appointed magistrate. More than once I have requested the government, even the Lord, to send us a truck full of them."

"The Lord can only do so much," the priest said. "But what about the commissioner and the governor? Have they written back to you?" he added insincerely. He knew the answer.

"Who knows? They might have," she replied, in a tone that suggested rather a yes than a no. "But now that the storm has swept every access road to our village, I doubt we'll ever again see a postman around here—or anyone else, for that matter." She thought about the actual implications of what she had just said: no more merchants, no more occasional visitors, no more passing travelers, no more men ever again. The dismal prospect made her anxious. "We must do something about those roads immediately," she asserted, fetching her notebook and a stub of a pencil from a drawer.

"First things first, my child," the priest suddenly interposed, before the magistrate could add *Have access roads rebuilt* to her long, useless list of priorities. "Procreation must be our number-one priority." He motioned to the altar boy to step outside, then sat across from Rosalba. Together they discussed the issue at length, concluding that Mariquita's women had to bear boys soon, or else their village would disappear with the present generation. The magistrate suggested that Santiago Marín "do the job."

El padre shook his head, looking as if he'd just been cursed. "May God forgive that . . . man."

"Oh, Padre Rafael," Rosalba groaned. "Are you still bearing Santiago Marín a grudge for what he did?" She rolled her eyes and breathed an impatient sigh, oblivious to her condescending manner. "Wouldn't you agree that being in quarantine, alone with his grief, was enough punishment for that poor man? Good Lord! It must take a great deal of courage, *and love*, to do what he did. And that's exactly why I'd rather think of Santiago as one of us, a widow. The Other Widow."

Feeling offended, el padre met Rosalba's comment with impervious silence. He looked the other way and began playing with his fingers, which lay on top of his prominent stomach.

"Besides," Rosalba continued heedlessly, "he's the best chance we have to get a woman impregnated."

El padre abruptly stood up. "Never!" he roared, hitting the magistrate's desk with his palm. "A man who's sinned against the Lord by lying with another man will never father the future people of Mariquita!" He reached into his pocket for a handkerchief and patted his forehead with it, his hands trembling.

The magistrate observed the priest quietly and decided she'd wait for the little man to calm down. She was used to el padre's bad temper. One time, long ago, he'd torn out the few strands of hair left on his head because he'd run out of wafers for the Eucharist. "Oh, what a disgrace!" he had said. How did they expect him to celebrate mass without the Body of Christ to offer? Was he supposed to just skip Holy Communion, the most significant part of the liturgy? In the end Rosalba, as always, had solved the problem. She made tiny, thin arepas and suggested that el padre bless them. At first he was insulted: "The Body of Christ a piece of corn bread?" But Rosalba made him understand that hosts were nothing but thin pieces of bread, and at length he accepted her offer. With all the confusion, however, the priest forgot to bless the arepas, and as a result the women swallowed in church the same thing they'd eaten for breakfast at home, only smaller. Ever since that day arepas had become Mariquita's hosts, sometimes sweet, sometimes salty, and, when available, flavored with cheese.

The priest took a couple of deep breaths and sat again.

"What about Julia Morales?" Rosalba said. "Underneath those skirts there's a fine man." She emphasized the word *fine*.

The priest rolled his eyes. "Are you not listening to me, Magistrate? Procreation cannot be forced. It's bad enough that it won't be an act of married love, but it has to involve, at the very least, a degree of tenderness and affection that only a real man can give to a woman."

"I don't know what to say then," the magistrate confessed, crossing her arms. "Maybe we should consider the boys. Che and Trotsky will be fifteen this year."

"They're children," el padre said.

There was a long silence in which they avoided each other's eyes. After a while el padre sighed, shaking his head. "Well . . . ," he murmured. "No, I can't do that." He covered his face with both hands, as though he were going to cry. "I can't do that. I can't, I can't, I can't," he kept saying between his fingers, shaking his head frantically. But then, overcoming his guilt as only good Catholics can do, he said loudly and confidently, "One must face up to one's responsibilities. If this is God's will, Thy will be done." He stood up, a martyr's expression on his pink face, and gazed through the window at the cloudy sky. "I must do it!"

The magistrate objected to the idea. "I think it'd be terribly harmful for your and your church's reputation, but also for our community. You're the embodiment of—morality and chastity, Padre." But the priest insisted it was a divine will with which they must not interfere. Rosalba didn't pursue the matter further. She was almost certain that el padre's idea would encounter heavy resistance among the villagers. She'd let the women argue with the obstinate priest.

In the evening, the priest pealed the church bell strenuously, calling for a town meeting. The women of Mariquita had grown weary of such gatherings, because nothing important was ever said. Oftentimes the magistrate just reminded them to sweep and mop their floors, keep their backyards, clip their nails, comb their hair or inspect their children for lice. They attended the meetings, however, because there was nothing better to do. Tonight, Rosalba read a series of short paragraphs written by the priest for the women of Mariquita. The first paragraph informed them—rather, warned them—that Mariquita was in danger of disappearing if they didn't reproduce. "There's hope, though," the magistrate said. "El padre Rafael is willing to break his holy vow of chastity to help Mariquita stay alive."

A murmur of confusion was heard in the crowd.

A second paragraph explained that el padre would risk having to spend, after his death, a much longer time in purgatory than he deserved, just to give back to the community that for all these years had supported his church. Following that there was a short sentence announcing the beginning of the Procreation Campaign. "The objective of the campaign," the magistrate read, "is to impregnate twenty women during the first cycle." She added that she and el padre would be praying that a good percentage of the newborns were male. Then she read the rules: Only women older than fifteen and younger than forty could participate. They had to register with Cecilia Guaraya, the magistrate's secretary. Proof of age would be requested upon registration. Once the registration was official, the participant would be placed on a waiting list and told when she could expect to receive the visitation. The list would be permanently posted in the magistrate's office. Out of respect for God, all religious images should be removed from the room where the holy act would be consummated. No feelings would be involved in the holy act: el padre wouldn't be making love to them, he'd just be making babies, hopefully boys. And finally, the women should consider donating any food to help el padre stay fit and strong during the entire campaign, which would last a few months.

CONTRARY TO WHAT the magistrate supposed, the villagers didn't publicly object to el padre's idea. And contrary to what el padre supposed, no woman registered during the first few days after the announcement. They couldn't even conceive of the idea of going to bed with a priest, let alone *their* priest. "It'd be like making love with God," the Morales widow said. But that didn't discourage el padre. Every day at mass, he reminded the women of their duty to the human race and accused them of being selfish. "If I'm willing to make the sacrifice, why can't you do the same?" It wasn't, however, until he assured them God had granted him special permission to break the Sixth Commandment that the procreation visit list began to grow.

A young girl named Virgelina Saavedra was number twenty-nine.

*   *   *

Virgelina and Lucrecia, her grandmother, lived in a shaky house across from the market. As a child, Virgelina had been left in the care of her grandmother, who'd brought her up to be a housewife, servile and submissive. Shortly after Virgelina turned twelve, Lucrecia's health deteriorated, and the girl was required to take care of both of them. The old woman spent her days peering through the curtains at the women in the market, guessing what they'd be saying and fabricating amusing stories she later told her granddaughter as if the women themselves had shared them with her. Virgelina listened to the stories while she did housework, nodding from time to time. The girl had a morning routine: she woke up at the crack of dawn, mouthed her prayers, started the fire in the kitchen, made breakfast, swept the floor with a bunch of leaves and bathed if there was water. Occasionally she'd bring water from the river, but most of the time she relied on the rain to fill up three water barrels they kept in the back of the house. After completing her morning chores, the young girl went to school, where the schoolmistress had named her "Best Student" two years in a row. Virgelina only had three dresses, all black and conservative, which she had inherited from her late mother. She was small, quiet and well-mannered, and she was only fourteen.

Lucrecia had managed to convince Cecilia that, though underage, Virgelina was fit to bear a boy. "My great-grandmother bore nineteen boys," she'd said to Cecilia. "And my great-aunt's second cousin bore eleven boys. We come from a family that knows how to make boys."

Cecilia, who was notorious for her rudeness and inflexibility, surprisingly made an exception. She had a soft spot for two kinds of people, the elderly and the ones who paid her compliments.

In the mornings Lucrecia looked like a mummy. She had arthritis, which was exacerbated by the night wind that blew in through the cracks in the doors and roof. So every night before bedtime, Virgelina wrapped her up from neck to toes in ten yards of white cloth. Her grandmother had kept the fabric from when she was Mariquita's best seamstress. But regardless of the effectiveness of the therapy on her joints, the old woman promptly found new afflictions to grumble about: food never agreed with her stomach, noise gave her headaches, her kidneys hurt when it rained. Or pettier complaints: too cold, too hot, too sweet, much too sweet.

SINCE THE VISITS had begun, twenty-eight women had made room in their beds for the little priest, who, as rumors went in the market, was blessed with a large penis though he was a mediocre lover. "He finishes before you notice he's started," Magnolia Morales had told her friends during their nightly meeting at the plaza. One widow had had a late period, but it proved to be a false alarm. No one had yet claimed to be pregnant.

THE DAY VIRGELINA was to receive her visit, Lucrecia woke up complaining more than usual: "I can't breathe," she said. "My leg hurts." "I'm drowsy." "I'm nauseated." At least twice Virgelina was on the brink of telling her to stop fussing, to be quiet for a minute or two, to shut her old beak because today, especially today, she wasn't in the mood for her whining. But instead she kicked Fidel and Castro every time they crossed her way, and when she left for school, she slammed the door with all her might. After lunch, when the old woman woke up from her customary siesta crying and saying that she couldn't open her eyes, Virgelina ignored her. She dragged a chair outside and started knitting a quilt, worrying about the visit: that night would be her first time with a man.

As she knitted and purled she recalled, one by one and in perfect order, the seven steps her grandmother had contrived for her defloration. Virgelina had been forced to recite them several times, and each time her grandmother made her reverse the order of them, or combine two steps into one, or cut or add new steps in case something didn't work. Her first sexual experience had been meticulously planned, leaving no room for impulse, intuition, or the sudden passion that recently she'd begun to feel. Virgelina didn't know why, but lately her nipples had begun to itch. Now, every night after blowing out the candle in her room, she found herself stroking her nipples with the tips of her fingers until she felt as though she had a colony of angry little ants marching inside each breast, biting her flesh, eating her up. As she knitted, she imagined the priest's hands cupped on top of her small breasts, and the thought was so vivid that she could actually feel his fingers squeezing them hard. Suddenly, an electric current traveled briskly through her body, making her throw her hands and needles in the air. She rose and rushed inside the house, covering her bosom with her arms. She'd never felt anything like it before. She stood against the wall in the kitchen and took a deep breath, then another, and then another. Eventually she forced herself to remember that those fingers—el padre's—were connected to a couple of flabby arms, which were connected to a small trunk with a protruding belly, which was connected to a large bald head with an ugly pink face, with a long nose and tiny chicken eyes half covered with drooping eyelids. When at length she went outside to retrieve her sewing instruments, she felt somewhat relieved.

In the afternoon Virgelina rubbed her grandmother's eyes with warm water, but it didn't help. The woman's eyes were hermetically sealed. "I'll go get Nurse Ramírez," Virgelina said. The old woman replied that it wasn't necessary, that it was a sign from heaven, a warning that God was still mad at her for something only she knew.

Later on that night, the following conversation took place in their kitchen.

"Thank you for dinner, mija. Your soups are much better than your mother's, may her soul rest in peace."

"Drink your coffee, Grandmother. The cup is right in front of you."

"I can't drink coffee this late anymore. Last night I was up until dawn hearing the cries of all those poor men."

"What men, grandma?"

"Mariquita's men. Haven't you heard their poor wandering souls? May God have mercy on them."

"May God have mercy on us. We're still here, suffering."

"My child, you're too young to talk about suffering. When I was your age I was the happiest girl—"

"Yes, I know. A handsome man was courting you, but your father didn't approve of him because he was a Liberal. Two years later you were forced to marry my grandfather, who, of course, was a Conservador, and who, of course, beat you day and night. You see? I've learned the whole thing by heart now. Instead, why don't you tell me once and for all how Mother and Father died?"

"This kitchen is too cold. Where's my blanket?"

"You have it wrapped around you. Let me look for some cinnamon to make you a hot tea. That'll warm you up."

"And my walking stick? Where's my walking stick?"

"It's in your hand."

"Are you ready for your visitor, mija?"

"I am, but he won't be coming until eight."

"I just heard eight bells."

"I counted seven."

"It's better to be ready ahead of time. Remember that he's a busy man these days."

"I know, Grandmother. Where did I put the cinnamon?"

"Are you wearing rouge on your cheeks?"

"Uh-huh."

"Do you remember all the steps, mija? Tell me all the steps."

"Not again, Grandmother. Instead you tell me how Mother and Father died. I don't understand why it's such a secret."

"Did you clean the entire house like I told you?"

"Every corner."

"What about the bedspreads?"

"All clean. And I burned eucalyptus leaves in the outhouse and

brought enough water in case he wants to wash. Oh, here it is: the cinnamon. It was mixed with the panela. Let me heat the water."

"Did you remove the picture of Jesus on the cross from your bedroom?"

"No. Why should I do that? You said it would be a holy act."

"It will be, but the Lord doesn't need to witness it."

"I'll remove it, then, but before I do that, please tell me how Mother
and Father died."

IT TOOK VIRGELINA a great deal of perseverance to get her grandmother to tell her, in an exceptional moment of lucidity, the story she
wanted to hear. The old woman had avoided talking about it for years,
but today Virgelina would become a woman, and she was entitled to
know the truth.

"Your father killed your mother," Lucrecia said straightforwardly,
as though that was both the beginning and the ending of the story.

Stunned, with her hands joined over her mouth, Virgelina fell into
an old rocking chair she kept next to the stove.

Then, in a small but firm voice, Lucrecia gave her granddaughter
the details: "One morning, some thirteen years ago, your father woke
up and found his breakfast cold on the night table. Next to the cup of
coffee there was a note from your mother saying, 'My dear husband:
these are the last eggs I cook for you. I'm leaving you for someone
who'll never beat me. All best, Nohemí.' Your father went crazy." Lucrecia said that the enraged man had gone from village to village looking for his wife and daughter—Nohemí had taken little Virgelina with
her—until he found them near Girardot. And that he had brought them
back to Mariquita on a rainy night in the middle of June. "The morning
after," Lucrecia went on, "I found a bundled-up little baby crying at my
doorstep. It was you. I picked you up and rushed to Nohemí's house,
only a couple of blocks down. But it was too late." When she arrived,
she said, the house was in a terrible mess: broken glass everywhere,
broken vases and chairs, broken everything. She had found Nohemí

in a puddle of blood in the kitchen, her throat slit, and in back of the house, Virgelina's father hanging from a tree, with Nohemí's note lying on the ground right below his dangling feet.

When Lucrecia finished the telling, Virgelina wondered: Who was the man with whom her mother had fled? Had she been in love with him? What had become of him? She wanted to ask her grandmother, but the woman had slipped back out of lucidity and was shouting to the ceiling, "Lord, oh Lord. Forgive me for begetting a sinful daughter. Forgive me, for I didn't bring the lost sheep to Your flock." And then, with her sealed eyes toward Virgelina, she bitterly said, "Your mother's behavior brought shame to my name. That's why God's sending misfortune unto me!"

*   *   *

EL PADRE RAFAEL knocked on their door with the first ring of the church bell, and by the time the eighth ring was heard, he and his altar boy were already sitting in the living room with Virgelina. The priest had his legs crossed and a delighted expression on his rosy face, like he'd just tasted candy. Hochiminh's round face, on the other hand, was perfectly blank. He'd laid the enormous Bible on his lap and rested his plump arms on it. The Bible itself was much more likely to display a trace of a smile than he was. The light of a candle on the table illuminated Virgelina's face, which was indeed smeared with rouge, making her fearful expression even more dramatic.

When asked, Hochiminh mumbled that he was neither hungry nor thirsty. He didn't want coffee or cinnamon tea. He was fine. El padre said he'd take a "sip" of water. Just a "sip," for he knew how arduous it was to carry it all the way from the river. He spoke condescendingly, addressing Virgelina's breasts, smiling salaciously. The girl disappeared into the kitchen, where her grandmother sat unmoving and wrapped in her blanket like a poorly carved statue.

"He wants water," Virgelina grumbled. She went about the kitchen, looking for the vessel where they kept their drinking water. It was on top of the only table, before her eyes, but the girl was so agitated that she didn't see it. "Where did you put the water?" she asked, in a tone that betrayed her foul temper. The old woman turned her head to the right and then to the left, but didn't acknowledge the question. Virgelina rolled her eyes at the bundle of clothes her grandmother was, and kept looking for it, slamming pots and pans and banging skillets. She couldn't find it. "Where's the water?" she yelled. Lucrecia didn't reply. Virgelina walked up to her, grabbed her by the shoulders and shouted the same question once again.

Lucrecia pushed her away, brandishing her walking cane as if it were a sword. "What? What's happening?" she said in a small, broken voice. "Who's there?"

"It's me! Where's the damn water vessel?"

"Who's there? Say something," repeated Lucrecia.

"Oh, dear Lord," Virgelina groaned.

Evidently their Lord had decided, in the past few minutes and on top of everything else, to take away her grandmother's hearing. Virgelina sat at the table, weeping, then she saw the vessel sitting in front of her. She reared up, poured water into a cup, spit in it, stirred it with her index finger and ran from the kitchen, stumbling along the dark hall that separated the rooms. When she was gone, Lucrecia opened her eyes wide and walked to the door and pressed her ear against it to better hear the conversation taking place in her living room.

"Thanks, my child," said the priest, taking the cup with both hands. He quickly gulped down its contents. "Will your grandmother join us for the Bible reading?"

"She's not feeling well."

"I'm sorry to hear that. Is there anything I can do to assist her?"

"Nothing, unless you can perform miracles. Can you, Padre?" Virgelina said with remarkable harshness.

El padre chose to receive the girl's reply silently. He asked Hochiminh to look up Genesis 1:28 in the Bible, and when the boy found it, he moved the Bible onto his own lap, put on his reading spectacles and began to read by the flickering light of the candle:

"Then God blessed them, and God said unto them, 'Be fruitful and multiply; and replenish the earth and subdue it; have dominion over the fish of the sea, over the fowl of the air, and over every living thing that moveth upon the earth.' " He crossed himself and, putting away his spectacles in a concealed pocket on the left side of his soutane, added, "Praise be to God!"

"Is that it? Can I go now?" Hochiminh asked. The priest assented, and both boy and Bible fled without so much as a wave.

In the few seconds that passed between the moment Hochiminh slammed the door and the moment the priest said, "Shall we, my child?" Virgelina, in her mind, debated whether or not her mother had been wrong to leave her husband. Until that afternoon, she'd only heard good things about her mother. People in the village raved about Nohemí's innumerable great qualities but seldom mentioned her father. What a wife and mother, Nohemí! What a devoted Catholic, Nohemí! What a kind and generous soul, Nohemí! What a remarkable human being, Nohemí! They spoke so highly and sympathetically of Nohemí that Virgelina, who'd never seen a picture of her mother, imagined her as an angelic figure with long hair, rosy cheeks and a permanent smile. She had set up an altar to her mother in a corner of her bedroom, and she prayed to her every night. The altar had three levels, and it rested on piled-up boxes. On the top level she placed a small image of the Virgin Mary—who represented her mother—a rosary, and a white candle she only lit when she offered a sacrifice. On the middle level she kept a plastic bowl to hold the ladlesful of soup she offered up daily to her mother—she was very fond of soups, Nohemí!—and when she found them, yellow marigold flowers, the flower of the dead. On the bottom level Virgelina arranged a cup full of water and several little charms and trinkets she acquired at the market, in honor of her mother's spirit.

But today, after her grandmother's confession, Nohemí's image had swiftly deteriorated in Virgelina's mind. How good could a wife have been who abandoned her husband? Virgelina reflected. And how good a mother, who risked her daughter's life by having an affair with God knows who?

"Shall we, my child?" the priest said, rising. He gracefully took the candleholder with two of his fingers and handed it to Virgelina, then motioned to her to go ahead, he'd follow.

As Virgelina entered her bedroom, closely followed by the priest, her head suddenly cleared. It occurred to her that both her mother and grandmother had had a free choice when they selected their paths. What they could've or should've done didn't matter anymore, because back then, at that moment when they had to decide which path to take, in their own minds both women had made the right choices. She, Virgelina, had no right to condemn them.

Feeling empowered by her realization, Virgelina was able to see that she, too, had the right to make her own decisions. At this very moment several paths presented themselves before her: she could stay in the room with the priest, doing as her grandmother had told her to do, without complaining. She could run away like her mother, without looking back, hoping no one would ever find her. She could tell el padre the truth—that she was terrified—and politely ask him to leave. She could suffer "it" in silence until "it" was finished, then get the biggest knife from their kitchen, thrust it into el padre's chest, draw his heart out and place it, all bloody, on the top level of her altar, next to the white candle. A sacrifice that big would certainly appease God's fury against her grandmother; it might even prompt Him to give Lucrecia back her sight and hearing.

She closed the door with the tips of her fingers and turned around, ever so slowly, to face the eager priest.

VIRGELINA LAID THE candleholder on the night table. They stared at each other in the flickering light. Only the bed stood between them. From where he stood, the priest could see a small part of the girl's lips and chin, and the outline of her small right breast. From where she stood, Virgelina made out an inquisitive eye fixed on her right breast, a trembling nostril and half a mouth smiling lustfully at her.

"Come over here, my dear," el padre said, patting the bed with the palm of his hand. "Come . . ."

The room was so still she heard the throbbing of her own heart. And then, almost in a whisper, the echo of her grandmother's voice repeating the steps for Virgelina's defloration began resounding in the girl's mind.

Step one: Tell him you're a virgin so that he'll be gentle.

"I'm a virgin, padre," Virgelina blurted out.

"I beg your pardon?"

"I'm a virgin."

He chuckled. "I wouldn't expect anything different from you, dear." He walked around the bed, eliminating the space that divided them, and stood confidently before her. One of his hands rested on her hip while the other searched up and down her back for a zipper. It found buttons, undid them, and after a couple of swift motions Virgelina's dress fell to the floor. She jerked her body a little and wrapped her arms around her chest.

Step two: Kiss him on the lips, then put your tongue inside his mouth and move it in circles.

Without releasing her firm grasp from around her bosom, Virgelina pushed her lips together the way her grandmother had instructed her, closed her eyes and thrust her face outward, again and again, like a bird pecking at a piece of fruit, hoping that eventually her mouth would reach his. Recognizing what the girl was trying to accomplish, el padre took her head in his hands, and, standing on his toes, began to kiss her with great tenderness. Virgelina allowed el padre to go about his business, but she wouldn't put her tongue inside his mouth. How could her grandmother think she'd do such a revolting thing? But el padre wanted to feel her tongue. And so their lips engaged in a violent fight: his twisting around, striving vigorously to push hers open; hers making strenuous efforts to resist. Virgelina had always thought that kisses had flavors, and that when two people liked the flavors of each other's kisses, they fell in love and kissed and kissed until one of them died or their lips dried out. Her first kiss, however, tasted like spittle and blood because el padre Rafael, frustrated with Virgelina's reluctance, bit her lips fiercely.

Step three: Grab his hands and put one on each of your breasts.

She didn't need to aim the priest's shaky hands anywhere. They knew what to look for, where to go, what to do, when to rest and how to stroke. They traveled slowly across her back, stopped at the knot she made with the ends of the pieces of cloth she wore as a brassiere, and untied it with great skill. Next, they yanked down her underwear faster than she could say no. Virgelina tried to blow air toward the candle on the night table, but it was too far away. Instead she shut her eyes as firmly as she could. And then she felt his lips again, this time sucking the angry little ants that had just begun to bite her breasts again, making her nipples itch.

Step four: Undress him.

The soutane el padre Rafael wore for his procreation visits was the kind worn exclusively by bishops, archbishops and cardinals. He'd bought it at an auction when he was young and optimistic, thinking one day he'd rise to the highest echelons of the clergy. Later, when he finally understood that he had neither the connections nor the determination to get ahead in the Roman Catholic Church, he started wearing the special soutane whenever it pleased him. It was tailored in black linette and featured purple and gold metallic brocade cuffs, five pleat inserts front and back, gold metallic piping, a removable tab collar and a full button-front closure, which served a good purpose in el padre's nocturnal duties.

Virgelina decided to wait for the priest to rise before disrobing him. At the moment he was on his knees, his slimy tongue between her legs, causing her to make little nervous flutters with her entire body. But when it became obvious that the man wasn't going to stand up anytime soon, she drew him up by holding her hands in his armpits. Sweating profusely, el padre removed the tab collar—which he liked very much, since it eliminated the need for an underlying clerical shirt. He unfastened the top button of his soutane, but was promptly interrupted by Virgelina's dexterous knitter's fingers. *That's our job, Padre*, they seemed to say, and moved downward, freeing the first seven buttons from their holes. She knelt down and continued undoing the lower ones, her fingers gracefully descending along the golden piping. When she unfastened the last one, she looked up and watched the naked little man come out of his soutane with a majestic gesture, like an arrogant queen dropping her velvet mantle for her vassals to pick up.

Step five: *Check how excited he is.*

Standing in front of him, Virgelina remembered what her grandmother had told her to look for: "His penis will be erect, and you must touch it to make sure it's hard." The old woman had added, "If his penis isn't stiff, kiss him some more and touch him here and there, like I told you."

The priest was excited, very excited, Virgelina concluded after touching his swollen penis and hearing his howling. He gently pushed her onto the bed, and without taking off his white socks and worn sandals, positioned himself on top of her. El padre was smaller than she was and had a paunch, and yet his body fit into hers almost perfectly: a fist into an open hand.

Step six: *Commend yourself to God and let him do the rest.*

Virgelina's grandmother had been vague about what "the rest" was. The girl had seen dogs mating as well as cats, and thought "the rest" would be the same: a game of power played by two in which the male scored by putting its member inside the female's sexual organ, while the female scored by getting pregnant. Virgelina's biggest fear was the pain she might feel during the bout—the cry of the cats she'd seen mating was terrifying—and her grandmother's advice, "Bite the pillow and hold back," hadn't given her any comfort. She decided she'd let el padre score at once and get the game over with as quickly as possible.

Mounted on top of her, el padre rocked his hips in a way that was everything but sensual, more like scouring, like scrubbing off a stain.

"Do you like it?" he whispered in her ear. She didn't reply. He kissed her mouth, her nose and eyes, her chin. "Do you like it?" he insisted, a bit louder this time, for she might not have heard him before. Not a word back, a gesture. Virgelina was striving to make herself believe that the man lying atop her was an entirely different man from the one who had given her first communion not so long ago. He kept scrubbing and kissing, asking the same question and getting the same silent answer.

But then, without a warning, he thrust down on her with all his might, until a part of him disappeared in her flesh, and blood flowed down Virgelina's legs. She screamed. She felt her insides being split, as if by a giant nail, and she screamed with pain.

"It feels good," the priest said, lying still on her stomach. She dug her nails into his back and shouted to him to please remove *that* from within her, "Please." But he didn't; instead he started moving in and out of her. She tried to push him aside. "For the love of God!" He didn't hear her supplication; he continued thrusting into her, gathering speed inside her body, and so she fiercely scratched his face and sank her teeth into his chest. "Stop!" He stopped abruptly and shouted, "How dare you?" He slapped her twice across the face, then grabbed her hands, spread her arms and held them down firmly with his own hands, his fingers twined in hers, before resuming the furious motion of his hips: up and down, right to left, back and forth and around again (she wept, thinking of her grandmother's sacrifice), fuming, biting, breaking, tearing, (she wept, thinking of her mother's sacrifices), digging into her flesh, faster and faster until his legs tightened and he exploded inside her, chanting, "Oh, God. Oh, God. Oh, God . . ." (she wept some more, this time thinking of her own sacrifice).

Step seven: Close your legs and cross your feet so that the seed won't escape from within you. Stay in that position for a reasonable length of time.

Beneath the priest, Virgelina sobbed and shivered. "Is there anything wrong, dear?" el padre asked, suddenly noticing her wailing. She shook her head. He let go of her arms slowly, as though afraid she might attack him again, but the girl didn't move. Then he got down off her, picked up his soutane and promptly enrobed himself in it, his back to Virgelina. "I enjoyed myself very much," he said softly as he fastened the tab collar. "I hope that your grandmother considers putting your name down for a second visit." He introduced each button in its respective loop, bending down slightly to reach the lower ones. "I promise it won't hurt next time," he said, addressing the wall, and that's when he saw it. Before his eyes, hanging on a rusty nail, was the picture of Jesus dying on the cross. With all the distress caused by her grandmother's confession Virgelina had forgotten to remove it. El padre was stunned to see it.

"It is finished," Virgelina suddenly said and sighed with relief. The three Biblical words made the priest shudder. He swiftly turned around, and what he saw filled him with horror: lying face upward with her head slightly tilted to the right, her arms stretched out to the sides, her legs joined together and her feet crossed, Virgelina looked like Jesus crucified, bleeding and moaning, dying half naked upon an imaginary cross.

The priest hastily crossed himself and ran off, stumbling first over Fidel and Castro, who had the peculiar habit of sleeping by the doorway, and then, when he was out of the house, over stones the size of dogs and dogs that lay like stones in the street. He ran and ran without looking back, shouting, "Lord, oh Lord, have mercy on me. I'll never do it again!"

Indifferent to the priest's reaction, Virgelina collected the little strength she had left and sat up on the bed, wincing. Her body shook, and her hands trembled. She gathered the white, bloodstained bedspread from underneath her and used it to wipe down her inner legs, rubbing the thick cloth so harshly against her skin that it hurt. She slowly rose and began folding the bedspread with great care, until it was but a small, compact square of red-stained fabric. Then she knelt down in front of the altar and placed the cloth on its top level, next to the white candle that tonight burned fitfully.

And finally, as she confidently waited for her grandmother to walk into her room shouting that God had worked her a miracle, that all her pains were gone and she could see and hear again, Virgelina, hands clasped under her chin, began mouthing prayer after prayer until the white candle died and the night covered their house with absolute darkness.

Bernardo Rubiano, 26
Right-wing paramilitary soldier

"What's going to happen to me?" I asked the guerrilla. I was on my knees, drinking water from a creek we'd just found. He was taking me to his camp.

He yawned, stretching his arms one at a time, then said, "They won't kill you, if that's what worries you." Earlier that day I'd walked into a guerrilla ambush, and the rebel had made me his prisoner. He moved a little closer to me and squatted down, his gun firmly held in one hand. "You'll be *interrogated*, though," he added in a sinister tone. "If you spit out everything you know about the paras' whereabouts, they won't hurt you much. But if you don't—" He paused, brought his index finger up to his throat and made a dramatic slicing motion.

He was now hardly a yard away from me, squatting. He looked thin and gaunt. I thought I could take him. I intentionally gulped more water to make him thirsty. He cupped his free hand, and without taking his eyes off me stretched his arm out to get some water from the creek. But he was a bit too far away, so he stretched his arm a little farther, just enough to lose his balance and fall on his side. I threw myself upon him, lashing at him with my fists. He fought back hard and somehow ended up on top of me, panting, sweating and shouting that he was going to shoot me, although his gun had disappeared in the struggle. I fumed and roared. I bit and tore and raked until I was on top of him. Then I started hitting him. On the head and back and face and stomach, as hard as I could. He shouted and panted and yelped and sweated and writhed in pain, but I didn't stop. Not until I saw the gun, lying on the grass. I jumped up, took hold of the Galil, and pointed it at him.

"Please don't," he begged, his hands up. "Please." I'd heard many men beg for their lives. This one was no different. "Take my watch. Here." He took it off, laid it on the grass and gently pushed it toward me. "Please don't kill me. My boots. Take my boots." He started undoing the laces of his black jungle boots, but then remembered something even more valuable to trade. "Want this?" He ripped his shirt open, exposing a silver chain with an array of little amulets hanging from it. "It'll protect you from misfortune." He tore it off his neck. "Here." And threw it at my feet. "Please don't kill me. Please don't. Please—"

I squeezed the trigger. Gently, but the bullet went through his mouth and shut him up just the same.

CHAPTER 8

The Plagues of Mariquita

Mariquita, June 20, 1999

THE MAGISTRATE'S ANNOUNCEMENT FOR the Next Generation decree went something like this: "In yet another effort to preserve our dear community, and after consulting with my advisers, I, Rosalba viuda de Patiño, magistrate of the town of Mariquita, resolve that as soon as all four boys in our village—Che López, Hochiminh Ospina, Vietnam Calderón and Trotsky Sánchez—turn fifteen, they'll be compelled to enter a competition. The women of Mariquita will decide which of the young men shall be granted the right to marry a female of his choice, to constitute a family for the preservation of the moral and social purity of our town. The three unselected young men will be ordered to serve as Mariquita's full-time begetters for an undetermined period of time, during which they'll no longer be autonomous individuals but rather government property, workers whose sole duty will be to father boys, and who'll be provided with food and lodging and nothing else for as long as we need their labor."

Following Rosalba's declaration, the four boys were ordered, on pain of banishment, to stay away from women until their fate was decided, which would be on the morning of June 21, 2000, a day after Hochiminh, the youngest of the four, would turn fifteen.

Although she was responsible for drafting the Next Generation decree, the magistrate thought the entire thing was absurd and uncivilized: How can anybody in her right mind, she asked herself, oblige one of those children to make love to someone like, say, Orquidea Morales, such an ugly thing? But she felt she had to make amends to the women of Mariquita for the "complete" and "ignominious" failure of the Procreation Campaign, in which twenty-nine women had been intimate with el padre Rafael for three months, and none had become pregnant. "I was deceived by el padre Rafael into believing that he could beget boys; or girls, for that matter." the magistrate admitted before the crowd that swarmed into the plaza to learn about her new decree. "I would've never endorsed el padre's idea had I known he was as sterile as a mule."

Everyone in the plaza applauded Rosalba's harangue; everyone but the priest, of course. He thought the magistrate's remarks were a declaration of war, and in retaliation, he stopped hearing confessions and giving communion altogether. The embargo of the two sacraments worked wonders for el padre, especially on the older widows, who after two weeks without confessing their peccadilloes felt as though constipated. They begged the priest's forgiveness again and again until, satisfied, the little man absolved them of all blame and resumed giving the customary array of those invisible graces called sacraments. Still, the magistrate refused to apologize.

DURING THE ENTIRE year after the Next Generation decree was announced, the villagers debated whether or not it was needed or even wanted. From behind the pulpit el padre Ráfael declared time after time that he was against it, that it was a desperate measure from a desperate magistrate. "Forcing our boys to engage in sexual activity with women who are not their wives is wrong. It goes against the principles of Catholicism, but also against the boys' rights."

The older women, too, openly condemned the Next Generation decree in the market, while trading a cheap trinket for a pound of onions or a papaya for a handmade bar of soap. They couldn't understand why any woman—old or young—could possibly want to beget more men. Had they forgotten how the men had mistreated, ignored and diminished them? Didn't they remember those creatures with broad-brimmed sombreros that would go drinking rather than stay home nursing a sick son? The same creatures with unkempt mustaches who'd rather pay a whore at La Casa de Emilia than make love to their devoted and decent wives.

Certain unnamed widows discussed the magistrate's peculiar decree secretly, in the privacy of their bedrooms, under lavender-scented sheets, after making love and before one of them had to depart in the middle of the night, protected by darkness. They shared the same view as the older women, and maintained that if not having men around meant that Mariquita had to end with the present generation, perhaps an entire generation of harmony, tolerance and love would be preferable to an eternity of misery and despair—not to mention war.

Old maids also chose to talk about the Next Generation decree at night, only they did it on their doorsteps, while they spun cotton or separated good beans from bad ones for the following day's soup. They were somewhat ambivalent toward it. Indeed they welcomed the possibility of becoming mothers, even if it involved being intimate with a callow youth. But at the same time they felt that having a child—boy or girl, it didn't matter—wouldn't change their despised status as old maids. What they wanted, really wanted, was to be someone's girlfriend or fiancée, someone's wife. They wanted to belong to a man, to be claimed as his property. They declared that the first verb their mothers had taught them wasn't *to be* but *to belong*; therefore belonging would always come before being.

The younger women, on the other hand, didn't talk so much about the decree. They talked about the boys, and they did it every time they saw the small cluster of them in school taking dictations from the teacher Cleotilde, or bringing water from the river in earthen containers, or working their mothers' orchards, or playing soccer in teams of two. But they also talked about them every night during their customary after-rosary meeting, when they sat in a big circle in the middle of the plaza playing games, trying new hairstyles, or, as their mothers said, "Feeding the mosquitoes." Oftentimes they simply rated the boys, making a parody of the anticipated competition ordered by the magistrate. In their version, which they called "Míster Mariquita," each girl was asked to rank the four boys in trite categories, such as Cutest Face, Most Adorable Smile, Sweetest Personality, etc., and then compare their results amid peals of laughter.

But not everything the girls did during the months before the competition was amusing. Virgelina Saavedra saw in the upcoming event an opportunity for profit. She took bets of different amounts and goods on the results of the competition. She herself bet a romance novel illustrated with photos—which she treasured—that Che López would win the right to choose a wife and form a family. Meanwhile, Magnolia Morales took it upon herself to circulate three different waiting lists (one for each unknown procreator) to determine the order in which each girl would eventually have a naked boy in her bed. She purposely kept the list from old maids and widows, for she decided the former had had every chance to secure a man in their prime (and squandered it), and the latter had already enjoyed their share of men in this life. This, naturally, gave rise to controversies, quarrels, verbal confrontations and even a fistfight. As always the magistrate had to intercede, first drafting and then announcing one more of her brilliant decrees: as long as a woman was menstruating regularly, she had the right to be on any of the three lists and to marry the one eligible boy, should he happen to select her. Period.

*   *   *

MAGNOLIA MORALES WAS the first woman to arrive in the plaza on that fatal Sunday in June of 2000. She got there a little before daybreak, wearing a shapeless robe of sacking she'd sewed herself. The gusting morning wind made the mango trees tremble, and the many leaves on the ground caused Magnolia to slip, but she didn't fall. She spread a blanket on the ground, in front of the improvised platform that had been built the day before by order of the magistrate. The eagerly awaited competition wouldn't begin until eight that morning, but Magnolia had promised her sisters that she'd be the first one to show up and that she'd keep a place for them in the first row.

Luisa arrived next, about half an hour later, then Cuba Sánchez, then Sandra Villegas and Marcela López, and by the time the first rooster crowed, women had appeared from different corners of Mariquita, as though carried along by the wind. They sat around the platform, dark rings under their eyes from not enough sleep, and alcohol on their breath from drinking too much chicha. The night before they'd celebrated Hochiminh Ospina's fifteenth birthday with a great fanfare not seen or heard in Mariquita in a long time. It must be said that Hochiminh's birthday was the last thing on the women's minds (Hochiminh himself had not been invited to his birthday celebration). It was the event that would take place the morning after the boy's birthday that they were anxiously awaiting; an unprecedented competition that would make Magnolia, Luisa, Cuba, Sandra, Marcela, Pilar, Virgelina, Orquidea, Patricia, Nubia, Violeta, Amparo, Luz, Elvira, Carmenza, Irma, Mercedes, Gardenia, Dora and many other young girls, widows and old maids of Mariquita immensely happy.

But while the women sat around the platform in the plaza, chatting merrily and making their last conjectures, Che, Hochiminh, Vietnam and Trotsky had begun to experience, separately, the adverse effects of the tremendous anxiety caused by the contest that would decide their fate. For several months the four boys had been the subject of discussions, speculations, assumptions, controversies, fights, bets and even jokes. Their thoughts and feelings about the magistrate's decree, however, had never been consulted. Their anxiety had been building for an entire year, and they'd grown awfully apprehensive. On this memorable morning, the proximity of the event and the mounting pressure placed on each to win had worked them up to a state of near hysteria where anything was possible.

THEY SAY THAT Che López woke up at two on that Sunday morning and couldn't go back to sleep. He didn't suffer from insomnia—he could sleep soundly for twelve hours. The night before he'd planned to get up at six, earlier than usual, because he had to win the right to marry the girl of his choice, Cuba Sánchez. To achieve his goal, he thought, he needed to trim his hair, clip his nails, and, with a piece of coal and great care, add some density to the faint shadow he had for a mustache. He was fifteen, with black hair and eyes, a small colorless face and a full erection hidden in his white cotton pajamas.

Restless, he lay on his back, staring at the ceiling, yawning. The moonlight coming through a hole in the ragged curtain illuminated his swollen crotch. He rubbed it hard with the open palm of his hand, thinking of the warm, mushy, moist flesh of the watermelon he'd bored a hole into—and made love to—the day before. He pulled down his pajama trousers, wrapped his hand firmly around his penis, and began to stroke it zealously. But something wasn't right; his hand felt a little too big around his penis. Maybe it isn't fully erect, he thought. He held it between his thumb and index fingers and squeezed to check its hardness. It felt as bone-solid as only a fifteen-year-old penis can be. The boy moved slightly to the right so that the moonlight shone on his penis, and for a moment had no doubt that it looked smaller, by three-quarters of an inch at least. Maybe it's my hand that's growing, he supposed, and continued masturbating, imagining big, juicy watermelons lined up on the kitchen table, waiting to be penetrated. After some time, a long, unrestrained moan escaped from his mouth, and his hand stopped moving. He remained motionless for a few seconds, his lungs gasping for air. But something else wasn't right; he didn't feel any sticky liquid on his hand, and his penis appeared to be dry. He quickly shifted his body toward the right side of the bed and lit a candle. He looked closely for any evidence of ejaculation. He didn't see anything on his reduced penis, nor his hands, the bed sheets or his pajamas. Armed with the candle, he checked the naked walls, the shiny floor, under his bed; he even checked the ceiling—nothing.

Every Friday after class Che and the other three boys of Mariquita went swimming in the river. They often measured, with a ruler, the size of their penises before going into the cold water, and then after. They were always amazed to see how their penises shrunk. A week before, they had decided to do something different. They held a contest to decide who could ejaculate the farthest. They picked an open space on the riverbank and marked a spot. One at a time they stood on the spot, masturbated and shot. Che won with a seven-foot-six reach, followed by Trotsky with five feet, three inches, then Vietnam with five feet, and finally Hochiminh with three feet, eleven inches. Che boasted about it for the entire week; he even called for a second contest because he wanted to break his own record, but the other boys ignored him.

On that Sunday, however, at two thirty in the morning, Che firmly believed that his penis was shrinking, and that he had no semen.

DAWN WAS BREAKING, and gusts of wind were capriciously changing the order of objects in patios and backyards: flowerpots, plastic containers, clothes from the washing lines and even washing lines themselves drifted in the air for a little while before hitting a wall or landing in someone else's yard.

Meanwhile, they say, Hochiminh Ospina was having a frightening dream. In his dream he was swimming naked in the river with his friends from school, racing to see who was the fastest to get to the bank on the other side. Hochiminh worked his arms and legs vigorously, but his body—as fat in his nightmare as it was in real life—didn't move forward. He saw his friends disappear in the distance, their arms and legs splashing. He tried harder, with his arms fully stretched and his hands perfectly curved as they thrust firmly into the water, and yet he didn't advance an inch. Suddenly his body began to whirl around on the surface, faster each time. A powerful eddy had formed, and its circular movement was sucking him into its center. He struggled fiercely against it, moving his arms and legs as fast as he could. He felt a shooting pain in his chest, possibly caused by the strain he was putting on his muscles, but he didn't stop moving; he couldn't, or the eddy would swallow him up. The pain became acute, as if someone were pressing heavily on his chest and piercing his nipples at the same time. He continued swimming tenaciously against the whirlpool, enduring the ache, until the rooster in back of his house woke him up with its rowdy crowing.

With his eyes fixed on the ceiling, relieved that it only had been a bad dream, Hochiminh thanked God for the roosters. However, as the rest of his body began to rouse, he felt an intense pain in his nipples. He brought his hands to his chest instinctively and became horrified. His hands didn't land flat on the skin of his chest, as they generally did; this time, he thought, they arched over two large mounds that had appeared overnight, like boils. Hochiminh jumped out of his bed and quickly lit the candle that was on the night table. He lowered his head until his double chin touched his cleavage, tilting it slightly from left to right and vice versa with his eyes wide open. The proximity of the view caused him to imagine that his breasts looked larger than they were, and he wept quietly. How was he going to explain these to his mother and sisters? And what about the contest? Up on the platform he'd be nothing but an object of ridicule. This couldn't be happening to him. He, who had been an altar boy. He, who recited a Hail Mary and a Lord's Prayer every night before going to bed. He, who was a good student, an obedient son, a good brother to his two sisters, and a good grandson to—well, on a few occasions he'd stolen silver coins from his grandmother's purse, right in front of her exhausted, half-blind eyes, while she said rosary after rosary. This had to be a divine punishment. After saying a few prayers with fervent devotion, Hochiminh put on his late father's bathrobe and threw a large towel behind his neck, making sure the ends covered his breasts. He grabbed the candle, opened the door of his bedroom slightly, just enough to see that there was no one in the corridor, and hurried to the outhouse.

Outside, the boy undressed in front of a full-length mirror and gave free rein to his imagination. He saw two fleshy protuberances, each with a large nipple at the end, stare back at him. He cupped his hands under them, feeling their weight. They were as heavy as oranges. He squeezed them hard, trying to deflate them, but the excessive pressure made them hurt and the sharp new pain seemed to insist that they were a part of his body; two self-contained organs that, quite possibly, were there to perform some specific functions. Perhaps, a more pragmatic Hochiminh reckoned, they'd shrink if he soaked them in cold water, like his penis did. He ran across the patio, naked, to the large barrel they used to collect rainwater, and went into the water, immersing his pudgy body from the neck down. A few minutes later he came out, shivering. His nipples had become stiff, and the pain in his chest had stopped, numbed by the cold water. But his breasts remained large and firm—or so he believed.

THAT SAME MORNING, they say, Vietnam Calderón didn't get up until his mother tickled his heels. The boy was redundant with laziness, slackness, tardiness and other words ending in *ess* that amounted to nothing good for his character. In the outhouse he found, as usual, the washing basin and towel his mother left for him every morning. He scrubbed his armpits and between his legs, cursing at her for making him wash daily; then went to his room and put on clean clothes his mother had chosen for him. A few minutes later he sat at the dining table in front of a stale piece of corn bread and a cup of hot chocolate. His mother sat beside him, holding a cup of coffee and repeating, one last time, her "useful tips" on how to win the competition.

"Listen to me, Vietnam," she began, a hint of irritation in her voice. "When you're up on the platform, don't pick your nose or rub your crotch, like you *always* do." The boy nodded his head mechanically. He looked rather tense, but his mother decided he was just not keen on the contest or her tips. After all, he wasn't too keen on anything in particular. Everything he did was marked with such indifference that the teacher Cleotilde had said he'd make a good politician.

"...And please, Vietnam, for once in your life wear a smile on your face. Are you listening to me?"

"Yes, Mamá," he finally replied in the falsetto voice of a little girl. He cleared his throat and said it again, "Yes, Mamá." It sounded just as delicate.

The widow took a sip of coffee before asking, "What's the matter with your voice?"

"I don't know. It was—" He stopped, cleared his throat again and tried one more time. "It was normal last night."

"You sound like a girl, for Christ's sake!"

"Leave him alone," said Liboria, Vietnam's grandmother. "Boys' voices start breaking when they turn fifteen." Old Liboria lay stretched in a hammock slung from beams across the dining area. She was always in the hammock, aging slowly while suspended in the air, like a good sausage in a butcher's shop.

Vietnam drank his hot chocolate in sips, letting every mouthful burn his throat. "It was normal yesterday," he repeated, soprano-like.

"Stop talking like that, Vietnam!" his mother admonished him, her index finger in the air.

The boy's face turned red. He coughed, grunted and made every guttural sound he could think of. "It was normal yesterday," he repeated.

Visibly upset, his mother finished the coffee in one gulp, reared up and plodded into the kitchen.

In the back of the house, in front of the mirror his father had pasted up on the wall many years ago, Vietnam gargled with salty water. "Testing, uno, dos, tres." He gargled more. "Testing, uno, dos, tres." But his voice remained impossibly high-pitched. Desperately, he pushed his index finger down his throat and moved it in circles until he vomited his breakfast and tears came to his eyes. He wiped the tears away with the heel of his hand, then went to get water to clean the mess he'd made. It was back there, as he fetched water from the laundry sink, that Vietnam felt a stream flowing down his legs. He forgot about the water and rushed to the toilet, his legs held together from the hips to the knees. He was so embarrassed to have wetted his pants that when he pulled them down he saw not urine, but blood, staining his trousers red, running down his inner thighs. He looked at his penis and noticed blood still gushing from it. He became frightened, not just because of the scarlet color of his blood but also because of his total inability to restrain the discharge. "I'm dying," he wailed.

"Vietnaaaaaaaaam!" shouted his mother from the kitchen. "Hurry up. You're going to be late for the contest!"

"I'm coming, Mamá," he shrieked.

"Stop talking like that, Vietnam! I'm warning you!"

"Leave him alone," his grandmother grumbled from her hammock.

THEY SAY THAT when Trotsky Sánchez's mother walked into her son's room to wake him up, she found him weeping on the edge of his bed. He used one of his hands to cover his diminutive slanting eyes, and kept the other clenched on his chest, close to his heart.

"What's wrong, mi cielo?"

" . . . ! . . . . . !! . . . . . !!!" Trotsky gabbled.

She came closer to his bed and stroked his hair. "You're frightened about what might happen at the contest, aren't you?" She sat next to him, embraced him and wiped away his tears with her impeccable white apron. "My heart tells me you'll win, Trotsky, and a mother's heart is never wrong."

The boy unclenched his hand and looked at it over his mother's shoulder: what he was hiding was still there. He closed his hand tightly again and let out a shriek.

"Everything's okay, cariño. Mamá's here."

But the boy had empowered his imagination to take him to a place where nothing was okay. Earlier that morning, before sunrise, Trotsky had awakened wanting to urinate. He pulled the chamber pot from under his bed and placed it on the mattress. He stood in front of it, still somnolent, and inserted his right hand into his pants, looking for his penis. His hand landed on his young pubic hair and quickly traveled the pubes, hunting for his member. It moved all over, his five fingers extended in every direction. He found his testicles, warm and shriveled, but not his penis. Annoyed, he lit a candle. His sleepy eyes and hand were now in search of the elusive penis, but they couldn't find it. Trotsky became fully awake, almost alert. He pulled his trousers down to his knees, and with wide eyes and both hands he examined his pubic area thoroughly, splitting small sections of his pubic hair. His penis simply wasn't there. In fact, there was no indication of any penis ever having been between his legs. In his state of confusion he even looked for it in sections of his body where ordinarily it wouldn't be, like his navel, his armpits, and behind his ears. Trotsky opened his eyes wide and covered his mouth with both hands the way his mother did when someone mentioned guerrillas and paramilitary soldiers. He still felt the need to urinate, but how? Perhaps his penis had retreated beneath his skin like his testicles did sometimes, leaving the scrotum empty and wrinkled. He pulled up his pants and walked to the outhouse.

There he stood in front of the latrine, not knowing what to do, until at length he squatted on his heels, hoping that his penis would pop up from under his pelvis. But his urine found a different way out of his body. It came out in a steady flow through his rectum, just as warm and yellow as always. Trotsky cried all the way back to his bedroom. He sat on the edge of his bed waiting to wake up from his nightmare. He even pinched his arm to make sure he was awake. Then he saw it: his penis! Trotsky saw his penis lying on the floor, next to a pair of beat-up black shoes he'd inherited from his late father. Perplexed, he bent over to get a better look at it: a flaccid outgrowth the size of a silkworm with a dark mole in the center. Somehow it had detached itself from his crotch while he was sleeping, and traveled from the bed to the floor.

Contemplating his apathetic penis in his mind's eye, Trotsky discovered he was afraid of it. If it had been able to remove itself, it might be capable of much more. It might crawl and twist like a worm; it might fly sightless, like a bat; it might even attack the boy, its master. After some time, and after convincing himself that his penis wasn't qualified to perform such difficult tasks, Trotsky overcame his fears and picked it up from the floor. He held it tenderly in the palm of his hand, observing it from every possible angle. It didn't appear to have been cut off; its base was perfectly sealed, and the top looked exactly as it had when Trotsky saw it last, its head covered with extra skin contracted into folds. Holding his loose penis in his palm made the boy feel deeply sad.

He wept and wept until his mother entered his room.

THEY SAY THAT the four boys met at the doorstep of Nurse Ramírez' house sometime before eight. They'd rushed, separately and without telling anyone, to the infirmary, which was, in fact, the nurse's living room, soberly decorated with her late husband's medical school certificates and a large, cobwebby picture of the human skeletal frame, and which had a separate entrance also on the street. The nurse answered the infirmary's door in her late husband's pajamas. She was rather buxom and had a mass of shining black curls that clustered about her rotund face.

"Shouldn't you all be heading to the plaza?" she asked in a squeaky voice, visibly bothered by the boys' early presence. They hid their faces without replying. "You're just terrified of all those silly girls and their stupid competition, aren't you? Go on! You'll get over it." The boys whined and didn't move. Nurse Ramírez rolled her eyes at them and said, "All right, all right, damn it! Has anyone been shot?" They shook their heads. "Good, because I can't stand the sight of blood. Come inside and wait until I get dressed."

Mariquita's nurse was squeamish about blood, vomit, diarrhea, pus, rashes and other people's genitalia—her own she found quite desirable. Needless to say, she wasn't a good nurse. In fact, she was not a nurse at all. She was the widow of Dr. Ramírez, Mariquita's only physician for over thirty years, and she'd half learned, from him, only the very basics of medicine—how to take a patient's pulse and blood pressure, how to read a thermometer and use the stethoscope, and how to give injections. She refused to learn how to give mouth-to-mouth resuscitation. Eight years before, after the guerrilla attack in which Mariquita's men disappeared, the widow of Dr. Ramírez had been of no help. That day she tried to assist her neighbors and friends in treating their wounds, but she became nauseated after seeing so much blood and went home to grieve over her own losses. A few weeks later a serious epidemic of influenza arrived, killing seven children and three old women in the first week. That time, however, she treated several patients and succeeded in stopping the epidemic from spreading. The Pérez widow even claimed that "Nurse" Ramírez had saved her life. Since, every time someone was injured or fell ill, "Nurse" Ramírez was called in.

While waiting for the fastidious nurse to come back, the boys pretended they weren't in the infirmary waiting for the fastidious nurse to come back. Che bragged about his powerful, far-reaching ejaculation, "Be ready, guys, because I've been practicing for our next contest. I'm shooting farther each time." The comment echoed in Trotsky's ears. He tried to remain calm, though he couldn't help biting his nails. "That was a dumb competition," he grumbled. "I'll never do it again." Meanwhile Hochiminh, in one of his late father's shirts—which looked rather large on him—and with a huge book clutched firmly against his breasts, occupied himself by memorizing the names of bones from the skeleton's picture: "Ster-num, il-i-um, sac-rum . . ." Vietnam, for his part, refused to talk. He wrote on a piece of paper, "I caught a severe throat infection and lost my voice," and held the note up for his friends to see it.

NURSE RAMÍREZ COULDN'T bring herself to examine the boys. She called them into her office one at a time and listened to their symptoms. What she heard was so terrifying that she immediately locked them in the waiting room. In her mind there was no doubt that she was faced with some mysterious, ghastly epidemic. She grew apprehensive, her hands began shaking involuntarily, and she felt a compulsive desire to wash herself. She took off her clothes, put them in a bag and sealed it, then gave herself a sponge bath, scrubbing her entire body several times. She got dressed again, feeling a little calmer, and took out of a drawer an old medical reference book, a relic that had been handed down from generation to generation in her husband's family. She wanted to look up the disease, but where to start? It occurred to her that someone else should get involved.

WHEN THE MAGISTRATE arrived and learned the bad news, she wanted to see the boys, but the nurse wouldn't let her. Rosalba insisted.

"But you didn't examine them. How do you know they're not lying?"

"Lying? Would you lie about something like that, Magistrate? If you had only seen their faces. They looked terrified. Hochiminh was covering his breasts with a large book, poor thing. And Vietnam couldn't even talk. How disgraceful!"

"Ramírez, I must see the boys," Rosalba requested firmly.

"Magistrate, you go inside that room, and you'll have to stay in it with those infected boys for forty days," Nurse Ramírez returned, in a harsh tone that to the magistrate's autocratically trained ears invited confrontation. But the circumstances were so dire that even Rosalba recognized that they called for serenity and compliance. She gave the nurse her word that she wouldn't see the boys but demanded the key to the room where they were kept. That way she could feel as though she were in control of the situation. She hid it in her bosom, then went to get the police sergeant, Ubaldina viuda de Restrepo.

The sergeant wasn't given specific details about the boys' medical condition—discretion wasn't among her attributes. She was sent to look for the other three men of Mariquita (Julio Morales, Santiago Marín and el padre Rafael), and to bring them to the infirmary for a full medical examination.

THE SERGEANT FOUND Julio Morales—Julia, as he was better

known—among the crowd of women waiting for the contest to begin. He was, as usual, dressed as a girl, her black hair arrayed with colorful flowers. "The magistrate wants to see you immediately," the sergeant whispered in the girl's ear. Julia gestured to her to go ahead; she'd follow her. Which she did with her back perfectly straight, her hips swinging side to side rhythmically, and each of her bare feet landing exactly in front of the other with every step—a bewitching gait that put the ungainly sergeant, with her linen pants, plaid shirt and worn leather boots, to shame.

Santiago Marín, the Other Widow, was found in his backyard, working on his small but flourishing garden, where he grew the best tomatoes in town. Ever since the night he sent his lover Pablo on his last, nonreturn trip, Santiago had grown introspective and quiet. He hadn't turned mute like Julia; he just didn't talk unless he had something meaningful to say. Today, after listening to the sergeant, Santiago put on a clean shirt, let his long hair down and left for the infirmary, escorted by Ubaldina.

El padre Rafael was the last man brought to the infirmary. The sergeant had found the priest eating breakfast at Cafetería d'Villegas, and after she informed him about "something terrible" scourging Mariquita, he begged for a few minutes with the Lord. Ubaldina walked him to the back entrance of the church. They didn't want to be seen by the crowd gathered in the plaza—the women, by now, were getting impatient with both the boys' tardiness and the fiery sun's promptness. The sergeant waited outside the church, whistling old songs and stroking the butt of the old revolver she carried in her waistband. Four songs later el padre came out, and together they walked toward the infirmary.

THE BOYS' MOTHERS were also sent for. They needed to be notified about the boys' medical condition and the ordained quarantine. The four widows demanded to see their children, threatening to kick down the door of the room in which they were kept if the magistrate didn't let them in. While Nurse Ramírez and the sergeant occupied themselves with the potential multiple detentions, Rosalba decided it was time to confront the crowd of women at the plaza. They'd become so rowdy and unrestrained that their uproar could be heard from every corner of Mariquita. It was hardly ten in the morning, and the sun was already flaming. Rosalba went along dreary streets carpeted with thousands of leaves the wind had snatched from the mango trees earlier that morning. There was not a soul in sight. The contest had paralyzed the village's activities, which on a regular Sunday morning weren't many anyway: a few street vendors and a handful of God-fearing widows who attended the early services. Rosalba wondered how the women gathered at the plaza would react to the news. They'd grown resilient after enduring so many adversities over the years, but this really was the end of their hopes. If Nurse Ramírez was right about the boys' disease, the women would never be with a man again. Or bear boys. Or girls. Or anything else. After today, they'd have to decide whether they wanted to rot in this wretched village waiting for male relatives or suitors that might never come back, or boldly cross those intimidating mountains clustered around them and find not a village, but a large city where guerrillas couldn't kidnap every man at once, where there were enough healthy men to impregnate them, and electricity and running water and cars and telephones. Maybe even one of those electric machines that made cold air and blew it on you. Rosalba would give anything to sit next to one of those right now.

But what would these poor peasants do in a large city with no land for sowing? They'd end up working as domestics or prostitutes, the only professions for which countrywomen seemed to be qualified when they moved to the city. What would those provincial women do among so many sophisticated ladies and cultured gentlemen? People would laugh at them, at their ragged clothes and bare feet. They'd make fun of their plump, corn-fed bodies, their coarseness, their legs covered in mosquito bites. And if the plain women were to say that they'd come all the way from Mariquita, the sophisticated ladies would ask, "Mari what?" and roar with laughter.

No. These poor, simple women would never leave Mariquita. They'd stay right here, immersed in this routine where even the musty air they breathed smelled the same day after day after day; where everyone knew their names and their weaknesses; where no one was rich or sophisticated—merely less poor, less unrefined—and it didn't matter anyway because in the end they were all marked for doom. Yes. They'd stay here, in purgatory. Because that's what Mariquita really was. Purgatory. Only no one had realized it yet. No one but the magistrate.

"I have dire news," Rosalba said to the crowd, looking unusually composed. "The boys," she added, watching the women's puzzled expressions, which in a second or two would turn into suffering. She proceeded to explain in great detail what had occurred to each boy, or rather what the nurse had told her. She told the women about breasts that mysteriously appeared and penises that shrank or left without so much as a warning. For an instant she considered taking advantage of the improvised gathering to ask the women to sweep the streets and alleyways. The many leaves made it unsafe for people to walk. But when her announcement was greeted by hysterical shrieks, Rosalba realized asking the women to sweep leaves might not be the most sensible thing to do.

Brokenhearted, Magnolia propped herself against a robust tree and wept. Not far from her, Luisa buried her face in Sandra's bosom. Elvira and Cuba nursed their mutual sorrows on each other's shoulders. Other women hid their faces behind their hands and wept through their fingers. What now? The four boys had been the only hope for all of them. From now on they wouldn't have any expectations. They'd sit and watch days run into weeks into months into years. . . . And then one day, after a lifetime of loneliness, they would die; bitter old maids who never knew what it felt like to have a man other than the priest panting around their necks, his bristly face brushing against their breasts or between their legs.

"What has befallen me?" Magnolia Morales cried, kicking and hitting the blameless tree with her fists. "What a disgrace! What a terrible misery! I'll never be happy." But with her sobs came a certain relief: for the very first time in her life Magnolia confronted her biggest preoccupation. She tenderly stroked the scabrous surface of the tree as though it were her man bidding her a sad farewell. And she cried some more.

At that moment Nurse Ramírez arrived from the infirmary. Her face was shiny and sweaty and her eyes sunken. She was followed by el padre Rafael, Julia and Santiago. Santiago carried a large book between his hands. The nurse stood on the platform next to the magistrate and announced that she had examined the three men. But in reality, since they hadn't complained of any symptoms, she'd merely asked them to undress and, from a certain distance, verified that everything was what it should be and where it should be. "None of them is missing anything. They're complete and intact," she announced to the crowd, under the obvious impression that she was the bearer of good tidings. But her tidings didn't bring any relief to the women's grieving. They'd never thought of Julio and Santiago as men—neither had Julio and Santiago—and as for el padre Rafael, that was all in the past; a nasty, shameful past of which no woman wanted to be reminded.

But the nurse wasn't finished. She reported that she had found something. A lead, she said, in an old medical reference book that was like a Bible to her. "I presume that our boys are suffering from a condition known as . . ." She signaled to Santiago to come closer with the book. "Let's see," she said, opening it on a page marked with a corn husk, pulling her face away from it to better see the small print. "Here it is: Babaloosi-Babaloosi. A mysterious condition seen once in the late 1800s in a remote region of southern Africa. Babaloosi-Babaloosi is believed to have gradually turned infants of the Zukashasu tribe into exceptional creatures that were neither men nor women. The creatures, known as Babas, eventually became the tribe chief's advisers due to their impartiality in all matters."

"Please stop," el padre Rafael called. "This whole thing is absurd. Are you all blind? Can't you see that this is a punishment from God?"

He walked up to the magistrate, looking as though he was experiencing muscular dystrophy on his face. "You must do something about all this nonsense," he hissed.

"Ramírez, please continue," Rosalba said to the nurse. Furious, the priest stepped aside. He crossed his arms and shook his head repeatedly. The nurse went on.

"Babaloosi-Babaloosi was confirmed by the English doctor Harry Walsh, who began studying it during the last decade of the nineteenth century. Unfortunately, Dr. Walsh died of malaria in 1903, leaving inconclusive theories about the selective disease. The Zukashasu believed it to be a miracle, but medical records classified it simply as a mysterious condition of unknown origins." The nurse stopped and asked if anyone had questions.

"Where's Africa?" Francisca said, raising her hand in the air.

The nurse shrugged her shoulders and scanned the crowd, looking for Cleotilde. The schoolmistress always had an answer for every question.

"Africa is located south of Europe, between the Atlantic and the Indian Oceans," the old woman answered from the back. Francisca was just about to ask where Europe was when the priest spoke.

"Does your book say what happened to this wondrous tribe?" His words were filled with contempt.

The nurse took notice of el padre's question but overlooked his sarcastic tone. She faced the book again and read, "The Zukashasu tribe was exterminated by their neighbors, the Shumitah tribe, in an ethnic war that killed thousands of native Africans in 1913. Nevertheless, they are remembered as one of the most successful forms of society ever seen in that continent." She paused to look up and then said, in the ingenuous voice of a young girl, "Imagine that: an impartial human being, someone who won't take sides because they are neither male nor female. I think the world needs people like that." She closed the book, convinced she'd ended her speech with a profound sentence.

An absolute silence spread throughout the plaza as the women began speculating. First, they tried to picture what an impartial human being would look like; and then they tried to conceive of a society with no prejudices, ruled with fairness and honesty. But nothing materialized. They had never seen either.

"No one's as impartial as God. He doesn't judge us," the priest interrupted their thoughts, in the same tedious and sermonizing tone he used daily in church.

"But your God doesn't live in this town, Padre," Nurse Ramírez returned, feeling under attack. "He gave up on us, and you're very stubborn to still believe in Him."

"You'll burn in hell, you blasphemous woman!" the priest shouted. He turned to face the crowd and said, "Turn a deaf ear to foolish fairy tales. The Bible says—"

"The Bible says nothing we can understand or relate to," the nurse interposed suddenly, her cheeks flaming with rage. "How many times has manna rained from heaven when we've been hungry? How many of our dead relatives have been brought back to life? Your fairy tales are no more believable than mine, Padre." Both the nurse and the priest turned to the magistrate, as though seeking support, and the crowd, which had detected the delicious prospect of a serious confrontation, also looked at the magistrate (nothing made their problems smaller than witnessing the difficulties of others).

But Rosalba didn't respond immediately. She seemed to be considering both el padre's and the nurse's arguments. Whatever she said next, she knew, could calm them down or infuriate them even more. "I say we should write our own Bible," she finally proposed with a giggle. "A Bible that speaks to us, that tells about towns devastated by guerrillas and paramilitaries. About doomed villages of widows and spinsters and penises that disappear overnight."

Except for el padre Rafael—who rolled his eyes—and a handful of pious widows, the crowd found the idea amusing. The women nodded and murmured to one another, and some even laughed quietly. And so Rosalba, encouraged by the somewhat positive response to her witty remark, went on, "We perform our own miracles, after all. Don't we feed great crowds with very little food? Don't we walk on water every October and November, when we have those hideous floods?" She chuckled.

"The only miracle we haven't mastered yet is how to cast out demons," Nurse Ramírez interrupted, giving the priest a vicious look. The crowd had a good laugh at this last comment.

"I want a Bible that doesn't disgrace women who love women," demanded Francisca from the crowd.

"Or men who love men," the Other Widow echoed from the platform.

And as more people began to enthusiastically shout their ideas for Mariquita's Bible, the priest began gabbling away in Latin: "*Sanctus Dominus Deus Sabaoth . . .*" He slowly fell on his knees. "*Miserere nobis. Dona nobis pacem.*" Stretched his arms to their full length. "*Pater noster, qui es in coelis . . .*" He turned his face toward the sky, hoping for a violent thunderstorm to break at that moment, but the sky had never before looked so clear.

LATER THAT DAY, kneeling alone on the bare floor of the chapel, el padre pleaded, "Why, Beloved Father? Why are You letting them abuse Your name? They're only swearing against You so as not to face the truth in a dignified way. And why don't You allow Your humble congregation to be fruitful and multiply? All we want is to follow Your mandate, oh Lord, to replenish the earth with Catholics and have dominion over every living thing upon it. Why have you sent this plague to scourge us?"

He went on and on with his litany.

Then something unusual happened: while contemplating a painting of Moses with the two stone tablets of God's law, which hung askew on the wall, el padre was imagining how onerous it must have been for poor Moses to be entrusted with such a burden, when a radiant sunbeam filtered through the window, blinding him, and at the same time, miraculously, laying the truth before his eyes. He remembered that in the Old Testament, God rescued His chosen people from slavery with twelve dramatic plagues, and then parted the waters of the Red Sea so that they could escape from the land of Egypt. Why, of course! That's what God had intended when he sent that first plague, the guerrillas, to Mariquita in 1992. The rebels forcibly recruited and kidnapped most of the men, sinful creatures who skipped mass and went wenching to that house of sin, Doña Emilia's. Why, of course! The boys' sudden disease was the Lord's way of punishing the women for their horrible sins; for lying with each other and not believing in God. Everything made sense now: his own mysterious barrenness, Che's shrinking penis, Hochiminh's breasts, Vietnam's menstruation, Trotsky's self-ruling genitals—they were all plagues. The Plagues of Mariquita.

"The light!" he murmured, his eyesight already cleared. "I've seen the light!" God may not have made Himself manifest in the middle of a flame, or talked to him directly from on high (that was a privilege of real saints that he could not expect), but the Lord had disclosed His will to el padre nonetheless. He'd done it through a modest sunbeam and el padre's prodigious mind and perception. "I've been chosen by God to be the Moses of Mariquita!" he concluded ecstatically. "Praise be to God!"

Overwhelmed with his new knowledge, but unsure as to what his mission in Mariquita might be, el padre decided to look for guidance in God's Book itself. He sat on a pew with the massive Bible resting on his lap, and eagerly began reading the second book of Moses called Exodus. Meanwhile, the crowd in the plaza outside got louder. Their impertinent noise crept against the walls of the chapel and rumbled like a draft through the cracks and crevices of it. El padre rose and looked into the plaza through the metal grating. Dozens of women sat by the platform under the mango trees, jabbering about new Bibles, Babaloosi-Babaloosi, and Zukashasu. Before long, el padre thought, they'll be worshiping idols in human form, like those plagued boys. Or even worse, idols of animal likeness, like . . . like themselves!

He went back to the pew and continued reading Exodus with in-creased devotion until, in chapter 32, verses 26 and 27, he found the answer to his question. Filled with awe, el padre abruptly brought his hands to his mouth, closed his eyes and stayed like that for a few minutes. Then he rose, straightened his back and lifted his chin, and, addressing the window through which God's sunbeam had enlightened him, he softly said, "Thy will be done."

*   *   *

El padre Rafael wasn't a wicked man, just plain stupid. He'd gotten an idea into his head. Two ideas, in fact: he was a modern Moses, and he was on a divine mission to save the people of Mariquita. On that account, he overcame his pride and went to see the magistrate in her office.

"I want to pay a religious visit to the boys," he began with certain haughtiness. But after meeting the magistrate's stern gaze, he quickly reconsidered his approach and softened his tone. "The nurse said you have the key to the room where they're kept, and I think it's very important that they receive the Holy Eucharist. They need to be at peace with God, Magistrate."

"You can't go in there, Padre," she replied lethargically.

"And why is that? Is it because you dread my presence will . . . interrupt the boys' *mutation* into—"

"Spare me your sarcasm, Padre," Rosalba interrupted. "I don't believe in any of that Babaloosi business any more than you do." She rose and walked slowly up to the window. There she stood, with her arms folded on her chest, looking at nothing in particular.

"Why, I'm relieved to hear that!" he returned. The magistrate's confession had lifted his spirits. "A brilliant community leader like yourself can't give credence to mundane explanations of divine mandates."

"I've also stopped believing in your God, Padre," Rosalba replied instantly and with absolute conviction, as if saying the first line of the Creed.

El padre Rafael walked about the room silently. He made different faces and quick gestures with his hands and head, all of which suggested that he was having an earnest conversation with himself. The magistrate's revelation hadn't taken him by surprise. In the past few years he'd noticed a significant decrease in the women's faith. The great majority of them still attended mass once a week, but el padre knew that at least half of them did it for a different reason. In a small community of thirty-seven widows, forty-four old maids, ten teenagers, five children, Julia Morales, Santiago Marín and the priest himself, going to mass was a social duty. Women must be seen in church or else openly declare themselves nonbelievers—as Francisca had done after she found a fortune under her bed—and bear the consequences of being excommunicated. The fact that Mariquita's highest authority had candidly admitted to not believing in God meant that soon it'd be socially acceptable for anyone not to attend the religious services, and consequently el padre Rafael would no longer be needed. He, however, would not be discouraged by that (hadn't Moses had to endure a similar situation?). El padre Rafael had been assigned a divine mission by the Lord Himself, and he would carry it to its logical conclusion.

"Magistrate," he said ceremoniously. "You said you don't believe in the nurse's tale, but you also don't believe in . . . *my* God. Then, may I ask, how do you explain the boys' strange condition? Because you know their condition is real."

"No, Padre. I don't know if it's real. I haven't seen them. No one has. They merely mentioned their symptoms to Ramírez, and she immediately locked them up, without examining them. You know how squeamish and fastidious she can be."

"I sure do. But if the boys went to see her in the first place, it was because . . ." He narrowed his eyes and, lowering his voice, said, "You're not suggesting that they made it all up?"

Rosalba shrugged. "I only say they've been known for their shrewdness."

"Well, there's only one way to dispel your doubts, Magistrate," el padre said confidently.

Rosalba considered the priest's proposition for a short while, then turned aside, reached into her bosom and took out the key to the padlock that kept the four boys captives. "I want it back in an hour," she said, handing it to him.

EL PADRE WENT back to his dwelling, located in the back of the church. It was a small, stuffy chamber with bare walls and a single window that had been jammed for years. Not a single image or crucifix hung there. On top of his chest of drawers were a basket full of tiny arepas and a jug half-filled with chicha. The corn tidbits and the fermented corn beverage were donated and delivered to him every Sunday morning by the Morales widow. She also tidied up his room.

He pulled, from under his bed, a wooden trunk filled with all sorts of junk: plastic washbowls, rusty tubes and iron fittings, empty bottles of different sizes, a hairpiece he'd used when he started losing his hair, a wig he'd worn when he lost it all, a table lamp and even lightbulbs from when Mariquita had electricity. He rummaged about in the trunk, clearly searching for something. He emptied the whole trunk before happening upon the object he was looking for: a medium-sized bottle with the screw top tightly wrapped in adhesive tape. He held the bottle up to the light coming in through the window. It was filled with some liquid. "Hallelujah!" he said, kissing it. Then he put it in the pocket of his soutane.

Disregarding the mess he'd created on the floor, el padre went to the chest of drawers. He clutched the jug against his body as best he could, grabbed the basket of arepas and hurried out to the street, toward the infirmary.

CHE, HOCHIMINH, VIETNAM and Trotsky were overjoyed when they saw the priest. They were true Catholics; they knew that when everything else failed, they could always count on God—or at least on one of His emissaries. El padre promptly padlocked the door from the inside and began scrutinizing the boys, one by one, for some sign of the dramatic plague the Lord had sent on them. Aside from their reddened eyes and frantic expressions, they looked perfectly normal. But el padre knew better than to trust his own eyes: the devil worked in deceptive ways. He laid the inoffensive basket and the inoffensive jug on an old desk and stood behind it, facing the boys. He made them sit and began speaking about God and His will. He spoke in the language of the Bible, a language too sophisticated for them to understand. Something about darkness and kingdoms, madness and plagues, destruction and chaos. And maybe angels. Then he talked about the Holy Eucharist. Again incomprehensible. So much that Hochiminh wondered if el padre were speaking in tongues. When he was finished, he made each boy go to a corner and say three Hail Marys and a Creed. "For penance," he said, though he hadn't heard their confessions. Meanwhile he took the bottle out of his pocket and opened it. With great caution he emptied its contents into the jug of chicha and watched it dissolve quickly. He replaced the top tightly on the bottle and put it back in his pocket.

Once absolved from all their sins, the boys were asked to line up in a row facing the improvised altar. They arranged themselves according to height. Vietnam, the shortest, on the far left, then Trotsky, Che and finally Hochiminh. They bowed their heads, and each one clasped his hands before his chest. The priest thought they looked like angels—except they didn't have wings or blond hair. To be real angels, they had to have blond hair.

El padre raised his hands in the air and began a conversation with the Almighty. "We come to You, Father," he said, "with praise and thanksgiving, through Jesus Christ Your Son." He made the sign of the cross over both the basket and the jug. Then he added, "Through Him we ask You to accept and bless these gifts we offer You in sacrifice." He joined his hands, closed his eyes and remained silent for a moment.

When Hochiminh noticed that the priest was getting ready to break the bread, he, who had been an altar boy—a mediocre one, but an altar boy nonetheless—instinctively began singing, "Lamb of God, you take away the sins of the world: have mercy upon us . . ."

El padre took an arepa out of the basket, and since he didn't have a paten in which to place it, broke it over the desk. He carefully let a little piece of it fall in the jug and mouthed a few more of his incomprehensible words. He took the arepa, raised it up before his face and asked the boys to come closer, and closer still, until the obedient creatures were up against the edge of the desk, hit in the face by el padre's sour breath. He took a tiny arepa out of the basket and showed it to them. "The body of Christ," he said.

"Amen," they replied in unison. One by one the four boys received communion.

Then, the priest grabbed the jug with both hands and gave it to Vietnam, saying, "The blood of Christ."

"Amen," the boys answered again. Each boy lifted the jug to his lips, swallowed a generous gulp of chicha—sweet, aromatic, slightly peppery—and retired to a corner where he knelt down.

"Let us pray," said el padre. He extended his hands and closed his eyes tightly. But instead of praying, he anxiously waited for the church-like silence of the room to be broken by the first warning sound.

Vietnam's breathing became very rapid, then slow and irregular. He began coughing in spurts.

The priest chanted, "May the blessing of Almighty God . . ."

Trotsky felt numbness in the throat. His heart pounded disorderly against his constricted chest. Bewildered and fearful, he ripped off his shirt, muttering angrily.

" . . . the Father . . ."

Che wanted to scream for help—his insides were burning—but his jaw was stiff, and the words drowned in his throat.

" . . . and the Son . . ."

Hochiminh shrieked with pain. He vomited violently, his face beaded with sweat.

" . . . and the Holy Spirit . . ."

The four boys managed to straighten up and take a few steps toward one another. They didn't want to die on their knees.

" . . . come upon you . . ."

One by one they collapsed on the floor, where they convulsed in pools of vomit before falling unconscious.

"Go in the peace of Christ!" el padre commanded, his voice a strident scream. Then silence. A silence so funereal that a chill ran up his own spine. He opened his eyes: the room was dark, empty of life. He hastened to kiss the surface of the desk and made the customary reverence. Then he went to the door. As he put the key in the padlock, he turned and glanced over his shoulder at the macabre scene: Four boys with protruding eyeballs and purplish, sweat-drenched skin. Four boys with their mouths covered in foam and blood. Four still boys.

El padre heaved a long sigh.

The key turned easily in the lock.

The room became icy cold.

And in the misty air, a strong smell of shit and bitter almonds.

Camilo Santos, 41
Roman Catholic priest

The military "unit" sent to respond to the massacre consisted of
a second lieutenant, six armed soldiers, a susceptible young doctor and myself. Soon I saw why: the village was nothing but a few
crumbling houses covered with flaking white paint, and a patch of
dirt with no trees or statues they called a plaza. The smell of death
oozed from every corner.

"You came too late," an old woman with no teeth mumbled as
soon as we got out of the truck. She was kneeling behind a bloody
heap of human parts she'd collected, trying to fit them together as
though they were the pieces of a jigsaw puzzle. Scattered across the
dirt road were several mutilated bodies and parts. The young doctor laid his first aid kit and bag of instruments on the ground and
leaned against a tree to throw up. The soldiers, a little more used
to the horror of the war, walked around asking useless questions of
the surviving witnesses, as if finding out which group had perpe-
trated the butchering was our priority.

"Where are the injured?" I asked the same woman.

"You're looking at them," she replied, a hand pointing toward
herself, the other toward a group of women—widows, mothers and
sisters—who walked around turning torsos over onto their backs,
picking up their men's pieces, sobbing. "Everyone else is dead," she
added.

Suddenly, a little girl sprang up from within the small crowd.
"The head, Grandma. I found Papa's head!" she announced, almost
enthusiastically. She walked up to the toothless woman and handed
her the bloody head of a man. The woman took the head with both

hands, calmly, and looked at it on all sides before setting it, face up, on her lap. "We're still missing the hands," she said to the girl. "We can't bury him without them. He had such beautiful hands . . ." The girl scratched her head. She looked around, then at me, as though asking me for advice on what to do next. I, too, looked around. I, too, didn't know what to do next.

The old woman took out a handkerchief and gently began to wipe the blood from the pale face lying on her lap. Then she looked up and, staring at the Bible in my hand, said, "Padre, we need you to pray for our men's eternal rest. Please start saying your prayers now."

I looked at the helpless woman, at the ill doctor and at the indifferent soldiers, and suddenly realized what I had to do next. I went back to our truck and traded my Bible for a shovel.

Sometimes even God has to come second.

CHAPTER 9

The Day Time Stopped

Mariquita, June 23, 2000

B EFORE SUNRISE, A GROUP of ten widows secretly gathered in the
school to discuss how to kill the priest. Some brought knives and
heavy clubs from their homes. Others picked up large stones from the
ground. They couldn't agree on a specific method, so they decided that
each woman would contribute to the man's murder in her own way.
They split into two groups of five. The first one, led by the Sánchez
widow (Trotsky's mother), went to the main entrance of the church.
The other, with the Calderón widow (Vietnam's mother) at the head,
strode purposefully toward the back of the building.

Armed with a stone, the Calderón widow pounded at the back door,
which led to the priest's chamber. "Come out, you child murderer!"
she shouted. "Come out now, scoundrel, or we're coming in!" The
other four women did the same, calling the priest all sorts of names.
The group in the front also ordered that el padre come out, threatening to set the church on fire if he didn't.

Terrified, el padre Rafael rang the church bell strenuously, a desperate call for help from the sergeant, or the magistrate, or his most
devoted followers, or, perhaps, from God. Only the first two took notice
of his clamor. Magistrate Rosalba and Police Sergeant Ubaldina went

to the women, pleading with them not to get carried away by their anger.

"We must avenge our sons' deaths," the Sánchez widow shouted.

"We won't let that bastard get away with killing our boys," the López widow echoed.

Rosalba asked the enraged women to consider that an eye for an eye was simply wrong, and that having to bury their four boys the day before had already been a terrible tragedy for Mariquita. She so pressed them that they agreed not to murder el padre on the condition that he leave Mariquita immediately.

The magistrate and the priest had a short conversation through the small metal grating of the main door.

"You must go right away," Rosalba said.

"That's not fair, Magistrate," he replied in a shaky voice. "I've dedicated—"

"You have no moral right to talk about fairness or anything else," Rosalba interposed. "I'll give you half an hour to vacate, or else I'll let the women come inside and get you." She joined the growing crowd outside the church and silently watched the little man bring out a rolled-up mattress, a rocking chair, his enormous Bible, a small crate of chickens, sacks, boxes, bundles and bags, and load them on his old mule—a gift from the Restrepo family on el padre's twentieth anniversary of service to Mariquita in 1991. By the time he finished, the mule could barely stand.

Afraid the women might repent of their weakness and lynch him, el padre hesitated before approaching them. They had gathered on both sides of the main street, hardly leaving any room for him and his mule to pass. He took a deep breath, armed himself with courage and, leading the mule, moved gingerly through the crowd, his head lowered just enough to protect his eyes from the light rain that had begun to fall. As he passed, the women's rage became more fierce. The Calderón widow spat in his face, then broke into tears. The Ospina widow tried to leap on him, but two women grabbed her by the arms. "Murderer!

Murderer!" she shouted, her voice choked by sobs. The rest of the women made a remarkable effort not to stab him, or hit him with their clubs, or strangle him with their bare hands. Instead they prayed loudly that he'd die a slow, painful death with no one to look after him.

The priest didn't dare say adios. Not even to the magistrate, who had supported his church all these years and tolerated his constant meddling in her affairs. His round-shouldered, bandy-legged form grew smaller, and smaller still, until it finally disappeared in the mist that settled over the road leading to the south. When he was gone, the villagers sighed with relief. They turned around and began to walk slowly toward the church. Toward nothing.

They soon discovered that el padre Rafael had taken everything his beast could carry, and then some. In addition to his belongings he'd also stolen chandeliers, images, paintings, crucifixes, candles, the chalice, the basketwork folding screen that had served as confessional for many years, the ragged tuxedo and shabby wedding gown worn virtually by every couple married in Mariquita since 1970, and, in retaliation for the hostility the entire village had shown toward him—the emissary of the Lord God Almighty—the birth certificates of every person born in town. He left nothing but the wormwood-riddled pews, and a profound distaste for Catholicism in the mouths of nearly every woman in Mariquita.

AFTER EL PADRE left, the few remaining believers kept going to church just like always. They walked around the old building, looking at the holes in the bare walls where rusty nails had held images of their beloved saints, kneeling before shadows left by oversized crosses, whispering Hail Marys and humming hymns.

Cleotilde Guarnizo, the schoolmistress, had taken it upon herself to toll the church bell at six every morning, then again at noon and one more time at six in the evening. One morning, after a few weeks, she encountered an obstacle: the church clock had stopped at one minute after twelve the night before. The teacher, who'd never owned a watch, couldn't tell the exact time. She searched in vain for the large silver key to wind the clock, but all she found was its empty case. El padre, she realized, also had taken the key. "Damned padre," she muttered.

Upon hearing the bad news, the magistrate commissioned Police Sergeant Ubaldina to go from door to door looking for a working time-piece or a transistor radio. Ubaldina found every pendulum of every clock floating in mid-swing, broken; every hour, minute and second hand of every watch standing still; and every transistor radio collecting dust on shelftops and corner tables, their batteries long dead. A few widows had cannibalized their radios for parts. The Morales widow, for instance, had used the knobs as buttons for a dress, and turned the metal pieces and wire twists into bracelets that her daughters traded for eggs at the market. The Villegas widow had planted a beautiful violet in the carcass of her radio, then placed it on the windowsill of the modest cafeteria she owned, where it bloomed four times a year next to an old picture of Pope John XXIII.

In the same way Eloísa, the bar owner's widow, had replaced the insides of her wristwatch with a faded picture of her slain husband's face. Every time someone asked her what time it was, she would look at the picture inside the watch, heave a long sigh and finally utter in a melodramatic tone, "It's too early to love him and too late to forget him." The other women thought the widow's answer hilarious. They often stopped her on the street just to hear her say it. But Eloísa, a born capitalist, turned her invention into a business opportunity, transforming nonworking wristwatches into photo frames in exchange for all kinds of food.

Right before nightfall, the sergeant went to the magistrate's office to tell her what she'd found, or rather what she hadn't.

"With all due respect, Magistrate," Ubaldina said, "I suggest that you send someone to the city immediately to buy a new watch or batteries for the old ones."

The magistrate stood gazing forlornly through the window at the motionless church clock. She imagined Mariquita frozen in time: a town of widows and spinsters who would never again hear the crying of a newborn baby. A miserable village condemned to endless poverty. Nothing but a few run-down shacks without running water or electricity, scattered below a big mountain on the verge of swallowing them up.

"Perhaps you're right," the magistrate said with a frown. "Perhaps I should send someone right now . . ." But then her reverie took a different turn: Mariquita, frozen in time, a town that would never again see men, ruthless guerrillas or crime. A town inhabited by courageous, self-sufficient women who worked the land from sunrise to sunset, and who would never give up, not even in the most terrible circumstances. A town ignored by diseases and tragedies, forgotten by death.

The magistrate had a contented smile on her face when she added, "Or perhaps I should just wait a few more suns."

A FEW SUNS later, the sergeant went to the magistrate's office again, this time to tell her that the roosters, all of them, had stopped crowing.

"They're confused," Ubaldina said categorically.

"Ridiculous," the magistrate retorted. "What kind of stupid roosters can't tell when the sun's rising?"

"Roosters don't have brains like you and I, Magistrate," Ubaldina said, glancing up into Rosalba's unfriendly face. "They were used to seeing activity during the day, and quiet at night. But now days and nights are no different."

Indeed, in Mariquita a day was no longer a day. Freed from the tyranny of the church clock, the women weren't all bartering at the market, or saying their prayers in church, or tending their gardens; they weren't even all awake. And when night fell, not every woman slept, or tossed and turned in bed, or secretly made love to another woman, or whispered prayers in the darkness. The difference between day and night was within each woman, and it changed from moment to moment. Mariquita had become unpredictable, like a hailstorm in the middle of June—except by now no one could remember when June was.

*   *   *

THE MORNING AFTER the roosters stopped crowing, the magistrate rushed out of her house to investigate the time situation. She wore her Sunday dress, which after so many Sundays was no longer milk white but pale yellow and frayed at the sleeves. So much had happened recently that she wasn't certain of how many days or nights had passed, and so dressing for a Sunday just felt right. She had chosen to remain faithful to the conventional system of reckoning day and night, because she felt it was her responsibility to record events at least by the color of the sky. A white dog scratching at its fleas in the middle of the main street seemed to confirm the magistrate's conviction that everything in Mariquita was just fine.

So what if those stupid roosters don't want to crow? she thought as she walked along the streets. If we've learned to live without men, we can learn to live without cocks. At that moment she caught sight of a naked woman running toward her. She had long, shiny black hair, which from a distance seemed to be floating, and her flaccid breasts moved up and down alternately, like a seesaw. Rosalba stopped instantly, as if she had seen a guerrilla standing in her way. But as the naked woman came closer, the magistrate recognized Magnolia Morales.

"What do you think you're doing," the magistrate snarled, "roaming the streets naked like a madwoman this early in the morning?"

"And how do you know it's early in the morning?" Magnolia replied, catching her breath.

"Well, the sun just came out."

"Time only exists in your mind, Magistrate." Magnolia's voice was so soft it was soothing. "Someone told us that when the sun rises, it is morning, and when the sun goes down, it is night. Someone said we should wake up at dawn and go to bed at nightfall, and that we need to eat breakfast, lunch and dinner at certain times. But, Magistrate, try telling a mango tree not to ripen its fruit until you're finished with the oranges. Try telling a rose not to shrivel until your eyes get tired of its beauty." Her voice began to rise gradually. "Tell a cow to yield more milk." And before long she was yelling, "No one will ever again tell me when to do anything! I am free of time, like a rose!" After she was through, she squatted on her heels and, without taking her eyes from the magistrate's disturbed face, emptied her bowels on the ground with a smile of pure satisfaction.

The magistrate wanted to say something. Say, perhaps, that mangoes and roses, like those stupid roosters, didn't have brains; but when she realized what the girl was doing, she decided Magnolia didn't have a brain either. Disgusted, she walked away, covering her nose with one hand and wiping the sweat off her forehead with the other.

ROSALBA TURNED RIGHT at the first corner she encountered and hurried down a desolate street. She hadn't walked half a block when she saw the old Pérez widow in her usual outfit: a black, long-sleeved, overly conservative dress with a lacy collar, at least two sizes too large. She was on her knees, cutting daisies from the Jaramillo widow's front yard

"Good morning, Señora Pérez," the magistrate said politely. "What day is it today?"

The old woman glanced at Rosalba over her shoulder, as if the magistrate were her shadow. Then she shrugged, saying, "When you're old as I am, you just live the same day every day."

"I understand," the magistrate said condescendingly, "but tell me, is it day or night?"

"Every moment is the right moment for praising Christ our Lord."

Rosalba rolled her eyes and took a deep breath. Then she tried again, "Is it time for breakfast or dinner?"

The widow shrugged once again, curving her lips. "See those birds over there?" She jerked her sharp chin at a couple of pigeons pecking at a piece of guava under a tree. "I'm just like them. I eat when I find something to eat." She stood, turned her back on the magistrate and plodded away, a tidy bunch of flowers in her left hand.

Rosalba didn't know what to say. She followed closely behind the old woman until something came to her mind.

"Where are you going with those flowers?"

"To church," the old woman answered without turning around. "I'm going to offer them to God." The magistrate tried to remember whether she had ever offered anything to God. In the past she had been a devout Catholic who had attended mass almost every day, said prayers almost every night, and observed almost every one of the Ten Commandments. But had she ever offered anything to God? No, in fact she had been angry on several occasions when she noticed moldy bits of corn bread or rotten guavas, mangoes, onions and tomatoes on top of improvised altars inside the church. "It's disgusting and un-sanitary," she'd told el padre, who promised to clean the altars more frequently to avoid vermin.

"Are you making a promise to God, Señora Pérez?"

"No." Señora Pérez sounded annoyed. "I just go to church every day and offer flowers to Him."

"Every day? And have you received anything in return?"

The widow stopped abruptly and turned around, her saintly face transformed by a sour expression. Then she said, "Unlike you, I don't crave wealth or power. My reward is larger: I'm securing a good place in heaven, and when I pass on I will have a preferential place next to the most virtuous souls." Saying this, the widow turned back again and walked away, warbling a song to God.

The magistrate leaned on a lamppost—or rather a post, because the lamp part had been stolen many years ago—and watched the old woman gradually drift away. How terribly sad, she said to herself. That poor woman has gone through life with a single purpose in her mind: to prepare for death!

THE SUN APPEARED to be playing hide-and-seek with the magistrate. Only twice, maybe three times, had the sun turned to show its face, but except for the magistrate, no one in Mariquita seemed to notice.

"Good night, Magistrate!" Francisca shouted as Rosalba passed. She was in her nightgown, brushing her long hair in front of the open window as if the street were a mirror. Rosalba didn't reply. Instead she cupped a hand to her forehead, shading her eyes, and looked at the sun. She held the pose for a little while, then continued walking.

"Good afternoon, Magistrate!" called Virgelina Saavedra. She and Lucrecia, her senile grandmother, were sitting on rickety chairs outside their house, the girl knitting a quilt, the old woman looking dead, taking a siesta. Rosalba gave them half a smile and went on.

"Good morning, Magistrate," said Santiago Marín, the Other Widow. He was sitting on his steps, shirtless and barefoot, his long hair loose around his shoulders. Rosalba was relieved to hear someone say, at last, the word *morning*.

"Good *morning* to you, Santiago!" she chirped. "Can you tell me about what time it is?"

"Huh, let's see." Santiago rose and reached under a dirty rag and pulled out a paper bag. Inside were tallow candles, which he counted, nodding his head. Then he glanced at the candle burning on the ground before announcing: "It's four and three-quarters candles."

Rosalba impatiently waited for Santiago to render that nonsense about candles into something intelligible, but he didn't seem to think this necessary. He took a candle from the paper bag and lit it using the dying flame of the candle on the ground. Then he placed the new candle on top of the old one and gave Rosalba a close-lipped smile.

"So? What time is it?" she asked again, a hint of exasperation in her voice.

Only then did Santiago realize that she wasn't familiar with his method of calculating time. He moved slowly toward her and began to explain, "You see, Magistrate, in the kind of time I keep, events are triggered by the duration of a lit candle." He held the paper bag up in the air. "I burn one candle at a time and usually go through ten candles every sun. I light the first candle when I wake up. Before it goes out, I'm already tending my vegetable garden. I often burn two more candles while working, another while I'm cooking lunch, and one more after lunch, while I rest. I go through two more candles at work before sunset, and then two more before going to bed."

"That only makes nine candles," the magistrate sharply remarked.

"The last candle is for the Virgin Mary."

"And what happens if the wind blows one of your candles out, and you don't see it?"

"Nothing happens. I simply light it again when I see it's out."

"And what if you oversleep? What if you wake up when the sun is already high over your head?"

"Then I get to use less candles," an annoyed Santiago answered derisively, then he flicked back his beautiful long hair and disappeared into his house.

Insulted, hands on her hips, Rosalba looked up and down the street. Once she was completely sure nobody was looking, she stooped, blew out Santiago's fifth candle and then walked away, with each step gently swinging her large bottom in the breeze.

THE CAFETERÍA D'VILLEGAS, the only eatery in town, was empty when the magistrate arrived. Its owner, the Villegas widow, was folded into an old wooden chair, staring at a fragile violet in a flowerpot that rested on the windowsill. The cafeteria existed, basically, for the five families of land workers who had no one to cook for them, and who paid for their meals with their produce.

"What's for lunch?" the magistrate asked.

"I haven't cooked anything yet," the widow said bitterly, without taking her eyes off the plant.

"But why? It's midday! Your customers should be here soon."

"Not anymore. They come whenever they please. One orders lunch, another orders breakfast and a third wants to know what's for dinner. Everything's backward in this damned town." She sounded very angry. "I'm very angry," she said.

"I'm starving," Rosalba announced. "I don't care what you cook for me." She walked to the counter, poured water from a vessel into a large blue plastic cup and brought it to a table next to the Villegas widow. There she sat facing an old picture of Pope John XXIII.

"If it weren't for the violet, I, too, would have lost track of time," the Villegas widow said. "Do you know that this particular violet blooms every ninety suns?"

"Do you at least have any rice cooked? People eat rice with every meal."

"I've watched the entire process three times already, and it never fails. It takes ten suns for the buds to be in full bloom, twenty more for their color to fade and after that, ten more suns for the flowers to die. Sometimes they're purplish, sometimes bluish, but they're always lovely."

"In Italy they don't eat much rice," Rosalba said, contemplating the fat pope. "They eat spaghetti day and night." She imagined the pope eating a full bowl of spaghetti for breakfast. "I don't know about you, but I like rice better."

"I like purplish better," the widow returned. She waited a few seconds before continuing, her voice much lower now, "According to my calculations, I'll have flowers for seventeen more suns, which means that in twenty-five suns my daughters can start plowing. And then . . ." She stopped and began silently counting on her fingers. "In thirty-three suns they can begin to sow!" she announced. "I'd better write this down." She reared up and vanished through a beaded curtain.

Rosalba was furious. How dare she ignore the magistrate's request for food. Her eyes went from the cup full of water on her table to the fragile violet, from the fragile violet to the pope, and from the pope back to the cup full of water, again and again, as though negotiating a bothersome decision with her conscience.

After a while, the Villegas widow emerged and was relieved to see the magistrate had left. Then she noticed the plastic cup lying on the windowsill, empty. She was devastated by grief when she realized that her flowerpot was flooded with watery mire, and her precious violet was swimming in it.

BACK IN HER house, the magistrate had just started making a pot of potato soup when she remembered that early that morning she'd used up the salt in her kitchen. She picked half a dozen mangosteens from her orchard, put them in a basket and went to the market to trade them for salt. The marketplace was depressing. A few small tomatoes and yuccas and some dry oranges lay on empty sacks spread on the ground. The magistrate walked about asking for Elvia, the López widow, also known as the salt woman. Elvia had learned, from her Indian ancestors, how to obtain salt from a saltwater spring located on a hillside near Mariquita. She boiled the springwater in a large copper pan for hours until it condensed. When the water had cooled, there'd be coarse salt at the bottom of the pan. It was bitter and grainy, but good enough to season and preserve food.

"The salt woman hasn't been here yet, Magistrate," a woman missing all her front teeth told her.

"Is she coming soon?"

"I don't know what time she's keeping," the woman replied, shrugging.

This sort of answer regarding each woman's time had become quite common, and to hear this over and over upset the magistrate.

She traded her mangosteens for a few tomatoes and walked away.

ALONG THE EMPTY streets of Mariquita the magistrate went with her head down and her shoulders hunched, feeling despondent: her village had turned into a Babel without a tower. How could she ever govern a community where time was a candle, a plant, or the movement of someone's bowels, for that matter? How was she ever going to carry out any of the grand things she'd conceived for her town of widows, when ninety-four people couldn't even agree on when morning was morning, when night was night? Perhaps if she closed her eyes and walked the other way, she would forget about all this. Maybe that was the only way to go through life. Yes, maybe Rosalba had solved the mystery of existence: every time you encounter an obstacle in your path, all you ought to do is shut your eyes and walk in the opposite direction. Maybe Rosalba's mother had been wrong all along when she said that there was no worse blindness than that of those who refused to see. Maybe Rosalba didn't need to see, to *really* see, the bad things that happened around her.

Or maybe she did.

Up and down the quiet streets the magistrate went, looking like an ant with her thin arms and legs and her large behind, feeling like a failure as she finally saw, *really* saw, exhausted women working the parched fields in the scorching sun, breaking their backs so their families wouldn't starve to death; old shacks defying gravity with their cracked, weed-infested walls; scrawny dogs and cats that kept mysteriously disappearing as food became scarce. . . .

Along the empty streets of Mariquita the magistrate went with her head down and her shoulders hunched, feeling overthrown as she finally heard, *really* heard, the clucking of the Sánchez widow's hens, trained to lay eggs in the widow's bed; and the grunting of Ubaldina's pigs, all of which were hoarded inside the woman's house to prevent them from being stolen. . . .

On a sunny afternoon of a day no one recalls, in a town the existence of which no one remembers, a poor magistrate dressed in her Sunday clothes wandered up and down the streets, looking like an ant, feeling like a failure.

Rogelio Villamizar, 25
Right-wing paramilitary soldier

His name was Góngora, and he was just an ignorant campesino, like me. But he'd been with the forces much longer and become a squad leader. I was assigned to his detachment; that's how I came to witness what I'm about to tell you.

We'd been chasing a guerrilla column in the jungle for several days, and they seemed to have been swallowed by the wild vegetation. We were about to give up and return to our base when we ran into a small group of Indians, five or six. We knew the Indians in that region fed rebels and often hid them in their reservations. The Indians were naked, their bodies covered with paint. They ran when they saw us, so we shot at their legs. All but one managed to escape into the thick scrub. The brilliant colors on his skin made him an easy target. He was a small man with long hair, and he looked even smaller after we tied him to a tree. A bullet had hit him in the left thigh and he was making grimaces of pain. We stepped aside and let our squad leader do what he liked the most.

"Where are the guerrillas," Góngora asked him. The Indian opened his mouth as though he wanted to speak, but he made no sound. Góngora walked up to him and slapped him twice across the face—nothing humiliates an Indian more than being slapped in the face. Góngora asked him the same question again. This time, the Indian's answer was an awful gurgling sound. Pissed off, Góngora hit him in the face with the handle of his revolver. The Indian made that horrible noise again, and his face twisted into a pained expression. Blood was gushing from his nose and mouth, and still he wouldn't tell our leader what he wanted to hear.

Góngora shouted a stream of abuse at the Indian, then put the tip of his revolver on the Indian's brow and said, "I'm losing my patience. Where are the damn guerrillas hiding?" The Indian started making louder and more annoying sounds, his eyes suddenly brimming over with tears. Most prisoners would have talked by now, if for nothing else, so as not to prolong their misery: they all know that after blurting out, they'll get killed no matter what. And so I marveled at this Indian's loyalty and bravery. The sounds he made, annoying though they were, seemed to be the only ways he could safely express his fear without betraying anyone.

Góngora took a few steps back, aiming his revolver at the Indian's head. I looked into the Indian's eyes: he stared blankly past our leader, past us. Then I looked at my comrades, and then at Góngora. But when he pressed the trigger, I just looked away.

Later we found out that the guerrillas had cut out the Indians' tongues.

CHAPTER 10

The Day Time Became Female

Mariquita, date unknown

THE MAGISTRATE HAD BEEN sequestered in her bedroom for several suns now, severely depressed. She had been defeated in her attempt to govern Mariquita. She was a worthless, stupid, arrogant, self-centered middle-aged woman who'd been given the opportunity of a lifetime and miserably failed. The two major events of her so-called administration—the Procreation Campaign and the Next Generation decree—had ended in disaster. The village still had no running water or electricity or a working phone, and all its access roads were now overgrown with thick shrubbery. Mariquita might as well have been erased from the nation's map.

All this caused Rosalba to have strong feelings of guilt, though her dominant emotion was fear: fear that her tenure as magistrate was at risk. Soon someone would plot to overthrow her, someone younger, more intelligent and better qualified.

During the length of her depression, Rosalba had refused to see her few friends and acquaintances. Only her boarder was allowed to come into her bedroom. Vaca brought Rosalba food three times a sun, gave her periodic reports of the people who had stopped to visit or to inquire about the magistrate's health, and impatiently listened to

Rosalba's self-abuse. One morning, however, fed up with Rosalba's whining, Vaca went to see the nurse.

"The magistrate's stopped loving herself," Nurse Ramírez said after listening to the long list of symptoms Vaca named. She prescribed a cup of marjoram tea eight times a sun, frequent sponge baths, and wearing clean clothes and makeup, if she could find any in the market. And so Vaca went back home, dragged Rosalba out of bed, to the patio, gave her a cold bath and made her lie naked in the sun, like a washed sheet, to dry. She then helped Rosalba put on a red dress and did her graying hair in a chignon at the back of her head, a good inch and a half higher than usual, so that the back of Rosalba's neck showed.

THIRTY-TWO CUPS OF marjoram tea later . . .

Darkness had begun to spread languidly over Mariquita. Feeling a bit more animated, the magistrate went outside and sat on her steps. The street was empty, and only a steady pounding sound was heard in the distance. The Ospinas must be grinding maize, Rosalba thought. She imagined the sturdy Ospina widow beating kernels repeatedly with a heavy flail.

The sound of footsteps interrupted Rosalba's thought. She leaned forward, squinting her eyes at the approaching shadow, until she recognized the expressionless face of the schoolmistress. Cleotilde hadn't come once to visit. She hadn't even asked after the magistrate's condition. But Rosalba couldn't blame the old woman for her indifference toward her. If anyone in town could claim to have been ill-treated by the magistrate, it was Cleotilde.

"Good evening to you, Señorita Guarnizo," Rosalba said in an unusually cordial tone of voice. The teacher merely acknowledged her with a motion of her head and walked past her as fast as her seventy-four years and goutish toes allowed her. "Would you like to join me for a bowl of soup, Señorita Guarnizo?" Rosalba shouted. "Vaca always makes a little extra."

Cleotilde stopped abruptly. She wanted to say yes, she'd be pleased to, but the request had taken her by surprise—she couldn't remember the last time the magistrate had invited her into her house—and despite the teacher's natural eloquence, no words came to her mind.

"Please, Señorita Guarnizo," Rosalba sounded almost humble. "I need your wise advice on some matters that are tormenting me."

Wise advice, advice, vice, ice, ce . . . The words echoed in the teacher's mind. She turned around, not entirely convinced it was she the magistrate was talking to. But the pitiful scene before her eyes cleared all her doubts: sitting all alone with her eyes fixed on her own feet—chapped and swollen in the shabby sandals she wore—with the dilapidated facade of her house as her only backdrop, the once-arrogant magistrate looked utterly dejected. Cleotilde tilted her head down and lowered her spectacles with her index finger. "It pleases me to hear that my recommendations are appreciated around here," she remarked.

Rosalba gave a timid laugh, then, addressing the teacher's knees, said, "Your recommendations aren't just appreciated, Señorita Guarnizo. They're treasured."

Treasured, easured, sured, ed . . . The flattering sounds resonated in Cleotilde's ears along the hallway toward Rosalba's dining room.

Later on, after they'd eaten two bowls of soup apiece, and the magistrate had apologized several times for Vaca's lack of talent for cooking, the two women sat in tall wicker armchairs in the living room drinking coffee and analyzing the "disastrous effects," as Cleotilde put it, that the "time dilemma," as Rosalba put it, would have on Mariquita if it weren't tackled promptly.

"Have you thought about any possible solutions?" Cleotilde inquired.

"Oh, several," Rosalba lied. "I'm just not happy with any of them, and I thought you and I could . . . perhaps come up with some tonight."

"I'd like that," the teacher returned, "but it's getting late, and I must prepare my ethics class for tomorrow. I'll come back tomorrow afternoon."

Visibly disgruntled, Rosalba rose and began walking in circles, glancing at the endless number of lists that hung neatly arranged on every wall of her house: lists of priorities, an updated count of widows and maidens, schedules for the cleaning and disinfecting of the village's homes, inventories of medications needed in the infirmary, records of her own unpaid and long-overdue salaries, lists of stray dogs and cats with a full description—which was brought up to date periodically as they kept mysteriously disappearing—and lists of lists. She had recorded the entire history of Mariquita since the men were taken away, in a journal made of pointless lists.

Suddenly, it occurred to her that the reason why she'd failed was that she had spent every single day of her magisterial career planning the things that she'd do the day after. She had sacrificed her *today* to a *tomorrow* that soon became *today*, and which was immediately sacrificed once more to another *tomorrow*, again and again, ceaselessly.

"No, Señorita Cleotilde," an energetic Rosalba finally said. "Mariquita's time can't wait until tomorrow. We must work on it now."

"But . . . what about my class?"

"Oh, skip it."

"But my students will—"

"Tell your students that you were sick, or that you were on a different schedule. It's only an ethics class, for God's sake!"

The schoolmistress frowned at this last remark.

*   *   *

MAGISTRATE AND SCHOOLMISTRESS spent the night and several candles thinking and conferring with one another about time. They talked about Santiago Marín's burning candles and the Villegas widow's blooming violets, and acknowledged the urgency of establishing a single system that allowed everyone in town to measure, in equal fashion, the duration of events.

"I still think that you should send someone to the city to buy a watch and a calendar," the schoolmistress observed. "The universal concept of time has been successfully used for hundreds of years." She supported her recommendation by talking in great detail about the theories of a Mr. Isaac Newton and a Mr. Albert Einstein, and she quoted them with such a degree of familiarity that the magistrate assumed the two men had personally discussed their hypotheses with the old woman.

"What you're suggesting," Rosalba said as soon as the teacher gave her the opportunity to speak, "is that we go back to the traditional male concept of time, in which time is all about productivity."

"In a way, yes, but—"

"I refuse to replicate that concept, Señorita Guarnizo. We live in a male-free world." She paused briefly, as to organize her thoughts, then added, "You know what I'd like to do? I'd like to create a female concept of time: the Theory of Female Time of Rosalba viuda de Patiño and Cleotilde Guarnizo." While she spoke her hand flew in the air as if she were printing her words on some invisible surface. Things had begun to look a little more promising for the magistrate. If she pulled through this crisis, she thought, she'd be able to prove to the villagers that she still was competent and resourceful.

IN DISCUSSING THE purported female concept of time, magistrate and teacher declined to make use of cyclical changes in their own environment, like migratory species, the recurrent proliferation of mosquitoes, or the predictable metamorphoses of the red-and-yellow butterflies that populated their region. "What if they become extinct?" Rosalba argued. They recognized the alternation of day and night as a natural and tangible method for keeping time, one that they would like to keep.

"What about climate?" Cleotilde suggested. "We have two pretty consistent periods of rain and drought."

"I don't know about that," Rosalba replied. "The weather has become so unreliable in the last few years that even the trees have grown confused. They don't know whether to order their flowers to bloom or their leaves to fall."

And then Cleotilde had a brainstorm.

"How about menstruation?" she said, and almost immediately experienced a great deal of satisfaction. She was confident that menstruation, being an exclusively female condition, would be a suitable idea for the magistrate's female concept of time. But she also proposed it out of some twisted desire to get even with Rosalba, who, the teacher had no doubt, was currently going through menopause. Some twenty years before, Cleotilde herself had undergone the change of life. She had endured the physical discomforts that came with it, but the emotional symptoms had taken her by surprise and forced her into a severe depression. She felt incomplete, half a woman, half finished. She decided that the magistrate was feeling the same way.

"Huh!" Rosalba mumbled after hearing the teacher's proposal. "I don't know that our community's time can rely on menstruation. Everyone's cycle is different." But both women knew everyone's cycles were identical. Soon after time stopped in Mariquita, the women's periods had synchronized. It occurred unexpectedly, as if nature, anticipating the chaotic situation that would follow the absence of time, had judged it its duty to grant all women an accurate way to keep the same schedule. And although nature hadn't yet succeeded in its ultimate goal, ever since, every twenty-eight suns, all washing lines in Mariquita displayed the white rectangular pieces of cloth that women wore as undergarments during their periods.

"If there's one thing that women can rely on in this village, it is menstruation," Cleotilde said. "Of course, you wouldn't know anymore." She paused to give Rosalba a complicitous look before adding, in a comforting whisper, "Rest easy, Magistrate. I won't tell a soul. We all go through it at some point."

Rosalba decided to ignore the schoolmistress's sardonic remark. "Your idea doesn't offer anything new to the theory we want to create," Rosalba said. She wouldn't admit it, but the one thing about the menstruation calendar that really troubled her was to have to depend on other women—younger, fertile women—to tell her whether it was day three or day twenty. If only I were ten years younger, she thought, I would be not only Mariquita's magistrate, but also its walking calendar.

"Maybe so," Señorita Cleotilde replied, "but a thirteen-month, twenty-eight-day calendar will make time calculation and recording very simple. Besides, if we keep time synchronized with the phases of the moon, Mariquita's calendar will remain in use and accurate far into the future."

Rosalba giggled. "Do you really believe that a bunch of women dying slowly in a far-flung corner of the world have any future?"

"Of course we have a future. Whether it's good or bad is a different thing." She pushed her spectacles up her nose.

"The future's only in . . . in the reveries in which we indulge ourselves," Rosalba said ponderously.

"That's ridiculous!" Cleotilde groaned, shaking her head repeatedly. "If we don't have a future, we might as well reverse time, go back to the past. That way at least we'd know where we're heading."

This last observation, ludicrous though it was, had a great impact on Rosalba. The magistrate looked first serious, then contemplative, then perplexed, then dazzled and then serious again. For a while the only sounds in the room were produced by the drops of rain that had just begun hitting the window steadily. But then, abruptly, Rosalba exclaimed, "You're brilliant, Señorita Cleotilde! Absolutely brilliant! We'll go back in time. Yes, we'll adopt the menstruation calendar you proposed, except we'll make time flow backward."

"But, Magistrate, we can't make time flow backward. It's just—"

"Our female calendar will begin with the last day of December and end with the first day of January. Better yet, we'll replace those boring names of the months with thirteen of our own names." Overly excited, Rosalba rose from the chair.

Overly concerned, Cleotilde rose too. "I was just making a hypothetical argument, Magistrate. I didn't intend for you to take it literally."

"How about if we start with the month of Rosalba and continue with the month of Cleotilde? Is that fair? Because if you want, we can start with the month of Cleotilde. It doesn't matter to me."

"Magistrate, what I meant to say was that—"

"I know what you meant to say, Señorita Cleotilde. You meant to say that when time moves backward, people have a chance to change the course of their lives. That's wonderful thinking! We'll go back in time, fix the many problems there are in our history, and create a prosperous future for all of us."

Shaking her head, Cleotilde took a deep breath.

"Now, how far in history should we go?" Rosalba went on. "First, I'd like to delete all of our stupid civil wars. Really, there's no need to fight among ourselves. Same with that silly battle for independence of 1810. We'll never be anybody's colony, so such a battle should never take place. And what about the Discovery Day? How horrible that was! I'd really like to efface that whole passage from our history. We should not be discovered for another thousand years or so. Or maybe we should be the ones who discover Europe. What do you think, Señorita Cleotilde?"

Señorita Cleotilde thought that the magistrate had finally gone crazy. She was just about to say that when Vaca walked into the room, holding a tray with two bowls and a couple of spoons.

"Breakfast," she announced.

"Great!" Cleotilde said. "I'm starving. What is it?"

"Hot soup."

"Again?" she sounded disappointed. "I always eat an egg in the morning. Don't you have any eggs?"

"If I had an egg, I'd have eaten it myself," Vaca said. She set down the tray.

"Well, I hope that at least there's some kind of meat in it," Cleotilde insisted. "Is there any?"

"Maybe," Vaca returned, shrugging her right shoulder.

"There's more meat in a mosquito's leg than in this soup," Cleotilde complained bitterly as she stirred the clear broth splashed with bits of cilantro. She tried to eat it with the spoon, but there was nothing solid in it. So she lifted the bowl and literally drank the soup in one gulp. When she was finished, the schoolmistress got up and began smoothing down her short hair with the backs of her hands.

"You're not leaving, Señorita Cleotilde, are you?" If the schoolmistress left, Rosalba thought, she would not be back until the next sun—if at all. By then the project would have lost momentum.

"Yes, Magistrate, I am. You already have a solution to the most urgent problem. That is if you can call a backward calendar a solution to anything. I trust you can figure out the rest on your own."

"I really think you ought to stay," Rosalba said, in a tone that sounded more like a warning than a request. "How else are you going to claim that Mariquita's female time is half your idea if you don't help me draft a document with the specifics of it?"

This last sentence felt like a slap across the teacher's face. "*It is* half my idea," she snarled. "I intend to help you draft the document. I just need to get some sleep before we start working on it." She removed her glasses and massaged her eyes with the back of her index fingers.

"Take a siesta in my bed," Rosalba suggested. "It's quite comfortable."

Cleotilde hated sleeping in other people's beds. She had a sharp sense of smell that made it impossible for her to sleep while engulfed in the offensive odors that were likely to emanate from someone else's bedclothes and mattress. As tired as she was, she decided that she'd rather work on that document now than sleep in the magistrate's malodorous bed. She locked her hands behind her back and for a while walked back and forth across the room, thinking, until at length she slid a piece of paper and a stub of a pencil across the table toward the magistrate, saying, "Rosalba, I'm going to give you dictation."

"I beg your pardon?" the magistrate replied. She didn't know what had startled her the most: being called by her first name, or being asked to take dictation.

"Write this down, dear: To establish a Time Committee of five young, comma—" She paused to allow Rosalba to write the phrase, but the magistrate, still confused, began mumbling something unintelligible. Disregarding the magistrate's bewilderment, Cleotilde went on with her dictation, " . . . healthy, comma—"

"Excuse me, Señorita Cleotilde," Rosalba attempted an objection.

"Dear, please raise your hand if you wish to formulate a question or if you wish to be excused." The schoolmistress waited a few seconds for Rosalba to raise her hand, but since the magistrate didn't do so, she proceeded with the next phrase. Eventually Rosalba started taking terms and conditions down, crossing out and rewriting until they had a draft of a bill that satisfied both of them.

IMPLEMENTING FEMALE TIME wouldn't be an easy task, the magistrate thought. Especially now that every woman was keeping her own schedule. Just getting all the villagers together to announce the decree would be difficult. Rosalba knew she'd encounter some resistance among the most stubborn villagers. She'd have to work really hard to persuade them that having a communal time scheme would help improve Mariquita's productivity, and therefore the living conditions of every family. But she'd have to work the hardest to convince them that keeping a lunar calendar in which time flew backward would eventually help each one of them get a second opportunity on earth.

But did she really believe that? Rosalba asked herself. Did she really think that an archaic calendar turned backward would be good for everyone? Maybe not. What significance would it have to someone like Magnolia Morales, who had said that time only existed in one's mind? Probably none. And would a systematic calendar appeal to the Pérez widow, who had declared that she lived the same day every day? Definitely not. Maybe Magnolia and the Pérez widow were right in their own eccentric ways. Women were idealistic and romantic by nature, and even though men had always seen those characteristics as faults, perhaps it was time for women to dignify them as unique female qualities and make use of them in their daily lives. Female time, Rosalba thought, should allow an infinite number of individual interpretations, so that it could exist simultaneously as the official system for the entire community, and boundless in each woman's idealistic, romantic and fertile mind.

The magistrate shared her latest thinking with Cleotilde, who was still walking back and forth across the room with her hands clasped behind her back.

"I like that idea," the old woman said, "but I think the villagers should have at least one parameter, or else we're going to end up with ten Magnolias running around naked, claiming that time is a . . . bare nipple or something like that. I suggest we ask that every month each woman chooses a virtue she wants to master or a defect she wants to eliminate, and that she apply her mind to it." She now sank into a chair, convinced she had said something important and definite.

Soon afterward, the two women engaged in a long conversation about morality, justice, faith, dignity, rectitude, generosity, tolerance, devotion, determination, patience, strength, hope, responsibility, trust, optimism, wisdom, prudence, understanding, tact, intuition, sense and many other things they considered virtues. Next, they spoke about vice, sinfulness, evil, virulence, mordancy, corruption, depravity, abuse, wickedness, iniquity, cruelty, abomination, conceitedness, degradation, lechery, rancor, bitterness, mediocrity, egotism and many more things they considered faults. And after so much talk about virtues and faults, Rosalba and Cleotilde resolved that instead of "months" and "years"— which they considered meaningless words—female time would be introduced as "rungs" and "ladders" to self-improvement. But unlike the intimidating ladders to success or fame established by men, these ladders would go down and down only, because, Cleotilde declared, "Except for God, no one has ever found glory on high." The women of Mariquita would never feel coerced into stepping up. Instead they'd be encouraged to go all the way to the bottom, where one's mind, character and soul would meet perfection, and most importantly, where perfection would have as many definitions as there were women.

*   *   *

SUDDENLY, SOUNDS FROM the outside intruded: there was a commotion in the streets. Rosalba and Cleotilde could hear, in the distance, the raucous voices of the women of Mariquita repeating the same phrase over and over.

"What are they saying?" Rosalba asked

"I'm not sure," the teacher replied, her hand cupped around her ear, "but they're enraged."

Rosalba sighed. "There's always something."

"Shouldn't we find out what they're up to out there?"

"Let them kill one another. We can't leave this house until we have an acceptable drawing of the calendar." She handed Cleotilde a piece of paper and began sharpening a pencil with a knife that needed sharpening itself. "Can you draw freehand, Señorita Cleotilde?"

Before the schoolmistress could reply that "of course" she could, there came a thunderous tapping on the door, and presently Vaca stormed into the room.

"Magistrate, you need to go outside immediately," Vaca began, catching her breath. She explained that a group of villagers, taking advantage of Rosalba's absence, had gone to Cecilia and demanded that a vote be taken for a new magistrate. Cecilia had tried to dissuade them, but they complained that Rosalba hadn't done a darn thing for Mariquita, that what they farmed wasn't nearly enough to feed everyone in town, and that most people had already forgotten what milk tasted like. Furthermore, the younger women accused the magistrate of having allowed el padre Rafael to execute a scheme to deceive them, while the older ones charged her with letting the priest get away after murdering their innocent boys. They'd so pressured Cecilia that she'd called a quick election in which Police Sergeant Ubaldina had been elected the new magistrate of Mariquita. "Cecilia just announced it," Vaca said.

"They're still striding around the plaza with Ubaldina on their shoulders, giving cheers for her."

And just like that, without warning, Rosalba was forced to confront her greatest fear. Fortunately, things were much more different now. For the first time in several suns Rosalba felt in control. Not only had she regained her self-confidence, but once again she was near achieving something exceptional for Mariquita. This time she wouldn't allow anyone or anything to ruin it for her. She would go out there and reason with them. The women, she was certain, would reelect her by acclamation.

*   *   *

OUTSIDE, THE HEAT was stifling. The light rain that had fallen earlier had made the air heavy and sticky. The windows of most houses were wide open, not so much to allow the slight breeze to circulate as to let the heat out. Walking down the street with Vaca and Cleotilde, Rosalba encountered nothing but two dogs curled up in the shadow of a tree, sleeping, and a long line of hardworking ants. Except for them, there was nothing alive on the streets.

When the three women reached the plaza, however, they heard singing and saw revelry around Ubaldina. The villagers had skipped over their individual schedules and gathered to celebrate, with a rowdy party, the election of the new magistrate. Rosalba tried to speak to a few of them, but they barely acknowledged her. She wasn't being overthrown: she was fading away. Rosalba quickly abandoned the idea of reasoning with them and went to plan B. She drew her pistol from its holster, aimed it at the sky and fired one of the two bullets she had left. As if there were magic in the resounding detonation, the women stopped celebrating and scurried into the church, the only place where they felt safe—especially since there was no priest. Only Cecilia Guaraya remained motionless in the middle of the plaza. She held a scrap of paper with the results of the voting.

"What did I do to you that you have betrayed me?" Rosalba asked Cecilia. The hot pistol was shaking in her hand.

"Please, Rosalba, don't be angry with me," Cecilia pleaded, addressing the magistrate's gun. "The women of this village are dead set on rebellion. I agreed to call an election only if your name was included on the ballot." She held the piece of paper out to Rosalba. "You came in second," she said.

Rosalba snatched the paper out of Cecilia's hand and glanced over it. "Oh, great!" she said contemptuously. "I came second, with two worthless votes." She scrunched the piece of paper into a ball and threw it back at Cecilia's feet. Then she put her gun away and went to the church, escorted by Vaca and Cleotilde.

Inside the house of God, Rosalba advanced up the aisle with a stately gait. Her authoritarian aspect elicited the women's fear, not their affection. There was no sound or movement except the blinking of the many eyes that followed Rosalba all the way to the pulpit, where she stood behind the naked, half-rotten desk from which el padre Rafael used to conduct the service. Cleotilde stood by her side.

"I'm here to take full responsibility for my mistakes and oversights," she began humbly. "Ever since I was appointed magistrate, I've struggled to have full control over our village, to overcome all sorts of obstacles and make a new life for ourselves without our men. I have gone astray in my beliefs and have done some things wrong. There are other things I should've done that I didn't. But now I'm finally able to see that my job in Mariquita, though unpaid, is to organize our community, to make sure that the Moraleses don't have leftovers while the poor Pérez widow eats what she finds when she finds it. To see to it that Perestroika stays healthy enough to yield sufficient milk for each of us to have at least a full glass every week. To ensure that every family has a house and that every house has a roof and that every roof keeps out the rain. I've learned many things that now will make me a much better magistrate for our village. All I ask is to have an opportunity to fix the mistakes that are fixable, and to make amends for the ones that are beyond reparation. If you agree that I deserve an opportunity, please step forward." She gazed sincerely at the crowd.

There was a long silence as the villagers considered the magistrate's words. Some women were skeptical. Rosalba's tone brought back to them unpleasant memories of courteous politicians, broken promises and denied privileges. But a few others believed in Rosalba's candidness and full intentions, especially now that the schoolmistress—whose credibility was intact—seemed to be endorsing her.

"You deserve a second opportunity," said Vaca from the first row. She walked toward Rosalba and stopped in front of the desk.

"I'm with you, Magistrate." The voice came from the very back. "To me, you are and will always be the only magistrate." It was Cecilia, who had followed Rosalba into the church and now walked up the aisle. She, too, stopped before the desk. Rosalba met her with a sympathetic look.

After a short wait, Doña Victoria viuda de Morales came into view. "We also think that you deserve a second chance," she shouted. She pushed her two oldest daughters—Orquidea and Gardenia—forward. "And you have our unconditional support." She now began struggling with the two youngest—Magnolia and Julia—who were notorious for their stubbornness. Doña Victoria whispered all kinds of threats in the girls' ears, but they resisted fiercely until at length the widow gave up.

Nurse Ramírez and Eloísa viuda de Cifuentes came forward next, followed by Lucrecia and Virgelina Saavedra. One by one more women began to join the group, their heads lowered in shame as they stated their support for Rosalba.

Magnolia and Julia Morales, Ubaldina and the mothers of the four dead boys had gathered on the right side of the church. They stood still and defiant, their heads held high. Rosalba realized that she had to shift her strategy if she wanted to win over the dissenters.

"How very sad," she said in a low voice, speaking to herself rather than to those before her. "If the spirits of our beloved Vietnam, Trotsky, Che and Hochiminh were to appear among us, they'd be very disappointed. They wanted us to live in perfect harmony." She stopped her discourse briefly to feel her throat with her hand, as if she were having trouble swallowing. Then she continued, "Their youth didn't stop them from teaching me, through their noble actions, that loyalty, respect and cooperation are the answer to success. It's very sad that they gave their innocent lives for nothing. May they forgive you."

The mothers of the boys, united by their tragedy, joined their hands and wept together. Eventually, they too moved to stand with the crowd of women who supported Rosalba's authority, leaving Ubaldina with no choice but to forget her magisterial aspirations and join the rest. Disappointed in Ubaldina, Magnolia and Julia left the church.

Rosalba was satisfied with how she'd handled the critical situation. This time, however, she didn't allow pride to stop her from seeing the truth: the revolt hadn't been an isolated incident but rather a serious warning of the extent to which the villagers were prepared to fight for food and shelter, the most basic human rights. She approached the women and personally thanked them for ratifying her as the ultimate authority in town. Then, taking advantage of the improvised gathering, she and Cleotilde explained to the villagers what they had been working on. They promised that the female calendar would be ready the next morning, and that it would mark the beginning of a new and splendorous era for Mariquita.

*   *   *

BACK IN ROSALBA'S house, after having eaten a meal of stewed lentils and white rice, Rosalba and Cleotilde began making the sketch of Mariquita's female calendar on a yellowed piece of paper.

First, Rosalba drew a ladder with thirteen rungs and gave each rung a female name, which she wrote in her neat and beautiful cursive handwriting. The top one she called Rosalba, of course—this time she didn't bother to ask the schoolmistress's opinion. The next one down she called Cleotilde, and then, in order, Ubaldina, Cecilia, Eloísa, Victoria, Francisca, Elvia, Erlinda, Rubiela, Leonor, Mariacé and Flor.

Then, on each rung, she drew four vertical rows of circled numbers (six on each), starting with number twenty-four and ending with number one. They represented the many suns of every rung. A fifth row with four empty circles symbolized the length of an average menstruation cycle. This last row, they agreed, would be called Transition, and it would be the most important period of every rung.

A faint ray of moonlight filtered through the grimy glass, reminding the two women that night had fallen.

"Can I tell you a secret, Magistrate?" Cleotilde said abruptly, removing her spectacles. Rosalba lifted her eyes from the sketch and nodded. "I remember feeling dirty and ashamed every time I had my period," Cleotilde said. "There were times when I felt so ashamed that I wished I were a man."

Rosalba also confessed to one of her secrets: "My husband slept in a separate room while I had my period, as if I had a contagious disease. To me, menstruation was a curse."

"Well, it won't be a curse anymore," Cleotilde said cheerfully. "From now on menstruation will be a time to celebrate femaleness."

The two women rose and stood across from each other, their bodies upright, their feet slightly apart and their hands by their sides. Scattered on the large table that separated them were the pieces of paper embodying the fundamental principles upon which female time was to be conducted thenceforth, and the final illustration of the first female time calendar ever, which would be set in backward motion at dawn. Standing there, Rosalba and Cleotilde looked like two statues of national heroines. The air of confidence that blazed from their eyes seemed to confirm that they, too, were women of admirable exploits; female versions of Simón Bolívar—Colombia's glorious liberator and first president.

"Is there anything else we need to discuss?" Cleotilde asked out of courtesy.

The magistrate shook her head. She used her lips to point at the pieces of paper on the table and said, "I think it's time to put all of that into practice." She offered to walk Cleotilde halfway. They hurried down the empty street until they reached the church building, which looked immaculate by the light of the moon. There they stood still, facing each other in the same way they always had: with their backs straight, their brows furrowed and a defiant look in their eyes. Only on this particular occasion nothing but a few inches and the invisible air kept them apart.

"Thank you much, Señorita Cleotilde," Rosalba said sincerely, even though the rigid expression of her face showed no appreciation. "I simply couldn't have done it without you."

"I am pleased to have been of help to you and to Mariquita," Cleotilde replied. She, too, was sincere. She, too, didn't show it.

The two women said good night and began to walk slowly in opposite directions along the desolate road. Their bodies, although shaped differently, cast two identical silhouettes that grew closer and closer as Rosalba and Cleotilde moved apart; climbed up the white facade of the shabby house of God; reached the tower, where a forgotten clock stood motionless; and finally, as the two women disappeared in the dusk, became one gigantic shadow that spread over the sky of Mariquita, covering equally everyone and everything beneath it.

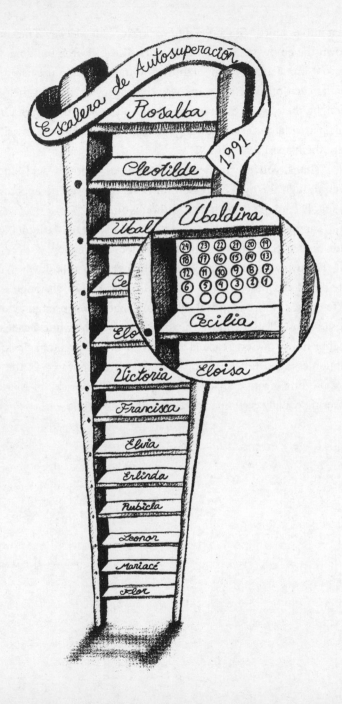

Plinio Tibaquirá, 59
Peasant

My son moved to the city as soon as he turned fifteen. He said he wanted a job where he didn't have to carry a machete tied around his waist. There, he met his friends, the revolutionaries. The next time I heard from him, he was in jail. I traveled a whole day on foot and another day on a bus to visit him, but when I got there, they told me guerrillas weren't allowed any visitors. Thieves could get visitors! Murderers could get visitors! But not guerrillas! I asked to speak to the sergeant in charge. They made me wait outside. They thought I'd get sick from the sun and the heat and go home. I bet none of them had fathered a child.

The sergeant told me the same thing: guerrillas weren't allowed visitors. I said to him, "Pardon me, sir, but my boy needs me now more than ever. I can feel it. I'm his father. You see, guerrillas have fathers too." I was crying when I said this last phrase. He made no reply, but ordered one of his men to take me to see my son. "Only for five minutes," he said to the man. I followed a young soldier through many gates and long corridors. There were stinky cells on both sides, and behind their rusty bars, there were faces, faces with blank expressions, faces of men that were not my son.

Finally, the young soldier pointed to a dark cell. "There," he said. I stood behind the bars, pressing my face against them, but I couldn't see anything because there was no light inside. So I whispered his name, Felipe. Three times I whispered his name before I heard a sound, a wail. "It's me, son. Your father. I'm here for you." He made that terrible noise again, louder this time. He was telling me he was very happy I was there, but that he was in so much pain he couldn't even speak, only make that noise. I begged the soldier to let me in. He said no. I asked him for a flashlight. He didn't have one. Besides, he thought it was better that way, because my son wasn't "presentable" that day. I imagined my boy lying on the ground, chained and beaten up, forced to relieve himself next to where he ate and slept.

I went back the following morning. No one knew anything about my son. His name wasn't in their files. Was I sure that was his name? They were very sorry, but no, Felipe Andrés Tibaquirá Gutiérrez had never been there. And no, they'd never seen me before.

I must have dreamed it.

CHAPTER 11

The Cow That Saved a Village

Mariquita, Rosalba 5, Ladder 2000

T HE MAGISTRATE TURNED OUT to be particularly amiable that morning. She distributed among the crowd palm-frond fans she had made herself, and personally poured cupfuls of cool water to help mitigate the unmerciful heat. She shook hands with every curious woman who approached the large table she'd set up outside the municipal office, and promised all of them that they would never regret signing the two-page document she was so persistently waving under their noses.

"This is Mariquita's Communal Agreement," she said, the words rolling out of her mouth with ease, as if she were introducing her best friend to them. "By signing it, you'll be committing yourselves to vesting the ownership of all your possessions in the community of Mariquita as a whole."

The vagueness of the explanation made the women's expressions change. Most older widows didn't read and barely knew how to sign their names; therefore, when it came to signing documents, they mistrusted everyone—especially the magistrate, with her elaborate sentences and preposterous decrees that almost always got someone, if not everyone, in trouble. They eyed Rosalba with suspicion and began whispering to each other, alternating nods with shakes of their heads. Finally, the Solórzano widow, who owned Perestroika, ventured to say, "We'd like to know what *vesting* means, Magistrate."

"Oh, *vesting* is just a fancy word," Rosalba said at once, throwing her hand in the air. "It's kind of like . . . bartering, only better because you only have to give once, but you'll keep receiving benefits for the rest of your life." She smiled an almost maternal smile.

"Hmmm . . . ," the Calderón widow murmured. She owned three mules, which she hired out for carrying loads of harvested products in exchange for half of the products the mules carried. "What am I expected to trade?"

"Whatever you own, Calderón," Rosalba replied with a shrug. "Anything." She was making a great effort to look and sound casual about the hidden implications of the agreement.

"And what do we get in return?" the Sánchez widow inquired. She owned a good number of chickens and brood hens that earned her, her two daughters and her old mother a living.

"Whatever you don't have, Sánchez," Rosalba replied. Then, in a strategically smart move, she put the document aside and grabbed a water jug. "Vesting is a good thing for everybody," she said, and began refilling the women's cups with fresh water. "A really good thing for everybody." She kept repeating this over and over as she walked among dozens of large palm-frond fans that moved rhythmically in the women's hands, blowing Rosalba's words into the thick, humid air.

BEFORE THE SUN reached its highest point in the sky, all the villagers, including Rosalba, had signed the Communal Agreement; or, if they were illiterate, said out loud, "Sí, acepto," in front of the schoolmistress, who signed their names and served as the official witness.

Except for the magistrate, all the women went back to their houses to hide from the sun. Rosalba preferred to lie down in the shade of a tree in the plaza, hoping for an unlikely breeze. She was pleased to realize that contrary to Señorita Guarnizo's predictions, developing a collectivist economic system in Mariquita was going to be an easy task after all. She began to outline, in her mind, the general plan that would help her accomplish this goal. First, she would collect all domestic animals and take them to join Perestroika in the Solórzano widow's backyard, which would become Mariquita's first communal farm. Next she would divide the arable land into parcels of different sizes, each of which would be assigned to a group of women with specific instructions on what to cultivate. Then she would hold an early meeting to inform the villagers that everyone was required to work and/or produce something, in her own capacity, for herself and for the benefit of the community. Those who had no special skills, like the half-deranged Jaramillo widow, would be assigned to clean the houses and wash the clothes of those who did, or sweep streets and alleyways. And if a woman were too old or physically disabled, like the Pérez widow, she'd be asked to entertain the villagers every evening by telling them old stories or folktales, so that Mariquita's traditions would remain alive. She was so lost in her thoughts that she no longer felt the implacable noon heat, or heard the unbearable buzzing of the mosquitoes in her ears, or felt their painful sting that after so many years still left festering wounds on her fair skin. The worst is over for Mariquita, she thought. The storm's finally abating.

BUT WHEN ROSALBA, Cecilia and Cleotilde started going from house to house to collect all domestic animals, they encountered heavy resistance among the villagers.

"You touch one of my chickens, and I'll wring your neck," the Sánchez widow said.

"That piece of paper I signed didn't mention Perestroika's name," the Solórzano widow argued. Even Ubaldina, the police sergeant, refused to part with her pigs.

Doors were slammed. Threats were made. Insults were shouted.

The next morning Rosalba called for a meeting in the plaza to clarify, once and for all, what "vesting the ownership of one's possessions in the community of Mariquita as a whole" meant, and the implications of having signed the agreement. But the meeting soon turned unpleasant. When the women heard in simple, unadorned words what Rosalba's plan was all about, they divided into two groups: the majority, who owned nothing but their meager wardrobe and therefore supported the plan; and a smaller group of seventeen who claimed they'd been misled into signing a vague, wrongful document to deprive them of what little they had. And while the former group gave three cheers for the magistrate, the latter group rebelled, calling her a liar and a thief.

Rosalba remained calm until the tension abated. Then she made an unexpected announcement: "Each one of you has two choices: to stay in Mariquita and abide by the rules of the agreement you signed, or to leave. If you decide to go, I'll give you until sunrise tomorrow to collect whatever you own and leave once and for all." She paused briefly to loosen the lump that had formed in her throat, and then, raising her voice gradually, she added, "Now, if you decide to stay, know that you'll be a part of a prosperous community where no one will ever again miss a meal. You choose!"

Immediately after the confrontation, the rebellious villagers secretly met at Ubaldina's house.

"If we're going to leave, we must leave as soon as possible," Ubaldina remarked. "Rosalba's insidious and vindictive, and she'll set the village against us."

"She already has," the Sánchez widow said in her successful voice, the voice of a widow who had started out with a single brooding hen and currently had twelve hens, seventeen chickens, and at least a dozen eggs every morning. "I hate the idea of giving up my house, but I hate even more the idea of sharing with everyone what I have earned all alone."

Comments were made, explanations given, questions asked and answered and at length a decision was reached: "We'll leave before sunset. Everyone, go home and start packing."

When the magistrate was informed about the dissidents' plan for a hasty departure, she secretly met with the schoolmistress to draw up a plan.

"We must do something to retain them, Señorita Guarnizo," Rosalba began in a frantic tone. "If they go, Mariquita might not survive. They'll take our milk and cheese and butter, our pigs and goats, our eggs."

Cleotilde listened carefully, without interrupting, and when the magistrate stopped, she said, "I think the ethical way of dealing with this crisis is by—"

"I don't care whether or not it's ethical," Rosalba burst out. "I haven't accomplished one thing in my life without having to lie or cheat some." She turned her back on Cleotilde and, addressing a non-judgmental wall, added, "Every time I tried to do something the right way, I failed miserably. I try to be honest with everyone and to lead a life of good moral principles, but I can't."

"Well, perhaps you can use your *notorious* persuasion powers to talk the rebels into staying," Cleotilde suggested.

But the situation, Rosalba reasoned, was too crucial to be dealt with honorably, and after proposing a number of dishonest ways to get her way (which ranged from kidnapping the three most influential widows to using the last bullet in her pistol to threaten them) she ended up using her "notorious" persuasion powers to convince Cleotilde to tell a lie with her. "A small, white lie," she said. "For the sake of Mariquita."

BEFORE SUNSET, A long procession hurried down the main street. Santiago Marín, the Other Widow, his mother and two sisters led the caravan, followed by a group of young women who carried on their backs large bundles of corn and stacks of raw cotton. The heavy produce—yuccas, potatoes, plantains and coffee beans—they put in sacks, which they distributed among the Calderón widow's three mules. Behind the mules came a group of thick-bodied matrons carrying rolled-up blankets on their wide shoulders, and pots, pans and kettles tied around where their waistlines ought to have been. The Sánchez widow struggled with a cardboard box filled with clothes on her head, and what seemed to be a whole poultry farm concealed upon herself. The Solórzano widow dragged Perestroika along the street, or maybe it was Perestroika—loaded with its owner's personal belongings—who dragged the widow. More widows with more household goods, pigs and goats, cats and dogs and even an old parrot that would eventually make a decent soup, marched down the street in a boisterous and colorful farewell to Mariquita.

At the end of the main street, the caravan turned onto a long, narrow path that took them up a small rise and ended in "the border," an almost impenetrable clump of trees and shrubs that had sprung up where the road that led to the south used to be, and which now served to separate, or rather hide, Mariquita from the rest of the world. But when Santiago Marín and his mother were about to enter the dense thicket, they heard the unmistakable commanding voices of Rosalba and Cleotilde. "Halt! Halt!" they shouted repeatedly. The two women tried to walk fast, but the soles of their shoes were so thin they felt like socks on their feet, making them move slowly and clumsily on the unpaved road.

"What can they possibly want from us?" Aracelly viuda de Marín said.

"I think we should keep going," one of the Ospina girls suggested. "It's getting cloudy."

"Let's wait for them. Maybe they want to come with us," Santiago said, giggling.

They all agreed and began laying their bundles and sacks on the ground.

When they reached the border, Rosalba and Cleotilde stood side by side before the group. "First, I want to thank you all for pausing your . . . abrupt journey," Rosalba began in a conciliatory tone. She had a large book clutched against her chest. "Since it looks like rain, and I know you want to reach a safe place before nightfall, I'll be brief. Earlier this afternoon, Señorita Cleotilde and I were leafing through a history book when we came across a section that narrates a very important episode in the history of our village. Isn't that true, Señorita Cleotilde?"

"Uh-huh," the schoolmistress uttered, addressing the women as well as their animals, all of whom stood in uproarious disorder over the small rise. "It's a wonderful story that every Mariquiteña should know. We wish to read it to all of you before you leave town." Santiago and the women looked at one another, saying, with their mute expressions, that they wouldn't stay for another one of the magistrate's tedious lectures. "Please," the teacher begged, staring at Santiago. She knew he couldn't refuse an old lady's request, especially one asked in beseeching tones.

Looking exasperated, Santiago sat on the large bundle of corn he had been carrying. His action signaled to the women to do the same. They began settling on rolled-up blankets, pots and boxes, finally ending in a rough semicircle with their belongings next to them. Perestroika and the mules moved to the sides to eat tall grass and leaves. The magistrate handed the book she was holding to the teacher. "I think it's better if you start," she whispered. "I'm a little nervous." Rosalba had deliberately told all kinds of lies to all kinds of people in her life, but she couldn't remember anything as important as Mariquita's future ever depending on one of her fabrications. At the moment she doubted the effectiveness of the fiction she and Cleotilde were about to tell, and regretted not having thought up something much more spectacular.

Cleotilde reached for her spectacles, which lately she kept hanging from a silver chain around her neck, put them on, cleared her throat, opened the book (an atlas, of all things!) on a random page, and began telling the story:

"Once upon a time, in a small village called . . . Taribó, currently known as Mariquita, there was a beautiful young girl named . . . Caturca, who was the only child of a celebrated Indian chief. One morning, after coming back from a tour around her village, Caturca went up to her father and asked, 'Father, why do you and I have leftovers on our table when some of our own people have nothing to eat?' Her father was a well-intentioned man, but not very smart, and so he couldn't answer Caturca's questions. The young girl asked her father's advisers the same questions, but they also weren't too bright."

Cleotilde had been addressing small and large crowds her entire life. She knew when to raise or lower the tone of her voice, when to pause, when to look at her audience, which words to emphasize. It was not surprising then, that at the moment everyone seemed captivated by her telling.

"The next morning, escorted by a group of servants, Caturca left Mariquita in search of answers. She traveled through exotic lands where she learned about many different cultures, customs, beliefs and governments. She dwelt with the very poor as well as the very rich; spent suns among the civilized and the barbarous; had long conversations with intellectuals and ignorant country people. When Caturca finally returned to Mariquita, she was no longer a young, ingenuous girl but a cultivated, wise woman. Her father, now a feeble old man, abdicated and made her the new chief of the village."

At this point Cleotilde stopped. "The magistrate will continue now," she said. Rosalba took the atlas with both hands and turned the page, as though expecting to find the continuation of the story in it. Faced with the map of North Central Europe, she had no alternative but to continue the telling.

"During Turca's reign—"

"Caturca," the teacher interrupted. "Her name was Caturca."

Rosalba feigned a smile and began again, "During Caturca's reign her village became the most prosperous community in the area. She freed the slaves and abolished servitude, and though she remained their chief she declared all villagers equal. She redistributed all the land and houses so that each family had a house in which to live and a piece of land to work. Women were asked to teach men how to cook, clean and do other housework, and men taught women how to farm, hunt and fish. Then, men and women took turns working the land and keeping house, and the villagers became more considerate toward each other."

The women were becoming restless and distracted. The Sánchez widow had noticed a new line on her left palm and now wondered what sort of things it might tell about her future. Meanwhile Ubaldina watched, with increasing interest, a dog trying to mount one of her pigs.

"Only then did Caturca take the one last step that would make her ruling system perfect: she eliminated the position of chief and became a regular Indian in the village, and a regular Indian she remained up to a ripe old age."

Rosalba closed the book in a dramatic fashion and, putting on a cheerful expression, asked, "Wouldn't it be wonderful if Mariquita went back to Capurca's ruling system?" She scanned the crowd looking for an answer. "What do you all think?"

"I think that you mispronounced the Indian's name *again*," Santiago Marín observed relentlessly. "It's Caturca. Ca-tur-ca." The two Ospina sisters got the giggles.

"Can you think of anything . . . better to say?" Rosalba said in a challenging tone.

"Sure. I think that it's going to rain and that we should get going." He rose, and the women rose, and they quietly began to collect their goods and gather their animals with the clear intention of continuing their journey. To the magistrate, their indifference felt as if someone had spat in her face. She wanted to hurl all kinds of insults at them—to tell them that they were hard-hearted, rapacious vultures; that they were much more stupid than Caturca's father and his advisers; that, by the way, Señorita Cleotilde and herself had made up that ridiculous story about Turca, Purca, Catapurca or whatever they wanted to call that damned Indian; and that as far as she was concerned, they could all go to hell with their scrawny chickens and stinky goats, the selfish, ugly, greedy bitches. . . . But she had promised Cleotilde she would remain calm and handle this special situation with the composure and grace of the distinguished lady she ought to be.

And so poor Rosalba stood there for a while in silence. Her face showed lassitude, a tangible consequence of both the tension produced by the confrontation with the women and the extreme heat. Her body assumed a relaxed, comfortable posture, as if she were waiting to be lifted by the wind. When the crowd was about ready to resume their journey, Rosalba suddenly began to speak in a soft but resolute voice: "Do you really think that behind those mountains you'll find a paradise without violence or poverty awaiting you?" She shook her head several times. "A place like that, you must create yourselves. And you can't do it with just a few people. It takes an entire community, like the one Señorita Cleotilde and I imagined for Mariquita. When we imagined that community, we were counting on your willingness to sacrifice a little to create here, where you and your children were born, that paradise you think is waiting for you somewhere else.

"If you still want to leave, I wish you good luck, but be aware that you're merely changing one kind of misery for another, and in the end, choosing the kind of misery you can live with will be the only freedom you'll have left." Rosalba handed the atlas to Cleotilde and gently touched the old woman's shoulder in a subtle demonstration of gratitude for having lied for her. Then she started walking down the rise, back to Mariquita, devastated by sadness.

Cleotilde marveled at what the magistrate had said. Rosalba was notorious for her incompetence, her eccentric and capricious decrees that resolved nothing and complicated everything, and her long speeches in which nothing meaningful was ever said. The speech she'd just given, however, had come from a different Rosalba—an older, seasoned and more intellectually mature Rosalba who, Cleotilde sensed, was growing aware of the corrosive effect of passing rungs and ladders on her flesh; but who, instead of seeking relief in invisible gods, was strongly binding herself to reality, doing work that justified her existence, but that also empowered her to go on living.

Suddenly a heavy rain began to pour down. It fell fast and in enormous drops while streaks of lightning rent the sky. The women seized their belongings and ran to the closest building, Doña Emilia's abandoned brothel, to take shelter.

And then something extraordinary happened.

With an abrupt motion, Perestroika freed herself from the Solórzano widow's grip and started walking down the slope after the magistrate, dragging along the road a thick rope that was tied around her neck, mooing loudly. Then, as if the cow's lowing were a secret call to revolt, mules, pigs, goats, cats, dogs, the parrot and other loose birds scurried away across the road to join Perestroika and Rosalba. The women left the protection of the former brothel and ran after their animals, shouting at them to come back. Only the dogs stopped, but not to show obedience. They bared their teeth, ready to snap at their mistresses' legs if they came any closer. The remaining creatures, the ones that were tied up, became extremely agitated. They grunted, growled, barked, howled, or made whatever sound they could in open solidarity with the others. The uproar was such that the women, afraid it all might end up in an unfortunate tragedy, turned the protesting animals loose. The creatures immediately joined the riotous caravan led by the magistrate.

Rosalba couldn't help being slightly moved by such a display of loyalty. Suddenly, she remembered a famous story from the Bible she'd heard many times, and though she no longer believed in God, she allowed herself to feel like Noah, leading the animals toward a safe haven from the Flood that would drown the world. She continued walking, now with increasing confidence and a jubilant smile that sparkled in the night with each strike of lightning.

Meanwhile, the crowd of women had rejoined the schoolmistress beneath the eaves of the brothel. They stood against the discolored stucco walls, contemplating the merciless rain that washed away leaves, branches and tree trunks mixed with earth, gravel and stones.

"I'd never seen anything like it," the Calderón widow said. "Those dogs acted like they were possessed."

"We can't leave without our animals," the Solórzano widow declared. She paused to wipe the excess water from her forehead with the ragged sleeve of her dress. "They are the reason why we decided to leave Mariquita."

"I don't know about you, but if Perestroika wants to stay here, I'll stay with her," the Solórzano widow announced. "It's better to share her milk than to lose her."

The group grew quiet, but after a long silence filled only by the rain, the Sánchez widow spoke her mind. "I think she's right. If my hens won't follow me, I'll follow them. All I ask for is to be provided with four eggs every sun, one for me, one for each of my daughters and one for my mother. The rest you can share among yourselves."

"My sister and I can make arepas and tamales for everyone," Irma Villegas declared. She looked at her sister for approval.

"Yes, indeed," Violeta Villegas returned. "As long as we can get enough maize and some meat."

"You can have as much of our maize as you want," the Ospina widow volunteered.

"Well, then the same goes for my pigs," Ubaldina said coyly. "I think I'd rather share their meat with my own people than sell it to strangers."

"If anybody would like tomatoes, onions, yuccas or potatoes, please come to us," the Other Widow offered.

The sharing disposition appeared to be contagious. Each family announced what they would contribute: farm and homegrown produce, home-cooked food, manufactured merchandise and knitted goods. They soon realized that there wouldn't be enough of everything for every woman in town, which they decided wouldn't be fair. Therefore, they agreed to cultivate more fruits, nutritious vegetables and grains. "We'll need more people to work the land," the Ospina widow said, and almost immediately two sturdy young girls volunteered. The women also agreed to increase the production of domestic animals and dairy products. Perhaps even start a farm where they could keep all the animals, collect the eggs, raise chickens, turkeys and pigs, milk Perestroika and make butter and cheese. "I'll be glad to run the farm," the Solórzano widow said. "But I'll need . . ."

Look at them, Cleotilde said to herself. Talking about creating an animal farm, sharing their produce and working together, like it's their original idea. What geniuses!

But as difficult as it was for her, Cleotilde kept her thoughts to herself. Let them think it was all their idea; let them take all the credit. That, she concluded, was what wise women did.

"I think we've been a little too greedy," Ubaldina said to the group, her voice full of regret. "Don't you agree?"

At that moment lightning struck close to where they stood. The bolt was promptly followed by a deafening thunderclap that made the women believe that nature, in its own furious way, had just answered Ubaldina's question. In absolute quiet they gathered their things and started down the slippery rise, walking as fast as they could to catch up with the large caravan that was already turning onto the main street.

Cleotilde held the open atlas firmly over her head and walked out in the rain with her characteristic gait, slower than the others, but still staunch and purposeful. She splashed water as she went along the muddy, difficult road that soon would put all ninety-three women and Santiago in an extraordinary place: the thriving community of New Mariquita.

Jacinto Jiménez Jr., 26
Guerrilla soldier

We were scouring the mountains for paramilitary soldiers when
we came upon a caravan of displaced Indians. The elders walked in
front, dragging their bodies up the trail, some pushing and pulling
each other. Then came the children, all naked. They had rolled-up
blankets on their shoulders and drove small herds of pigs and goats.
The women came next, their babies in their arms, pots, pans and
chairs strapped to their backs with hemp cords. Last in the long line
were the men, about ten of them. They wore conical woolen hats
and colorful robes, and they carried loads on their backs in large
blankets tied around their foreheads.

"Where are you all heading for?" Cortéz, our leader, shouted at
the men from a distance.

The Indians went on, quietly, as if they hadn't heard or understood the question.

Cortéz yelled at them to stop. "Where are you fucking going?"
he sounded angry.

"Anywhere," a middle-aged man with a sad face and a vacant
look replied in a faint voice, without stopping or even raising his
eyes from the ground. He was their chief. His hat was taller and his
robe white, and he was the only one who had a mule to carry his
load.

"Halt!" our leader yelled again.

The men stopped abruptly.

Cortéz approached the group with his indifferent pace. "Are
you running away from paramilitaries or from guerrillas?" he asked,
addressing the Indian chief.

The Indian stood still next to his mule, staring at the ground, as though thinking. He knew the wrong answer could get him and his people killed.

"Are you running away from paramilitaries or from guerrillas?" Cortéz repeated, louder this time, and put the tip of his gun on the man's temple. The other Indians watched, terrified.

The Indian chief swallowed saliva two or three times but couldn't bring himself to respond. The side of his face I could see was beaded with sweat.

Cortéz snapped back the safety catch of the gun.

"From—from the war, *sir*," the man faltered at last. "We're running away from the war."

Cortéz snatched up the Indian chief's hat and put it on the mule's head. Then he looked at the other Indians and bared a few teeth, as if in a smile.

"*Now* you can go," our leader finally said, putting his gun away.

CHAPTER 12

Widows in Love

New Mariquita, Ubaldina 1, Ladder 1998

E LOÍSA VIUDA DE CIFUENTES got out of bed before dawn as usual, and just as usual arranged three large pillows in a line down the middle of her bed and covered them with bedclothes. That way in the semidarkness, from the doorway and with her head slightly tilted toward the right, the bulge gave her the illusion that Rosalba, the magistrate, lay amid her lavender-perfumed sheets.

She stood naked by the door contemplating the silhouette she had fabricated, and imagined that she and the magistrate had just finished making love. It wasn't unusual for Eloísa to see the bulge's midsection heave or the entire thing turn onto its side. Later, after giving it some consideration, she would admit to herself that those movements were nothing but an optical illusion. But in the morning, before drinking her first cup of coffee, it was imperative that she lived her fantasy thoroughly, no matter how crazy it seemed.

Eloísa was in love with Rosalba, but nobody knew; not even Rosalba.

The church bell rang in the distance: a single set of five chimes that indicated to the villagers that it was time to rise and start getting ready for work. Inside her kitchen, Eloísa set a few logs on the ashes in the stove and put on the kettle. At that moment she felt something warm and damp running down her legs. She slid her hand along the inner part of her right thigh and confirmed, with great concern, that she had gotten her period a sun early.

Eloísa was a member of the Time Committee. One of her duties was to report to the magistrate her first discharge of blood every twenty-eight suns, which needed to coincide with that of the other four members of the committee. After drinking a full cup of coffee Eloísa walked out into the patio with a towel on her shoulder. She stopped in front of the large barrel she used to collect rainwater and noticed that it was empty. She remembered seeing it almost full the night before. Her boarder, the selfish Pérez widow, had gotten up before her and used it all to bathe herself.

Eloísa had been burdened with taking in the Pérez widow after a storm destroyed the old woman's shack several rungs before. She hated sharing her house—especially with the Pérez widow—but didn't complain because she, Eloísa, had signed that damned Communal Agreement, and she was a woman of her word. According to the document, "nobody owned anything because everybody owned everything," or at least that's what Eloísa had gathered from Rosalba's speech. To Eloísa, signing the piece of paper also meant having to work, with three other women, a plot of land that had been abandoned since the men disappeared. The four women's hard work kept the community supplied with coffee beans, avocados, papayas and squash, and even produced a little extra to be stored, together with other dry foodstuffs and fibers for blankets, in an adobe granary that the magistrate had had built in the ruins of a deserted house. But the new law wasn't all bad. For instance, Eloísa no longer had to bid against other women to procure food. She didn't even have to cook anymore. Every morning three matrons received from the magistrate a large basket full of fresh vegetables, fruits, grains, and eggs and meat when available. They cooked breakfast and dinner. Only raw vegetables were eaten at lunchtime.

*   *   *

AFTER CURSING THE Pérez widow in her head, Eloísa went back to her bedroom. She dampened the towel with the drinking water that she kept on her bedside table and scrubbed her body where it needed to be scrubbed. Then she set forth, naked as she was, to report her early period to the magistrate.

A few rungs before, Eloísa had become the first widow to go stark naked in public. "It took thousands of generations for the female body to reach perfection. Why should we hide it under a costume?" she had alleged.

The magistrate could have penalized her for public nudity, but her own body went numb and her mouth dry with admiration and desire after seeing Eloísa's breasts. Rosalba thought they were marvelous: their light brown color, their firmness, their size and shape like a ripe grapefruit cut in half. They were so extraordinary that they might well have taken thousands of generations to reach such a level of perfection.

On one occasion, after being pressured by the town's most pious women, Rosalba had stopped Eloísa on the street and made it clear to her that some parts of the female body must be covered, if only because they were very sensitive. But the magistrate was disarmed by Eloísa's reply: "I can't think of any part of the female body that's less sensitive and more misused than a butt, and yet women have covered it throughout history."

Being fully clothed soon began to seem strange, unnatural. For some it was simply a fair and practical solution to the growing problem of having to spend energy weaving new clothes, but for others it was just no longer conceivable that women were the only creatures in the world that had to cover the upper and lower part of their bodies. The older women were cautious. They believed nudity was just a trend—like miniskirts had once been—and they were not just about to become the laughingstock of the village with their dried-up posteriors and deflated breasts, the nipples of which lined up with their belly buttons. They cut the sleeves of their blouses and shortened the length of their skirts, and that was as far as they would go.

*　　*　　*

THE CHURCH BELL rang again. Two sets of five chimes each, which indicated that it was time for the villagers to stride toward the communal kitchen to which they had been assigned, to get their first meal. The bell-rings code had been developed by the schoolmistress, who also had volunteered to ring the bell until she had no strength left to pull the long rope tied to the clapper.

Feeling hungry, Eloísa reasoned that reporting her period could wait and instead hurried down the street toward the Morales's kitchen. She arrived at the same time as the magistrate, who randomly ate in all three communal kitchens to ensure the quality of the food served and the promptness of the service. To Eloísa's pleasure and surprise, the magistrate showed up completely naked, though covering her crotch with her appointment book. Eloísa had been working on Rosalba for rungs. Every time the magistrate complimented Eloísa on her olive-colored Indian skin and the many beautiful moles on her body, Eloísa replied, coquettishly, that she was certain the magistrate had many far more beautiful moles hidden underneath her clothes. Rosalba's clothes had gradually begun to shorten a little here and a little there, and eventually she had gone down to her underwear.

"Your body puts the blue morning sky to shame, Magistrate!" Eloísa said enthusiastically. The same line—or a slight variation of it—had been used by Eloísa's husband in a poem he'd written to her. Rosalba looked up at the blue morning sky. There was nothing in it but a lazy sun and a flock of white birds that kept flying in circles over the village. Then she looked down and laughed nervously, feeling as though her nudity was a rash that had suddenly started expanding all over her body. Eloísa stepped to one side and motioned with her fully extended arm. "After you," she said. Rosalba walked sidewise through the door holding the book tight against her stomach and sat at the first table she came upon, followed closely by Eloísa.

The long table was partially covered with a piece of white plastic and several black flies that appeared to be glued to it. Orquidea, the oldest daughter of the Morales widow, emerged from the kitchen wearing one of her conservative long-sleeved brown blouses and a matching long skirt and carrying three large baskets filled with arepas. She stopped abruptly in front of the magistrate and shook her head disapprovingly. She distributed the baskets almost symmetrically along the table and quickly disappeared into the kitchen. A moment later, her sisters Gardenia and Magnolia and the widow herself peeped out through the doorway and had a chuckle. Rosalba missed it, for Eloísa had engaged her in a conversation about the history of the heart-shaped birthmark she, Eloísa, had under her right breast.

A chunk of butter dancing on a chipped plate and two bowls of hot egg soup were delivered to the magistrate's table by Julia, the youngest child of the Morales widow. She wore a tight red dress with a revealing neckline (though there was nothing to reveal), and she had a fresh purple orchid tucked behind her ear. After placing the two bowls on the table Julia tapped Rosalba on her shoulder, and with a few simple gestures and her expressive eyes let her know that she looked wonderful without clothes; that she—Julia—supported the magistrate's decision wholeheartedly; and that she—Rosalba—shouldn't pay any attention to her sisters because they were fat, ugly, mean and envious spinsters, or something to that effect.

The dining room filled up soon. Contrary to what Rosalba expected, her nudity didn't get much attention. The women who didn't arrive early enough to sit at any of the three tables carried their food outside and looked around for empty buckets and flowerpots, which they soon converted into seats. Their kitchen was not scheduled to get milk that morning, so they all drank their coffee black. Francisca pretended to squeeze her bare dark nipples into her cup. It was an old joke, but it still got good laughs out of the crowd.

Three sets of five bell rings were now heard, instructing the villagers to head for their specific workplaces. The Morales sisters began clearing the tables, while the women got up in orderly fashion, without interrupting their loud conversations and guffaws of laughter. Eloísa and Rosalba agreed to remain seated until the majority of the crowd was gone. Eloísa took the opportunity to tell the magistrate, in a slightly regretful tone, that she had gotten her period that morning. The law ordered that any member of the Time Committee who became irregular should be immediately substituted and never again considered for the task. She dreaded the public humiliation that most certainly would come with being dismissed.

"Don't worry," Rosalba whispered in Eloísa's ear. "I'll break the law just this one time."

As Rosalba spoke, one of her aged, freckled hands landed on Eloísa's bare thigh and swiftly slid down to the woman's knee, then just as swiftly flew back to the table. She meant it as a caress, but to Eloísa it felt like the magistrate was wiping crumbs off her leg.

INSIDE HER OFFICE the magistrate walked back and forth, fighting her secret feelings for Eloísa. Was it mere physical attraction? Infatuation? Love? Whatever it was, it wasn't right. Rosalba was of the opinion that sex between two women was unnatural. She was aware that some women in her village *occasionally* slept with each other, and she'd decided that as long as they were discreet, she wouldn't meddle in their sexual affairs. That was before she saw Eloísa's breasts. Those breasts, she thought, should be New Mariquita's emblems. They should appear on New Mariquita's flag and on the coat of arms. In fact, they should be the entire coat of arms. Period. Perhaps, Rosalba thought, she shouldn't worry much about her feelings for Eloísa. After all, appreciating Eloísa's body, watching the sensual way in which Eloísa wet her lips with her tongue as she spoke, and feeling Eloísa's skin brush hers during breakfast were nothing but little sources of pleasure, like tying knots in a piece of string before weaving a shawl. Rosalba had never woven a shawl, but she had started dozens of them. It was the knotting phase that gave her pleasure; forming the little knobs along the strings of wool. Actually, weaving itself might ruin her enjoyment. Perhaps that's how she should manage the situation with Eloísa: keep doing the little things that brought her pleasure, but refrain from weaving.

She was lost in reverie when Cecilia walked into her office. "The Solórzano widow just stopped by," Cecilia said. "She came to report that one of the she-goats gave birth to a healthy kid this morning."

"Ceci, my friend, there's something I want to ask you," Rosalba said, ignoring the news. "Let's pretend that you have feelings for someone, anyone, but those feelings are of an unnatural kind. What would you do?"

"You've feelings for Eloísa, don't you?"

There was no use in denying it to her perceptive secretary. "Yes. I think . . . I think I do." Rosalba's voice was full of guilt, as though confessing to a felony.

"Eloísa seems like a very passionate and romantic woman," Cecilia stated; then she instructed Rosalba to, first, "Give her a bunch of flowers." Second, "Send her a poem written on a perfumed sheet." And third, and most importantly, "Don't tell anyone."

MEANWHILE, IN THE fields, carrying broad baskets tied around their waists Eloísa and Francisca had started picking coffee. Eloísa was a skilled coffee picker who collected a little over seventy pounds of cherries sunly, twice as much as the other coffee pickers.

"You're not asking me, but I think the magistrate is in love with you," Francisca said in a low voice. The two women were working on parallel rows. Because the trees stood between them, they could barely see each other's faces.

"You're right," Eloísa replied. "I'm not asking you."

Francisca ignored this harsh reply. "I wonder what's like to be in love with another woman," she said. "Do you think it's wrong?"

"No. Love is a beautiful thing that can never be wrong, just like hate can never be right."

Francisca fell silent. She stood quiet for a while but then, abruptly, as if her mouth could no longer contain the words, said, "Cecilia and

I are madly in love." Hearing herself say it out loud, Francisca felt liberated. "Cecilia and I are madly in love, Cecilia and I are madly in love," she repeated again and again until she saw Eloísa standing in front of her, laughing hysterically. They laid their baskets on the ground, and Francisca began telling Eloísa about her long-term romance with the magistrate's secretary. "We've been *together* for a ladder, six rungs and thirteen suns now." It had all started, Francisca said, before the New Mariquita, when she still did housework for Cecilia in exchange for room and board. "One sun, I was untangling Ceci's hair when the comb broke and a piece of it fell into her bosom. I started laughing, and we made some silly jokes about it, but then Ceci dared me to retrieve the piece of brush. I said to her, sure, but only if you let me do it with my teeth. We've been together since." And when the Communal Agreement had come into effect, Francisca said, she and Cecilia had requested to be allowed to stay together under the same roof, arguing that they got along very well and could share the house and its duties on even terms. "But there's a problem," Francisca added. "As much as I want to shout in the middle of the plaza that we're in love, Cecilia wants to keep it a secret. She thinks that what we're doing is a sin."

When Francisca finished her telling, Eloísa admitted to having deep feelings for Rosalba. "But there's no story to tell," she said. They promised each other to keep it all a secret until the circumstances were favorable for all four.

THE MAGISTRATE DECIDED to do what her secretary had suggested, except she inverted the order of the steps. A poem, she thought, would be the perfect way to start courting Eloísa. She spent the entire afternoon shut away in her house, writing and rewriting love verses. Before going to bed, she read them and decided that they were nothing but a rhyming list of the things she liked about Eloísa. She tried writing them again, and again she came up with a list, different from the first, even melodious, but a list nonetheless. She sat on the edge of her bed and tried to call to mind any poems she might have learned or heard during the course of her life. She remembered but two: patriotic, repetitious pieces she had recited in school.

If she had gone to sleep any sooner, she might never have thought of the verses that her late husband had written to her when he started courting her. Rosalba had kept them along with old letters and telegrams he'd sent her on the few occasions he went away. She was convinced that those yellowish pieces of paper would be the only proof future generations would have that men had once inhabited the village now known as New Mariquita. She pulled a sturdy chest from under her bed, unlocked it and looked through the writings, being careful not to crumple or tear up any of the priceless documents. The letters were dull, but the poems still captivated her. They gave her a yearning desire to love and be loved again. One in particular caught her attention, for she thought it described her feelings toward Eloísa much more beautifully and clearly than anything she could ever write. It was a two-stanza poem entitled "Say You Do," neatly written in cursive calligraphy and signed, "Yours Faithfully, Napoleón."

Rosalba copied the poem word for word onto a lavender-perfumed sheet of paper. When she finished, she rolled up the sheet, tied it with a red ribbon and put it in a drawer. Then she went to sleep, and she slept soundly.

Ubaldina, First Sun of Transition

The incessant ringing of the church bell announced the beginning of the four-sun term called Transition. Female time required that on the first sun of Transition, women write their personal goals for the next calendar rung and allow time for self-evaluation.

On this morning Eloísa was awoken not by the bell but by heavy knocks on her bedroom door. Before she had a chance to respond, her boarder entered the bedroom.

"The magistrate stopped by earlier and asked me to give this to you," the old woman said, tossing the rolled-up sheet on the bed. Then she shut the door with a slam and disappeared quickly to avoid the daily scolding about how she seemed to enjoy slamming doors.

Eloísa hastened to untie the ribbon and read the poem.

SAY YOU DO
(A poem dedicated to the very graceful Eloísa)

Your charms have defeated me,
my darling, I need to know,
do you love me, do you love me,
as much as I do love you?

Please say you do,
say you'll be mine forever,
say you love me, say you need me,
and the skies we'll reach together.

Yours faithfully,
Rosalba viuda de Patiño
(Magistrate of the village of New Mariquita)

Eloísa read it three times, and each time she wept with joy. Anybody who could express her feelings in such a romantic way had to be a great lover. Like the magistrate, Eloísa, too, kept the letters and poems that Marco Tulio, her late husband, had written to her. She believed that love letters and poems, like flowers, shouldn't be simply thrown away but replaced with fresh ones, and before this morning she hadn't been given a fresh love letter or poem, much less a bunch of daisies to replace her withered ones.

After reading the poem, Eloísa decided that this morning she wouldn't make a phony Rosalba out of her pillows and blankets. She got out of bed promptly and danced all the way to the patio, holding on to an invisible partner.

* * *

LATER ON, IN the coffee fields, Eloísa told Francisca the news about the poem Rosalba had sent her. They chuckled and made little jokes about it like a couple of schoolgirls. "I always thought the magistrate was an insensitive woman," Francisca confessed, "but after hearing what she wrote to you, I have no doubt that she's passionate and romantic." And then she told Eloísa the two things she needed to do: First, "Reply to her poem with a poem of your own written on a perfumed sheet." And second, "Give her a bunch of fresh flowers."

SITTING AT HER desk in her office the magistrate had begun writing her personal goals for the next calendar rung: *One: Have Eloísa be the last thing I see when I go to bed. Two: Have Eloísa be the first thing I see when I wake up.*

Oh, but that couldn't be. Her two goals implied sleeping with Eloísa and quite possibly having sex, and that, she remembered, would be as bad as weaving a shawl. Unless, of course, Eloísa and she slept together without touching. Or maybe they could touch just a little: an arm might brush against another arm; a leg might gently rub against another leg; their lips, slightly pursed, might touch softly and at once part without making that smacking sound that would turn it into a kiss. *No kisses.* A kiss was the equivalent of lacing two strings together, and Rosalba had no interest in weaving. *Thank you very much.*

As she thought of her goals, the magistrate became more anxious and confused. She hadn't heard back from Eloísa, and her concern was growing into a fear of rejection that she hadn't experienced since she was a maiden. Perhaps she had been precipitate in sending the poem. Maybe Cecilia had been right, and Rosalba should have given Eloísa the flowers first. Or maybe all of it had been a big mistake, and Rosalba should never have entertained the idea that Eloísa, a handsome younger woman with splendid breasts, would be interested in sleeping with an older and graceless thing with sparse graying hair and a large behind.

She arose and stood looking out through the window at the distant fields of maize and rice. None of that had been there two ladders ago. Back then, all she could see from her window was misery and desolation. She remembered that for several Transitions she had the same single goal on her list, *To see from my office window a field full of large golden ears of corn*, at a time when most villagers' goals were to find the strength to leave Mariquita and start a new life somewhere else, or to find their old husbands or new ones.

Back then all Rosalba had needed to achieve her goal was a pair of strong hands and determination. But now it was different. In order to accomplish her present goals, she thought, she would need youth and charms she no longer possessed. How could she compete with the beauty and grace of younger women like Virgelina Saavedra?

She was weeping by the window when she heard a knock on the door, followed by the creak of rusty hinges, followed by small footsteps, followed by a question asked in a hesitant voice that Rosalba didn't recognize: "Magistrate, are you in there?"

Rosalba wiped the tears from her eyes with the heel of her hand. "Who is it?"

"Francisca, Magistrate. Can I come in?" The last time Francisca had been to Rosalba's office, she'd been seeking advice after having found a fortune under her bed.

"What do you need?" the magistrate shouted from inside her office, but Francisca was already opening the door that led to it. "Shouldn't you be working on your personal goals, Francisca?"

"I only came to give you this," she said, handing her a folded piece of paper.

"What is it?"

"It's a note from Eloísa, Magistrate, but I swear I don't know what it says."

Rosalba snatched it from her and tossed it in a drawer. "Well, thank you much," she said matter-of-factly. "Now, if you will excuse me, I have goals to write."

Rosalba waited to hear the door being closed, then took the folded note out of the drawer and read it.

KISS ME GENTLY
(This poem is dedicated, with all my heart, to the always beautiful and jo-vial Rosalba viuda de Patiño, magistrate of the village of New Mariquita)

Last night I dreamed of your kisses
Oh! Your kisses were so sweet
that when I opened my eyes
I found sugar on my lips

I can't wait until night falls
hence I'm going to take a nap
if only in my dreams you kiss me,
kiss me gently, don't wake me up.

Very truly yours,
Eloísa viuda de Cifuentes
Identity Card # 79.454.248 from Ibagué.

Rosalba read the poem, then brought the piece of paper close to her bosom in a tender fashion. "She likes me," she said. "Of course she likes me. I'm a fine woman." How could a smart woman like Eloísa resist spending a night with Rosalba? How could she not notice that the magistrate was bright and brave, loving and neat? And no, Rosalba's breasts weren't really that flabby, not for her age anyway. And yes, her behind was large indeed, but so was her heart.

Ubaldina, Second Sun of Transition

On the second sun of Transition women were expected to share their goals with a sponsor of their own choosing referred to as a madrina, who was expected to advise her protégé on how to carry out her goals.

At their home, a two-room house with two front windows covered with thick curtains that were permanently closed, Cecilia and Francisca lay in their pushed-together beds, sharing their goals with each other.

"My new goal is to make it public that we're in love," Francisca said.

Cecilia sat upright and stilted on her bed, her face turned toward her lover. "Francisca, we have talked about this before, haven't we? Whatever happens in this house is nobody's business. If you mention our secret to anyone, I swear to God you'll regret it. You've been warned, and that's that!"

But that wasn't that. Francisca rose and stood in front of Cecilia with her arms crossed over her chest and her right leg slightly forward. "I told Eloísa," she said.

Cecilia rose to face Francisca, panting. "How dared you tell Eloísa about us after I told you not to? María Francisca Ticora Rodríguez viuda de Gómez, you've betrayed my trust." She started walking back and forth across the room, holding her head between her hands. Then, from a corner, she said, "I will never forgive you." And soon afterward, from the opposite corner, she added bitterly, "And I won't ever again rub your dirty feet."

"Good!" Francisca replied, arms akimbo. "You're lousy at it anyway. And now that's that!" She stormed out of the room.

And, at least for that sun, that was really that.

ELOÍSA AND ROSALBA had gone out, separately, to pick flowers for each other. Eloísa remembered that the daisies her husband tucked between her breasts came from the Jaramillo widow's front yard, so she went to the same place. As she cut the flowers, she visualized her long, delicate fingers placing each flower between the magistrate's breasts, in the same tender way Marco Tulio had laid them in her cleavage. When she had enough daisies, she decided to personally deliver the bunch to the magistrate's house.

While picking orchids in the woods, it occurred to Rosalba that

Eloísa might be of the same thinking as Napoleón, her late husband. He had never picked flowers for Rosalba but instead gave her flowerpots with violets in bloom. "If God had wanted flowers to be used as accessories," he used to say, "He would have made them grow behind women's ears." In her courtyard Rosalba had violets, camellias and begonias. She would take the one with the most flowers to Eloísa.

VACA STOOD STILL beneath an aloe that was perpetually suspended above the door for good luck. Except for her prominent jawbone—always working—nothing about her moved. She had truly become the embodiment of her nickname. Her real name was of Indian extraction: long and unpronounceable. People knew her as Vaca, but in her presence they called her only Doña.

"Buenas y santas, Doña," Eloísa greeted her in a melodious voice.

Vaca lowered her big eyes and fixed them on the bunch of daisies that Eloísa held against her breasts. "What can I do for you?"

"I'm here to see the magistrate."

Vaca considered this for a moment, then said, "The magistrate's got an office and a secretary. Rosalba's got a house and a boarder. Which one are you looking for?"

"I'm looking for Rosalba."

"She's not here."

"Would you give her these daisies for me?"

Without making an audible reply, Vaca took the bunch of flowers away from Eloísa and swiftly turned around and went into the house.

"Please keep them in fresh water!" Eloísa shouted from the door, but the voluminous figure had already disappeared from sight.

THE MAGISTRATE'S DELIVERY of the plant to Eloísa's house was not a pleasant experience either.

"Quit banging the door, for God's sake!" the Pérez widow roared from inside the house before appearing in the doorway. Rosalba stood on the steps, holding with both hands a large flowerpot that contained a small camellia tree blooming with showy yellow-colored flowers. The Pérez widow, fully dressed, looked up and down at the naked magistrate and rolled her eyes. "Yes?"

"I'm here to see Eloísa, Señora Pérez."

Señora Pérez brought her clenched hands to her waist and gave Rosalba a disapproving look. "Is that it? You interrupted my prayers because you want to talk with Eloísa?"

"Actually, I want to give her this camellia tree. Isn't it beautiful?"

The Pérez widow heaved an impatient sigh. "Eloísa's not here, so you and your bush can go look for her someplace else."

"I'd rather leave the tree with you. If you don't mind, that is."

"Well, I do," the woman snapped. "Bring it in yourself and put it wherever it pleases you." She went inside, muttering trifling complaints.

Rosalba laid the flowerpot in the hallway and left.

Ubaldina, Third Sun of Transition

In the beginning of female time, the magistrate and the schoolmistress had insisted that on the third sun of Transition, each woman find something about herself that made her unhappy and apply her mind to it. But the women decided against it, claiming that unless a woman's traits affected her relations with others, she should simply accept herself the way she was. Rosalba and Cleotilde weren't happy with the decision, but since the majority had agreed on it, they let it go. As a result of that, on the third sun of Transition the villagers had half a sun for themselves.

Rosalba knew that in her spare time Eloísa liked to go swimming. On her way to the river, Rosalba imagined Eloísa coming out of the water, the sun shining on her wet skin, her long black hair dripping cool water down her back. Once there, Rosalba stood on the bank, next to a large rock, scanning the clear waters for the woman she wanted to see. She made out five heads floating on the surface like large bubbles, the bodies connected to them distorted in the water. Eloísa wasn't one of them.

"Get into the water, Magistrate," Virgelina Saavedra called. "It's nice and warm."

Rosalba waved at her and smiled but didn't move. She felt unsure of herself in the girl's presence. Virgelina, the gaunt little girl who'd once put a stop to el padre Rafael's Procreation Campaign, had grown into the most beautiful woman in Mariquita. Rosalba resolved to go back home, but when she turned around, she saw Eloísa coming down the road.

"I didn't know you liked swimming, Magistrate," Eloísa said.

"Oh, I love swimming. I just never bring myself to do it."

"Well, let's swim, then."

Rosalba soon found herself surrounded by six women younger than herself, which made her very uncomfortable. She kept her body as low as she could and raised nothing but her head from the water; not even her arms, because suddenly she was all too aware of the stubborn wiggles of loose skin that hung from her underarms. Her body, she remembered nostalgically, was the same body that once had driven the three bachelors of Mariquita wild, to the point that they tossed a coin to decide who would have the chance to approach Rosalba first. It was the same body that kept her husband Napoleón home, next to her, while most married men were getting drunk at El Rincón de Gardel, or visiting the prostitutes of La Casa de Emilia. That body was now older, softer, grown a little square and wider at the hips. What a mistake this had been, coming to the river! She wanted to dissolve into the water. But she couldn't, so she let the current take her down a little farther from the group. Eloísa followed her.

"Thank you for the beautiful camellia, Magistrate." The clear water covered her body up to a little underneath her breasts, accentuating their shape and color.

"Thank *you* for the poem and for the beautiful daisies, Eloísa. And please, call me Rosalba."

"I'd like to call you something else."

Rosalba blushed. "And what would that be?"

"I don't know . . . maybe Corazoncito?"

"Ha, ha!" Rosalba wiped the excess water off her face with both hands. "I think I'd prefer it if you made up a word. A word that's just for me."

"But why? Corazoncito must be the sweetest word in the whole world."

"In the world you created with Marco Tulio," Rosalba replied, feeling somewhat jealous of Eloísa's dead husband.

Eloísa considered this for a moment. "You're right," she said. "I never thought about it that way. How about . . . Ticú? No, Ticuticú? How about Ticuticú?"

"Ticuticú? Does it mean anything?"

"I just made it up. It means my sweetheart, darling Rosalba."

"Well, then I love it."

Eloísa laid her hands on Rosalba's shoulders, and at the count of three, they submerged themselves together in the water, like little girls. Eloísa cupped her hands and gently slid them down to Rosalba's breasts, which floated round and smooth in the water, and it was precious and extraordinary to discover how well hands and breasts fit each other. Eloísa's fingers pressed, feeling the throbbing of Rosalba's flesh, then let go, leaving on them ten slight indentations that presently vanished on the paleness of Rosalba's skin.

Their heads now rose above the water, and their lips quivered as they smiled at each other nervously. Under the water their hands joined, taking turns to stroke and be stroked, fast, clumsily, acting on a wild impulse they could contain no more: Eloísa and Rosalba were two widows in love.

Ubaldina, Fourth Sun of Transition

On the last sun of Transition nobody worked. Not even the cooks: the villagers were encouraged to eat fresh fruits and raw vegetables. At sundown, everyone was asked to come to the plaza to take part in a celebration that honored femaleness. Feeling restless in her bed, Rosalba decided that she was in no mood for celebrations. She had come to realize that her feelings for Eloísa were much stronger than she'd originally thought, and it filled her with fear and some anger. For ladders her obsession with tying little knots in a string without ever weaving a shawl had worked just fine, but when she'd tried to apply the same notion to her feelings for Eloísa, she discovered that doing the little things that brought her pleasure alone, without wanting to go further, was simply impossible. She now wanted to make beautiful love to her. But it was unnatural. *Is it really?* And she was the magistrate, a public figure. *But I have feelings just like anyone else.* She spent the entire sun in bed, trying to come up with a solution to her problem. Eventually she did.

Every rung a different household was in charge of organizing the celebration. Tonight it was the Ospinas, and they had exceeded all expectations. The plaza was brightly lit, its four sides surrounded by tallow candles and festooned with chains of flowers: purple orchids, yellow daisies and white lilies dangled from the lowest branches of the mango trees.

When the women arrived, they split up into four groups that at first glance appeared to have been improvised, but that in reality had long ago been determined by the women themselves in direct ratio to their ages, and, less frequently, according to the type of work they did, their liking of potatoes or their disliking of onions, the number or kinds of maladies that constantly affected them, and many more factors.

The actual celebration was quite predictable, and this rung's wasn't an exception. It started, like it always did, with a drink. The women stood in line to get a full cup of chicha from the Villegas widow. The widow prepared the fermented maize drink at least five suns prior to the event to ensure its characteristic sharp, peppery flavor. Next, as always, the schoolmistress made everyone yawn by reading poems by some Alfonsina Storny. When Cleotilde was finished, the attention focused on Francisca, who entertained the audience with her usual jokes and imitations. "Do the teacher," a woman would say, and Francisca would walk slowly with her back straight and her neck thrust forward, twirling an invisible mustache with two of her fingers. On this occasion, Francisca did the Pérez widow, Vaca, Julia Morales, the magistrate and, though no one requested it, a woman that was long gone: Doña Emilia, the town's madam. The music was by the four Morales sisters' "band." The girls only knew half a dozen tunes, which they played over and over with their curious instruments made of old cooking pots and pans and lids. The women sang along and danced to the band's lively rhythm. When the music stopped, the four groups of women quickly settled down to listen to the magistrate's customary discourse. She always started with the same sentence: "A new rung is about to begin, and with it comes a new opportunity to improve ourselves as individuals. . . ." By now most women had memorized it.

Rosalba rose from within the crowd and advanced slowly toward the front row, from where she was to deliver her speech. Before leaving her house, she had coated her entire body with eucalyptus-scented oil to repel the mosquitoes and other insects. As she walked among the women, the flickering light of the tallow candles reflected all over her shiny skin, making her look like a mythical goddess about to go up in flames.

She stood in front of the crowd, a blissful look on her face, and began talking:

"I'd like to express my gratitude toward the Ospina family for the effort they put into organizing this term's celebration of womanhood." The variation of her speech aroused the immediate suspicion of the villagers that the magistrate was up to something. "I don't think our plaza has ever looked as beautiful or felt as cozy as it does tonight." She looked around, smiling gracefully at the chains of assorted flowers hanging from the trees. "I'd also like to make an announcement," she continued. The villagers were now certain that Rosalba was about to surprise them with a shocking statement: maybe an outrageous new decree. They held their breath and listened attentively.

"I'm in love with Eloísa," she said, plainly and simply, holding her head up high. The crowd stared at her in stunned silence, then started bowing their heads, slowly, as though with growing shame.

"And I'm in love with Rosalba," Eloísa shouted from the back. The women turned their heads, again slowly, toward where the voice had originated. Their prying eyes followed Eloísa as she walked toward Rosalba and planted a kiss on her mouth.

"I'm in love with Cecilia," Francisca said out loud.

This time the women turned their heads not toward the confessed lover, but toward her woman. The pressure was such that Cecilia had no alternative but to stand up and, with her eyes fixed on the ground, admit to her sin: "I'm . . . in love with . . . with Francisca."

"Virgelina and I are also in love," Magnolia Morales declared. Both women rose to their feet and each put her arm around the other's waist, smiling.

"And so are Erlinda and I," said Nurse Ramírez. She extended her hand to the Calderón widow, and together they rose from the ground.

Other couples timidly disclosed their secrets, and when they ceased, a few single women started declaring their love for one another. The feeling was so contagious that some decided, at that very moment, that they were in love with the women sitting next to them and told them so. Even the ancient women, who hadn't loved or been loved in ages, felt once again the strength of passion burning in their shrunk bodies.

The new couples as well as the old ones slowly began to disappear behind doors or vanish into the darkness of the night. And the few women who remained single, whether it was their choice or not, soon went back to their houses, to their bedrooms with their empty beds and clean sheets that would never get stained with blood or perspiration other than their own.

Only Santiago Marín and Julia Morales remained in the plaza, surrounded by orchids, daisies and lilies, and by the dying flames of tallow candles. They lay on the ground gazing at the sky, waiting for the twinkling light of a star to shine so that they could make a wish. And when the stars finally came into sight, Santiago wished that somesun, somewhere, he could be reunited with Pablo. Julia wished for the sun when she, too, could shout, like the women had done tonight, that she was in love—only with a man.

The flames of the candles surrounding the plaza died one by one, each with a hissing sound and a rapid succession of blue and yellow sparks.

The melting tallow solidified on the ground, leaving behind a strong smell of burned fat that presently dissolved into the thin air.

And the night, now full of stars, swallowed the fierce moaning of New Mariquita's passionate women, and the gentle murmuring of its widows in love.

Gerardo García, 21
Right-wing paramilitary soldier

A mass grave had been dug, and most of our enemies' bodies thrown into it. Only a dismembered corpse still lay on the ground waiting to be accounted for. I was on my knees beside it. A little farther to my right, smoking a cigarette, there was "Matasiete," a commander who was notorious for his harshness. (He was a war machine who killed guerrillas and then sat to eat his ration next to their dead bodies.) My job was to strip the bodies, check them for dog tags or ID cards, birthmarks, eye and hair colors and other distinctions, and report them to Matasiete, who wrote these findings in a large notebook for our own records.

The corpse I now had in front of me was small, a boy's. It was missing both legs from the knees down and the left arm, and I couldn't make out much about the face, which was completely smashed. "Young," I said to Matasiete. "Seventeen, maybe younger." The jacket pockets were empty, but a Swiss Army knife hidden on the belt had miraculously survived the soldiers' search for valuables. I slipped it into my pocket.

"Strip it down," Matasiete said indifferently. I removed the boy's tattered jacket and what was left of his pants. Most of his torso was smeared with dried blood. A small, laminated image of a baby Jesus was hanging from a cord around his neck. It wasn't unusual (we soldiers carry all sorts of charms and amulets), except this one looked exactly like mine: the same size and length, the same brown leather cord, and, affixed to its back, the same black-and-white photograph of my mother.

My mother had given my little brother and me identical charms when we were younger to protect us from misfortune. I suddenly felt a lump in my throat. He'd only just turned sixteen. (When had he joined our enemies' ranks? Why hadn't I stayed in touch with him?) I couldn't admit to Matasiete that he was my brother—I'd have been labeled as a guerrilla informer and most likely executed—but I also couldn't let my brother become just one more "unidentified person" on our ever-increasing list.

"García Vidales," I mumbled, pretending to be reading a dog tag.

"What? Speak louder," Matasiete commanded.

I choked back, waited a little, then said, "García Vidales Juan Diego. Born 1982." My voice shook a little. Matasiete wrote down the information and got up and motioned for me to dump the body into the grave. I suddenly wanted to smell flowers, marigold and carnations, because my little brother was about to be buried, and that was what Christian burials smelled like. I only smelled blood and death.

"Forgive me, Dieguito," I whispered. I knew he could hear me. I dragged him to the edge by his only arm and gave him a gentle push with the tips of my fingers. I watched his body tumble down the wall and land awkwardly on top of his comrades.

Then I began shoveling dirt over his grave, saying the Lord's Prayer in my head.

CHAPTER 13

The Curious Gringo

New Mariquita, Francisca 20, Ladder 1996

ALL MORNING LONG JULIA Morales had been lying in a hammock slung between two trees in the middle of the plaza, twirling her hair around one finger, taking deep breaths, looking south. She wore a tight, faded blue dress that exposed her thighs. From time to time she swung, giving a lazy push from the ground with one of her delicate feet. Once, when a beam of sunlight struck her face, she got up and carried one side of the hammock to a different tree, then lay down again, staring longingly south, the direction the smell was coming from.

One by one her three older sisters had come around to tell her to stop fantasizing and go to work. "Smell? What smell?" her oldest sister Orquidea asked harshly. "The only thing I smell is your laziness." Gardenia took a more aggressive approach: "Get up right now, you sluggard cow. I'll give you something to smell. Here, smell this," she said, showing Julia her naked posterior. And Magnolia, who had the faculty of viewing everything in relation to herself, said, "I don't smell anything. If there were something to smell, I would've been the first one to smell it."

Julia was not in the least troubled by what her sisters said. She knew what she smelled, even if no one else could detect it: a robust, slightly acrid, alluring, pungent mixture of lime peels, mineral salts, perspiration and musk . . . large amounts of musk. The smell filled the air, getting stronger as the sun wore on. She had no doubt that a man was approaching town, and she was determined to be the first one to welcome him to the village of New Mariquita.

*   *   *

THE AMERICAN REPORTER wore a pale guayabera shirt that was large on him and a pair of loose khaki trousers hacked off below the knees, fraying at the edges. A canteen half filled with water was slung over his left shoulder. His hair was long and yellow and greasy and gathered in a ponytail, and he had two weeks' growth of flaxen stubble. His sneakers were nearly hidden under coats of fresh and old mud that made it impossible to tell their color or brand name. His feet were blistered, the left one badly, causing him to walk with a limp. There was an air of refinement and intellect about his face, a severely sunburned face with sky-blue eyes and a small nose. He had been traveling the country for the past six months, interviewing guerrilla, paramilitary and national army soldiers, as well as civilians touched by the Colombian conflict. He was thirty-one and answered to the name of Gordon Smith.

Walking ahead of him were a barefoot boy and a scrawny mule loaded with a medium-sized yellow duffel bag. The boy liked to be called Pito, and his mule was Pita. Pito wore a sombrero with a chewed-off brim and ragged shorts. Nothing else.

"Slow down," Gordon shouted to Pito. "Please."

"We're almost there, Don Míster Gordo," the boy said. He stood with his legs splayed, anchored in glutinous orange mud, wondering why the funny-talking gringo insisted on being called "Gordo" when he wasn't fat.

Gordon looked at his watch; they had been riding for almost seven hours. "I've heard you say that three times before," he replied, shooting the boy a suspicious glance.

Pito ignored both the comment and the look. "Sure you don't want to ride Pita again? She's a little old but still very strong."

"Gracias." Gordon shook his head. Riding the beast had made him nervous and dizzy, but he was too proud to admit it. Instead he'd told the boy that the mule didn't look strong at all and that he felt sorry for it, which was true enough. Pita looked starved, weak-legged and poorly watered, and had a loose shoe on her right rear foot.

They continued their journey up and down the hills, among long stretches of woods and through narrow, rarely used trails that crisscrossed capriciously and often turned to sludge, making the journey even more unpredictable and puzzling. From time to time Gordon pulled out of his shirt pocket a scrap of paper with a poorly drawn map of the region they were passing through. He stared at it, turned it upside down, looked around and put it back in his pocket.

Only two days before, while interviewing a Communist guerrilla defector in the village of Villahermosa, Gordon had been introduced to an older, neurotic, pink-faced man who claimed to know of a tribe of ferocious female warriors living in a small village deep in the cordillera. Intrigued, Gordon agreed to buy him a few drinks in exchange for the telling of the entire story.

"They're Amazons," the crazy-looking man said while biting his nails in a compulsive manner. "Listen to this: pigs, cows and horses have disappeared, but also men like you and I. Uh-huh, all vanished from the face of the earth after being seen near where those creatures live. Country people are terrified of them. Entire Indian tribes have moved far south to avoid them. Even guerrillas and paramilitary groups don't go near them. Believe me when I tell you, gringo. They're direct descendants of the Amazons." The story turned even more fantastic with each beer the man drank. By the time their meeting ended, Gordon, somewhat drunk, had made up his mind to go out into the cordillera to look for a tribe of grotesque, man-hating, heretic, cannibalistic women of gigantic proportions.

The next day, after sobering up, Gordon recognized that the story was preposterous. Even so, there was something in it that fascinated him, something that seemed perfectly plausible in a country that had been at war for nearly forty years: the existence of a town inhabited solely by women. He went to the neurotic old man's house and paid him to draw a map of the area supposedly inhabited by the tribe. Then he hired a boy and a mule to take him there.

At the moment, after a seven-hour ride, Gordon thought the map looked the same from every angle. Fortunately, Pito didn't need a map. He knew all the paths and shortcuts from having led cattle along them since he was a child, and from spending the last four years delivering secret coded mail between the groups of guerrillas scattered throughout the mountainous region. He'd been the fastest, most reliable courier the guerrillas had had. But recently, the heavy presence of the national army had forced the rebels to abandon the zone, leaving Pito out of work, which is why he had agreed to take Gordon across the mountains in the first place.

They had ridden a good distance when they reached an expanse of level land. The mule hastened its pace and soon Pito saw why: a thin stream ran almost soundlessly along the flat. They washed their faces and drank some water, which had a metallic taste.

"Well, this is it," Pito said. "See those woods over there?" He pointed to a tight clump of trees and shrubs at the end of an impressively steep rise.

"What is it?" Gordon asked, squinting to better see what the boy was pointing at.

"The entrance! That man said it was at the end of the first rise after the Tres Cruces flat. This is the Tres Cruces flat, so that must be the entrance over there."

Gordon contemplated the sight for a moment. "It looks like we're going to need machetes or something to get through it. It seems almost impenetrable."

"Don Míster Gordo," Pito said, adopting a solemn tone. "You hired me to get you up to this spot right here in one piece, not to help you go across."

The little bastard wants more money, Gordon thought. He produced from within his crotch a small plastic bag where he kept, rolled up and secured with a thick rubber band, a wad of bank notes. He began undoing the bundle.

When the boy realized what the gringo was doing, he shook his head. "I'm not going in there no matter how much money you give me. I've been told what's over there. Those women eat people like you and me for dinner."

Gordon gave a loud laugh. "Don't tell me you believe all that."

"I do. And you better believe it yourself. You don't know nothing about this country." With a dignified expression on his small Indian face, he unloaded Pita and handed the duffel bag to Gordon.

After muchas graciases were exchanged and hands grasped and shaken several times, Pito stepped aside. He watched Gordon slowly limp up the steep rise with the bag on his back. "God be with you, Don Míster Gordo," he whispered to himself. He walked over to Pita and took the reins, but he didn't mount. He kept staring at Gordon, hoping the gringo would see reason and choose to return to town. If he did, Pito decided, he'd take him back for half the price.

But Gordon didn't stop. He hadn't come this far to flinch at the last minute. Besides, he needed a new story, something interesting and exciting. It was with this thought in his head that he began tearing his way through the undergrowth, ripping at the vines with his own large and delicate hands, pushing into the thick tangle of leaves and branches and woody material until he disappeared into it.

*   *   *

DURING BREAKFAST THAT morning, Doña Victoria viuda de Morales had made excuses for her daughter with Rosalba by saying that Julia didn't feel well. Her other three daughters, she promised, would do Julia's work in the communal kitchen until she recovered.

Orquidea protested in private: "So I have to toil all morning at the joiner's workshop, and still come during my break to do that loafer's work?"

"That's right," Doña Victoria asserted, and then, slamming a basket full of red onions on the counter, she added, "Here, chop these before you go."

Orquidea had recently been transferred from her mother's kitchen to the joiner's workshop as part of a new campaign started by the council of New Mariquita, which consisted of training every worker to perform several different tasks. Gardenia had been sent to the fields and Magnolia assigned to follow the roof-patching team. Julia, however, had been allowed to stay doing kitchen work, because Doña Victoria convinced the five council members that it was Julia's special touch that made each and every dish from her kitchen so scrumptious.

Julia Morales, the most beautiful of the four Morales girls, was despised by her sisters on account of her good looks. She had big, rounded hazel eyes flecked with gray, which glowed against her brown skin. Her nose was small and lightly turned up at the tip, like a doll's, and her lips full and well-defined. Her gait was so spectacular that watching her walk unescorted around the plaza was often the most anticipated event of the sun. Julia was taller than most of the women in town, and she had the most refined manners. She also had beautiful black hair that rippled in long waves to her waist, and a large penis hanging between her legs.

Julia's astounding transformation was the product of her own self-discipline, perseverance and dedication. She'd spent entire suns following her mother and sisters, paying great attention to how they moved, adopting and improving on their feminine mannerisms. And although Julia couldn't articulate any sounds, she listened intently to her sisters' speech patterns, which she translated into a series of smooth and delicate motions of her body and limbs. The result was an exquisite and precise sign language that to the eyes of a foreigner might have seemed as though Julia Morales was performing a mysterious dance from a faraway land.

*   *   *

FROM WHERE HE stood, Gordon saw a dreamlike village of white houses with bright tile roofs of orange and red, flowering mango trees, a few well-defined roads and a church, the spire of which broke the otherwise perfect harmony of the view. Green hills rose behind the village; several plots of maize, rice and coffee and the runners of potato plants dotted the stretch of fields on the hillsides.

There were no Amazons in sight, or women, or anything that resembled either. Gordon looked at the palms of his hands: they were bleeding. His lacerated arms and legs and ripped pants also testified to his struggle through the thick undergrowth. He wiped his hands on the front of his guayabera shirt and felt the bloody wounds chafing against the fabric. His face was unharmed; he had used his duffel bag to protect it from the strong prickly vines and the gigantic leaves covered in bristles that repeatedly bounced back.

Moving slowly forward, Gordon heard distant shouts and female laughter, but he didn't see anyone. He noticed that the height of the dwellings was standard, which clearly eliminated the remote possibility of running into a giant. He kept descending the hill, cautiously, considering what he would say when he met the first group of women, and wondering what kind of reception they would give him. They'd certainly be stunned, but would they welcome him or greet him with contempt? And what if they asked the reason why he was there? Should he admit to being a reporter? That might get them on the defensive. Maybe he should claim to be lost and show them his bloody hands; surely they wouldn't hurt an injured man.

By this time he had entered the village and was limping along a small street. The houses he passed by were all uniform: they had white facades with a front door and a large window, the frames of which were painted green. All doors and windows were open, and Gordon had the odd feeling he was being watched through the curtains. He could no longer hear the shouts and laughter he'd heard earlier. Suddenly he saw something move farther down the road: a large bundle hanging between two trees with something alive in it. Gordon kept going, a little apprehensively, looking behind him again and again. Before reaching the corner he made out that the bundle was a hammock with a handsome woman sleeping in it. Gordon drew near her, moving slowly and silently because he didn't want to wake her up. At that moment he heard a loud cry from behind. When he looked back he saw an army of naked women rushing out of their dwellings, screaming furiously and running toward him with sticks and stones.

WHEN GORDON WOKE up, he saw nothing but the dazzling white of a ceiling. He thought he was dead, his soul floating on air, among clouds. Little by little he began tracing in his mind the sequence of events leading up to this moment. The woman in the hammock. The cry. The army of naked screaming women. Then blackness.

So, where was he now? There was only one answer: the women had captured him, and he was in prison.

Faint sunlight came through two small windows set at irregular intervals. Still dizzy, Gordon brought himself to a sitting position and examined his body. They hadn't hurt him; he had no new wounds or injuries, and he could move all his limbs. He looked around and saw a large and empty space. It didn't look at all like a jailhouse. Actually, it looked more like a church, but with no benches, crosses, statues or religious images of any kind. The walls were utterly stripped, and the cement floor, where Gordon lay, was impeccably clean and smelled of lavender. Lying there in his dirty clothes and shoes, with his wounds still oozing blood, Gordon thought he was the only untidy element in the room.

Realizing that he was alone, he rose and started for the door, holding onto the walls for support. He bent a little to look outside through the small metal grating, and his eyes opened wide at an extraordinary sight: a large crowd of naked women standing across the street, jabbering away in undertones. Some of them held hands like sweethearts. A smaller group of five older women, four of them naked, were going through the contents of Gordon's duffel bag. He watched one of them take out his T-shirts one by one and hold them up to the light like film negatives, then pass them on to the other women. They didn't seem interested in Gordon's mini tape recorder. They examined it from all sides, shrugged and set it aside, unable to explain its use. A can of Coca-Cola, however, caused a sensation. They held it horizontally, with two hands, and rotated it, giving big approving smiles. Gordon watched this process with genuine curiosity, but also wariness.

A deafening cry sounded, and all heads, including Gordon's, turned toward the source of it. The roar came from the young girl in the tight blue dress that he'd seen sleeping in the hammock earlier. Two women took hold of the girl while a third tried to muzzle her with a handkerchief. The girl wriggled like a worm, kicked and gnashed her teeth and made wild guttural sounds. Gordon thought she was stunning. Suddenly the girl stopped struggling, her wrath turning into a long, disconsolate wail. Exhausted from restraining her, the two women relaxed their grip. The girl immediately freed herself from them, knocking them to the ground in the process. Then she ran toward the front door of the church.

Gordon had just enough time to step aside before the girl violently pushed the door open. She cast a quick glance over the long, empty room, and when she spotted him, she threw herself upon him, locked her hands around his neck and passionately kissed him on the mouth. At that moment, the other women began entering the building in small clusters, pushing and shoving for the chance to see close up the blue-eyed foreigner while the rebellious girl clung to him like a limpet.

"Julia Morales," a matron of majestic proportions and broad hips shouted, elbowing her way through the crowd. "Let go of the Míster and step aside. Now!" The girl did both, not without frowning and pursing her lips together. The matron stood arms akimbo in front of Gordon, who was frozen.

"Who are you where do you come from who sent you and what brought you here?" she said, all at once, as if all four questions were of equal significance.

Gordon said nothing. He was so astonished and bewildered that he couldn't have articulated anything in his own language, much less in Spanish. Instead he observed with curiosity the women's harmonious nakedness—their tan breasts that ended in large, chocolate-colored nipples; their long torsos and dark stomachs, some flat, some prominent; their pubes hardly covered by short, dark hair and their smooth and solid limbs. He thought that they were an exquisite race.

"Well?" the wide-hipped woman said, her face turned to the crowd, "it looks like our friend here is mute."

Only then did Gordon realize that she was one of the five women who had been going through his bag. She had an indisputable air of authority and determination. If she could display those attributes while in the nude, he reasoned, she had to be the law. "I'm not mute," he replied in a conciliatory tone.

"Ohhhh!" the crowd whispered in unison.

"Then who are you?" the woman asked again.

"Name's Gordon Smith," he replied. A few giggles came from the spectators.

"Come with me to the municipal office, Señor Esmís," the same woman said. "You must state your business to our community's council."

She walked ahead, forcing the nosy women to clear the way. Gordon limped behind her, his muscles, joints and bones hurting. This time he noticed, with growing admiration, the small plaza shaded by massive mango trees and surrounded by wooden benches, half of them facing east, the other half facing west; the homogenous style of the houses, their chalky facades and bright floral decorations hanging from windows; the cleanliness of the sidewalks and unpaved roads. And amid these almost utopian sights appeared the girl named Julia. She walked along with the crowd, slightly ahead of Gordon, from time to time glancing at him over her shoulder in a coquettish fashion. Her features, he thought, were refined and delicate, like those of the women of his own race. But there was something wild, almost bestial, in her rounded hazel eyes flecked with gray, something especially alluring about her thick blue-black hair and shiny brown skin. He wished that she, too, were naked.

WHEN HE ENTERED the building, Gordon glanced around quickly. There were two rooms, the first one small and empty and the other furnished with a long rectangular table and four benches, all made of rough, bark-covered wood. A lamp sat in the middle of the table. The walls were bare except for the back one. It was half covered with a large damp patch, which, the matron explained, was a recurrent problem that the plumbers hadn't yet tackled. "Do you happen to know anything about plumbing, Señor Esmís?" she asked. Gordon said he didn't and apologized for it. The furnished room also had one window through which several young faces were already appearing and disappearing, blowing kisses and giggling. Gordon recognized Julia's among them and gallantly waved his hand at her. The wide-hipped woman hastened to close the window, shutting out the flirtatious girls but also the remains of the sun.

She grabbed the lamp and took off its glass globe to light the wick. "I'm Rosalba," she suddenly said. "I used to be the town's magistrate. The only one who made decisions. Now it's five of us. A council, we call it." She lighted the wick and replaced the glass globe. "This used to be my office, only much nicer than this. My desk was one hundred percent pure mahogany. Really pretty. I had it over there." She lifted the lamp with one hand and with the other pointed at the wall with the damp patch. Gordon looked at the wall and arched his eyebrows in a vague expression that could have been either of admiration or plain indifference. Before long they heard a knock at the door. "It must be the others," Rosalba said. She placed the lamp on the table and went to the door. Three women entered the room, two of them carrying Gordon's yellow bag, which they handed to him. A fourth woman, old and fully dressed, wearing thick spectacles and leaning on a cane, followed them at her own pace. "Ladies, please take your seats," Rosalba said. They sat two on each side. Rosalba sat at one end of the table and indicated to Gordon that he should sit at the other end, across from her. "Señor Esmís," she began. "We're New Mariquita's council: this here is Cecilia, over there is Señorita Cleotilde, that's Police Sergeant Ubaldina, here Nurse Ramírez, and I'm former magistrate Rosalba."

"Nice meeting you," Gordon said coyly, bowing his head. This courteous gesture seemed to have made a good impression on everyone but the Indian-looking woman named Ubaldina, the police sergeant.

"What brought you here, Señor Gordonmís?" Ubaldina inquired, giving him a suspicious look.

He studied the women's faces for a second or two, and decided that except for the police sergeant, they seemed amiable. There was no reason to lie to them. "I'm a journalist," he said. "I work as a correspondent, writing news and articles for magazines and newspapers. I've been covering your war for some time now. I've interviewed guerrilla, paramilitary and army soldiers as well as their families, and written stories about them. Those stories I sell to newspapers and magazines mostly in the United States, but also—"

"Who sent you here?" Ubaldina interrupted. "And what do you want from us?"

"A few days ago I met a man, a crazy man who told me a bunch of lies about you and your village. He said this town was inhabited by giant, man-hating, masculine women who grew beards and mustaches and were capable of impregnating themselves. He said that you were heretics who liked to torture your enemies before eating them alive. I didn't believe much of it, but I figured that the part about this being a town inhabited only by women had to be true. And to me that sounded like a very interesting topic to write about: a town of women in a land of men." He paused briefly for dramatic effect. "So I asked him to draw a map for me and give me directions, and here I am." He stopped, raised his face and cast a quick glance over the five sets of eyes that were fixed on him. "That's the whole truth, ladies," he said with his right hand raised, as though he were swearing an oath in a courthouse.

The five women didn't appear surprised by Gordon's account. They looked at one another repeatedly, displaying no feeling on their faces, saying nothing.

"So . . . now that my presence here has been explained, I'd like to request that I be granted permission to live in your community for a short period," Gordon said. "I'd like to write a story about your village, and I'm willing to work in exchange for room and board."

"What's the name of the man who told you about us?" Ubaldina asked, ignoring the reporter's request.

"Rafael. Rafael Bueno. He said he used to be a priest and that this was his parochial district for a long time, until you tried to eat him alive."

The women looked at one another again. They now wore an expression of pure rage on their faces.

"Infamous wretch," said the oldest woman, the señorita, hitting the floor with her stick.

"We should've thrashed him good and hard."

"We should've killed the bastard."

"Yes, and fed him to the dogs."

"Or to the pigs."

It was obvious to Gordon that Rafael Bueno had done something very hurtful to the women. He wouldn't ask what, though. Not now, anyway. At this moment he could only hope that his request had registered with the council and that their reply was a positive one.

"We need to discuss this man's request," Ubaldina said. Then, addressing Gordon, she added, "Privately." He grabbed his bag and started toward the door.

"Julia Morales is going to eat him alive out there," Rosalba warned the council. Gordon stopped abruptly and looked back. "I didn't mean it that way, Señor Esmís." She giggled. "I assure you we don't feast on human beings."

After realizing that sending the reporter out would create even more commotion, the councilwomen asked Gordon to remain in the room and went outside themselves. He watched them through a crack in the door. They stood together under a mango tree, surrounded by the restless crowd, discussing their views and jerking their heads like disturbed chickens. After a while, they came back into the municipal office wearing solemn faces and sat in their respective places without giving the reporter any hint about the decision they had reached. Contrary to what he expected, Ubaldina, not Rosalba, was the one who ultimately stood up and spoke.

"I'll be straight and brief, Señor Gordonmís. I'm responsible for maintaining peace and security in our community. Your uninvited presence has caused a great deal of disorder, and quite honestly we can't expect anything good from an individual sent over by the man who murdered four of our children. We'd ask you to leave now, but it's getting dark, and someone as white as you can easily be spotted by all sorts of dangerous night creatures. We've decided to give you until sunrise tomorrow to leave our community, and we hope never to see you again."

"Señora Upaultina, I assure you that I—"

"Ubaldina," she said. "My name is Ubaldina."

"I've come in peace, Señora. Ubaldina. I'm a good guy."

"Nothing good has ever come through that thicket," Ubaldina retorted, and then sat down with her arms crossed, signaling the end of the discussion.

Before Gordon could say anything more, the woman they called Nurse Ramírez asked him to follow her to the town's infirmary. "I'm responsible for the community's health care, and so I'll clean and dress your wounds and sores."

"After that, you'll follow me," the one named Cecilia said. "I'm responsible for the community's diet, and so I'll take you to one of our communal kitchens, where you'll eat a warm meal."

"I'm the administrator," Rosalba said. "I oversee everything, but especially our community's farming and housing. I'll make sure that you get a clean room furnished with everything you might need for tonight."

"And I'm responsible for the community's school and the town's bell," said the old Señorita Cleotilde. "In other words, I'm the clock of New Mariquita. I'll see to it that you get up early enough to leave our village before sunrise."

AFTER BEING RELEASED from the infirmary, Gordon was taken to the community's second best kitchen: the Villegas's. The Morales kitchen was rated number one, Cecilia said, but she had been instructed to keep him away from Julia Morales.

By the time Gordon and Cecilia arrived, only three couples were in the dining room, feeding one another what remained of their meals. Wearing matching aprons on top of their nude anatomies, Flor (formerly the Villegas widow) and her spouse Elvia (formerly the López widow) welcomed Gordon and sat him in a corner table all by himself. The reporter was fascinated with the community, its operating system, its people and customs. Since Ubaldina had forbidden him to speak to any of the villagers more than was necessary, he dictated his thoughts, in English, into his miniature tape recorder. Cecilia didn't object to it. She was unusually friendly and kind toward him, and soon Gordon understood why:

"Señor Esmís, you said you've been interviewing guerrillas. I was wondering if perhaps . . . if maybe you've come across my son. His name's Ángel Alberto Tamacá, and he joined the guerrillas a long time ago. He's tall, and—"

"Do you know for sure if he . . . if he's alive?"

"My heart tells me he is," she said. "Do you think there's any way that I can get news to him that I'm alive too?"

"I have some connections. Write him a note and give me all his information. I'll do my best to have it delivered to him. If he's around, you know?"

The few diners present looked curiously at Gordon, as though surprised to see him eat the same things they were eating: a meal of rice, fried yucca and a small piece of a roasted, strong-flavored meatlike thing the origins of which he didn't dare ask because he was afraid to learn the answer. When he was finished, he complimented the cooks. Elvia said it was an honor to have such a distinguished gentleman dining in their humble kitchen.

Gordon and Cecilia were getting ready to leave when Julia Morales arrived. She now had on a red polka-dot dress. The dress was old-fashioned and had a few patches, but was tight in all the right places. The girl stood by the door with her hands on her hips and gave Gordon a daring look followed by a timid smile, disconcerting him. It all appeared to be part of a well-devised seduction plan that was working beautifully. His eyelid began twitching, and this symptom, as well as an erection that wasn't as visible on account of his loose pants, clearly indicated how much he desired her. Cecilia hastened to stand in front of the reporter, as though her small figure could keep the long-legged man from seeing anything. "Hurry up, son," she said to Gordon, though addressing Julia. "Rosalba is waiting for us in the church." Julia crossed her arms and leaned her back against the doorframe, making room for them to pass. As he went by, all Gordon managed was a wink. He walked off with Cecilia right next to him, thinking that Julia was the most exotic creature he'd ever seen.

THE REAR OF the church had been fitted out with a hammock and a blanket. Next to it, on an upside-down wooden crate that served as a night table, sat a lit lamp, a rag and a piece of soap.

"Is there a bathroom in here?" Gordon said.

"No, Míster Esmís. Not in here," Rosalba said. "We only have one bathroom in the village. It's a communal bathroom with ten showers and ten latrines, so clean you wouldn't believe it."

"Great! Can you show me where it is?"

"I'm sorry, Míster Esmís, but you're not allowed to use it. Another council decision. You'll have to use that empty bucket." She pointed at two buckets, one filled with water, which had been set to the side. "There are more blankets in that corner if you need them. Nights are getting much cooler. I hope you have a good night and a safe trip back tomorrow." She said this with a lingering smile. Her lips parted, as though she wanted to say something else but couldn't. She waited for Gordon's reply—a close-lipped smile—and then turned around and walked toward the door looking somewhat sad.

He followed her with his eyes till she left the building, and was surprised to realize that he had paid no heed to her nudity. Amazing how quickly the human eye adjusts, he thought, and for a moment he imagined himself and hundreds of people walking naked down Fifth Avenue in New York City, stopping now and then to see their genitals and buttocks reflected in the tall show windows of fancy stores that sold everything but clothes. He chuckled, then walked over to the empty bucket and peed in it. Next he took off his dirty sneakers and socks and got in the hammock with his long legs hanging down on each side of it and a beat-up copy of García Márquez's *One Hundred Years of Solitude*, which he'd been reading and rereading for some time now. There he lay stretched out, looking at the white ceiling upon which the light of the lamp had created an immense sun in soft yellow tones. He read for a little while, then put out the light of the lamp and in utter darkness swung himself a little with his feet till the motion gradually sent him to sleep.

GORDON WOKE UP in a sweat in the middle of the night, removed his clothes out of instinct, and then, completely naked, tossed and turned in the hammock, breathing heavily and moaning. He was ill. Suddenly, he felt a soft, small hand on his burning forehead and cheeks. Then a wet cloth, patting his face and neck, his arms, his chest. It must be a dream, he thought in his delirium. A few drops of water fell on his lips, which parted to let them in. He felt more patting on his face and neck, more water falling on his lips, and then a kiss: smooth, fleshy lips lightly pressing against his, traveling to his ear, down his neck and back to his mouth, where they lingered. A wild scent in the air made him think of Julia, and he quickly realized he wasn't dreaming. She leapt onto the hammock, and he felt her light and smooth naked body struggling to settle itself on top of him. She was twisting her bony hips like a cat. Gordon also twisted his hips, passionately at first and then violently—for he had just felt an unexpected and unwelcome swelling in the midsection of the body lying over him. Theirs was a furious battle, a battle of aroused hips in which Gordon, betrayed by his libido, eventually lost all his power of resistance. The soft and small hands that just a while ago had stroked his forehead now landed firmly on his chest for support, while a couple of muscular calves encircled his waist with rocking motions. Julia sat on his crotch and began to dance in a seductive way, drawing all of him toward her with increasing strain as though something inside her was claiming him. And so he moved inside her and she wailed, and she wriggled and squirmed and her muscular calves tightened around his waist as she pushed herself down on him. They moved together in an invisible mambo, the hammock swaying under the weight of their restless bodies, he moaning, she wailing, until they exploded, he inside her, she on his abdomen, and a wild feline scent instantly filled up the otherwise empty room.

Julia glided over Gordon's body and quietly laid her head on the man's chest, listening to the throbbing of his heart. He ran his long fingers through her long, thick hair. "What's your real name?" he asked. She didn't answer. Or perhaps she did in her own language of graceful motions that Gordon never saw, for there was no light to see them by. And so they lay there in a feverish silence, listening to each other's hearts, until Gordon fell into a deep sleep that kept him from hearing the click of the door when she left.

*   *   *

BEFORE SUNRISE, THE teacher Cleotilde found Gordon lying naked outside the church, shivering. An army of red ants surrounded his body, determined to carry it back to their nest. The old woman knelt down to feel his forehead: he was burning with fever. His lips trembled and his teeth chattered as he mumbled something incomprehensible. She grabbed him by one of his arms with the intention of dragging him inside the building, but her bones were too old and his too heavy. She frowned under her thick spectacles, less concerned with the reporter's condition than with the impossibility of his leaving town at sunrise as he'd been ordered. She went inside the church and rang the bell, signaling rising time. Then she went to Rosalba and Eloísa's house and told them about the sick reporter. "I suggest we call a council meeting to decide what to do with that man," she said.

"There's no time for meetings," Rosalba replied in her former magisterial tone, which reappeared occasionally and involuntarily, to the annoyance of the other council members. "Eloísa and I will assist Míster Esmís. You go get Nurse Ramírez," she ordered Cleotilde. "And hurry up." Cleotilde was no longer brave enough to confront Rosalba as she used to do. Off she went, tapping her cane and muttering a long and incomprehensible complaint. Outside the church, Rosalba swept the ants off Gordon's body, then grabbed him by the legs while Eloísa seized him by the arms. Together they carried him inside, both women stealing furtive glances at the man's large genitalia, but acting as though they saw penises and testicles every sun. They couldn't lift Gordon back in the hammock, so they piled up a few blankets in a corner, laid him on them and tried to cover him with a thin blue sheet, but he was sweating profusely and refused it. He complained of an excruciating headache and pain in his muscles, joints and behind his eyes.

Before long, Cleotilde arrived with Nurse Ramírez, who wore nothing but a mask and a pair of gloves she had made long ago from a discarded white plastic tablecloth patterned with a variety of colorful fruits and vegetables. She brought along her late husband's old medical reference book and bag of instruments, and a notebook in which she'd been recording her own findings and herbal remedies for every malady she'd seen and treated. When the nurse saw the naked man lying on the pile of blankets, she stood in awe. The only naked man she had ever seen was her late husband. Seeing another one after so many ladders suddenly stirred up something in her, a sort of desire that was similar—though not quite the same—to what she recurrently felt toward Erlinda, her present partner. The difference lay in its intensity. The desire she was feeling at the moment was much stronger, almost irrepressible, shameful. She made a tremendous effort not to reveal it to the other three women in the room. With her brow sweating and her hands shaking, Nurse Ramírez knelt down next to Gordon and examined him thoroughly to the best of her ability, which wasn't much. And when she pressed her ear against the man's chest to listen to his heart, her aroused nipples brushed the man's feverish skin, making her own vital signs go out of control. She found that the man's pulse was accelerated, his blood pressure low and he had a high fever. (She couldn't tell exactly how high his fever was, because every line and number above forty degrees Celsius had faded from her husband's thermometer with use and time.) Once she finished her examination, she covered Gordon from his waist down with a sheet and asked him a series of questions, some of which were completely irrelevant to his affliction, like, "Is everyone in your country as pale as you are?" She wrote all his answers in her notebook, including, "No, they're paler," and then compared them against previous notes and against the medical reference book. Finally, through the piece of plastic covering her mouth she gave her diagnosis: dengue fever.

"Please tell me it isn't contagious." Rosalba said.

The nurse replied that it wasn't. The dengue virus could only be transmitted from the bite of an infected mosquito, and a mosquito could only catch the virus after biting an infected human. Therefore the one precaution they must take was to make sure that the Míster didn't get bitten by any kind of mosquito.

"Is it hemorrhagic dengue?" Gordon asked in a faint voice. He knew that type of dengue was often fatal.

She said that it wasn't, but that it could turn into it if they weren't careful. She would prepare a potion to ease the intensity of his symptoms, but he should know that there was no specific treatment for dengue. He had to rest and drink plenty of fluids until he recovered, which would take ten to fifteen suns.

Rosalba ordered Cleotilde to ask the cleaning and maintenance team to shut the two windows of the church and hang a large mosquito net over Gordon's improvised mattress. Eloísa excused herself and left for work. She led a team of sturdy plumbers who had taken on the almost impossible task of restoring the old aqueduct. Nurse Ramírez asked Rosalba to please watch over the Míster for a while. She had to collect all the herbs she needed for the potion and then pay a visit to the Pérez widow, who had sent word that this time she was *really* dying.

"You go ahead, Ramírez," Rosalba said. "Do what you need to do. I'll take care of Míster Esmís until you're back."

Upon hearing the news about Gordon's condition, Julia Morales went to the church with a pot of soup and gestured to Rosalba that she wished to volunteer to take care of him.

"We don't need help taking care of him," Rosalba told Julia through the small metal grating. "Leave the soup on the steps if you want. I'll make sure Míster Esmís knows it's from you."

Julia shook her head. She wanted to feed him the soup herself, herself, herself. Three times she beat upon her chest with her palm.

"I already told you, Julia. Leave the soup on the steps and go back to work."

The girl turned red with anger. She began making a series of swift gestures with her free hand—and especially with her middle finger—

which she complemented with a variety of grotesque sounds in an insufferably high-pitched tone. Finally she sat on the sidewalk with the container of soup between her legs and buried her face in her hands, crying and sobbing.

Softened by such pitiful scene, Rosalba offered to let her in on the condition that she leave as soon as Gordon ate the soup. Julia agreed and went in, all smiles after her tantrum. She laid a blanket next to Gordon, under the mosquito net, and fed him very slowly so that she could stay longer tending to him. She made him drink cup after cup of dark grape juice that the López-Villegas couple had delivered. "A natural virus-killer," Flor Villegas had said. Gordon fell asleep, and when he woke up he stared at Julia indifferently, as if she were painted on the wall. But that didn't discourage her; she continued patting his sunburned face with a wet rag, bringing relief to his red, swollen eyes and his parched, chapped lips.

From the opposite corner, sitting on a wooden folding chair with her arms crossed over her stomach, Rosalba watched the ingenuous girl with sympathy. Poor silly girl! she thought. As soon as that gringo is cured, he'll go, and you'll be left with a broken heart. Even if he likes you now, once he finds out what's between your legs, he'll despise you for having the same thing he's got.

Before going home, Julia gave Gordon a passionate kiss on the mouth—a lost kiss that was never acknowledged nor noticed, because the recipient of it was delirious, and Rosalba had fallen asleep on the chair. A while later, when Rosalba woke up, she found Gordon on his knees fighting with the mosquito net, struggling to get up. She ran to his side.

"What are you doing, Míster Esmís? You're going to hurt yourself."

"I've got to pee," he mumbled, a hand covering his genitalia.

"Here, do your business in here." She grabbed the bucket, already reeking with Gordon's urine from the night before, lifted a corner of the net and handed it to him.

He took the bucket in one hand and turned around on his knees and breathed deeply. A loud, prolonged splash filled the room.

"It's getting dark in here," he said, setting the bucket at the lower end of the mattress, within the netted area. "What time is it?"

Rosalba hadn't been asked that question in ladders. "It's almost the end of the working day." She noticed Gordon was going through his bag, looking for something. He took out a pair of boxer shorts and swiftly slipped into them. He was having a lucid moment, she thought, but before night fell he'd be burning with fever again.

Still on his knees, Gordon began to scrutinize each corner of the spacious room. "What makes this building a church?" he suddenly said. "There isn't one thing in here that makes me think of God."

Rosalba also looked around the room and smiled, obviously pleased with the emptiness of the view. "We call it the church out of habit," she said, "because that's what it once was. Just like we used to call God God and heaven heaven."

"What do you call God now?"

"We don't call it anything. It's just an empty word, like this church."

"And heaven?"

"Also empty. Without God there's no heaven, or hell. Life's better that way."

Gordon gazed curiously at her. "Do you worship anything?"

"Nature. We've learned to fully appreciate the beauty and benefits of our land, our plants and animals."

Gordon sat on the mattress with his back against the wall. He was too tired to pursue a discussion about belief. "Where did she go?" he said.

"Who?" Rosalba reached for the lamp.

"The girl who was here before."

"Julia? I expect she went back to work." She lit the lamp and set it on the upside-down crate next to him.

The nearness of the light reduced Gordon's visibility beyond the net but let him see clearly everything within. He noticed several holes in the fabric. "She can't talk, can't she?"

"No."

"What's her real name? I mean, *his* real name?"

Rosalba stared at the reporter through the meshed fabric, as though she wanted to see or learn something personal and unique about him. So he knows about Julia, she thought. He might be a different kind of gringo after all: a curious one, who's willing to experiment with new things, new sensations. All gringos can't be narrow-minded, materialistic and full of themselves.

"Julio," Rosalba emphatically said. "His name's Julio something. I don't remember his middle name. We've been calling him Julia for so long that I—"

"How long?"

"Hmmm." She shrugged. "I lost track of it. All I know is that it all started on the day the men disappeared."

"The men, right. How did they disappear?"

"Guerrillas."

"Did the guerrillas kill them all?"

"They might as well have."

"They took them away, didn't they?"

"It's too long a story to tell," she said, making an effort to look weary and uninterested.

She was playing hard to get; Gordon was sure of it. Two could play that game. "Don't worry, then," he said. "Maybe some other time." He let his body slide down the wall until his back was flat on the mattress and his body partially covered by the thin blue sheet. Soon afterward, the bell announced the end of the working day; five thunderous and reverberating strokes that, from inside the empty church, sounded more like the beginning of the end of the world.

While the echo of the last chime was still resounding in their ears, Rosalba shouted, "Do you really want to hear how our men disappeared?"

"Only if you feel like telling," he shouted back, a cunning smile on his face.

She straightened her spine against the chair's back, shifting her matronly extra weight. She looked up at the white ceiling as though for inspiration, then began the telling of her story:

"The day the men disappeared started as a typical Sunday morning in Mariquita. . . ."

ELOÍSA, NURSE RAMÍREZ and her spouse Erlinda Calderón stopped by after dinner. They had on ponchos of sacking that old Lucrecia, the community's seamstress, had tailored for every villager to wear on chilly evenings. Eloísa kissed her Ticuticú and handed her a plate with her dinner and an extra poncho.

"How's the Míster doing?" the nurse asked. She held a small earthen container in her hands.

"He was quite alert for a good part of the afternoon," Rosalba said. "I even told him a story, and he loved it. But he's delirious again."

"That's typical of dengue fever," the nurse declared. She walked over to Gordon, relieved to see he was now wearing shorts. She felt his forehead and checked his body for rashes, which, she explained, were also typical of the disease. Had he vomited? No? Very good! Had he complained of headaches? Well, that was common. Muscle pain? Sure, that was also common. Nurse Ramírez poured into a cup some of the formula she had prepared—an infusion of chrysanthemum and honeysuckle flowers, marijuana and mint leaves, and burdock and anise seeds—and forced the thick mixture down Gordon's throat. "I'll tend to him tomorrow," she volunteered.

"Good," Rosalba said. "I'll make sure he gets plenty of juices, maybe even a good soup from the Morales's kitchen. And I'll stop by after dinner to tell him another story." She put out the light of the lamp and sang, "Good night, Míster Esmís." Soon they were gone.

*   *   *

AFTER HEARING THE first story, Gordon told Rosalba that he'd like to write a book about New Mariquita. And so every evening after that and for eleven consecutive suns, Rosalba made it her duty to tell Gordon a story about her town of widows, and Gordon made it his to listen to it and tape it and, when feeling strong enough, take notes. Rosalba's privileged memory covered the better part of Mariquita's history since long before the men disappeared, but her stories were to some extent unreliable; a singular combination of her own experiences coupled with several different versions and—this was the unreliable part— assumptions she had put together in the absence of facts. Fortunately for Gordon, it was easy to tell when Rosalba was speculating by her passionless tone and lack of details, but also because Rosalba—who otherwise was a confident storyteller—would stumble over the words or look the other way as she told them. Every time Gordon was seized by doubt, he would discreetly pencil in a question mark next to the suspicious line, or cue himself on the tape if he was recording it. He'd check her version against that of Julia—his special friend—when he had the opportunity.

Rosalba's telling was interrupted many times each night. Councilwoman Ubaldina, for instance, often stopped by to examine and evaluate Gordon's improvement. Aroused women of different ages also came around every evening after dinner, hoping to catch a glimpse of the semi-naked man, bringing presents of flowers, mangoes, oranges, bananas, hearty soups or blood sausages and puddings—the mere appearance of which nauseated Gordon. He himself interrupted Rosalba often to repeat a word he didn't know or hadn't caught, to ask her specific questions about the story, to clarify a confusing anecdote or have her repeat a section of the story that he liked. It was not unusual for Rosalba to jump from one story to another, or to wander from the point and begin endless discussions about herself. On those occasions, the reporter had to resort to his journalist's subtle ways to lead her back to the subject matter: "That's most interesting, Señora Rosalba, but you were saying that . . ."

And so it was in this way that Gordon learned about how Mariquita's men disappeared and Julio got to be Julia, but also about the crisis that followed the men's withdrawal from the village: the prolonged dry spell and the cutting off of electricity, the shortage of food and water, the epidemic of influenza that killed ten people, and the gradual departure of nearly half the adult population and their children. He learned from Rosalba about the passing military commission that had designated her as the town's new magistrate; and about the brothel madam's persistent attempts to keep her business afloat in a town of widows and spinsters. He learned about the mysterious schoolmistress who refused to teach history, and about how Santiago Marín became the town's Other Widow. About the hypocritical priest who first developed a procreation scheme and later killed the town's only four boys. About the widow who found a fortune under her bed just as the town's economy was slowly reverting to a bartering system. About the day time stopped, and the sun time became female, and about how a cow named Perestroika saved the magistrate's plan of economic, political and social restructuring that turned a rotten, meager town into a prosperous and self-sufficient community.

IN THE SAME way Rosalba made it her duty to tell the reporter a story every evening, Julia Morales made it hers to create, together with Gordon, one more story for him to write about: theirs. Every night after the village had gone to sleep, Julia scurried along the desolate streets toward the church. The first few nights she contented herself with running the tips of her delicate fingers all over Gordon's body in the absolute darkness of the room, while he slept under the narcotic effect of the nurse's concoction. But as the man's health began to improve, the girl demanded more from his hands and fingers, from his hips and tongue and lips. And when they kissed and made love, she sucked him in, breathed in the air he breathed out, and filled herself full of him night after night after night.

*   *   *

Twelve suns later, Nurse Ramírez informed the councilwomen that Gordon had fully recovered from his illness. She made the announcement over breakfast in the Morales's communal kitchen.

"Well, then, I'd better go escort him up to the thicket right now," Ubaldina said. "I want to make sure he leaves once and for all." She put down the arepa she was eating and stood up.

"I have a proposal to make," Rosalba said suddenly. She looked at Ubaldina and pointed to the wooden bench, prompting her to sit down again. The other three women turned inquisitive eyes to Rosalba. "As we all know, Míster Esmís is the first real man we've seen in many ladders." Rosalba thrust her head forward and lowered her voice to avoid being heard by the people in the table next to theirs. "Naturally, some of our finest women have shown interest in him. I propose that we take advantage of his being here to get two or three women pregnant. I'm sure Míster Esmís wouldn't mind doing us a favor after all we've done for him." Ubaldina looked as though she was ready to object, and so Rosalba went on whispering reasons why the council should consider her proposal. "Our population is getting old; with every ladder that goes by, another woman in our community loses her ability to bear children. In about forty ladders, our youngest girls will be menopausal, and all of us will be dead, and there will be no one to continue what we started." Once again Ubaldina attempted to express her disapproval, but Rosalba wasn't finished. "Besides, can you imagine how beautiful Míster Esmís's children would be, with his golden hair and blue eyes? With his tiny nose and white complexion? Especially with his white complexion. They'd be absolutely gorgeous!"

The nurse and Cecilia looked at the color of their own limbs and stomachs and awkwardly folded their arms, covering a small part of their brown nakedness with more of the same. Cleotilde remained still. She'd been in her skin for too long to suddenly be ashamed of it. But Ubaldina, the darkest, most Indian-looking of all five, seemed to be insulted by Rosalba's comment. "I feel very fortunate to look the way I do," she said in a dignified matter, her chin raised just enough to show her impressive cheekbones in all their grandeur. "I think of it as a blessing from the gods, and I strongly believe that our future generations should look like us: black-haired and brown-eyed, with a beak like ours, and their skin should be dark so that it can endure the harshest sun, and thick so that it will last much longer."

Now it was Rosalba who felt discriminated against, her pale skin and green eyes excluded from Ubaldina's prototype of Mariquita's people of the future. "I only mentioned Míster Esmís because I happen to think he's a handsome man, but if you don't agree, that's fine with me. I still think someone here must bear a male child or two if we want our community to survive."

"I say we should try our luck again with our two men," Ubaldina said. She was referring to the one occasion, two ladders back, when Santiago Marín and Julio Morales had been persuaded to make an effort to impregnate a woman of their choice. Santiago picked Magnolia Morales, while Julio, as though returning the favor, chose Amparo Marín, Santiago's youngest sister. The two women were instructed by their own mothers to treat the men gently, because Santiago and Julio would only respond to tenderness and love. The encounters took place on the first waxing moon of the ladder, when the women's probabilities of becoming pregnant were at their best. Magnolia and Amparo did everything they could and knew to excite their respective men, but neither their grace and kindness first, nor their sensuality and lechery later, aroused any response.

Rosalba gave an affected laugh. "You do that. Try your luck again with those two." She pushed the plate with her untouched breakfast away from her. At that precise moment, Julia Morales came up to their table with a fresh pot of coffee, offering refills.

"The Míster has to go today," old Cleotilde emphatically said. Julia's hand, the one holding the pot of coffee, began trembling, but the councilwomen were so absorbed in their discussion that they didn't even notice the girl's presence. "But we should wait until after breakfast, when the women are at work, or his departure will end in uproar."

Nurse Ramírez and Ubaldina indicated with their heads that they were in accord with Cleotilde. Cecilia remained still, neutral. "Let it be on your heads then," Rosalba said, throwing her hands in the air. As for Julia, she quickly disappeared through the kitchen door.

*   *   *

GORDON LOOKED UP and noticed enormous dark clouds filling the sky. He was sitting on a bench in the plaza, his duffel bag on his lap and his arms resting on top of it, like a resigned traveler waiting for his bus to arrive. He had bathed and shaved and put on clean clothes that Julia had washed for him. His sneakers, too, had been cleaned by the diligent girl, exposing their Nike logo, fading blue color and heavy wear. The dark bags under his eyes had faded, and a healthy rose color bloomed in his cheeks.

The smell of freshly brewed coffee was still in the air, though breakfast was long over. His had been delivered to the church from the Morales's kitchen, and it had arrived with a little surprise: a neatly folded note hidden underneath a fat arepa. The note was from Julia, and it read, "Today is our day."

So when Gordon saw Ubaldina appear from around a corner with a derisive smile on her unfriendly face, and Rosalba, Cecilia, Nurse Ramírez and Cleotilde following her, he wasn't the least bit surprised.

"Your time's up, Míster!" Ubaldina shouted from a distance. She shooed him with the backs of her hands quickly and repeatedly. Gordon remained still on the bench, undisturbed, self-controlled, staring at the small Indian woman as she moved closer. He knew his aplomb would make her nervous, and so he decided it'd be his little revenge for her constant and unjustified hostility toward him. But the woman, sensing that Gordon was up to no good, stopped a few meters away from him and pulled the ugliest, most frightening face she could manage: her slanting eyes popping out of their sockets; her mouth stretching wide enough to expose her remaining four or five teeth—so pointed and separated that they appeared to serve more as weapons than for chewing—and her long tongue coming out, making a repulsive twist, drawing back and coming out again, like a lizard's.

Gordon thought the sight was amusing. "I'm leaving now, Señora Ubaldina," Gordon announced. He placed his bag on the bench and rose. "But first I'd like to say good-bye to the señoras behind you."

"Well, you'd better be quick," Ubaldina said in a softer tone. "It looks like rain." She stepped aside and indicated to Gordon, with a polite gesture, that he could safely walk by her, toward the women.

There was nothing extraordinary about the reporter's farewell. He respectfully bowed before each woman—including Ubaldina—and kissed her hand, saying "Gracias" time and again. Cecilia handed him a letter he was supposed to deliver to her son Ángel Alberto Tamacá, and a bundle of food as big as the man's head. "It should last you a couple of days." She sounded and looked motherly. Gordon kissed her hand a second time. He walked up to the bench and grabbed his bag and began walking toward the rise. The five women stood at the bottom. Before walking into the thicket, Gordon looked at New Mariquita one more time, as though fixing the town in his memory to make sure he hadn't imagined it. Against the gray sky the village looked like a multicolored painting. He saw every red roof, every white house and every ash-colored road, the green plaza and the ivory church, the plots of maize, rice and coffee, and the women working them. The branches of the tallest trees swayed in the wind, and for a moment Gordon thought he saw every woman of New Mariquita stop what she was doing to wave a hand at him. He waved back.

*   *   *

IT WAS POURING rain. Julia Morales pulled her loose skirt up above her knees and waded through the brown water and leaves and branches that the thundershower brought down the small rise. She carried, tied to her waist, a small bundle of clothes and a smaller one of food, both of which she covered with the bottom of her folded skirt. She also carried a sheathed machete. She walked fast, though no one was chasing her. When she reached the top of the rise, Julia looked back. After today none of this would exist; she would never again walk up and down the same narrow streets lined with plain mango trees. Beyond the thicket, on the other side of the world, there would be many large cities with thousands of broad, paved avenues lined with rows of stately trees and bordered by impressive buildings. She would indeed miss her sisters and especially her mother, that loving woman who had devoted half her life to looking after her children. But Julia preferred missing them terribly to ending up like her sisters, embittered spinsters living on hopes of better suns, or rather dying with them.

The rain was now falling with great rapidity and violence, beating her face fitfully. Julia turned to face the path Gordon had hacked out earlier that morning. If she could speak, she would call Gordon's name right now. Scream it. Just to hear him say, one more time, "I can clear a path for you, Julia, but I can't help you go across the thicket. That you must do on your own. Only when you're strong and courageous enough to make it to the other side of the world will you be prepared to live in it." He was a good man, Gordon. A good and honest man who had confessed to feeling something very special for Julia; a kind of love beyond description—even for a writer like himself—that he refused to label. He'd promised Julia that he'd give their relationship a chance, and that he'd help her start a new life over there.

Before entering the path, Julia looked back one last time: in the middle of the torrential downpour her village had turned dim and blurry, indistinct. And at that moment, before her eyes, New Mariquita began to fade little by little until all Julia could see was the spire of the empty church that soon would disappear.

She turned around, but instead of following Gordon's path, she moved away from it, to the right, until she found herself facing the thicket, that dense clump of trees and shrubs that for ladders had blocked her way to a new life. She now unsheathed her machete and felt its sharpness on the back of her hand, then raised the long blade high above her head, over her right shoulder, and resolutely began hacking her way through the coarse vegetation, clearing her own path.

Germán Augusto Chamorro, 19
Soldier, Colombian National Army

I was hiding across from the tree, behind the bushes, when I saw
a guerrilla coming my way. He was about a head taller than me,
muscular, a tough guy. He walked slowly, looking in both directions,
again and again, as though exercising his neck. I thought it was my
lucky day because the man stood right in front of me. All I had to do
was pull the trigger, and this country would've had one less guerrilla. I waited, though. I wanted to make sure this wasn't a guerrilla's
dirty trick, and that he was indeed alone. Suddenly, the man burst
into tears. Just like that. That big, tough guy dropped his Galil on the
ground, sat down with his back to the tree and buried his face in his
hands, weeping through his fingers like a woman. I watched him,
quietly, wondering whether he was separated from his squad or had
just been looking for a place safe enough to cry (we men occasionally do that).

I waited long enough and then shouted, "Hands up." The guerrilla raised his hands in the air. I approached him cautiously. He
looked terrified. "You're crying," I said harshly, as though accusing
him of something awful. "Why?" The guerrilla didn't reply. I took
a step back and lowered my gun. "Why are you crying?" I insisted,
my voice surprisingly soft this time. He said his mother had died.
She'd died three months ago, but he'd only found out that morning.
"You're making that shit up," I said, leveling my gun. He shook his
head and asked me for permission to reach into his pocket. In it, he
said, he had a letter from his sister. "Okay," I said. He threw a folded
piece of paper at my feet, and I picked it up and read it. "I'm sorry,"
I said. Then I told him that I'd never met my mother, that she had

abandoned me on a church pew when I was three days old. He said the same had happened to his father and began telling me the story as if we were old friends. Soon I found myself sitting next to him on the ground, under the tree, listening to his story, telling him mine. We laughed at ourselves, at the war, at life, at our guns that for a moment were forgotten on the grass.

Suddenly, we heard steps approaching. We snatched up our rifles. I climbed up the tree, and he followed swiftly. Only when we were up in the tree did we realize that we weren't alone, that there was another man hidden in the tree, a paramilitary soldier. All this time he'd been hiding up there in his green uniform and ranger hat, watching us and listening to our tales. He smiled at us, lowered his gun and placed his right hand on his heart as a sign of peace. We had to trust that smile, that hand, that sign. There was nothing else we could do.

The three of us stayed still, holding our breaths, our chins tucked in just enough to see four men in green uniforms creep along in the scrub beneath us. Were they army soldiers? Guerrillas? Paramilitaries? We never knew, and we let them pass unharmed.

From above, all we saw was four men, men like us, running away, looking for places safe enough to cry.

CHAPTER 14

The Men Who Asked for a Second Chance

New Mariquita, Eloísa 13, Ladder 1993

DAWN WAS SLOWLY BREAKING over the small valley, and in the sky the moon still shone. In house number one, which occupies the entire block where the municipal office and the police station used to be, fifteen female couples slept placidly in the privacy of their compartments. Suddenly, in the one closest to the door, Virgelina Saavedra woke up, startled.

"Magnolia," she called softly to her partner, her delicate voice resonating in the emptiness of the room. Their compartment was furnished with nothing but a large bed made of planks, topped with a handcrafted mattress stuffed with cotton and straw.

"What?" Magnolia replied sleepily.

"Did you hear something outside?"

"Nothing."

Virgelina went to the window and peeped out. "I see shadows moving around the plaza," she whispered.

"It must be dogs."

"And I hear voices."

"I only hear yours. Come back to bed."

"Male voices."

Frightened, Magnolia sat up hastily. Together, hand in hand, she and Virgelina listened to the low, indistinct sounds carried by the wind.

MEANWHILE, ACROSS FROM them in house number two, where the infirmary and the old barbershop used to be, thirty-one women and Santiago Marín slept soundly.

House number two is a long and enormous room with no partitions except the ones established by the scant furnishings. In the rear of the building, three rows of hammocks hang parallel to each other and a few feet apart. All hammocks are suspended from hooks inserted into solid upright poles. The poles also serve to steady the house frame, and the hooks double as hangers for baskets or bags containing the villagers' only personal belongings: bracelets, necklaces, pieces of cloth used during Transition, clothing (if any), pictures and other surviving objects that remind the villagers of their departed loved ones.

The dwellers of house number two were the youngest women of the community, all single and rowdy, plus Santiago Marín and his mother Aracelly, the kitchen caretakers. The house's dormitory had been arranged in the very back, so that the youngest women's constant chattering would not be heard from the other two houses. Perhaps that's why, on the morning of Eloísa 13, 1993, no one in house number two heard or saw the men return.

A WHILE LATER, in house number three across from the church, Cleotilde Guarnizo woke up Ubaldina, who was sleeping on the hammock next to hers. Ubaldina grumbled something unintelligible and turned onto her side. "It's your duty to the community. Get up right away!" Cleotilde scolded.

"All right, all right, I'm coming," Ubaldina retorted. She yawned and scratched her head. Eight small, identically framed pictures hung on the wall before her. They were pictures of Ubaldina's family: her seven stepsons and her husband, all taken away by Communist guer-rillas. She approached the first picture and heaved a sigh. In it, her youngest stepson, Campo Elías Restrepo Jr., smiled as he cut a sad-looking cake. "My sweet baby, listen to me," she whispered. "Don't ever go to bed without saying the Indian prayers I taught you." She slowly moved along the wall, murmuring motherly advice to each of the first seven photos: "Remember to brush your teeth." "Eat your veg-etables." "Don't bite your nails." "Get enough sleep." "Keep smiling." "Look after your brothers." When she stood in front of the last one, her husband's, she said, "Rest in peace."

"Hurry up!" Cleotilde shouted from the other end of the row. "You're making me look bad." Cleotilde was now old and too weak to peal the church bell. Her biological clock, however, was still intact, so her present job was to make sure that someone, anyone, rang the bell on time throughout the sun. Today, for the third consecutive morning, Cleotilde had chosen Ubaldina to be the one to chime the communi-ty's time to rise and get ready for work.

For a brief moment Ubaldina considered objecting to old Cleo-tilde's unfair treatment. Why couldn't she pick someone else to ring the morning bell? "I'm coming," she said calmly, and put on a pon-cho of sacking and grabbed a lamp. Walking between the two rows of hammocks filled with sleeping and snoring women, Ubaldina was suddenly overcome with longing for her own house, or at least her own bedroom. At the next meeting, she decided, she would express to the entire community her growing need for privacy. She could almost hear the women's answer: "What's the purpose of a cooperative house if its dwellers live in individual compartments? Privacy is only justified for couples." If only things between her and Mariacé Ospina had worked out, they'd be sharing a private room in house number one. But after failing twice in her attempts to make love to Mariacé, Ubaldina had decided that she simply couldn't love another woman. Not in the sense Eloísa and her "Ticuticú" loved each other.

She walked through the rest of the cavernous house and pulled the front door wide. Four figures stood across the street like ghosts, startling her. She lifted the lamp in the air with a trembling hand. "Who's there?" she called.

"Good morning, señora," the figure on the left replied in a throaty male voice. He took off what appeared to be a hat as a sign of respect. "Sorry to bother you this early, but—"

"If you're guerrillas or paras, you've come to the wrong place," she interrupted. "No men here." She immediately regretted saying the last three words. A town of women surely sounded like an easy target for outlaws.

"We're neither, señora. We're good men."

"How many is we? Where's everyone else hiding?" She looked past them, blinking repeatedly.

"It's just us," the same voice declared. "Just the four of us."

"Uh-huh," she mumbled suspiciously, still looking around. "What do you all want?"

"We're lost, señora. We're heading to Mariquita. Do you know which way it is?"

The man's reply frightened her, and her heart started pounding rapidly. "No," she said instinctively, thinking that they must have been sent over by that wicked man, el padre Rafael. "Who are you, anyway?"

"Name's Ángel Alberto Tamacá," answered the same man, his face barely visible. The name sounded familiar to Ubaldina, but before she could place it, a different man spoke in a somewhat younger, more melodious voice.

"David Pérez," he said, touching the tip of his hat with his hand.

"Jacinto Jiménez Jr. here," the third man said. He simply raised his hand in the air, indicating where he was.

"And I'm Campo Elías Restrepo, your humble servant," the last man said, bowing his hatted head.

When she heard the last man's name, an electric shock traveled briskly through Ubaldina's body. She strained her eyes to better see him, but in the faint light of the lamp, all she could make out was his small silhouette. This can't be true, she thought. It must be a mean coincidence, a mistake. She started walking slowly across the street, holding the lamp aloft, hoping to recognize nothing about the four figures shrouded by the dawn mist. As she got closer the men took on definite human forms. A dust-caked arm appeared here, a leg there, then torsos and half-lighted faces of men that bore a certain resemblance to men Ubaldina had once known. She moved a little to the right, toward the last man, wanting to see him clearly. He was older than the rest, stooped and white-bearded, his lower lip jutting out and his eyes hooded under overhanging bushy brows. And though he wore his hat low over his forehead, a scar shaped like a tilde was visible above his left eyebrow. An old scar, Ubaldina knew, left by a stone thrown at him in a street fight when he was younger. She'd heard the story many times from the same man who now stood before her, aged and half broken, her husband.

She dropped the lamp with a crash, her entire body shaking as though with cold, and began walking backward, awkwardly, stumbling over invisible objects, her lumbering footsteps loud in the dawn quiet. When she reached the house, she held on to the doorway and said in a low, supplicating voice, "Please, go away."

Confused by her demeanor, the four men made no reply.

"Go away. Please," she said again.

But they were motionless.

"Go away," she said over and over, raising her voice each time. Her plea turned into a blaring cry that woke up the entire community right on schedule.

*   *   *

MOST VILLAGERS OF New Mariquita would agree that of all thirteen rungs of the ladder, Eloísa is the most delightful. The rains have already passed, but the dry season hasn't quite begun. Temperatures are mild and pleasant. The tree leaves are irresistibly green. In the mornings, the air is cool with dew, and the fragrances of grass and wildflowers waft through the village. During the rung of Eloísa most of New Mariquita's cooking is done outside. At sunup, after the first set of rings of the church bell, three large log fires are kindled in the middle of the plaza. Three cooks—one from every house—and their helpers bring out corn dough, eggs, chopped onions and tomatoes. Pots and pans are crowded together above the fire. Coffee is brewed, arepas molded and grilled, omelets prepared. Two sets of five chimes summon the villagers for breakfast. All ninety-three villagers squat around the pots. Breakfast is served in handcrafted earthenware of great quality. Some eat with their hands or holding their plates to their lips; others use utensils carved out of wood. Some say grace to their gods; others talk about the dream they had the night before. Some listen; others laugh. The church bell rings again, and the villagers start heading for their specific workplaces.

*   *   *

ON ELOÍSA 13, 1993, the three cooking fires weren't kindled until the sun was high in the sky and the great excitement caused by the return of the four men had diminished.

Immediately after hearing Ubaldina's frantic cries, the villagers had rushed out of their houses. Tamacá, Pérez, Jiménez and Restrepo heard their strident shouts first, then watched the women appear from every corner of the plaza, naked, brandishing heavy clubs and fishing spears. The men drew closer to one another, each facing a different side, a different group of wild creatures, and finally stood dumbfounded in the middle of the large circle that the savage-looking women had created around them. Tamacá and Pérez thought themselves among a tribe of angry native Indians. Jiménez imagined he was hallucinating as a result of his extreme exhaustion and weakness. Restrepo was too shocked to think.

The villagers started walking around the intruders, quietly and cautiously, scrutinizing their faces as though the men belonged to a different race they had never seen before. Suddenly, Cecilia Guaraya, who had just caught sight of Ángel Tamacá, dropped her spear and brought her hands to her face dramatically.

"Ángel!" she cried out loud, taking a few steps toward him. She had recognized him at first glance despite the deep hollow where Ángel's right eye used to be, and which now made that side of his face look like a skull. He'd gone bald, except for a few threads of hair that curled awkwardly on the sides of his head. He wore mean clothes, ragged and filthy and dampened with a mix of perspiration and night dew. "Ángel Alberto!" she shouted again, just to make certain that every woman present heard her good news: that after all these ladders Mariquita's former teacher, her son, had come back from the war. "I'm your mother, don't you recognize me?"

He shook his head and moved back a little. Who was this crazy woman claiming to be his mother? Who were these other naked Indians clustering around him? Why did they look at him in surprise? Where was he?

"I'm your mother, Ángel," she repeated. "Cecilia Guaraya."

Ángel examined the woman's face carefully; then suddenly he threw his arms around her and began weeping. "I'm sorry, Mamá," he sobbed, tears falling copiously from his one eye. "I'm so sorry." Cecilia didn't weep, didn't say anything. She simply held him tight and rocked him as he cried. Her poor son had spent half his life fighting for a hopeless cause, and all he had to show for it was the empty socket of his right eye.

The villagers now approached the men with increasing interest.

"Jacinto Jiménez, is that you?" Marcela said after taking a closer look at Mariquita's former magistrate's son. "I'm Marcela. Marcela López." She beat upon her chest repeatedly with her palm, then kissed him on the lips, as if her kisses were all the dumbfounded man could remember her by. When Jiménez finally understood that he was in his native village and the girl kissing him was indeed his fiancé, his first instinct was to cover her naked body with his own shirt. He didn't want the other three men to see his girl's breasts and shapely curves. She accepted the shirt cheerfully but refused to button it up. This upset Jiménez and caused the couple to have their first argument.

Marcela was disgruntled to discover that her fiancé had only changed physically: he was taller, his face was more gaunt, and his body looked stronger in the sleeveless T-shirt he wore. His hair had thinned and begun to recede, and his skin showed the consequences of having been overexposed to the perverse tropical sun. But Jacinto's nature was the same as always: hot-tempered, jealous and possessive.

By now the villagers had already identified the other two men: David Pérez, old Justina Pérez's grandson, and Campo Elías Restrepo, Ubaldina's husband and one of former Mariquita's wealthiest men. Rosalba quickly took charge: "Welcome to New Mariquita. I'm Rosalba viuda de Patiño. Do you remember me? My husband was Police Sergeant Napoleón Patiño." A few other women reintroduced themselves, but most chose to remain quiet. The men merely nodded, struggling to match the burly nude figures standing before them to the pictures of the women they had in their minds.

After reacquainting themselves with the men, the villagers began to feel more at ease among the visitors, and after a while they sat on the ground to hear some of the moving accounts of the men's experiences, ask them questions and answer theirs. Jiménez was sad to learn that his mother and two sisters had left Mariquita soon after the men disappeared. Pérez was happy to find out that his grandmother Justina, the Pérez widow, though awfully aged, crippled with arthritis and mentally unsound, was still alive. David Pérez was now twenty-nine and had turned out to be handsome: tall and big-eyed with an olive complexion. His long face and wavy, slicked-back hair gave him a refined, almost elegant appearance that set him apart from the other three men.

AT MIDDAY, A hearty meal of boiled root vegetables, rice and cured meat was served. Jacinto Jiménez Jr. sat next to his stubborn fiancée, still not speaking to her, and David Pérez by his insane grandmother, who had to be fed on account of her stiffened fingers. Ángel Tamacá sat beside his mother, his knees pressed together against his small chest, his sad left eye fixed on the ground. He felt quite uneasy with his mother's nudity, which looked magnified in the heat—swollen, droopy and sticky. Cecilia, who had barely spoken earlier, now became particularly chatty, and with every sentence she uttered, Ángel's mouth dropped further: ". . . And so el padre Rafael developed an absurd schedule to make love to every young woman. . . . He poisoned all four boys in the name of God. . . . The two of them came up with the concept of female time, and . . ." Ángel sat there quietly and expressionless, thinking, What happened to the Mariquita I knew? ". . . When Francisca and I realized we were in love with each other, we decided to . . ." What happened to my mother?

Sitting between Rosalba and Nurse Ramírez, Campo Elías Restrepo found himself engulfed in the acrid odors emanating from the two women's bodies. He knew he didn't exactly smell like fresh flowers himself, but he'd traveled a huge distance on foot and in the brutal sun, climbing steep ridges and walking through thick undergrowth. These women had just started their day and already smelled like horses.

Restrepo was angry. His wife had shut herself in the house since his arrival and categorically refused every appeal to come out and meet with him. He was the bearer of sad tidings for her: her youngest stepson, Campo Elías Restrepo Jr., had drowned some years before, after the raft in which he and his friend were escaping from the guerrillas had gotten caught up in a whirlpool and overturned. Ubaldina hadn't been present earlier when he shared the bad news with the villagers. Restrepo imagined that by now Ubaldina had heard the story from someone else and held him accountable for the tragedy. Perhaps he should slink inside the house and confront her. Or maybe he should just wait, let her grieve some and then demand that she resume her duties as his wife.

*   *   *

INSIDE HOUSE NUMBER three, Ubaldina lay in her hammock. Indeed she had already heard the upsetting news about her stepson, and now stared at the boy's picture on the wall, quietly weeping. Why her sweet boy and not her husband?

Ubaldina's marriage had been a sham. She had been the Restrepos' maid when Campo Elías's wife died. He'd deceived her into marrying him only to secure a nanny, a maid and a cook. Ubaldina realized this early in their marriage, but instead of sobbing her heart out, she devoted herself to his seven boys, all of whom grew up to love her as if she were their natural mother. Campo Elías, for his part, devoted himself to the twelve girls of La Casa de Emilia, where he spent most nights. In fact, it had been there, in the brothel, that the guerrillas had found him that fateful sun when they took the men away.

And now, after all these ladders, not only did she have to deal with the death of her stepson, but also with her husband's return.

THE FOUR MEN spent their first night in New Mariquita's former church. Rosalba and her partner Eloísa gave them hammocks, blankets, rags, buckets of water and a lamp. They instructed the men to take a hot piece of firewood from the fire still going in the plaza, and place it under their hammocks before going to sleep to keep them warm throughout the night. As soon as the two women left, the men freely discussed their first impressions of New Mariquita.

"By God, it's true that I didn't expect a whole bunch of women to keep the village going, but I also didn't expect them to wreck Mariquita and turn back the clock," Restrepo said contemptuously. "They're living like savages. We've a lot of work to do if we want to make this town livable."

"I'm not crazy about all the changes," David Pérez said casually. "But I don't think it's that bad either. Sure, they're living a simple life, but—"

"Simple life?" Jiménez interrupted. "They run around fucking naked! And did you see them holding hands and slobbering all over each other? Damn lesbians! I agree with Restrepo: we have a great deal to teach these women."

"You're fools to think we can teach them anything," Ángel Tamacá said. "They're doing just fine without us. Who are we to come back after sixteen years and demand that they change their way of living anyway?"

"Who are we?" Jiménez snapped. "We're the only male survivors of this damned village. That's who we are! Mariquita belongs to us, and we've got to take charge again."

"We have nowhere else to go, Jiménez," Pérez said. "We're considered criminals everywhere in this country. Maybe we should just try to adapt ourselves to living here."

"I already did a lot of adapting in the fucking guerrillas," Jiménez retorted angrily. "No woman's going to tell me what to do. I'd rather accept the government's amnesty. At least that way I can clean my record and live in a place where women respect and obey men."

"Go ahead and accept the amnesty," Tamacá said, an affected smile on his face. "Move to Bogotá and let them cram you into a dirty shelter. Let them clean your record and then throw you out on the street to get killed or die of starvation. Do you really think anyone in the city's going to rent a room out to you? Or employ you? Or even befriend you? The moment they find out that just a few months ago you were blowing up bridges and oil pipelines, killing Indians and farmers who supported the paras, they'll think you're little better than dog shit."

"The bottom line is that we're here," Campo Elías Restrepo interposed. "Now what are we going to do?"

Restrepo's question was followed by a long, contemplative silence that lasted into the following morning.

MEANWHILE, IN THE back of house number two, the villagers had reunited to give Ubaldina moral support and to share their first impressions about the men's return.

"I absolutely refuse to meet with that man," Ubaldina argued. "He was an abusive husband and father. He doesn't deserve me or any of his sons." She began sobbing.

"But you haven't talked to him, Ubaldina," the Morales widow said in a small, deferential voice. "Maybe he's a different man now that he's lost one of his sons." Doña Victoria was talking from her own experience. Her daughter Julia's unexpected departure had changed her. She missed Julia a great deal and still wept every night as if she had just learned the news, but Julia's absence, she often said, had made her a better mother to her other three daughters.

"Well, I'm a different woman now, too," Ubaldina retorted defiantly.

"The main issue is how long the men plan to stay here," the old Señorita Guarnizo reasoned.

"No," said Ubaldina. "The main issue is how long *we will allow* them to stay here."

"You may want your husband gone, Ubaldina, but I want my son near me," Cecilia objected. Then, addressing Marcela López, she said, "Don't you want your fiancé to stay?"

"Wait, please!" Rosalba called before Marcela had the chance to answer. "There's no reason to debate this just yet. We can't assume that the men are here to stay. First, we need to show them what we are now. We have our own system and regulations. They may not want to stay."

Cecilia suggested giving the men a full rung to explore the community. Nurse Ramírez said ten suns. Ubaldina called for five suns only. But it was the usually quiet Santiago Marín, the Other Widow, who brought the meeting to an end by convincing the entire group that three suns—one per household—were enough for the men to get to know the community and vice versa. Should there be a mutual interest, he said, both parts could negotiate a longer stay.

*   *   *

THE COMMUNITY OF New Mariquita has no chief or council. Major decisions are reached by consensus, in a participatory, inclusive decision-making process that allows all ninety-three residents to have a voice. The smaller, sun-to-sun decisions are made by the caretaker of each particular area. For instance, every house has a meal caretaker and a helper. They cook all three meals and make sure their housemates get all the food they need. Supplies of food for each kitchen are equally distributed by the store caretaker, who also threshes or husks grain, dries any surplus of meat and fish, and stores all sorts of food in large jars made of clay. In a like manner farm products are collected and brought to the store by the farm caretaker. She oversees the communal farm, the planting and harvesting of crops, and, with input from the community, decides what produce and animals need to be raised. Every caretaker position, every task and small chore, is rotated among the villagers on a rungly basis. Wool and cotton are allotted to old women, who are charged with the task of spinning and weaving.

Everyone acts on her own, but if a woman (or Santiago Marín) has a problem, she is encouraged to bring the issue to the community consensus process.

*   *   *

THE FOUR MEN, still on the guerrillas' schedule, got up some time before sunrise. They used the rags and the water in the buckets to wash their faces and clean their bodies, and after dressing in the same malodorous clothes they'd been wearing since they'd escaped their encampment, sat outside on the church steps and silently watched the village gradually take on distinct forms and colors as the sun began to shine on everything.

The plaza was still a bit shadowy when the door of the house directly across from where the men sat opened, and a figure appeared. She had a long, shapeless white piece of cloth drawn completely about her, which in the distance made her look like an apparition, and like an apparition she advanced slowly through the plaza toward the church. As she neared the men, she quickly tilted her head down and hurried her pace, entering the church by the back entrance. The four men looked at each other and shrugged, unable to explain her strange behavior. The woman rang the church bell and soon afterward reappeared. This time Restrepo rose and followed her, thinking it was his wife. She moved fast, but Restrepo was faster and presently caught up with her. Gripping her so she couldn't get away, he tugged hard at the cloth, stripping it forcibly from her body. But it was not his wife who stood naked before him, it was the Morales widow, and she was shouting hysterically for help.

Women from all three houses hastened to assist the disgraced widow. They wrapped her up quickly in the same white cloth she'd been wearing and just as quickly took her into house number one, the closest to the incident.

A little while later the church bell started ringing insistently, calling for an emergency meeting. The doors of all three houses opened wide, making way for three armies of naked women who strode purposefully and in absolute quiet toward the men. The unexpected and intimidating sight made the men rise at once and draw together. They stood perfectly straight and quiet, as if they'd been ordered to fall in, and watched in suspense as the women came closer and closer and finally stopped, barely a few yards in front of them.

"Please, let me explain what happened earlier," Restrepo rushed to say. He seemed nervous as he scanned the crowd, looking for Ubaldina. She couldn't have changed much.

"There's no need to explain anything, Señor Restrepo," Rosalba replied confidently. She was standing in the front row. "We know exactly what happened and the reasons that drove you to it. That said, we won't tolerate any outsider forcibly stripping one of our own, regardless of his reasons. You see, the village in which you used to live no longer exists. You're now in New Mariquita, an independent all-female community with . . . special social, cultural and economic characteristics, and close bonds with nature." This definition she had conceived not so long ago, while trying to explain to herself what, exactly, their village had turned into. But this was the first time she had said it aloud. She thought that it sounded grand and exceptional. She couldn't have picked a better opportunity to introduce it. "The fact is, we won't even consider admitting any one of you into our community unless we're certain that he fits in here and is willing to conform to our ways, our ideals and our rules." She shifted her eyes from man to man as she spoke, making an effort to regard them as evenly as possible. She was a fair woman. "Why don't we start with you, Señor Jiménez? Tell us what brought you here, and what you want from us."

Jacinto Jiménez Jr. took half a step forward. He was the tallest and most muscular of the four. He looked at his comrades first and then at the villagers and finally decided to address the head of a dandelion that the morning wind had carried from someone's garden, and that now lay half broken not so far from Rosalba's bare feet.

"I don't want nothing from you," he began. "I'm here to start a new life for myself, and I don't need nobody's permission to do so. I'll begin rebuilding my father's former house as soon as possible. Then I'm going to marry Marcela, and we're going to move into *my* house on *my* property." He took half a step back, joining his comrades.

Rosalba considered the man's abrupt statement for a moment, then said, "Mr. Jiménez, is it true that you disapprove of Marcela's nudity?"

"I sure do," he retorted angrily. "Whatever you all do is your business. You all can stand on your tits as far as I'm concerned, but no wife of mine is going to be seen naked by anyone but me." He crossed his arms defiantly. The villagers looked at Rosalba, waiting for her reply, but at that precise moment Marcela, hands on hips, stepped forward. She took off the shirt Jiménez had given her the sun before.

"You haven't changed a bit, Jacinto," she said scornfully. "You're still as arrogant and pretentious as ever. Too bad I'm not the same. I've come a long way since you were taken away. You just can't imagine the things I went through so that today I can stand like this, face to face with you, and feel no shame, guilt or fear." Her face turned bright red as she added, "I'd rather be an old maid for the rest of my life than be your wife for a moment." She tossed the shirt at his feet as though it were their engagement ring and went back into the crowd, followed by Jiménez's furious stare.

With a smug smile, Rosalba called the next man.

David Pérez, in a more obliging tone than Jiménez, said that it was his wish to get back his grandparents' little piece of land. "I want to rebuild our house for me and my grandmother. You all have taken good care of her, and I thank you for that, but now I'm back and ready to take on my responsibility." He confessed to feeling uncomfortable with some of the changes that had taken place in Mariquita, and added, "I don't know whether or not I'll be able to adapt to all of your 'special characteristics,' but I'm willing to give it a try. Just bear in mind that we got here yesterday. It's going to take some time." Oh, and that, by the way, he wanted to start a family. Would anyone be interested in marrying a brave and affectionate man?

No one was interested at the moment. David's answer, nonetheless, was received warmly.

Campo Elías Restrepo stepped forward before Rosalba called his name.

"What have you got to say for yourself, Señor Restrepo?" Rosalba said.

"As you all know," he began, "I once owned a few properties in town and many acres of land. Well, I'm back, and I think it's only fair that they be returned to me by whoever's working or using them. I promise I won't charge you back rent." He laughed alone at his own joke, then continued, "Like Comrades Jiménez and Pérez, I also want to rebuild my house and . . . you know, take my wife with me. Because she's still my wife, isn't she? Or are you ladies going to tell me that Ubaldina also became a . . . you know . . ." The crowd stared at him with contempt.

"Why don't you ask her yourself, Mr. Restrepo?" Rosalba suggested in a derisive tone, pointing at a small Indian woman who had been standing in the first row all this time with her back straight and her hands locked right underneath her navel.

Restrepo glanced at the woman and furrowed his brow. He looked at Rosalba in confusion, then back at the woman who was supposed to be his wife. She stood on a couple of shapely legs and, like a statue, seemed to be cast in bronze. Two graying braids framed her round little face. She had slanting brown eyes under heavy eyelids, a wide Indian nose and full lips. Her breasts, Restrepo thought, looked shy, yet firm and graceful for her age.

"Ubaldina?" he asked incredulously.

She nodded.

"You look . . . different," he faltered. "Good. You look good."

"Do you know this is the first time you've ever *really* looked at me, Campo Elías?" Ubaldina said. "Oh, I forgot, *Don* Campo Elías. Please forgive me for being so disrespectful." She laughed derisively.

He stood there quietly, remembering. He'd married Ubaldina because he wanted his seven boys to have a mother, and they'd always thought of Ubaldina as family. Their master-servant relationship, however, had changed little with their wedding. Not once had Restrepo looked at Ubaldina through different eyes than those of an employer. The few times he'd made love to her, he'd been too drunk or too tired to go to the brothel. He hadn't missed her all these years. The rare occasions he'd thought of Ubaldina, he'd pictured a homely woman in an apron silently cooking or cleaning, always looking down. But the wife he'd mistreated had gotten rid of her apron long ago. As he looked at her today, he saw a ripe, mellowing, attractive woman who'd felt deceived, cheated on and abused by him, and who was rightly rejecting him. Nothing he said or did now would change what he'd done in the past.

"Don't you have anything to say?" Ubaldina asked, cutting short the man's reminiscences.

Restrepo couldn't think of any words that could convey the way he was beginning to feel. He shook his head.

"It's better that way," she declared.

He stepped back and hung his head.

After a short, sensible silence, Ángel Tamacá was called to state his intentions to the villagers. As the broken man stepped forward, Rosalba couldn't help wondering what he—the one person who'd volunteered to join the guerrillas—could possibly want from their community. He had no house to rebuild or land to claim. Perhaps his former teaching job? But what could he possibly teach them? The virtues of socialism? They were already living them.

"All I ask of you is to give me a second chance," Ángel said humbly to the crowd without looking at anyone in particular.

"A second chance?" Rosalba asked. "To do what?"

"To be human," he replied.

The villagers nodded affably: Ángel's petition seemed genuine. He deserved a second chance. Amparo Marín was especially touched by Ángel's appeal, by his manly voice, his politeness, and the sad expression of his face. How could a man convey his feelings in such a sensitive way with so few words to say and only one eye to glint?

BEFORE BREAKING UP the meeting, Rosalba informed the four men about what would happen next. "We've had visitors in the past; mostly passing travelers and displaced families heading for the city. No one, however, has attempted to stay. This is all new to us, and naturally your acceptance in our community will have to go through consensus discussion. Only when we reach consensus will we be able to give you an answer."

"An answer to what?" Jiménez shouted. "We haven't asked any questions or made any requests. Have we? We're here to stay, and we don't give a damn about your consensus. You keep forgetting that Mariquita is our village too."

"Señor Jiménez," Rosalba said calmly. "Look around and tell me whether this is the same village you're claiming to belong to."

He looked nowhere but into her eyes, his lips trembling with rage. "We own property here. We're not going anywhere." He glanced at the other three men for support.

"We're peaceful people here, Señor Jiménez, but don't be mistaken:

we'll do whatever it takes to defend our community and our principles from rude intruders like you." Rosalba's voice now had a menacing edge to it.

He laughed derisively. "I'd like to see that. A bunch of delicate women fighting four *merciless* warriors like us. You know how many people we've slain? Hundreds! Thousands! A handful of you won't make any difference to our criminal records."

"Speak for yourself, Jiménez," Ángel Tamacá abruptly said. "I'm done with fighting. And I thought you were too." He moved aside, separating himself from the other three. David Pérez looked at Restrepo first, then at Jiménez, and finally shrugged his shoulders and joined Tamacá.

"You two are fucking unbelievable!" Jacinto said to Tamacá and Pérez. "After all the shit we went through to escape from the guerrillas, now you're letting a bunch of women court-martial you like you're criminals." He shook his head repeatedly, then, addressing Restrepo, demanded, "Are you turning against me too?"

Restrepo put his hand on Jiménez's shoulders. "I've got to take my chances here, son," he said under his breath. "I'm too old to start anywhere else."

"Don't let them fool you," Jiménez whispered back. "You know how women are. They're just taking revenge on us for being gone all this time, like we had a choice."

But Restrepo had made up his mind. He lowered his head and joined the other two. Jacinto stood there, all alone, staring at his comrades. His eyes filled with tears, and his expression softened. But when everyone thought he was about to give in and join the other three, he shouted at them, "You all can go to hell, you worthless traitors! Stay here, rot in this fucking hole with these barbarian lesbians. This will be your prison!" Tears began streaming down his face, but he kept shouting, his voice now choked with emotion. "Me? I'm going to clean my record. And I'll become a respectable citizen. And I'll be far better off than all of you, traitors!" Saying this, he started down the road, backward so that he could see their faces become blurry and smaller and finally disappear, sobbing and shouting, "Traitors!" again and again, his frantic calls blending with the shrieks of a flock of crows that at that moment flew past the village.

*   *   *

BEYOND THE THREE large communal houses of New Mariquita there are vestiges of the old town: roofless houses, or rather roofless adobe rectangles, because everything that once made them houses—doors, windowpanes and frames, and even the flooring—was removed and put to use in the new dwellings. The insides of these empty rectangles were originally infested with aggressive weeds that grew in grotesque forms of extravagant proportions, like aberrations of nature. But once the industrious women finished the construction of the three main houses, they turned their eyes toward the remains of the old village. Together they decided to knock down all the inside walls of every former house, then transform each carcass into an enclosed farming lot. The resulting lots were plowed and soon turned into productive gardens.

If on a given sun you have the fortune to sight New Mariquita from the top of a hill, you will feel like you're standing on top of an immense blanket patched together out of many remnants of fabrics in different shades of green.

*   *   *

THE SUN WAS already high in the sky when the customary log fires were kindled in the middle of the plaza. Breakfast was cooked and served, and as soon as the villagers finished eating, they were summoned to the church.

The three men stayed in the plaza, waiting for their fate to be decided. In Tamacá's ears, the word *traitors* kept resonating, and that made him remember that it had been Jiménez's idea to escape from the guerrillas. Jiménez had discussed his plan with Tamacá first, then with

Pérez, and finally with Restrepo. All four swore to stay together and be loyal to their plan, and for over a year they talked about it secretly and separately, going over each step of the escape, considering the grave consequences they would face if their plan was discovered. Jiménez made arrangements with a local peasant, and one day, before sunrise, all four met at the man's shack and changed into noncombatant clothes and ate whatever it was the peasant's wife cooked and took some food for the road and then started moving along the rocky shore of the large river that eventually led them to their final destination.

Perhaps Pérez and Restrepo, Ángel thought, were also feeling bad for having let Jiménez down. Maybe if they saw together the amazing things the villagers had done for the community (all of which his mother had described to him in detail), then all three would remain secure in their decision. "Let's take a walk around the village," he suggested.

Walking around New Mariquita, Ángel felt like a little boy in an amusement park. He pointed at every blooming garden on either side of the street with growing excitement. "Look, yucca!" he shouted. "Look over there, squash!" He went on and on, as if his only eye had suddenly gained the power of seeing things the other men couldn't see with theirs. Restrepo was most impressed by the community's aqueduct: a skillful artificial channel built where La Casa de Emilia used to be, which currently provided running water for all three cooperative houses, the communal bathroom, and the small laundry area. It was so ingenious that even the gray water was used for latrines built on stilts above the running water. The sheltered communal bathroom startled Pérez: ten individual showers and latrines built on a platform where the market used to be. The entire structure was made of fine wood treated with resin. They visited the infirmary, the granary, and the community's animal farm, then walked through plots of maize, rice and coffee on the hillsides that rose behind the village.

When they finished their tour, they went back to the plaza and lay in the shade of a mango tree. They were tired, and the sun made them somnolent, but their anxiety kept them from falling asleep.

INSIDE THE CHURCH, sitting in a big circle, the villagers were struggling to reach consensus on the first consideration. "We can't discuss any man individually," Cleotilde, the moderator, said, "until we all agree to having male members in our community." In the past, all the community's decisions had been voted on, which made the process quick but always left a group of people unsatisfied. Cleotilde had recently introduced the idea of consensus. "Our objective shouldn't be to count votes, but to come to a unanimous decision that all of us can live with, through civil discussion," she'd said in the philosophical tone she had adopted with age. Cleotilde's recommendation was ironically put to the vote, but a large majority quickly approved it.

At the moment, a large majority was in favor of having male members, but two women still opposed the idea: Ubaldina and Orquidea Morales.

"This might be our last opportunity to have descendants and keep our community alive," Rosalba said to the dissenters. She reminded Ubaldina that long ago she had rejected Rosalba's idea of having Don Míster Esmís impregnate a few women on account of his being white. "These men are your own color, Ubaldina. Think about it. It doesn't have to be Campo Elías."

Cecilia pleaded with Orquidea Morales to agree. "Please, Orquidea, don't deny me the chance to be with my son," she sobbed. Francisca, Cecilia's partner, adopted a more aggressive strategy with the stubborn woman. "Just bear in mind that you might need our approval if your sister Julia ever wants to be admitted back."

Ubaldina eventually agreed. Orquidea, on the other hand, said she would never ever agree to any man living in their community, and demanded that the villagers quit trying to convince her to agree and that the meeting be stopped or the subject changed. Orquidea was one of the community's oldest spinsters and arguably the most unattractive.

But when it seemed as if a decision against men living in Mariquita was imminent, the Other Widow, once again, came up with a solution that after some further consideration pleased the entire group: "Why don't we help the men establish a new community nearby, where those who want to live with them can do so? We can make the offer conditional on their accepting our terms." The idea was met with a profound, ambiguous silence that could have been either pure astonishment or dry skepticism.

"And what would be our terms?" Ubaldina wanted to know.

"We'd have to define them," said the Other Widow.

"Who would want to live with them, anyway?" Orquidea Morales said.

"Well, let's find out," the Other Widow replied. "Would anyone here consider living and working in an integrated female-male community with the same characteristics as ours?"

Soon every woman in the room found herself fantasizing about their sister community. Amparo Marín imagined herself living there, happily married to Ángel Tamacá, pregnant with his child. Pilar Villegas went a little further: she fancied herself and David Pérez surrounded by seven children of their own. The thought put a smile on her face. Cecilia pictured herself and Francisca, each with a basket of flowers, walking hand in hand over to the adjoining community to visit her son Ángel and his wife. Rosalba envisioned herself as a store caretaker, trading her granary's surplus of barley with her peer from "the other New Mariquita." Virgelina Saavedra tried, as a harmless exercise, to visualize herself living there and sharing her bed with a naked man instead of Magnolia, but the only image that came to her mind was of el padre Rafael mounted on top of her. She quickly put that thought out of her mind and, feeling guilty, grabbed Magnolia's hand and brought it to her lips, making a smacking sound. Even Orquidea Morales gave free rein to her imagination. She fancied herself living in the new community, blocking a consensus decision that would allow men to go naked.

"I would," Amparo Marín abruptly announced in her low-pitched voice.

"I would too," Pilar Villegas said, her index finger high in the air.

"Me too," Cuba Sánchez called from the other side of the room.

Santiago's idea reached consensus on the first round, and so did every other proposal related to it, all of which were enthusiastically discussed in the afternoon. Before the end of the sun, the three men were invited into the church to hear the villagers' decision.

ÁNGEL TAMACÁ SMILED, obviously pleased, David Pérez shrugged his shoulders resignedly, and Campo Elías Restrepo frowned distrustfully at Santiago as the latter delivered the consensus declaration. The conditions, Santiago said, were specified in a contract that each man must sign by the end of their meeting.

"What are the conditions?" Restrepo asked.

"Well," Rosalba hastened to answer. "Equality between individuals and between the sexes is number one."

"What else?"

"The new community must follow the same administrative system we have. No individual can own anything, the livelihood of every—"

"But what about *my* properties? I should at least have some sort of compensation. I worked hard all my life, and now that I'm old—"

"Your livelihood will be guaranteed until the day you die, Señor Restrepo. That will be your compensation."

"Hmmm . . ."

Santiago explained the project in detail, answered whatever questions the men had, and gave them a tentative schedule (which they didn't fully understand, for it was in female time). Restrepo's brow relaxed a little, and Pérez even wore a smile. Men and villagers agreed to sort out their differences and go to work on the new village as soon as possible.

The next morning, the three men paired up with a partner and went on different scouting expeditions to seek a location for the new community: Ángel Tamacá offered Amparo Marín his arm, and together they went north. Pilar Villegas took David Pérez by the hand and headed west. Campo Elías Restrepo asked Sandra Villegas—after Ubaldina said no three times—and they walked east. Finding the most appropriate site—a cooler grassland area close to the river, with scattered trees, grading into woodland—took twelve expeditions. Once discovered, the site was approved within a sun, and the next morning the villagers, together with the men, walked over with machetes and knives and cut weeds and cleared gardens, but didn't hack down a single tree.

Two suns later, a building team of twelve strong women and three men began the construction of the new village: the community of Newer Mariquita.

*   *   *

THE COMMUNITY OF Newer Mariquita is a work of art that took a ladder and a half to build. It's comprised of two cooperative houses; a community dining room where two meals are available every sun; a small plaza with small araucaria trees and four benches carved out of large trunks; a self-sufficient aqueduct; a large communal bathroom; a granary; a communal farm; and a small animal farm with six chickens, two turkeys, eight rabbits, and a young, rebellious rooster that crows indiscriminately throughout the day.

The twin houses face one another and from the outside look like rectangular temples with tall ceilings. The compartmented one is called Casa del Sol, the uncompartmented one is called Casa de la Luna. Each is over 130 feet long by 30 feet wide. The framework is made of lacquered wooden poles and bamboo lashed together with wire and string. The walls are covered with tree bark, and the steep-pitched roofs are made of palm thatch. On the inside, each roof is a suspended garden: purple orchids, yellow daisies, white lilies and violets hang from the top in clay pots. Each building has two doors. The one in front leads out to the plaza, and the one in back gives access to the trails extending to the river, the woodland and the sister community of New Mariquita, which is barely over a mile away.

*   *   *

ON THE MORNING of Mariacé 7 of the ladder 1992, Ángel Tamacá sent word that his partner, Amparo Marín, had gone into labor. Eloísa set the bell ringing, and a cry of joy was heard around the community and over the small valley. The villagers stopped what they were doing and crowded into the plaza, singing and dancing and congratulating one another.

Rosalba and Cecilia rushed to the store and filled two baskets with the largest oranges, the best-looking papayas, the reddest mangoes and the best slices of cured meat. They took their baskets and, together with all the villagers, set out for Newer Mariquita.

AMPARO MARÍN AND Ángel Tamacá lived in Casa del Sol. Until that morning, Amparo had been the community's meal caretaker for two consecutive rungs. Ángel was the community's animal farm caretaker. They shared the house with two other couples—Pilar Villegas and David Pérez, who only recently had agreed to move in together after a ten-rung courtship, and Magnolia Morales and Virgelina Saavedra, who, wanting a change, had moved from New Mariquita two rungs before, after Virgelina's grandmother died.

Across from them, in Casa de la Luna, lived six people: Campo Elías Restrepo, the maintenance caretaker, who saw his wife Ubaldina once a rung, and who had yet to hear anything nice from her but was hopeful he might one day win her over; Cuba and Violeta Sánchez, who had helped build the new village and now were in charge of its cleaning; and Sandra Villegas and Marcela López, who were best friends, and who together with Pilar, David, Magnolia and Virgelina took care of the communal farm, the vegetable garden and the orchard. The sixth resident was David's grandmother, the Pérez widow. She spent her days sitting outside in a rocking chair, saying her prayers mechanically. She had long forgotten what she prayed for and to whom.

*   *   *

WALKING DOWN THE footpath, through a small stretch of woods, the women began considering names for the new baby. They would suggest them to Amparo and Ángel.

"If it's a girl, she should be named after her two grandmothers: Cecilia Aracelly," said the aged, almost senile señorita, Cleotilde.

"No," Cecilia replied. "If it's a girl, her name ought to be Mariquita. After all she'd be New and Newer Mariquita's first baby ever."

"I agree," said Aracelly.

Rosalba was silent. Until now she hadn't even considered the possibility that the baby might be a girl. Ever since she'd learned that Amparo Marín was pregnant, Rosalba had decided it would be a boy. It had to be a boy for their community to have a chance to survive. She couldn't understand how the villagers could be so irrational. The new baby would be named after his grandfathers or his father or his uncle or cousin or any other man. It didn't matter as long as it was a male name, because the baby would be a boy. At a bend in the road, just before the descent that led to the new village, Rosalba finally said, "What if it's a boy?"

"Ángel!" Cecilia replied at once. "His name should be Ángel like his father and his grandfather."

"How about Gordon?" Rosalba said. "Like Míster Esmís."

"Gordon Tamacá?" Francisca said aloud. "It sounds awfully funny." The women laughed hysterically and soon began shouting their suggestions, which were the names of their departed sons, husbands, fathers and other men whose lives they wanted to immortalize.

"How about Pablo?" said the Other Widow. This was the first time Santiago had mentioned, in public, his lover's name since his death. The women stopped and grew quiet, as if Pablo's memory had called for a moment of silence. Rosalba, however, was so absorbed in thinking of male names that she didn't even hear Pablo's name being pronounced. She kept walking with the basket hanging from her arm and didn't stop until she reached the part of the trail where the village of Newer Mariquita came into view. There she stood, feeling increasingly anxious in the face of the looming news of the baby's gender, gazing fondly at the beautiful landscape of high mountains and seemingly endless reaches of trees and vegetation, inaccessible mountainsides and valleys, large pastures covered with tall grass and wild flowers, plowed fields, gardens, and a tiny village that lay slumbering in the heat. Then she saw Ángel in the distance. He was jumping up and down with excitement, waving his hands in the air. The baby had been born. Rosalba pressed the basket firmly against her body with both hands and held her breath for a short while until she heard Ángel's cries, "It's a boy! It's a boy!" he shouted, his words echoing all over the valley.

At that very moment, all the high mountains disappeared before Rosalba's eyes. The vast stretches of trees and wild vegetation, the untouched mountainsides and valleys, all vanished, as if by magic. Only an open, clear horizon stood between Newer Mariquita and the rest of the world. Rosalba gazed intently at the fantastic sight, experiencing its extraordinary simplicity and expansiveness. She was aware that it was just a vision, that the actual transformation wasn't in the distant view but in herself and how she now saw the world. The universe had given her new eyes, and she had used them to discover new philosophies of life, work and independence, new landscapes of harmony and order, wherever she looked. She now understood that Newer Mariquita would be not only an extension of land over the small valley but also an extension of the community's philosophies, their female concept of time and their strong senses of justice and freedom, and that it would signal the beginning of a communalistic system of government that would eventually extend itself across the mountainous geography of the country, throughout its flat-topped hills, its plains and jungles and deserts and peninsulas, until the end of time.

Rosalba was wiping the tears from her eyes when the group caught up with her. They, too, had heard Ángel's shouts and now were running to meet him, giving cheers for the new boy and his parents, for the two Mariquitas, for life. Rosalba took Eloísa's hand in hers, and together they followed slowly the group down the slope toward Newer Mariquita, feeling fulfilled.

Their race had been granted a second opportunity on earth.

Acknowledgments

A FIRST AND VERY special thanks must go to Hillary Jordan, a true friend and colleague, who read this when it was but a short story in broken English; who helped me improve that story and write several more, and helped me all throughout the process of giving those stories the shape of the present book, never wavering, not even when I did. Hill: your invaluable advice and enthusiasm, your immeasurable faith and love have been absolutely vital to the writing of this novel and to my own sanity. This book is yours, mine, ours.

Special thanks to the following people:

To Maureen Howard, for her wisdom and guidance, and for asking me the same question over and over until I finally got it. Magda Bogin, for her good judgment and suggestions, and for lending me her charming house in Tepoztlán where I wrote a chapter of this novel. Binnie Kirshenbaum, David Plante, Victoria Redel, Alan Ziegler and the faculty of the Columbia University Writing Division, for embracing my work with passion.

To friends and artistic soulmates who read this book, or parts of it, in various stages, and contributed their valuable observations: Allison Amend, Raul Correa, Elizabeth Harris-Behling, Antonia Logue, Michele Morano, Amy Sickels and Scott Snyder.

For their enthusiasm and trust, and for seeing what others couldn't, I am especially indebted to two extraordinary women: my agent, Lisa Bankoff; and my editor, Claire Wachtel. I must add here that a great part of the pleasure of working with them has been the amazing help provided by their super assistants: Tina Wexler at ICM; and Lauretta Charlton at HarperCollins.

For their grants and fellowships, I would like to thank the Henfield Foundation, the National Hispanic Foundation for the Arts, the Rolex Mentor & Protégé Arts Initiative, the Columbia University Writing Division, the MacDowell Colony, the Corporation of Yaddo, Blue Mountain Center, Saltonstall Foundation for the Arts, Millay Colony and the Hall Farm Center for Arts and Education.

For their moral support and friendship, thanks to Bogdan Apetri, Alejandro Aragón, Neilson Barnard, Patricia Cepeda, Kathryn and Gary DiMauro, Beth Dodd, Miguel Falquéz-Certain, René Jiménez, Jaime Manrique, Melissa Moran and the staff at Hell's Kitchen Restaurant, Claudia and Alfredo Sanclemente, Sue Torres, and Rob Williams.

My love and deepest gratitude to my mother and my grandmother for giving me the inspiration to write this book; to my brothers, Oscar, Hernán, Pepe and Carlos, and my sister, Margarita, and to my entire family for their love and belief in me.

Finally, for enduring my insane writing process with so much grace, for your infinite faith, love and understanding, and for creating a wonderful life for me outside my tales, *mil y mil gracias a ti*, José, with all my love.

Questions for Discussion

Sociology, religion, gender, politics, sexual politics, history, women's studies, Latin American studies. It's hard to imagine a more stimulating combination of discussion topics. I hope that the following questions will enrich your group's reading of Mariquita's parable of hope. —James Cañón

1. What does the opening scene reveal about the women of Mariquita?

2. In the first chapter, a guerrilla boy says to the Morales widow, "This is and will always be a land of men." What are the implications of the boy's statement?

3. After the guerrilla attack in which most men disappear from Mariquita, Julio César Morales becomes Julia Morales—and permanently mute. Discuss the symbolism behind his transformation.

4. When their men are taken away by communist guerrillas, the women of Mariquita lose their family providers. What else, in your opinion, do the women lose? What do they gain?

5. Is Rosalba right to take on the job of magistrate, or should that role have gone to someone else? What are Rosalba's strengths and weaknesses?

6. In what ways does Cleotilde de Guarnizo defy popular notions of older women?

7. Chapter five begins with Francisca having a dream in which the men of Mariquita return, only they're faceless and naked and each of them has a small penis and enormous testicles. Discuss the symbolism behind this image. What's the significance of the dream in Francisca's tale?

8. At the end of chapter six, Santiago takes Pablo to the river: "He fixed his gaze on Pablo's face, filling himself full of the man he loved, and gently began to release his hold on him, his solid arms slowly separating from the smallness of his lover's back, giving him to the current like a gift." In what ways is the novel as a whole about the importance of letting go of the past in order to move forward?

9. Love and sexuality are two strong themes in the novel. How do the women use their sexuality to their advantage? What is the most powerful love story in the novel and why?

10. What role does el Padre Rafael play in Mariquita's fate?

11. Discuss the hidden reasons why el Padre Rafael kills the four boys.

12. Chapter nine poses a question about the importance of time. Do you think time is an overrated concept? Do you agree with Magnolia when she says that time only exists in one's mind? If you were in the same situation as the women of Mariquita, how would you keep track of time?

13. Discuss the "Theory of Female Time" of Rosalba and Cleotilde. What are the benefits of it? What are the disadvantages?

14. In chapter eleven, a cow named Perestroika saves the village. What does the cow's name suggest for the future of Mariquita?

15. Is the idea of living in a society without men a far-fetched notion, or is it something that could be possible? Discuss.

16. Why do you think Cañón chose to intersperse the narrative with accounts of war? Does it add anything to the story, or is it distracting?

17. The book embodies many contradictions. It is at once lyrical and brutal, subversive and idealistic, satirical and affecting, wickedly funny and profoundly sad. Do you like this paradoxical approach? In what ways do you find this style effective or ineffective?

18. Is *Tales from the Town of Widows* a tragedy, romance, comedy, or tragicomedy? Discuss.

19. Cañón chose to write his debut novel in English, a language he learned as an adult. Do you think it would have been a different book had he written it in his first language? Discuss.

20. In an interview, Cañón said that the last line of his novel was meant to be a reply to *One Hundred Years of Solitude*'s last line, in which "races condemned to one hundred years of solitude did not have a second opportunity on earth." Discuss Cañón's last line and his attitude toward the future of his "race."

21. At the end of the book, Mariquita's all-female utopia is put to the test when four men return to the village, forcing the women to negotiate between the world they've lost and the imperfect, peaceful existence they've created. What do you think of the women's final decision? Does it seem like a realistic solution?

22. Do you think the story's ending would have been different if a woman had written the book? How would you end the story?

23. One of the biggest debates about this novel is whether or not it is a feminist work. What are your thoughts on this issue?

24. A reviewer described *Tales from the Town of Widows* as "prime magic realism a la García Márquez, Cortázar, and Vargas Llosa." Do you agree with that characterization? How would you characterize this book? How does this book compare to other South American novels?

25. Although Colombia has the second largest displaced population in the world after Sudan, its war—the longest and bloodiest civil war in this hemisphere—has gotten little attention on human rights and refugee issues. Do you think this book can play a role in achieving social justice in Colombia? Do you think a book of fiction can influence the politics of a region? How?